Ebook ISBN: 978-1-956335-27-9

Paperback ISBN: 978-1-956335-36-1

Audiobook ISBN: 978-1-956335-35-4

Ebook and paperback cover design by Molly Burton at Cozy Cover Designs.

Chapter header and scene break drawings by Etheric Tales.

Axia map designed by Sarah Waites at The Illustrated Page Design.

First published in 2026 by Ringtail Press.

www.melissajacksonbooks.com

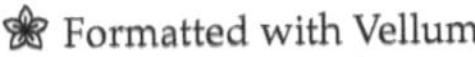 Formatted with Vellum

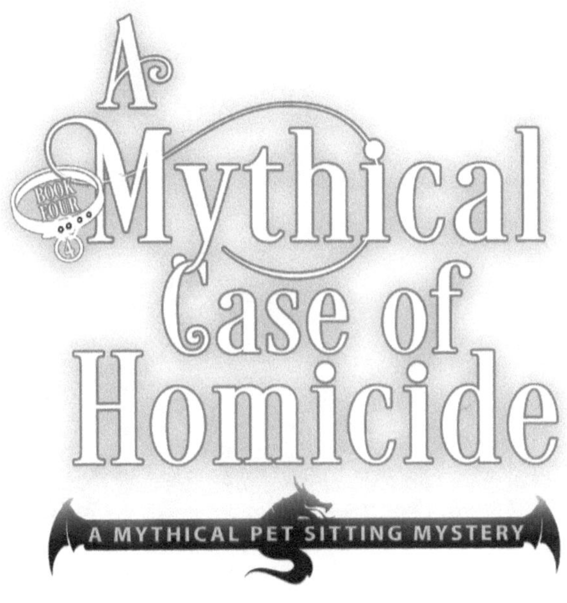

MELISSA ERIN JACKSON

SUMMARY

This year's festival season will be perilous.

Zombie cactus season has officially begun in Axia, and Deandra is *not* having a good time. The town is preparing for a festival to honor the versatile plant, and it's giving Dee—a recovering barista—Pumpkin Spice Latte–season flashbacks.

Most shop owners in Axia are taking part in the cactus-themed festivities, and Quinn and Rularo Greenwood are no exception. Their shop, InkCraft, is known for its alchemical inks that add magic-powered animation to business cards, signs, and even tattoos. Since the couple will be busy with the festival all weekend, they've opted to leave their salica at home, where the high-strung, magic-touched ferret will be more comfortable. They've hired a very reluctant Dee to aid in his care.

Though the ferret often uses the depths of Rularo's beard as a security blanket, he accepts Dee's calming presence as a passable, if weak, replacement. But when a customer of Rularo's dies because of a poison-laced tattoo, Peril is riddled with guilt, sure he could have saved his family from awful allegations had he been with Rularo at the time of the incident.

Uncovering who actually tampered with the tattoo ink is more complicated than Deandra and Peril anticipate. The more they dig, the more they're sure the incident is connected to a sapient-animal rights group that has been harassing festival attendees. With the clock ticking toward the end of the three-day festival, they must ferret out the culprit before the town's horde of cactus-crazed tourists depart Axia, leaving InkCraft in shambles … and taking their secrets with them.

READING ORDER

- **Book 1**: A Mythical Case of Arson
- **Book 1.5**: A Mythical Discovery
- **Book 2**: A Mythical Case of Murder
- **Book 3**: A Mythical Case of Theft
- **Book 4**: A Mythical Case of Homicide
- **Book 5**: A Mythical Case of Kidnapping

Flight Park
Wheeler Ave
Wendy's Apartment
Coterie Road
Angela's House
Mermaids' Club
Heather's Elixirs
Axian Nights Hotel
Eddy Way
McClaren
Telepost
Welcome Center
Grenal Way
Axia

il's House
Mythic Pet Kitchen
Paula's House
Starshadow's House
et Clinic xtension
Drug Store
Burned Building
Purl Way
Cruz's House
addel's ffice
Hogarth's Hoagies
ery re
Zombie Cactus
Telepad Station
InkCraft
Police Station
POLICE
Sensory astry
Axian 8
Oracle Park
Grandparents' House

CHAPTER ONE

Deandra paced the apartment. "This can't *possibly* be a good idea."

Wendy and Havoc sat on the couch watching her.

"We've done some pretty dangerous things since I came to Axia," Deandra said as she reached the hallway, then did an about-face and walked back toward the living room. "But this might be the most dangerous thing yet!"

"You're being a *little* dramatic," Wendy said.

Havoc chirped.

Deandra stopped beside the TV stand, hands on her hips. She glared at them both, then pointed a finger at her dragon. "Whose side are you even on?"

Potted plants with wide leaves flanked the TV. One of those leaves tickled her arm and she swatted it away. Even the flora in this apartment was plotting against her.

Havoc peeped worriedly and shot a questioning look at Wendy.

Wendy held her hands up in innocence. "You're on your own with this one, boy."

Havoc's muzzle bunched, and he growled low, faint tendrils of white smoke wafting from his nostrils. Wendy, unfazed, leaned over to scratch him affectionately under his chin. One of his back feet thumped a couch cushion as Wendy hit the right spot.

It was a strange sight for Deandra; while she saw a dragon, Wendy saw a dire wolf. When Deandra witnessed people physically interact with him, the glamouring magic woven into his collar did inexplicable things to reality. She saw some combination of what was *actually* there and what the magical collar made others *think* they saw. Wendy's hand was scratching empty space somewhere closer to Havoc's eyes, yet he still felt it on his chin.

Deandra gave her head a sharp shake. Yet another thing to go into the already overstuffed "too weird to think about" folder.

Plus, she was losing track of what was important. She was in danger. They *all* were.

"Cruz is going to get the third degree from Grandma, and he's going to run away screaming, and I'll never see him again!"

Havoc huffed another plume of white smoke from his nose, clearly having sided with Wendy.

Deandra gasped. "Traitor!"

Havoc offered a doggy smile, his tongue lolling out the side of his mouth. Deandra quickly averted her gaze, refusing to be manipulated by his adorable face. If no one was going to fight for her, then she'd fight for herself.

Before she could wage her next argument, though, Wendy said, "If you cancel dinner, Grandma is going to accidentally on purpose run into you next time. You know that, right?"

Deandra winced.

Last week, she and Cruz had been at lunch at Hogarth's Hoagies when her grandma walked by the building. Deandra had spotted her through the window, sandwich halfway to her mouth, in the same moment that her grandma had spotted *her*. Her grandma had stopped dead in her tracks, pointed in Cruz's direction, and mouthed "Is that him?"

Cruz had been too focused on his own sandwich to notice.

Deandra had nodded vigorously, held her sandwich in one hand, and used the other to mime holding a phone to her ear. She'd hoped her grandma would understand that Deandra promised to call her later. When her grandma just stood there, Deandra made a shooing motion with her free hand.

Wrong move.

Grandma January had hiked her purse higher, squared her shoulders, and marched inside the shop.

Deandra had plopped her sandwich onto her plate and then an elbow on the table before clapping a hand over her eyes.

Cruz had registered something was amiss mere seconds before Grandma January was standing beside the table.

"Deandra! My *darling* granddaughter! How lovely to *finally* see you. You've hardly returned my phone calls since recent ... developments."

Deandra had just talked to the woman the night before!

She'd lowered her hand to cast a pleading look at her grandma before offering Cruz a tight smile. "Cruz, this stunning woman is my grandmother."

Cruz had quickly wiped his hands and mouth on a napkin and then stood, holding out his hand in greeting. "You must be January. Dee has told me so much about you, Mrs. Eyre."

Grandma January shook his offered hand but leaned theatrically around him to pin Deandra with her piercing gaze. "Has she now?"

Cruz chuckled. "She has, though she undersold how stunning you *actually* are."

Grandma January's lips had pursed slightly as she stood to

full height. Anyone else might have thought she was put out by Cruz laying it on thick, but Deandra knew the opposite was true. Her grandma was also clearly pleased that the ambush hadn't flustered him.

Score one for Cruz.

"Would you like to join us?" Cruz had asked, once he let her hand go, motioning to the table.

"Oh, pah! You wouldn't want to spend your lunch with a decrepit old lady like me," she'd said, waving the offer away while readjusting the giant purse on her shoulder.

Deandra had tried not to roll her eyes. Her spry grandma only pulled the age card when she was trying to garner sympathy.

Grandma January had sniffed theatrically. "I've got a ton of errands to run. But when I saw my granddaughter here, I knew I had to pop in to say hello, as I wasn't sure when I'd get another chance. Harder to catch than an eel, this girl."

Cruz had turned to her then. "Deandra," he said, his tone reproving. "Have you been avoiding your grandmother?"

His wink had been so quick, she'd almost missed it. She'd already known from his tone that he was ribbing her to appease her grandma, which she appreciated, but she was also going to throttle him later.

"I've been busy, is all."

He'd looked aghast. "Too busy for *family*?"

Grandma January cocked a brow and gestured at Cruz, as if to say, "How does *he* understand and yet you don't?"

He'd turned back to her grandma then. "I'm sorry if I've encroached on your time with her. She hasn't been in Axia long, and I'm sure you missed her terribly while she was in the mundane world."

She smiled up at him and patted his arm. Deandra didn't miss how she lightly squeezed his bicep, as if he were a new car she was considering purchasing and giving the tires an experimental kick. "Well I can't blame you for wanting to spend time with her.

She's pretty special. Let's say you come to dinner on Sunday, and we'll call it even."

Turning back to Deandra, Cruz had winced slightly, clearly having realized he'd gotten backed into something he'd be hard pressed to say no to.

"We'd love to, Grandma," she'd said, though her gaze never left Cruz's face.

"Wonderful!" Grandma January said, hurrying over a few steps to grab Deandra's hand with one of her cold ones. Squeezing it, she'd whispered, "I'm looking forward to sharing pictures of the evening with your stubborn mother. Maybe *that'll* finally get her keister to Axia."

With a final squeeze of Deandra's hand and another pat to Cruz's arm, Grandma January had strolled off, giant bag nearly whacking a seated patron in the head.

Cruz had apologized after her grandma left. Deandra couldn't be mad at him. She knew he hadn't purposely roped them into a "meet the family" dinner before she was ready. They'd only been dating for two weeks. Deandra had foolishly thought she could avoid the meeting for a few months, but this was the problem with small towns. People were in your business, thanks to forced proximity.

Wendy loudly cleared her throat now. "Do I need to remind you *again* that you get weird when you like a guy?"

Deandra snapped out of her musings now to shoot a death glare at her cousin, who was as unfazed by this as she had been by Havoc's growling.

"Just admit that you're worried Grandma won't like him. You value her opinion, even if you're scared of it."

Deandra crossed her arms. After a prolonged pause, she said, "You know I hate it when you're rational."

"You're also worried *he* won't like *her*," Wendy said. "And, yeah, this is all a little fast, but you two are really good together. Just trust it."

Deandra let her arms fall to her sides. "I guess you're right. I mean, even Havoc gave him the stamp of trustworthiness already."

She realized her mistake a moment later, and her eyes widened.

Wendy gasped and scrambled off the couch onto her feet. She opened her mouth, shut it, opened it again. No sound came out.

Deandra grimaced.

Wendy rounded on Havoc. "I let you *live* here. We eat dinner together every night. I know your *secret*. I'm *protecting* your secret! And you let *Cruz* into the pod before *me*?"

Havoc was on his feet too, all four on the couch cushions. He peeped three times in rapid succession, then bunched his muzzle.

"I don't know what that means!" Wendy said. "Is this because I won't let you put your paws on the table? I'm sorry, but that one is nonnegotiable."

Havoc chirp-barked.

"I don't know what that means, either!" Wendy said, flapping her arms once before crossing them. "I'm super trustworthy. I'm so offended right now."

Havoc plopped onto his haunches, then snorted once, expelling smoke.

Deandra said, "Maybe you two are too much like siblings. You love your siblings, but you don't always trust them."

Wendy rounded on Deandra, jabbing a finger in her face. "Speaking of being too much like a sibling! When did Cruz get admitted into the pod? You didn't tell me!"

"Oh, look at the time!" Deandra said, glancing at her nonexistent wristwatch. "We only have an hour before dinner. I need to shower …"

"Deandra Hendricks!"

In a rush, Deandra said, "The day of the follow-up vet appointment. The day he, uh, asked me out."

Wendy stared at her as if she'd just been slapped—with a rotting fish. "That was like a month ago!"

"I didn't want you to feel bad!"

"How is lying better?"

"I wasn't lying! I was withholding information." Deandra sagged when Wendy hit her with a *look.* "Okay, that sounded bad. I'm sorry. I just didn't want you to take it personally. I assume he looped Cruz in because he helped him when he was sick—and also got him out of animal jail."

Wendy scoffed. "As if saving his life multiple times is a big deal …"

Some of the tension left Deandra's shoulders. Wendy wasn't *mad,* mad. "If it makes you feel better, the night Cruz first kissed me, Havoc sent him a very disturbing mental threat. I didn't see it, but Cruz said Havoc sent him thought-images of being burned in a hail of dragon fire—a promise of future violence if Cruz hurts me. There were apparently thought-smells of burning flesh and hair, too."

Wendy shuddered. "Well *that's* terrifying …" She glanced over at Havoc. "Good boy!"

He replied with a happy peep.

"We really *should* get ready, though," Deandra said. "Cruz is picking us up in forty-five."

Wendy jutted her chin at Havoc. "Guess you're my date tonight. I'd much rather hang with you than be a third wheel."

Somewhere in the middle of that declaration, Havoc's back foot had apparently grown very itchy. He gnawed at the yellow pad, the sound somehow both wet and aggressive.

Wendy sighed. "Honestly, I've dated guys with worse manners."

Laughing, Deandra headed for the bathroom to get ready.

At 6:45, Cruz strolled up the sidewalk to where Deandra and Wendy were waiting with Havoc. The dragon had been carefully stalking a beetle marching its way through the bark lining the

flower bed that hugged one side of the sidewalk. But when he heard Cruz walking toward them, he darted out in front of Deandra, entire backside swishing and wings flapping.

With barely a glance in the ladies' direction, Cruz dropped to one knee several feet from Havoc and held out his arms. "Hi, buddy!"

Deandra knew better than to fight it and let the leash go. The second the loop hit the ground, Havoc was off like a shot, tackling Cruz to the ground. He laughed as the wiggly dragon licked his face and neck, his tail whipping like a metronome behind him.

"I supply him with *shelter* from this dark, cruel world, and he's never *once* greeted me like that," Wendy said, arms crossed and foot tapping.

"He barely greets me—" Deandra tried, but Wendy cut her off with a flick of her wrist, a palm turned toward Deandra's face.

"Don't try to comfort me," Wendy said, her tone melodramatic. "I'm still unsure if I'm deeply offended or if I need to do some serious soul searching and reevaluate my character."

Deandra tried not to laugh, even though that was exactly what Wendy wanted. She figured her cousin wasn't mad so much as feeling left out. Not even Deandra was sure why Havoc continued to exclude Wendy from the pod.

After several more seconds of enthusiastic hellos, Cruz finally managed to get to his feet. As he brushed himself off, Havoc trotted back to Deandra.

"That was just embarrassing," Wendy admonished Havoc.

He chirp-barked, tongue lolling.

Cruz's gaze flitted back and forth between the ladies. "Oh. Hi."

Smiling and rolling her eyes, Deandra twirled one finger in the air to signal for him to turn around. He closed the distance before dutifully turning his back to her so she could swat away the lingering bits of leaves and dirt that clung to his gray button-up. He thankfully hadn't landed in any puddles of dubious origin.

"All clear," Deandra said, and he turned around. She grinned up at him.

He grinned down at her.

"Ugh," Wendy said, though she looked perfectly happy. "*Must* you remind me how painfully single I am?"

Cruz shot Deandra a look of disappointment and shook his head. "This happens every time you paw me in public; you upset onlookers."

"I only paw you in public when you roll around on the ground," Deandra pointed out. "Well, except for time you heard a squirrel literally screaming for help and you made me assist you in breaking into someone's backyard." She glanced at Wendy. "He crawled under a rando's house and came out covered in cobwebs."

"I wasn't breaking in," Cruz said. "*And* it wasn't a rando. I texted the owner before we let ourselves through the *unlocked* gate." Addressing Wendy, he said, "I've been the owner's vet for their venomous boxwood turtle for ages."

Wendy blinked dumbly at him, then leaned toward Deandra. "I can confirm that there's still stuff about Axia that's so weird to me, I don't know how to process it. You didn't mention the venomous turtle part." Giving her head a quick shake to presumably rearrange her marbles, she asked Cruz, "The squirrel made a full recovery, right?"

He nodded. "He was in a tiny cast for a week, but a tech and I released him into Oracle Park a couple of days ago."

Sunshine the fire newt popped into Deandra's head then, and while she hoped the little menace was faring well in the park, she also hoped the newt wouldn't sense weakness in the newly healed squirrel and harass it.

She hadn't seen scale nor tail of the newt since the week Deandra officially moved to Axia. She hadn't heard about anyone fleeing the park in terror with newt-sized holes burned into their clothes, so Deandra chose to believe that meant the newt was staying out of trouble like she'd promised.

"We should get going," Wendy said. "Grandma January needs as much time as possible to interrogate Cruz."

A crack fissured Cruz's usual mask of goofy nonchalance.

Deandra grabbed his hand and squeezed it. The sensation got him to refocus on her. Even though her nerves were frayed, too, she wanted to say something supportive to ease his anxiety.

"Do you want to escape the hub system and live a life on the lam so we can avoid this?" she asked.

He nodded. "Yes, please. We can get a van." After a thoughtful moment of silence, he said, "We'll need an income, though, and my stomach is too weak for dumpster diving. What's your skill level with creating useless items out of scrap metal?"

"Terrible, but I'll learn."

Wendy had walked away at some point and was loitering beside Cruz's car.

Deandra glanced at her, then at Cruz. She lowered her voice, even though Wendy was well out of earshot now. "You're sure you're okay with this? I know it's soon. Not that there's a rule for—"

He kissed her—quick but reassuring. With a hand cupping her face, he said, "I'm sure." He chuckled then. "If she doesn't like my answers during the interrogation, though, what are the chances she'll blast me into next Tuesday with a wind spell?"

Grandma January wasn't remotely a violent person, even when she was feeling fiercely protective.

"Zero. But I can't guarantee she hasn't researched your history so thoroughly that she has access to those fabled permanent records from elementary school."

Cruz shrugged, letting her face go. "The family lawyers had those scrubbed after the eyeball incident in third grade."

Laughing, Deandra squeezed his hand again, and they headed toward his car. Havoc trotted along on her other side.

At Deandra's insistence, Wendy rode shotgun while Deandra got into the back seat with Havoc. Cruz had removed the fabric tarp that usually covered the back seats, but the scent of Maxine,

Cruz's black lab, clearly lingered on the upholstery, given how intensely Havoc was sniffing it.

Cruz had just pulled onto the street when a pop song came on the radio that Deandra didn't recognize. From the conversation that sprang up between Cruz and Wendy, Deandra gleaned that it was a new song by a hub artist. The two launched into a nerdy conversation about how no one knew if the singer was someone who donned elaborate magical cosplay for her shows or if she *actually was* a minotaur.

When Cruz pulled up outside the house a few minutes later, Grandma January and Grandpa Morris were already on the porch. They were each in a rocking chair, mugs in hand. Grandpa Morris was smiling affectionately at his wife, whose eyes were closed as she laughed. A few moments later, they noticed their guests had arrived and got to their feet.

Havoc, all four feet on the seat, stood with his nose pressed to the glass as he stared at the house, his back end wagging so hard, it was a wonder the spade on the end of his tail wasn't whacking him in the face. Deandra unclipped his harness, then maneuvered around the wiggly lizard as best she could so she could open the door for him. The moment it was cracked open, he nudged it the rest of the way with his muzzle and was off like a rocket up the center walkway that bisected her grandparents' front lawn.

Grandpa Morris had descended the two porch steps and was sitting on the bottom one, arms out in a gesture that looked very similar to the one Cruz had employed earlier. Somehow mindful of her grandpa's age, Havoc kept most of his feet on the ground as he enthusiastically greeted him.

Grandma January stood on the top step, her shoulder leaning against the railing and her long cardigan sweater wrapped around her. She smiled down at the pair.

Deandra was slightly worried that Havoc would let her grandpa into the pod next. The choice would indirectly let Grandma January in, as that man kept nothing from his wife. As supportive as her grandma would inevitably be, she was not great with secrets. In less than twenty-four hours, Deandra's mother would know that, on top of her only daughter moving to a hub, she'd adopted a dragon—which were supposed to be extinct. When pressured, Deandra would cave faster than a sandcastle in a hurricane, and she'd end up telling her grandma *everything*.

Deandra didn't want anyone else to be burdened with the concern that powerful people—possibly dangerous people— might come to Axia one day to take Havoc from her.

Not to mention that Wendy would get her feelings hurt all over again if Havoc chose someone else before her.

The trio climbed out of the car. Deandra had planned to head toward her dragon, but Cruz calling her name stopped her. Wendy went on ahead.

Cruz gestured for Deandra to meet him behind the trunk. "I, uh, wanted to buy something to bring as a thank you, but I panicked a little, and I got more than one thing. Can you help me choose?"

Her curiosity was so intense, all she could do was nod. When the trunk opened, she did her best to stifle a laugh. A bouquet of flowers lay on each side of a plastic crate that held a pie, a tray of cupcakes, and two bottles of wine—one white, and one red.

She glanced up at him. "You're very sweet."

"I'm well aware of that. I'm an absolute delight. But that's not an answer," he said, brows furrowed as he stared into the trunk.

Deandra perused the offerings again and selected the maroon-maiden apple pie and the bouquet of sunflowers. Keeping hold of the pie, she held the flowers out to him. "These happen to be her favorite flower. I have no idea what her favorite pie is, but I tried maroon-maiden soda recently, and that stuff is like crack, so I'm choosing the pie for myself."

Laughing, he took the flowers. "Perfect."

Flowers in hand, he closed the trunk, and they set off for the house with their spoils in hand. Havoc had mostly calmed down and was snuffling in the front garden, not paying attention to anyone.

Grandpa Morris was on his feet, and he, Wendy, and Grandma January were huddled together at the base of the steps. When Deandra and Cruz reached them, Cruz held out the flowers to Grandma January.

"Thank you for the invitation, Mr. and Mrs. Eyre," he said.

Grandma January's eyes lit up at the sight of the bouquet. "Oh, these are beautiful." She took them and gave one bloom an appreciative sniff. "I hope you're all hungry. I made entirely too much food."

Grandpa Morris leaned toward Cruz. In a stage whisper, he said, "She wants you to like her, so she made dang near *all* of her specialties."

Grandma January's skin was too dark to easily tell if she was blushing, but between the way she buried her nose in the bouquet again and then glared narrowly at her husband over the top of the cellophane wrapping, Deandra guessed her grandma's face was hot. "Not *all* of them …"

Deandra said, "Grandma. Don't tease me. *Please* tell me those specialties include the garlic mashed potatoes."

Grandma January shrugged a shoulder, the picture of nonchalance. "Maybe …"

Angling a sweet smile up at Cruz, Deandra said, "If those garlic mashed potatoes *are* in that kitchen but they're in limited supply, please know I will knife you in the kidney for them."

Cruz nodded solemnly. "Not if I knife you first."

"So romantic," Wendy said with a snort.

Thankfully there *were* mashed potatoes, and they were available in abundance.

The evening was fun, the conversation was lively, and everyone got along.

And, most importantly, no one got knifed.

The 27th Annual

ZOMBIE CACTUS FESTIVAL!

JULY 17-19 FRI-SUN

GAMES & ACTIVITIES FOR KIDS

SHOPPING

LIVE MUSIC

FOOD, FOOD, FOOD!

ZOMBIE CACTUS PIE EATING CONTEST

CHAPTER TWO

It had only been two weeks since Cruz officially met her grandparents, but given how much the town had changed in those fourteen days, it felt as if that dinner had been months ago. She stood before a telephone pole now, glaring at the flyer stapled there. Light from a nearby lamppost cast odd angles across the paper, which were exacerbated every time one of the corners flapped gently in the breeze.

"*The 27th Annual Zombie Cactus Festival!*" the flyer read.

During Deandra's first weekend in Axia, Wendy had taken her to a store called the Zombie Cactus—named after the popular and versatile plant. Wendy had assured Deandra then that the flavor of the cactus was sweet and refreshing, and in the summer, Zombie Cactus Iced Tea season put the mundane Pumpkin Spice Latte season to shame.

Deandra had forgotten all about that until two weeks ago. Wendy hadn't been joking—and she'd also undersold it. This was about much more than a beloved flavor of iced tea. The town had been infested with zombie cactus, well, everything, and the festival was merely the event that kicked the season off, which would run from late July through the end of August.

The flyer before her advertised mundane things, such as live music and games and activities for kids. A zombie cactus pie-eating contest was scheduled for sometime during the three-day festival, which was hosted by the Mermaids Club.

It was the "Food, food, food!" label on the flyer, though, that spoke to the heart of the event. Every restaurant in the entire town apparently had special menus in reserve for the festival, as zombie cactus dishes and drinks were now on offer everywhere. Shop windows had been painted with renditions of the pink-and-white cactus fruit and saguaro-like cactuses, and, just yesterday, she'd spotted a mural that featured a row of ceramic pots that each had a zombified hand shooting from the soil and reaching for the light—or in several cases, reaching for a cactus-flavored treat to drag back into the earth until next year.

It wasn't until very recently that Deandra had learned the reason for the cactus's name. The body of the plant was a grayish-green color, reminiscent of the skin color most zombies had in movies. Deandra didn't know how she felt about food having the color palate of the undead.

Beyond that, the arms of the zombie cactus grew in an odd way back in the fae realm. Instead of having two to three arms that jutted into the air like a saguaro, the top of the zombie cactus was flat. From the back of the flattened area grew four or five shorter arms—or fingers—that stretched upward, for all the world looking like a giant zombified hand clawing its way out of the earth.

There was a bird species in the fae realm that exclusively subsisted on the zombie cactus's fruit, which looked similar to mundane dragon fruit. The flattened palm made a perfect platform for the bird's nest. The bird protected the plant from several large herbivores who were willing to brave a jab to the face by its needles in to get a taste of its sweet flesh, and in exchange, the bird was blessed with abundant fruit.

No matter what anyone said, Deandra thought the things were creepy.

The town hadn't been completely overrun with tourists yet, but there were more and more each day. In hopes of luring in zombie cactus enthusiasts, shop owners were employing all manner of advertising to drum up extra business. Some had chalkboard signs standing outside, either listing the zombie cactus products they sold or showing drawings of cactuses—some cute and smiling, others a little macabre and undead. Owners and employees wore cactus-themed headbands, hats, vests, shoes, and even full-body cactus costumes. Some shops even had inflatable cactuses out front, their undead fingers wiggling at passersby.

Oracle Park was slowly filling with carnival rides, game booths, and food trucks. Deandra hoped the grass would survive. She also hoped, again, that Sunshine didn't get agitated by all the new arrivals in her park.

Banners hung from lampposts, and flyers were affixed to windows, bulletin boards, and telephone poles like the one Deandra still stood in front of.

Deandra didn't have enough experience with zombie cactuses herself to harbor any *valid* ill feelings toward them. But the whole thing was giving her pumpkin spice–related flashbacks of her days as a barista. It wasn't as if the entirety of the mundane world threw a festival for the spice, but people certainly went feral for it every season.

At Urbean Edge, the coffee shop Deandra had worked at in Los Angeles, the owner had strongly encouraged everyone to adjust their wardrobe as necessary to match the "color aesthetic" of the much-loved spice. When Deandra moved to Axia, she'd happily donated a good amount of her orange and brown attire to Goodwill on her way out of the City of Angels.

Urbean Edge's customers, who were uppity *before* pumpkin spice season, seemed to get worse. The staff turnover rate with college kids was abysmal year round, but it always got dire just before pumpkin spice season started, meaning Deandra was working longer hours with more customers and custom orders to contend with—all with less help.

The whole of Axia going into zombie cactus mode was triggering a dormant PTSD in her. Some deep, irrational part of her assumed she'd soon despise the cactus on principle. But she figured she should at least try some of the seasonal offerings before waging a silent war on the plant and its fruit.

Granted, she was also a bit grumpy because, instead of being on the couch on a Tuesday night with her dragon watching the season five finale of *Faet of the Heart*, she'd been roped into helping Wendy at Heather's Elixirs.

The shop closed at eight. She checked her phone. Five minutes to go.

She'd been instructed that at eight, once the door was locked behind the last customer, she was to meet Wendy at the back door of the shop to help unload several massive orders that were all nearly a week behind schedule. They'd arrived today in waves during business hours, and the pallets of goods were taking up a considerable amount of space in the back parking lot. The shipments, naturally, were stuffed with zombie cactus products and decorations. Axia wasn't the only hub in the country that was celebrating the plant this summer, and there had been a backlog on orders across the hub system.

Heather, according to Wendy, had been a basket case for days, worried none of the shipments would arrive in time to fully deck out Heather's Elixirs with zombie cactus everything to capitalize on the flood of tourists that would be hitting the hub in three days.

Heather's stress had manifested in lashing out at employees. Two of Wendy's coworkers apparently almost got into a fist fight. Madison, Heather's teenage niece, had quit—again—this afternoon, running out of the shop in tears. When Wendy had called Deandra to beg her to help later, she'd been near tears herself.

Deandra thought she should get a Cousin of the Year award for pausing the season five finale and answering the phone when Wendy called half an hour ago. To be honest, Deandra had hoped Wendy was calling to ask if Deandra wanted her to bring home dinner. Instead, she got guilted into being helpful *and* donning pants. The injustice!

After checking her phone again and seeing that it was one minute after eight, she bid the Zombie Cactus Festival flyer goodbye and headed farther down Eddy Way toward Heather's Elixirs. When she reached the corner of Eddy Way and Coterie Road, she stopped. There were no fences or walls shielding the parking lot behind Heather's Elixirs, so it was easy to spot the numerous stacks of pallets that had been left in the lot. The plastic that wrapped the pallets had been torn loose from some of the stacks, the thick bands pooling on the asphalt like shed snakeskin.

The sight of so many boxes was intimidating enough, but the sound of shouting coming from somewhere beyond the maze made Deandra want to turn around and march her butt back home. She couldn't make out what was being said, but she recognized Heather's voice. The usually reserved woman apparently didn't handle stress well.

Wendy had mentioned that Heather's husband had been ill for a while, though, so Deandra figured the stress of the late shipments had sent her over the edge when she'd already been at her wit's end.

Creeping forward, Deandra tried to get a sense of what the altercation was about. By the time she reached the first stack of pallets, she determined that the argument was between Heather and her brother, and the topic was Madison.

"You're not hearing me. She hasn't stopped *crying*, Heather! And she won't tell us what you said to her!" he shouted.

"No, *you're* not hearing *me*. I don't have *time* for this, Terry," Heather snapped back. "We're stretched thin here as it is, and Madison isn't pulling her weight. I've told you *that* countless times, too, but you don't *listen*."

Deandra stopped in an aisle made by two stacks of pallets that were almost as tall as she was.

"She'd respect your boundaries if you actually set them," he said. "She's a willful girl."

"Your kid being a disrespectful brat is somehow *my* fault?" Heather asked, the question punctuated by a bitter laugh. "If she doesn't respect people's boundaries, it's because her teachers failed her!"

There was a long beat of silence. Deandra winced. She really wanted to run back in the other direction now.

"I don't know what's gotten into you lately, Heather," Terry said, his tone more incredulous than furious now. "She's your niece. You need to—"

"I don't *need* to do anything. I hired her as a favor to you and Beth. You know who doesn't respect boundaries? You. You take and you take and you take. You always have. And I guess that's on me, because I always let you. But I've got too much going on right now to deal with this on top of everything else. Madison is welcome to have her job back, but on *my* terms. I'll write up a contract, and she'll sign it. She violates any of my rules again, and she's out for good. No negotiating. Final offer. Take it or leave it."

Deandra bit down on her bottom lip. She couldn't see Terry or Heather from her vantage point, but she could still sense the fury pouring off Heather's brother like a fog.

"Fine," he ground out.

Deandra gave Heather a little mental cheer.

"Good. Now let us get to work. She can come in on Thursday

morning to sign the contract," Heather said. "Nine a.m. on the dot, and not a second later."

The click of leather soles on asphalt made Deandra jump. The sound was coming from her left, and she hurried forward a few steps, just in time to see a man walking in the other direction between the aisle of pallets one row over. While Heather had a new-agey vibe—loose, flowy clothes, almost all-gray hair that was constantly a bit unkempt, and chunky costume jewelry—Terry looked every bit the businessman he was. Deandra recalled that he was in the real estate business. He wore a crisp white button-up shirt tucked into black slacks. Lamplight winked off his shiny black leather loafers. His hair had gone salt-and-pepper, but it was neatly trimmed and gave him a wizened, sophisticated air.

He'd left the scene quickly, not noticing Deandra as she watched him go. He turned left onto Coterie Road on foot and quickly disappeared from view.

Deandra gave it a few more seconds to make sure Terry didn't come back with "And another thing!" on his tongue. When he didn't reappear, she hurried forward, quickly navigating her way out of the maze. She found a group of people huddled near the back doors of the shop, which were propped open with a pair of large rocks.

Heather was sobbing on a husky man's shoulder while three others—Wendy included—hyped the woman up for standing her ground.

"Woo! Go Heather!" Deandra said as she joined them.

Heather lifted her head from the man's shoulder and sniffed hard. Her eyes were bloodshot, and she looked exhausted. "Oh gosh. You heard all that? Did the whole neighborhood hear?" A deep red clawed up her neck and into her cheeks.

"Pah!" Deandra said, noting belatedly that she sounded like Grandma January. "I got here just as you really got going. I want to be you when I grow up."

Heather smiled and laughed awkwardly at the praise, but her face crumpled soon afterward, and tears slid down her cheeks.

The man with his arm around her pulled her a little closer. He was a heavy-set redhead with a well-trimmed beard. Deandra guessed he was in his thirties.

Once he'd calmed Heather down a little, Wendy clapped her hands three times in quick succession. "Now that Dee is here, we can really get started. What if we get you set up in the breakroom to relax a bit, Heather? We'll get you some tea, you can take a breather, and then, when you're ready, you can join us."

"But you don't—"

The man who had his arm around Heather said, "Don't start, Heather." He had a deep, resonant voice, and his tone was somehow both firm *and* affectionate. "We've all worked here for at least a year, and all of us have been through a Zombie Cactus Apocalypse before. Well, not Dee, but we'll get her up to speed. We need to get everything *into* the store first, anyway, right? So let us unload everything and then you can micromanage your little heart out."

Heather sniffed loudly. "I'm such a mess."

He gave her a squeeze. "You are. But you're *our* mess, so let us help, okay? Promise us substantial monetary bonuses, and we'll all be good."

"Despite not being an employee, I'll also take a substantial monetary bonus," Deandra added.

Heather let out another watery laugh, then cast her gaze around the assembled group. "I got very lucky in finding you all. Truly." She smiled at Deandra. "If you decide you'd like to take Madison's place, I will officially fire her right this instant. I don't care how mad my brother will be. Even if you *are* planning to participate in extortion."

Deandra shrugged. "I think I'd rather stick with my current job and also extort you for money from the sidelines. Best of both worlds."

The other young man held out a hand to Deandra. "You're very clearly related to Wendy, so I already like you. I'm Devon."

Deandra shook his offered hand. "Dee. Nice to put a face to the name."

He nodded. "Likewise."

He appeared human enough; at first glance, he looked like a twenty-something blond surfer who would have fit right in in her old neck of the woods in Southern California. He was tall, lean, and his mop of hair was disheveled in a very deliberate way that probably required a decent amount of mousse. What set him apart, though, were his eyes. He had goat eyes, which were familiar enough because of her interactions with Sarah, the owner of Pawsome Pals, but still wholly off-putting. He clearly had faun ancestry somewhere in his family tree. Unlike Sarah, who was full faun—complete with horns and furry goat legs—Devon no doubt could blend into the mundane world merely with the use of contacts. She did her best to focus on his freckle-dusted nose instead of his unsettling eyes.

Devon said, "You, me, and Wendy can start unloading the pallets, and Otis, maybe you can get Heather that tea?"

She wondered if Otis and Devon were the ones who'd almost gotten into a fist fight earlier. The larger man didn't seem to take any offense at Devon doling out tasks, but he was also focused on Heather.

"Which tea do you want?" Otis asked, steering Heather toward the propped-open doors.

As their voices faded inside, Deandra, Wendy, and Devon turned and stood in a horizontal line before the sea of boxes.

Devon gusted a long sigh from his spot between the cousins. "So ... I know this is one of the best moneymaking weekends of the year for Axia, but I have a confession to make."

Wendy and Deandra turned to look at him.

"I hate zombie cactus with every fiber of my being, almost entirely on principle."

Deandra laughed. "I hate pumpkin spice for the same reason. Honestly, I'm close to hating pumpkins in general. Which is extra infuriating, because pumpkin spice isn't even made from pumpkins! It's cinnamon and nutmeg." She scowled. "I *hate* nutmeg."

Devon's blond locks bobbed in her peripheral vision as he nodded.

Wendy said, "To be honest, I also hate this weekend. Heather going nuclear made a stressful time even more stressful. But I *do* love me a zombie cactus frozen lemonade. At any rate, we should name it—this weekend, I mean." She stared thoughtfully into the middle distance. "Cactolypse. Zompocolypse. The Great Cactus Invasion ..."

They slipped into contemplative silence.

"The Cactus Calamity," Devon offered.

"I appreciate the alliteration," said Deandra. "I feel like we need something slightly more gruesome, though. What about ... Cactus Carnage."

Devon pointed a finger gun at her. "Perfect."

Wendy rolled her neck and cracked her knuckles. "Then let the carnage begin ..."

BY THE TIME DEANDRA AND WENDY STUMBLED INTO THE APARTMENT later that evening, it was just after eleven p.m.

Deandra's hands were dry, she had a paper cut in the webbing between her pointer finger and thumb, and her shoes were covered in a faint layer of green glitter that she was sure would never come out.

Worst still, Havoc was airborne and spinning in dizzying circles in joy at their arrival.

While Wendy trudged off to the shower to wash green glitter out of her hair, Deandra hooked Havoc's leash to his harness and headed back outside, because he wouldn't let her sleep until he got some of his energy out.

She'd just stepped off the last step of the staircase when her shoe landed on something squishy. She slipped a bit, like a cartoon character who stepped on a banana peel. Flailing wildly, she managed to grab hold of the handrail before she hit the ground. When she found her footing, she lifted her foot in distaste, finding the remains of pulped dark-pink goo. Havoc gave the offending mess a sniff, then chirped happily before guzzling it down. The sickly sweet scent that wafted from it told Deandra it had been a frozen chunk of zombie cactus fruit. A discarded smoothie cup lay nearby.

She groaned.

Cactus carnage indeed.

CHAPTER THREE

On Wednesday afternoon, after walking Barnaby, her favorite alligator chicken, and taking Voidbringer to the flight park, Deandra headed to Mythic Pet Kitchen with Havoc. The pet store catered to exotic and mythical pets, which fit Havoc to a tee, regardless of which form he was in. Mealworms were still the most effective training treat for Havoc, so she was replenishing her supply. She'd also told Havoc he could choose a toy, as his go-to stuffed cow had been gutted recently, and Deandra was unsure if it could be revived.

She was convinced that Havoc had developed bloodlust—stuffing-lust?—from Maxine, Cruz's black lab, who was notorious for eviscerating her toys. Deandra would have to attempt to gently nudge him toward the tougher toys that lacked vulnerable soft bellies.

As she stepped through the sliding doors of the shop, her shoulders sagged. Not even the Mythic Pet Kitchen had escaped the permeating fog that was the encroaching zombie cactus invasion.

Just beyond the two cashier stations stood a massive free-standing shelving unit that stretched well over six feet tall. The colorful sign that arched above the shelves said "ZOMBIE CACTUS SEASON HAS GONE TO THE DOGS!" Which was odd, given that most of the products in the store weren't meant for canines. As she got closer, she noted the sheer variety of toys on display. There were zombie cactus fruit plushies, rubber cactuses, stuffed zombies, and gray cactuses with snarling mouths. Havoc, naturally, dragged her toward the display, tail wagging furiously, and almost immediately chose a severed-hand plushy.

Deandra tried to suggest something else, but he happily squinted up at her, stuffed hand in his mouth, as his wings fluttered. He was utterly enamored with his choice, and she would be a monster to deny him his zombie limb now.

Sighing, she gave him a nod, and he wiggle-walked toward the right side of the store. When there were live animals for sale, they were usually on this side, and Havoc liked to peer in at them. This was where Deandra had first learned about fire newts. There had been a display of eight terrariums; one had stood empty. Looking back, Deandra assumed now that the eighth one had once been occupied by Sunshine.

The display of zombie-cactus-themed toys wasn't the only change in the store. The right side boasted all manner of animals now. There were aquariums, terrariums, and cages full of unique creatures. A few of the cages held birds with feathers in colors Deandra swore she'd never seen before.

There were a few large cages, too. One held six small animals that looked like mundane kittens initially, but a closer inspection revealed scales, horns, antennae, or some combination of the three. Not to mention that all of them had fur in some hue of green. The cage had two ramps connected to platforms—similar to a winding staircase—to allow the cats to get to higher ground. Only one of the six was awake, though.

Instead of taking advantage of the multistoried enclosure, the other five were piled together in a fluffy bed on the bottom level, where they slept in a tangle of paws, horns, and tails. The conscious one was mostly teal in color and had two tall antennae that sprang from the top of its head between its pointed ears. All but one paw was white.

It had been drinking water from a bottle that hung from the side of the cage but started when it realized Havoc was lying on the other side of its enclosure. His belly was flat on the floor, and his muzzle was pressed to the wire mesh. Or, more accurately, he had his stuffed-limb toy pressed to the cage's side. His tail wagged hard. The kitten must have sensed that Havoc only wanted to say hello, because it cautiously made its way across the blankets that lined the cage's base. Its antennae flicked about independently, like eyestalks, and Deandra wondered what information the appendages were sending the kitten as it stumbled forward on its too-large paws.

One of the zombie toy's fingers poked through a square in the cage's wall. It was twitching a bit, what with Havoc's enthusiastic tail wagging. When the kitten was about a foot away, it finally spotted the gently waving undead digit and froze. It slowly lowered itself to the blankets, eyes trained on its prey. After a few seconds, the kitten wiggled its butt and then pounced.

The kitten, much like Havoc in his constant pursuit of insects, missed by a mile. It tripped over its own feet and slid chin-first into the cage's side. Havoc jumped back and dropped into play stance. The kitten mewed and darted to the side. Havoc followed it along the side of the cage. Before long, the two were chasing each other in dizzying circles. Deandra had quickly unclipped his harness so he wouldn't choke himself or get her feet tangled up in his leash.

All the commotion eventually woke up the kitten's littermates —especially when the pile got trampled by the teal kitten on one of its mad dashes around the cage. Most of them joined in the chase, running around and around the inside of the enclosure, while Havoc—his limb toy still in his mouth—pranced and bounced along the cage's exterior. Two of the kittens remained in the fluffy bed, though, wide eyes trained on the oversize dog ringing their temporary home.

As cute as the strange kittens were, Deandra would have to put her foot down if Havoc tried to take one of them home instead of the severed hand. Wendy would not be happy if she brought home a green cat that looked like something out of a sci-fi movie.

Plus, knowing Deandra's luck, she wouldn't realize until she got home with the alien feline that it had some bizarre magical power.

As if someone was listening to her thoughts, one of the terrified kittens still in the bed started to vibrate. It wasn't as if the cat was in the throes of a seizure; this wasn't that violent. It for all the world looked like the cat was turning into television static or was vaporizing into atoms. Before she could get out a word of alarm, the entire cage gave a pulse of bright blue light. Deandra blinked, and the vibrating kitten was ... gone. Another blink, and she saw it sitting on the topmost platform of its enclosure, staring down at its littermates, who still raced around the inside of the cage while Havoc pranced about outside.

Teleporting alien cats?

Nope.

"The cage is state of the art. When the kittens try to phase out of it, the cage's runes counteract their magic to keep them inside."

Deandra flinched and then glanced to her left, then down, to find a middle-aged man standing beside her, hands tucked behind his back. "I'm sorry, what?"

He was quite a bit shorter than her, giving her a clear view of his bald spot. He glanced up and smiled warmly. It was a human face, while also decidedly not. His skin was an olive-green color, and his pointed ears were covered in a smattering of long, coarse black hairs. His ears stuck out from either side of his head, rather than straight up like an elf's. What little hair he had was a chocolate brown. His eyes were a startlingly vibrant shade of green, but they were kind. Her best guess was that he was a goblin.

"Runes are carved into every wire. Vibrissa cats, especially as kittens, need to be contained in magic-regulated enclosures to limit the range of their phasing. You can't imagine the problems we ran into before we found a manufacturer for cages such as these. Cats were teleporting willy-nilly all over the store. Easy way for them to get hurt. The adults have more control over the ability, and they mostly use it to aid in hunting."

It took Deandra several long seconds to process all that. "Can they … phase through walls?" was the only thing she could think to ask, imagining a full-grown alien cat teleporting into someone's home looking for a human-sized snack. Her gaze shifted to the severed hand Havoc had yet to let go of.

The man chuckled. "Oh, Goddess, no. Can you imagine! They can only phase to a location in their immediate line of sight. And they're limited by distance, too. Different distances for different cats, depending on the strength of the skill and genetics and what-not. Kittens can travel just far enough for it to be a nuisance. The worst version of keep-away one can play is with a mischievous vibrissa kitten, let me tell you."

"How big do they get?" Deandra asked, imagining the size of cage needed to contain a tiger with the ability to teleport itself directly to its prey.

"Not much bigger than this, actually," he said. "Most don't get above five pounds. Really great housecats, once they grow out of the rebellious stage. You in the market for a new pet? Seems like your pup wants a friend ..."

Deandra glanced over at her "pup" to find him on his back, toy hand in his mouth, feet in the air. The original teal-colored kitten had stuck one of its white-tipped paws through one of the cage's square slots and was swatting ineffectually at the toy in Havoc's mouth that was just out of reach.

"They're adorable, but my roommate would strangle me if I brought home another animal," Deandra said. "The good thing about my job is that I get my animal fix during the day, and then I'm less likely to adopt one when I come here for supplies."

The goblin looked from Havoc to Deandra and back again. "Oh. *Oh.* I *thought* you looked familiar! You're the new pet sitter who's taming the mythical population left and right here in Axia, aren't you? I was so distracted by your pup wooing these grouchy kittens that the whole dire wolf puppy thing didn't register until now."

"You might be the first person who hasn't at least flinched when they meet Havoc," Deandra said. "And ... grouchy? Those little guys?"

The teal kitten's littermates were still amped up from their sprint around the cage and were now roughhousing and generally looking like happy kittens. Well, all except for the one on the highest platform, who was shivering from anxiety. That one was an emerald green, and it had a tiny teal nub of a horn poking out from each temple, as well as tall antennae. It lacked any scales.

"They're usually hissing and spitting at anyone who comes by to look at them," he said. "It's a shame. They really *are* great pets, but they need the right owner. Your pup calmed them right down. Which says just as much about you, honestly. Taming a dire wolf puppy is no easy feat!"

Deandra *wished* she could claim to be a dire wolf whisperer. She'd just gotten lucky that she'd been adopted by a dragon with such a sweet disposition. Unable to accept the praise, she merely offered a nonchalant shrug.

"I … uhh …" the goblin said, and began to nervously rub the back of his neck. "Listen. I have a … proposition for you. You can say no if it's not the kind of thing you're into."

Deandra's eyes widened.

When he glanced up at her, his eyes widened, too. "Oh! That sounded terrible." He held up his right hand, showcasing the thick black band that circled his ring finger. "Married! I'm married. Happily married!" His olive-green skin went a sort of muddy brown as he blushed furiously. "I swear I spend too much time around animals all day. It's made me even weirder than I already was."

"Hard same," Deandra said.

He laughed, his shoulders relaxing a bit. "What I meant to ask … is that I was wondering if you were planning to attend the Zombie Cactus Festival? In a professional capacity, I mean. We have an adoption event every year—it's great for business, *and* we find tons of homes for animals, too. I have several sister-stores in other hubs. A veritable fleet of vehicles have been on their way here for days; animals can't travel safely in telepads. The vibrissa cats are always the hardest to adopt out, if only because people are intimidated. But if you—and Havoc—would be willing to help us out in the booth, you can use it as an opportunity to upsell your pet-sitting business. Heck, I might even hire you myself. My wife and I just have mundane cats, which maybe wouldn't be exotic enough for you, but—"

"Mundane cats sound incredible," Deandra said in a rush, recalling her interaction with Peril the ferret all over again. She'd asked the universe or the Goddess or whoever was listening to send her a mundane pet to look after, and what had she gotten? A *talking* ferret.

"I'm more than happy to pay you for your time in the booth, too," the goblin said. "Once the vibrissa cats let their guard down, they're cuddle bugs. Havoc can wear them down, customers will be wooed by their cuteness, and then we can get these little guys homes."

Deandra glanced at the cage and immediately stifled a laugh. Havoc was asleep on his back, the severed-hand toy having fallen out of his mouth and onto the floor. The teal kitten had fallen asleep, too, its white-tipped paw still sticking out of one square of the cage while its little pink nose stuck out of another. The other kittens were sprawled out along the blankets in various places.

The scaredy-cat on the topmost platform had lain down but was still trembling slightly. Deandra suddenly wanted to make it her mission to find that one in particular a nice calm home.

"What days and times were you thinking?" Deandra asked.

The goblin lightly clapped his hands. "You'll do it?"

"I'm not sure I can commit to all three days, but we can help with a shift or two," she said.

"Oh, how wonderful." He held out a hand. "I'm Juniper, by the way."

She shook it. "Deandra, but you can call me Dee."

"Absolutely lovely to meet you, Dee. I'll let you get back to your shopping. We can exchange contact information when you're done. I'll check the schedule and give you a few options to choose from. The pay will be worth your while, too." He started to walk away but then scurried a few steps closer and whispered, "If your roommate attends the festival, point her out, and I'll shove a vibrissa cat into her arms. She won't be able to say no!"

Deandra had her doubts about that, but Juniper scampered off before she could say as much.

She gently roused her dozing dragon, got his leash reattached, and they set off to finish their shopping. Havoc, with his severed-hand toy back in his mouth, cast a few sad glances over his shoulder at his kitten friend, who was still fast asleep. Deandra did her best not to look at her dragon, sure his puppy-dog eyes would break her already weak will and then she'd have to explain to Wendy why there was a teleporting kitten on her dining room table.

After paying for Havoc's now soggy toy, two jumbo bags of

mealworms, and a case of canned cricket paste, Deandra was able to leave the store without a new kitten.

She loaded her items and her dragon into the car and flopped into the front seat, unable to get the image of that terrified little kitten out of her head. She grabbed her phone out of her purse that was sitting on the passenger seat and pulled up the text thread with Cruz.

> **Deandra**
> Do you want an alien cat?

Propping the phone on her dash, she started the car. Just as she started to back out of her spot, a squeak sounded from the back seat. The severed hand apparently came with a squeaker that Havoc had just now discovered. He squeaked it in rapid succession, issued a muffled chirp-bark of delight, and furiously squeaked it again. Oh boy. *That* was going to be a problem at three a.m., she just knew it.

She was pulling out onto the road when her phone started to ring.

Surprised, she hit the Accept button. "Hi. I figured you'd be working."

Cruz's voice piped out through the car's speakers. "I am, but I'm on lunch. Kind of."

"Meaning you're sitting in your car eating the day's spoils from the vending machine?"

Long pause. "No?"

She huffed a laugh. "Convincing."

"Is it less sad if I'm hiding in a supply closet eating pretzels instead of doing so in my car?"

"Jury's still out. Why are you in a supply closet?"

He exhaled a long, weary sigh. "We had to put an elderly animal down an hour or so ago. It was absolutely the right time, but I had the extra unhappy bonus of being able to hear his thoughts, which were a jumbled and confused mess. It happens with animals in old age, just as it does with people. It's just hard that I can *actually* explain what's happening to him in his final moments—something very few people get the opportunity to do —and in the end, it didn't really matter, because his mind was too far gone to understand anyway. He was a beloved patient here for many years. The owner is a wreck. The techs are a wreck. I just needed a few quiet moments to myself, I guess. Wanted to eat my stale pretzels in peace."

"And yet you called me," she said.

"You bring me peace, too." He immediately groaned. "Ugh, that was so cheesy. I didn't even think about it. It just ... came out."

She cracked up. "That *was* pretty bad. Want company? I'm not far from the office."

"As great as that sounds," he said, "I have surgery in half an hour."

"Too bad. Havoc could have shown you his new severed hand ..."

"I don't know if I want to address the severed-hand thing or the alien-cat thing first. I'm constantly amazed at how exceedingly good you are at providing zero context."

"Gotta keep you on your toes," she said, laughing, then told him about her interaction with Juniper and the vibrissa cats as she headed home. "I was only half joking about you adopting a cat. Though if Havoc had his way, we'd have left with one of them." Havoc paused in his excessive squeaking to issue a sad howl. "But I *was* thinking that an even better asset to have at the booth than Havoc would be a very talented and handsome zoolinguist who could talk to this nervous cat and maybe help find it a home?"

"Ah," Cruz said sagely. "I'm being exploited for my skills once again."

"I would have said that I made the suggestion because it's an excuse to spend more time with you, but we've already hit our cheese quota for this conversation."

He was quiet for a beat. "I'm in. I haven't interacted with a vibrissa cat since my days at the academy. They *do* make good pets, but they're cat ownership on hard mode. They require a lot of training and due diligence, in part because they're incredibly intelligent and stubborn in equal measure." He sighed. "I should be getting back, though. My pager just went off. I'll call you tonight, okay?"

"I will not know peace until you do," she intoned gravely. "Good luck with the surgery."

He laughed. "Bye, Dee. Bye, Havoc! I hear you squeaking back there …"

Havoc chirped once before returning to squeaking up a storm.

A minute later, she pulled into her parking spot at the apartment complex, shut off the car, and turned in her seat, determined to snatch the toy from Havoc, if only because she was developing a migraine.

Before she could, though, her phone started to ring again. Smiling, she turned back toward her dashboard, hoping it was Cruz. Her face fell as she saw the name scrolling across her screen.

Quinn Greenwood.

Peril's owner.

Oh no …

CHAPTER FOUR

"Hi, Quinn," Deandra answered, hoping she sounded friendly and not apprehensive.

"Hey, Dee," came Quinn's high and light voice. "I'm guessing you can figure out why I'm calling you …"

"Did you and Rularo decide to take that mushroom-hunting trip? Are you trying to get the heck out of town before the zombie cactus madness *really* gets going?"

Quinn laughed. "The mushroom-hunting expedition is still in the planning stage. And we would never dream of skipping the festival! The town council hired us to do the signage again. We'll have a double booth this year, too. We usually sell stationery and such, but this year Rularo is also going to offer flash tattoos on the other side of the booth. It's already one of our best weekends of the year, and Ru's tattoos are sure to help us do even better."

"Okay …" Deandra said slowly, getting the impression Quinn was stalling.

Havoc squeaked his toy ten times in rapid succession. She whirled in her seat. He was so startled by the quick movement, the toy fell from his mouth. Deandra contorted herself so she could grab it off the floor before he could. Havoc looked positively scandalized by the theft. Waving the soggy severed hand, she whispered to her dragon, "You know I love you to pieces, but you are *not* getting this back until this phone call is over."

Havoc huffed a very dramatic sigh that was punctuated by a thin plume of white smoke from either nostril. He stood up long enough to turn to face the back passenger side window, then flopped onto his stomach, head between his paws. He stared out the window as if contemplating how his life had come to this— suffering betrayal most foul by someone he loved. He groaned, world-weary.

Deandra rolled her eyes, then turned back around and deposited the cursed toy on the passenger seat near her purse.

Quinn spoke in a rush, her voice filling the car and redirecting Deandra's focus. "I'm sorry this is so last minute, but our sitter bailed on us. We had her lined up for months; that's why we didn't ask you when we saw you last. But she just called and said she's down with the flu. She didn't sound sick at all, if you ask me." She paused. "I'm sure Peril would be fine on his own, since we'll be home every night, but he just gets so stressed when he's alone all day.

"Normally Ru lets him burrow into his beard or hide in his shirt, but the event is outside, and Peril doesn't do well in the heat. He doesn't do well in crowds, either. And he's extra squirmy when he's anxious. It's just better if he stays home.

"Anyway, since he took a liking to you, we were thinking, if you could just drop by once or twice a day to check on him and hang out for an hour or so, that would probably make a world of difference! We'd hired the other sitter to stay at the house in eight-hour blocks each day, but I know you have other clients to care for. That's too much to ask of you with no warning."

Within seconds of hearing how distressed the woman sounded, Deandra had known saying no was out of the question. "I can do that. I'm helping Juniper from the Mythic Pet Kitchen at his booth a few times over the weekend, but I can check on Peril in between my stints."

Quinn issued a little gasp. "Wait, really? You can do it?"

"Sure," Deandra said. "Would coming by the house sometime today or tomorrow be okay, so you can show me around the house, his usual haunts, things like that?"

"Oh my Goddess, I might cry! I was so sure you'd say no. We'll pay you double because of the late notice." Deandra started to protest, but Quinn cut her off. "Don't argue. You're helping us out more than you know. Ru needs a clear head when he's doing flash with live ink, and knowing Peril is in your care will keep him steady."

Deandra wished she had as much confidence in herself and her supposed skills as everyone else did. She had no idea why Peril had taken a shine to her or if the interaction she'd had with the salica last month had been a fluke. Maybe the magic-touched ferret had just been having an especially good day and felt chatty. What if he took one look at her and fainted dead away in fright?

"I'll be at the shop until five tonight," Quinn said. "Would sometime after five thirty work for you?"

That would give Deandra enough time to walk Havoc, feed him, and make an early dinner for herself. Wendy wouldn't be home until after eight, as she was helping close.

"Sounds good," Deandra said. "Can you text me your address?"

"Yes, I'll do that the moment we hang up. Oh gosh! I'm so relieved; you have no idea."

Deandra plastered on her best approximation of a confident smile, even if Quinn couldn't see it. "See you soon."

After disconnecting the call, she grabbed the severed hand off the passenger seat and turned around to face her dragon once more. He was still staring out the window, miserable.

"Do you want this back?" she asked.

One of his cone-shaped ears flicked in her direction, but he otherwise didn't move.

Even if she found it mildly disgusting—why was it so damp? —she pressed her thumb and middle finger on either side of the palm. The toy squeaked. Havoc's head whipped toward her, head cocked. She squeaked it again.

He scrambled to his feet and poked his head between the front seats, butt wiggling.

"You've got to keep the squeaking to a minimum when Wendy gets home, okay?"

He wiggled harder, eyes trained on the toy.

"And we have to put it away when it's time for bed."

He wagged harder still.

Sighing, she offered it to him, and he snatched it out of her hand. He pranced around the back seat, the toy squeaking every other second. Deandra's eye twitched. She sent a silent prayer that his enthusiasm would puncture the squeaker's air bladder sooner rather than later, letting the undead hand die for good.

Quinn and Rularo lived near the northern end of town, not far from where Starshadow and the Hornsbys lived.

As she parked at the curb outside the Greenwoods' house, she gaped at the fenced-in garden. Even at first glance, Deandra would have pegged the house as belonging to people with an affinity for nature or earth magic. The yard outside the home was contained within a black wrought-iron fence, and a paver stone–

lined path ran along the inside of it. The grass grew in rough patches, in large part because the lawn was dotted with rectangular planter boxes arranged in two rows of three. The wood was painted a burnt orange. Vegetables and herbs grew in wild abundance from the boxes, and in some places, vines snaked out of a box and inched along the grass that was fighting for its life.

The only vegetable Deandra recognized was eggplant, though she thought they looked more blue than deep purple. She wondered how many of the plants were used for cooking and how many were ingredients for the Greenwoods' living inks.

She climbed out of the car and headed up the empty driveway, which wasn't enclosed within the iron fence. A few large oil stains marked where cars were usually parked. A green bicycle was propped up on its kickstand near a row of hedges that sat below the home's front windows.

The house itself was beige with emerald-green accents. Plants hung from the eaves at regular intervals, and they were as varied as they were plentiful. An earthy scent seemed to hover around the property, like damp soil, but it wasn't overwhelming. It reminded her of walking into the garden section of a hardware store.

The front door stood at the back of a small, recessed porch. Unsurprisingly, potted plants dotted the cement landing and two steps. She ducked under a hanging fern that had several furry tendrils reminiscent of the whorls of a snail's shell. Deandra's mother had always loved gardening, and even though Deandra hadn't inherited her green thumb, she'd always remembered the term "fiddleheads" to describe the young leaves on a fern, as they looked like the curled head of a violin or fiddle.

Rularo was not a small man; Deandra wondered how many times he'd whacked his head on the fern's pot while venturing toward the front door. A garage took up the space between the fenced-in front yard and the porch; perhaps he went in through there instead.

Deandra was about to ring the doorbell when she saw the small sign hanging above it.

Ring this at your own Peril.

She quickly pulled her hand back, equal parts confused and dismayed by the sign's warning. She opted to knock.

Several long seconds ticked by with no sound emanating from behind the black front door. Just when she was getting ready to text Quinn to make sure she was home, the door was yanked open. Quinn, barefoot and breathing hard, stood with one hand on the door's knob and the other on her side as if she'd gotten a stitch.

Quinn's pointed elf-like ears were more prominent than usual, as she'd pulled her curls into a tight ponytail today. Her mint-green eyes paired with her dark skin gave her an otherworldly aura, which was dampened somewhat by her bellbottom jeans and a beige shirt with a giant black and yellow sunflower on the front. Hello, Sunshine! the shirt said.

Quinn straddled the line of reality and fantasy so thoroughly, it made Deandra's brain glitch. It was almost easier to think of her as someone from the mundane world who was doing a spectac-ular job at fae cosplay.

"Hey, Dee! Thanks so much for coming by. Please, come in," she said.

Deandra cautiously stepped inside, not sure why she felt as if Peril would come flying at her at any moment, determined to gnaw her face off, when the salica was scared of his own shadow.

"Sorry for the mess," Quinn said as she closed the door behind her. "We've been in festival prep mode for weeks. Oh, is it okay to ask you to take your shoes off at the door? Quieter footsteps keep Peril calmer."

Deandra heeled her shoes off and left them on a rug piled with sandals, slippers, and boots. Rularo's were easy to spot; they were twice the size of Quinn's.

A kitchen stretched to the right, the floor lined with slate-gray stone tiles. The dark-brown marble countertops on either side of the rectangular room were absolutely heaped with vegetables and herbs. Some were in baskets, but most were stacked haphazardly. There were glass jars, plastic tubs, scissors, and spools of twine.

A pair of windows stood behind a double sink to the right of the kitchen. In front of the windows, from the ceiling, hung circular drying racks with clusters of herbs pinned around their edges at even intervals, like chandeliers. A five-foot-long mesh tube-like rack hung from the wall near the stainless-steel refrigerator. It looked a bit like a laundry hamper. Its exterior was solid save for a two-inch-wide column cut out of the center. The openings allowed for access to the six interior platforms lined with herbs, cut vegetables, and flower petals.

The wall opposite the doorway where Deandra still stood was lined with a dozen horizontal planks of wood. Drying herbs hung there, too, attached with clothespins. Small plaques sat above the rows, though they were too far away for Deandra to read what they said.

The table in front of the drying wall had three boxy machines in the middle. They were softly humming and lined with racks. Deandra figured they were food dehydrators.

Deandra wondered how the Greenwoods were able to cook in here.

Quinn heaved a breath behind her. "You don't even have to say it. I know! It's so much. We've started ordering food delivery every night because the kitchen has turned into an herb factory."

"Does Peril help himself to this buffet in the middle of the night?" Deandra asked.

"Thankfully, no! Salica can't digest plants, so he's strictly a carnivore."

Deandra was once again convinced she'd lucked out that

Havoc was an omnivore. Being able to feed him only plants or only meat would have been even more of a challenge.

Quinn said, "Unfortunately, he's not very food motivated. You can certainly try to use treats to lure him out of hiding, but it rarely works. There's a variety of meat treats in the fridge you can attempt if it comes to that, though. He's also pretty fond of a very expensive meat-based kitten food that's in the cabinet under the sink. You won't need to feed him this time around. Just a couple of check-ins a day to make sure he hasn't passed out from perceived abandonment will be more than enough. We'll feed him when we get home."

Deandra blew out a breath that puffed out her cheeks.

"The living room is this way ..." Quinn said, backing farther into the foyer.

Tearing her gaze away from the overwhelming sight of the kitchen, she followed Quinn. From the foyer, the kitchen was to the right, a hallway was to the left, and a large open-plan living room was straight ahead. The beige carpet was plush under Deandra's socked feet. The room was practically spotless, compared to the kitchen. A black sectional couch took up a good chunk of the middle of the room. Above the fireplace on the left side of the room hung a flat-screen TV. The volume was either low or muted, and on the screen was some kind of nature show. Currently, a massive swarm of starlings flitted before a pink-and-orange sunset, the birds shifting in unison, like a flying school of fish.

It wasn't until that moment that Deandra noticed a particularly odd feature of the house. Along the ceiling above the TV— and along the top of the walls of the entire room, now that she was looking for it—was a tunnel system. Deandra had had a hamster as a kid. A twisting tunnel system made of colorful plastic had been integrated into the wire cage. That was the first thing she thought of as she eyed the tunnels, though these were five times as wide as the one her tiny hamster had scuttled around in. The color of these tunnels was mostly clear, allowing them to blend into the walls and floor, rather than being the vibrant yellow, blue, and green of Hammy's "critter crawl" tubes.

Deandra turned in a slow circle, her gaze tracking the tunnel that ran along the wall into the den on one side of the living room and into the dining room on another. Her attention dropped to the plush beige carpet, finding that the tunnel system ran along the floor, too, hugging the wall. A closer inspection revealed that there were a few openings in the tunnels that ran along the floor, giving Peril multiple entry and exit points.

Quinn laughed softly. "I was wondering when you were going to notice those."

Deandra crept toward the den-like area to the left of the living room. The space overlooked the backyard. A couch faced the windows, and a row of low credenzas sat below them. They, of course, were topped with a clutter of potted plants. Other than a built-in bookshelf on the left of the rectangular room and what looked like a walking desk on the other side, the room was sparsely furnished. It probably made for a great reading room, especially in the warm months when the space was flooded with light. The tunnel system continued in here, with the tubes running above the windows and then curving toward the floor beside the door that led into the yard. The tunnel ended in a chute, and Deandra imagined the ferret using this section like a slide from an amusement park. The drop was nearly vertical, and she wondered if Peril ever came flying out of the chute like a cannonball.

"He's very dexterous," Quinn said from behind Deandra. "There are entrances spaced along the tunnels that span the entire house. Ru designed them based on Peril's specific requests, so they're all built to his liking. He's usually in the tunnels during the day, but he's got hidey places all over the place, as well as beds and baskets for him to sleep in.

"You don't have to worry about doing a head count, as he's usually so scared about having visitors that even *we* have a hard time finding him. He does have a tendency to lock himself in the bathroom for some reason, though, so if you can just make sure he hasn't managed that, that would help a lot. We're hoping that hearing you in the house will help ease his mind that he hasn't been abandoned for all time. So please make yourself at home. Watch TV. Play video games. Eat whatever food you can find—assuming you can navigate our disaster of a kitchen."

Deandra bobbed her head. "On the off chance he comes out, does he, uh, I don't know, like to play or anything?"

She knew that salica were something like the weasel-equivalent of draken. Though draken were descended from dragons and could no longer shift out of their human forms, salica were trapped in their animal form and had lost their ability to shift out of it. The magic-touched creatures had retained their human-like consciousness, though.

So perhaps asking if Peril "liked to play" was like asking if a feather attached to a string being dangled in a grown adult's face would qualify as suitable entertainment. For all she knew, Peril's favorite pastime was discussing the teachings of Aristotle.

For her own sake, Deandra hoped Peril was more interested in feathers than philosophers.

"He loves puzzles!" Quinn said. "There's a five-thousand-piece puzzle going on the dining room table right now. He was finishing the two-thousand ones too quickly. The small size of the pieces means he can use both his little hands and his mouth to carry the pieces around. And, like I said, he's very dexterous, so he's good about stepping lightly and not knocking all the pieces to the floor with his tail. When he first started doing the puzzles, he was very clumsy. Watching him now is almost like watching a dancer, he's so graceful."

Deandra honestly didn't know how to comment on that. Just when she thought things couldn't get weirder, they always did. She needed to stop being surprised.

"Honestly, if you get him to play with one of his puzzles during your visits, we might seriously consider paying you to just move in," Quinn said, laughing. "The bar is set so low with us, based on how he's reacted to other sitters, the goal at this point is just *let's hope he doesn't go comatose from anxiety.*"

How on earth did she keep getting saddled with the strangest of animal clients? And why did all these strange animals like her so much?

She silently sent a prayer into the universe that Juniper would call her sometime soon to sit for his mundane cats.

Quinn then took Deandra on a full tour of the house, showing Deandra Peril's most common hiding places, his favorite sleeping spots, several of the tunnel system's entry points, where to find his treats, and ending at the dining room table, where a giant puzzle—judging by the completed frame—was a third completed. The puzzle's box was nowhere to be seen, but from what Deandra could glean, the image was an all-white background dotted with hundreds of bright yellow bananas.

Deandra eyed the tunnel that ran along the top and bottom of the walls of the dining room. The topmost tunnel had an open section positioned near the middle of the table. Maybe Peril launched out of his tunnel in the dead of night, alighted on the table, and got to work in the quiet while Rularo and Quinn slept.

Quinn led her from the dining room through the stuffed-to-the-gills kitchen and into the foyer. She fished a key out of a pocket of her jeans and held it out to Deandra. A metallic beige ferret keychain occupied the ring, along with the house key itself. "You sure you're still up for this? I know it's a lot."

Deandra took the offered key before she could convince herself not to. "Yep. I just hope me being here is actually helpful and doesn't stress him out."

"I have a really good feeling about this," Quinn said, beaming.

They decided that Deandra would swing by twice a day Friday, Saturday, and Sunday. The Greenwoods would be out of the house from six a.m. to nine p.m. every day, so it was up to Deandra when to come by, as the visits were sort of a general wellness check more than anything else.

Particulars taken care of, Deandra was just about to slip her shoes back on when she heard a soft clack on the tile. Glancing down, she found a shiny gray stone sitting a few inches from her foot. It was no bigger than a quarter. Her gaze flicked toward the hallway a few feet away. A tunnel ran along the back wall of the corridor which led to the bedrooms and bathroom. Her eyes widened when she spotted Peril's little face poking out the mouth of a chute. His pink nose twitched.

Brow furrowed, she slowly bent down to pick up the small, smooth rock. There didn't seem to be any runes etched into it, nor did it do anything strange, like hum or heat up in her hand. It looked like a mundane river rock. Before Deandra could say anything, Quinn gasped.

"Oh, Peril!" she cooed. "Did you give Dee one of your rocks?"

Deandra glanced at the tunnel again, finding Peril still peering out from the opening in the tunnel. The chute of this particular tunnel would deposit him just outside the bathroom, and if he turned around to head the other way, the tunnel would eventually lead him to the master bedroom, where he had a hammock bed that hung in front of a window.

"Thank you," Deandra said, holding the rock between finger and thumb, not knowing what else to say. It was only Quinn's reaction to the gift that had tipped her off that the gesture might be a big deal for the ferret.

"Least favorite rock," he said, then abruptly turned and scampered away.

Glancing down at the rock now, she feared the gesture had been a veiled insult in ferret culture. Was giving someone your least favorite rock like getting flipped off?

Bewildered, she cocked a brow at Quinn, seeking clarification.

Quinn's eyes were watery, and her fingertips were pressed to her mouth. She looked from Deandra to the rock and back again. Lowering her hands, she said, "Aside from puzzles, he loves to collect rocks. We buy stones and geodes all the time—not necessarily anything rare, but ones we think are pretty. We often hide them in the yard for him to find. On his birthday and Yuletide, it's like an Easter egg hunt back there." She was thoughtful for a moment. "We adopted him when he was three. Adopting a sapient animal is … an odd experience. It's somewhere between a pet and a baby adoption, though the process is no less involved—perhaps more so, since the adoptee can technically vouch for themself even if society at large treats them as if they can't.

"We don't know what his early life was like. Someone found him near death on the side of the road near a hub on the East Coast, though it was a mundane street. It was a very, *very* lucky thing that the person who found him was familiar both with the hub system *and* salica. He would have been lost to the mundane exotic animal system otherwise.

"Anyway, he had several burns on his body—there's a spot on his back where the fur is a little thinner; it never fully regrew. One of his back legs was broken as well. He had surgery on it; there's a teeny tiny steel plate in his back leg. We're still unsure if he doesn't *want* to talk about his past, or if he truly doesn't remember, since he was so young. At any rate, because of all that, he's not the best at freely expressing softer feelings. Poor guy's got some serious trust issues. If he's prickly, it's a defense mechanism. I guess he figures if the other person is prickly back, he at least got in the first jab, you know?"

Deandra frowned down at the rock, wondering who had been so cruel to the ferret so early in his life.

"Regardless of whether that truly *is* his least favorite rock, the significance is that he gave it to you at all. He's never even given *me* one of his rocks," Quinn said.

"Well, I'm flattered," Deandra said, and meant it. She also hoped Peril was in earshot. As unnerving as it was to contend with a talking animal, she truly *did* want him to be comfortable around her. Plus, she liked Quinn and Rularo a lot, and if she could make their lives a little easier by caring for the ferret, she was happy to help.

After pocketing her rock and the house key, she got her shoes back on.

"I'll see you on Friday, Peril!" she called out. "Thanks again for the rock."

Deandra and Quinn both waited for a reply, their heads tipped back and eyes scanning. Nothing.

Shrugging, Deandra offered Quinn a smile. "Good luck with the festival prep. I might see you there in between checking on Peril. If I don't see you before then, I'll be sure to send you text updates about how he's doing."

Quinn's eyes were watery again. "This really does mean a lot to us. He's like our kid. The knot in my chest is gone now. I know he'll be okay. Now I can just focus on making a metric ton of ink. I was so stressed out after the sitter canceled on me today that I screwed up a batch of shadow wraith ink that had taken over two days to cure. If I get started today, I can probably get a new batch made in time. So, truly, thank you for giving me my sanity back."

Deandra wished Quinn luck once again and then headed out.

Upon reaching her car, she found a flyer stuck under one of her windshield wipers. It was for the grand opening of a clothing boutique that was happening this weekend. It didn't seem like the clothing shop catered to the goth crowd, yet the vibe of the flyer leaned heavily on the zombie part of "zombie cactus." Deandra commended them for doing their best to capitalize on the crowd that would be here this weekend, but the message was weird and muddied. They were hosting a costume party where "the best cactus wins!"

Why not the best zombie? Deandra had no idea.

There were also entirely too many puns.

"At the zombie cactus costume party, everyone will be <u>dead-on</u> with their outfits!"

"Feeling a little zombified? Worry not! Your outfit still slays."

"Ghoul, please! Your costume is drop-dead gorgeous."

Pulling the rock and house key from her pocket, she got into her car and tossed the flyer on her passenger seat along with her purse. After adding the Greenwoods' key to her key ring, she eyed the rock. She turned it over and over in her hand, enjoying the smooth surface as it glided along her fingertips. As worried as she'd been when she got here, she felt light now.

This strange new job in this strange new town had been exactly what she'd needed, she realized. For the first time in a long time, she felt like she was where she was supposed to be.

Axia somehow, despite how utterly bizarre it was, was the perfect place for her.

As she placed the rock on the seat, she caught a glimpse of the flyer again.

"Creepin' it real in my cactus glam," the weird flyer said.

Zombie Cactus Festival season was close to earning a tick on the con side of her pros and cons list, though.

Eh. No one was perfect.

CHAPTER FIVE

eandra had just wrapped up her only client for the day—
Barnaby—when her phone chimed with a text message.
After getting Havoc into the back seat of her car parked at
Angela's curb, she plopped into the driver's seat, fished her
phone out of her purse, and checked her messages.

Wendy
Help

Deandra
Please be more specific

Wendy
The good news: Madison showed up at 9 on the dot like she was supposed to. She's actually been helpful all morning! The bad news: Heather is driving us all insane

Deandra
Do you need help stashing her body? Providing an alibi?

Wendy
Ha. No. She's still with us. But the shop is so busy, she's on the floor more than usual and is micromanaging everyone. You'd think none of us knows how to do our jobs with the way she's harping on everyone. Normally she's in the back working on custom orders

Deandra
No one quit, did they?

Wendy
No, but even with all of us here, we're pretty short-staffed, given how busy it is. She even managed to call in Teresa (who lives in Kensey now) but who worked here last year

Wendy
Anyway, Otis is scheduled to set up the booth at the park within the hour, but it's a big job and he'll be there for hours if he has to do it alone

Deandra sighed.

Deandra
What time do I need to be there? Can you send me a map of the booth location?

The phone suddenly rang, and Deandra flinched so badly, she almost dropped it.

By way of greeting, Deandra said, "You know how I feel about surprise phone calls."

"How is this a surprise? You've been texting me for several minutes in a row. It's not like you're far from your phone."

"You're not supposed to argue with introvert logic, Wendy."

Her cousin laughed. "Well, your willingness to help Otis set up without even a *hint* of argument is exactly why I immediately called you, my introverted friend. Blink twice if you've been kidnapped."

"This would be more effective if this were a video call."

"I figured if I video-called you," Wendy said, "you'd have me arrested."

"Correct." Deandra shrugged, even if Wendy couldn't see it. "I know you've all been super stressed out, and I want to help. It's a light day for me, anyway. And Otis seemed nice enough. Plus, I can scope the festival out before it's full of people. It'll be like a behind-the-scenes look."

"Well, thank you. Honestly. Heather might be slightly less out of her gourd if she knows two of you are working on setup. Otis is loading up Heather's van right now, and then he'll head over there. Could you meet him in half an hour or so? You're done with your pet-sitting runs for the day, right?"

"Yep. I only had Barnaby today."

"Cool. Dinner is on me tonight, okay? I owe you one."

"All good," Deandra said. "I also demand a free dessert."

Wendy laughed. "Done. I'll text you the location. Oh crap. Heather found me. I was hiding in her office."

"Wendy Choo! We're drowning out there! You took your five already—"

Talking quickly, and steamrolling over Heather's reprimand, Wendy said, "I called Dee! She's going to meet Otis at the park to help with setup!"

There was a long beat of silence.

"Oh. Oh, that sweet girl. Wendy. Wendy, hon. I'm so … I'm so …"

Into the phone, Wendy whispered, "Oh gosh. Here come the waterworks. I'll text you as soon as I can get her to stop crying."

The call ended before Deandra could get a word out.

As she headed home to drop Havoc off, she hoped the festival itself wasn't as stressful as its preparation.

EVEN THOUGH THE WHOLE TOWN WAS DECKED OUT FOR THE FESTIVAL, the vast majority of the vendor booths were being set up on the eastern side of Oracle Park, a stone's throw from the police station. Setup for most vendors began on Thursday evening, with people from other hubs coming in through vehicle telepads with all their supplies as well as through mundane-travel entrances, like the one Deandra had used to visit Axia for the first time. Wendy had told her yesterday that there were strict schedules given to those travelers to ensure no unsuspecting humans on the mundane side of the veil would notice a procession of pickup trucks, cargo vans, and moving trucks traveling through dusty, seemingly abandoned fields before vanishing into thin air.

The hub's main telepad station also had a vehicle pad, and it was a mere block from the park. Schedules were strict for them, too, to help prevent traffic jams.

Wendy must have given Otis her number, because shortly after she arrived at the section of grass where she believed she was supposed to be, she got a text from an unknown number.

Unknown
Should be there in ten or so. Traffic is already awful. The werecats have been turned into traffic cops already. There's been a lot of honking and name calling out windows, but no one's thrown any punches yet. The old-timer vendors always leave setup until tomorrow morning, and that's when tensions get *really* high. Last year, a faun and a centaur got into a hoof fight because one thought the other stole his booth location. The faun was just in the wrong row. It's not every day you see a hoof fight

Deandra
Our assigned area has been very violence-free so far

She programmed Otis into her phone.

Otis
The day is still young

Deandra checked her messages from Wendy once more, to make sure *she* wasn't in the wrong location. She absolutely didn't want to get into a hoof fight.

From the map Wendy had sent, Heather's Elixirs had a double booth that was situated between a taffy booth and one for freeze-dried fruit and candy. The freeze-dried candy crew had already been hard at work when Deandra slowly walked up the makeshift aisle made by white pop-up tents and sections of grass with blue spray paint marking the four corners. A sheet of paper with "264" staked into the middle of the grass had marked it as Heather's Elixirs' spot.

"Hey," she heard now.

Deandra glanced up from her phone to find a middle-aged woman beside her. The lady was dark-skinned, and her hair was in box braids pulled into a ponytail high on her head. Even still, the braids hit her lower back. She wore a dark-green apron with "Enchanted Bite" written across the front in bright yellow. Her nails were the same shade of yellow, and she held a plastic bag in one hand and a small pair of plastic tongs in the other.

"Hi," Deandra said.

"How do you feel about being my next victim?"

Deandra's brows shot up.

The woman laughed. "I guess that sounds more ominous than I meant. Let's try this: Would you like to try a sample?" She poked the tongs into the bag and pulled out a misshapen light green glob that semi-resembled a piece of popcorn. Holding the odd thing out to Deandra, she said, "This is our newest attempt at a zombie cactus fruit puff. I haven't gotten a chance to try them yet; I pulled them out of the freezer just this morning. The last few batches, though, were … not it."

Deandra's nose involuntarily wrinkled. "Uh, sure." She held out her hand and marveled that the fruit puff lying on her palm was so light, her skin hardly registered it was there at all. Taking it between finger and thumb, she turned it this way and that. "What, uh, is it, exactly?"

"Freeze-dried candy. We make our own fruit chews and hard candies and then freeze-dry some of them. Completely changes the texture to something light and airy, a bit like cereal. The zombie cactus, though, as versatile as it is, seems to take offense at being freeze-dried."

Resisting the urge to sniff it first, Deandra popped the odd thing into her mouth and chewed. It behaved like a piece of cereal at first, breaking apart into little pieces. Then, all at once, it dissolved on her tongue like cotton candy. The flavor was first sweet, then tart, and then a little bitter. Then *very* bitter. She coughed.

"Oh, shoot!" the woman said. "Bitter, right?"

Deandra gave an involuntary full-body shudder. "It honestly tastes a bit like raw kale."

The woman sagged. "Another victim! I'm sorry. One sec." She

hurried to the right, where her pop-tent was, rounded the corner out of view, and then was back seconds later with another bag in hand. She handed it to Deandra. "These are strawberry. They're delicious. They always sell out. Free of charge for enduring that."

Deandra took the bag, and the woman fished one of the zombie cactus fruit puffs out of the bag she still held, popped it into her mouth, chewed slowly, then gagged. "Oh, Goddess above! That's even *worse* than the last one." She pointed her tongs at Deandra. "But you know what? We've been trying to put our finger on what that awful taste is, and you're right on the money: raw kale. Nasty." She stuck out her tongue, which now had a streak of green down the middle. "Can I give you a second bag of the strawberry for your trouble?"

Deandra laughed. "One bag was generous enough. I'll happily take these," she said, holding the bag to her chest. "Is that the only zombie cactus–flavored item you have? If so, the weekend might be rough going ..."

Chuckling, the woman shook her head. "Nope. We have dehydrated zombie cactus slices that sell like hot cakes every year, as well as zombie cactus fruit chews, popcorn powders, and hard candies. It just refuses to be freeze-dried. I'll figure it out eventually."

"Do you have enough time to change the label to kale puffs? Some people actually *like* kale."

She pointed her tongs at Deandra again. "You're a smart cookie. We'll make lemonade out of lemons. Or, well, kale out of zombie cactus. Whatever. You're a genius." Tucking the tongs under her arm, she held out her hand. "Where are my manners? What's your name? I'm Eileen. I run Enchanted Bite with my husband and kids. He'll be with me tomorrow. My kids are in there helping set up. This will be our ... fifth year here? Great event."

Deandra shook her hand. "Dee. I just moved to Axia a few months ago from the mundane world. This is my first Zombie Cactus Festival. My cousin works at the shop that goes with this tent." She gestured at the empty square of grass. "Things are hectic at the store, so I volunteered to help set up. I don't even *work* at Heather's Elixirs."

"Oh! Heather Wittly's store? I love that place. I'm here in Axia at least once a month just to shop there. Her temperature-control talismans changed my entire business model, honestly. Is *she* going to be in the booth this weekend? She never seems to be in the store when I go in. I'd love the chance to at least shake her hand."

Eileen sounded a touch flustered. Maybe meeting a fan of her work would calm Heather down some, but if the high-strung woman was inadvertently rude to Eileen simply because she was a stress case at the moment, it could shatter Eileen's view of her talisman-making hero. One shouldn't meet their heroes and all that.

"Not sure," Deandra hedged. "They're pretty slammed at the store. But I'll be sure to have my cousin pass on the kind words at the very least."

Eileen beamed. "That would be great. Well, I should get back to helping the kids set up before they stage a mutiny."

Moments later *"Moooom! Troy keeps eating all the samples!"* echoed from inside the depths of the tent.

Eileen rolled her eyes good-naturedly at Deandra, then walked off to join her family.

Deandra examined the bag of candies she'd been given, chewed the inside of her cheek as she contemplated trying one, then gagged slightly as the flavor of raw kale somehow flared up again. She opened the bag of strawberry candies and shoveled three into her mouth, if only to drown out the fuzzy vegetable taste.

She stilled.

The candies were *delicious.*

By the time Otis showed up, a third of the bag was gone.

In greeting, she shoved the candies at him. "Hi. Please take these away from me."

The big man dropped the handle of the wagon and took the bag from her. "Oh wow! How did you get these? They're always sold out by the time I get to the booth." He stuffed an entire handful in his mouth. His shoulders visibly relaxed and he groaned in delight. "Amazing."

After a second handful, he shoved the bag back at her, begging her to hide them. She did her best to shove the bag to the bottom of her purse, so it was out of sight.

They got to work.

THREE HOURS, FIVE TREKS TO HEATHER'S VAN, AND ONE SMASHED thumb later, Heather's Elixirs' booth was complete. Well, mostly complete. All the tables, banners, and display racks, shelves, and baskets were in place, as well as items such as bookmarks, coupons, candles, oils, soaps, and dried herb satchels. The pricier items, such as Heather's handcrafted talismans, wouldn't grace the tent until tomorrow morning.

Otis told her that the proximity of the human and werecat police to the festivities meant a large number of vendors planned to leave their wares set up overnight since the area would be patrolled, ensuring that anyone with sticky fingers would think twice about pilfering items from unmanned booths. But none of the employees of Heather's Elixirs thought Heather's sanity would hold out if someone made off with her goods in the dead of night.

Deandra and Otis stood at the mouth of the tent, hands on hips, as they surveyed their handiwork.

Otis stretched his arms high above his head, revealing sweat stains darkening the pits of his lime-green polo shirt, then let them fall back to his sides. "Can't thank you enough for volunteering as tribute. I would have been here twice as long otherwise. Those shelf things took forever to put together."

"I'd like to say I'm helping out of the goodness of my heart, but I'm doing it for selfish reasons. I'm hoping I can get free dinners out of Wendy for a month."

Otis chuckled. He was a big guy with a booming laugh. "Hey, as long as it indirectly helps me, I'm not gonna complain."

After she assured Otis she didn't need a ride, he grabbed the handle of the wagon, wished her a good day, and headed back toward Heather's borrowed work van. Wendy was going to meet Deandra at the park in twenty minutes or so for a thank-you lunch. The text that came in ten minutes ago had heavily implied that if Wendy didn't get out of the shop soon, she might commit a homicide.

While waiting for Wendy to arrive, Deandra took a slow stroll around the still-being-assembled tents. Eileen's family had finished an hour before, and Eileen had attached a tarp to the front of her tent, shielding the interior from looky-loos. It wouldn't stop anyone from dipping past the tarp if they really wanted to get in, though. Deandra guessed that Eileen would bring the bulk of her more popular flavors tomorrow. She wondered if Eileen had left all the kale fruit puffs inside, though, *hoping* someone would steal them.

As she wandered, Deandra saw booths for standard things such as jewelry, clothing, sweets, household goods, pet supplies, and crafts—both magical and mundane. There were more fantastical things, too. Horn accessories, fur dye, hoof-care products, alchemical powders, mood-enhancing bath bombs, and magic-reinforced animal cages.

Deandra stopped at the cage booth, reminded of the cage she'd seen at the Mythic Pet Kitchen where the vibrissa cats had been housed. She was motivated mostly by curiosity; she wanted to know how much a magicked cage cost. It couldn't be cheap, if runes were etched into every square of the wire mesh.

The tent in question must have been a quad, as Heather's was a double, and this one was massive. The tent wasn't one someone could buy on Amazon, she knew that much. It reminded her a bit of a circus tent, but the fabric was white—just like everyone else's. Deandra figured that was a rule the Axian Town Council had set to give the sea of tents an air of professional uniformity.

A woman holding the handle of a cage in each, uhh, hand suddenly walked past her and into the tent. She was a grimalkyne —a catlike species. Deandra had seen several of them the month before, as many had arrived in Axia to take part in Duncan Bettencourt's treasure hunt for the then-lost phoenix feather. This one was fully on the catlike end of the spectrum. She looked like a creature straight out of a fantasy movie or video game. She walked upright on two paws, and she was covered head to toe in navy-blue fur, save for her feet-paws and hand-paws, which were white. There were a few splashes of white on her face, too. Her head was that of a domestic shorthair. Deandra wondered if there were any grimalkyne who looked like vibrissa cats, complete with horns, scales, or antennae.

For clothes, she wore jean shorts—which had a hole cut in the back to account for her long, furry tail—and a plain black T-shirt. Her feet-paws were bare.

"You a vendor?" the grimalkyne asked as she walked by, her voice sounding surprisingly human while having an edge to it that was decidedly feline—which didn't make sense if Deandra thought about it too hard, seeing as cats couldn't normally talk. The grimalkyne's tone wasn't menacing, like a werecat's could be, but low and rumbly, like a cat's purr.

Deandra had flinched hard, startled both by her sudden arrival *and* her appearance. "Oh. Um. Kind of? Vendor assistant."

"Feel free to wander. We're still setting up, but we don't mind you having a look around. We offer a vendor discount, too, so if you see something you like, just let me know."

Shrugging to herself, Deandra stepped over the threshold into the tent's interior—and then froze. The space seemed to grow before her eyes. Maybe the tent had magical properties, just like the cages that filled it.

Birdcages hung from the tent's ceiling poles. Other cages were stacked on tables and elegant display stands. Some were wire mesh, like the one from Mythic Pet Kitchen, while others had solid walls made of metal sheeting or clear plastic. She figured the plastic wasn't of the mundane variety, but rather the same material that had housed the phoenix feather; something so resilient, it stood its ground against magical fire.

There were cages big enough to hold a horse and cages small enough for creatures the size of Sunshine the newt. Some cages were empty, while others were outfitted with platforms, ladders, ramps, and/or tunnels.

Two other grimalkyne moved about the space, arranging the cages, hanging signs, and decorating tables already topped with black cloths. Deandra inched her way toward a cage roughly the size of the one she'd seen in the pet store and read the description written on the white notecard clipped to the cage's front. The card listed the cage's dimensions, the type of runework that was woven into the cage bars, and the types of animals the enclosure was best suited for. Vibrissa cats were listed first.

Deandra did her level best not to balk at the mid-range four-figure price tag. She snapped a quick picture of it and sent it to Wendy.

The response was almost immediate.

Wendy
You can't have a teleporting alien cat, Dee.
Especially not if its cage costs more than rent!

Deandra
We don't have to get the deluxe cage. There are smaller ones! Plus you can't say no until you see one in person. They have antennae, Wendy! Antennae!

Wendy
How is a *dragon* not enough for you?

Deandra didn't actually *want* a vibrissa cat, but Wendy didn't need to know that. She pocketed her phone without replying. Tormenting her cousin was a treasured pastime.

After slowly walking around the maze-like booth for another few minutes, she stopped at a cage that looked more like a playpen, as the top was open. The attached card said if the animal tried to climb out, a protective dome of magic would flare to life above the pen, keeping the creature inside. There was also an option to order custom runework that would add features such as bright lights, vibrations, and even shocks to aid in training unruly creatures.

There was a warning that one should consult with their veterinarian before purchasing custom runework, to account for heart conditions and anxiety levels.

Among the beings listed as ideal candidates for this particular pen were baby yetis. Deandra pictured Kiwi on his back in the middle of the pen, throwing an epic tantrum because the magic dome had thwarted his plan of escape one time too many.

Deandra didn't know how she felt about sapient animals selling cages meant to keep other sentient and sapient animals confined. She couldn't tell if an odd line was being crossed here. But maybe this was no different from a mundane dog crate used for training purposes. After all, Juniper said the cage he had was for the vibrissa cats' safety until the felines learned better self-control.

Still, she found herself wondering what someone like Oleander Basnet would think of this booth's wares.

"Are you interested in a playpen?"

When Deandra turned toward the voice, she expected to see a grimalkyne. She was surprised to find a human-looking man beside her. He was her height, fair-skinned, and had short black hair. He was dressed casually in jeans and a black T-shirt. Deandra would have thought he was a fellow vendor if it wasn't for the words "Feline Protected" written on the right side of his shirt, under which was the image of a cage with a cat curled up inside on a fluffy bed.

"Do you, uh, work here?" Deandra managed once she tore her gaze from his shirt.

He nodded, hands tucked behind his back. "I'm one of the grimalkyne's sorcerers. I'll be here this weekend providing add-on runework should anyone want it."

"Oh," Deandra said eloquently. "Do add-ons take a long time?"

He shrugged. "Depends on what they want. Most custom work can be completed in a few hours. Anything more complicated than that will require the client to purchase the cage and the runework, and then we'll ship the cage to them once I've had the time to complete the work."

Deandra struggled with what to say next. It wasn't the fact that she was freaked out that she was standing next to a sorcerer.

Okay, yes it was.

What if he wiggled his fingers and turned her into a frog? Was that how sorcery worked? Deandra had no idea.

Whether he sensed she was panicking about his mere existence or had realized she wasn't in the market for a high-end magic cage, he'd clearly decided there were other things he could be doing with his time. He reached into his back pocket and pulled out a small silver wallet that held business cards. He extracted one and held it out to her. "I offer many runework services beyond enhancing cages. There's not much I can't do, rune-wise. I'm quite knowledgeable about fae flora and fauna." He gestured to the tent at large. "Hazard of this gig, in particular." He nodded at the card he still held. "All my contact info is on here. Happy to answer any questions if you have them."

Deandra took it.

Theodore Rochester

Affordable* runework for all your magical needs

*Please email or call about pricing

It included a website, email address, and phone number.

"We have just as much right to be here as you do!" came a shout from somewhere behind her.

"Ugh. *Not* again," Theodore muttered from beside her.

"What?" Deandra asked.

Thedore stalked past her, and she quickly turned to follow him. He crept forward and peered around the side of a particularly massive cage that had walls of metal sheeting. Deandra stood next to him, shielded by the cage, unsure what the sorcerer saw.

"It *is* him," Theodore muttered, more to himself, it seemed, than to her.

Deandra, curiosity getting the best of her again, sidestepped Theodore so she could see around him. The tent had four entrances, as far as Deandra could tell; the magic here was doing weird things with physics. Standing at the rear-most entrance was a grimalkyne with his back to Deandra. This one was snow white except for the tip of his tail, which sported a splash of dark purple. That tail was currently swishing in agitation.

Before him, just outside the tent, stood an elfin woman and a male faun. The faun didn't have horns as impressive as Sarah's, but they were still prominent. They were bone-white and were slightly curved at the ends, reminiscent of horns on a young ram. They stood out in sharp relief against his all-black fur.

"Who are they?" Deandra asked, glancing to her right. She started when she didn't find Theodore standing beside her. She turned in a slow circle, expecting to see his retreating form hustling around a corner or out of the tent altogether, but she didn't see him anywhere.

If it wasn't for the business card she still held, she would have thought she'd hallucinated him.

"We're only here as a courtesy."

Deandra peered around the cage again. Given the way the faun had his chest puffed out, she guessed it was him who had just spoken.

"The Alliance of Sapient Animals will be here in force this weekend. We wanted you to know that we'll be informing participants of your exorbitantly priced portable prisons. If you find yourself wondering why sales aren't what you've enjoyed in the past ..." Dramatic pause. "*We* happened."

The woman thrust a flyer at the grimalkyne so abruptly, the cat grabbed it with his paw, probably before he realized he'd done it. Flyer distributed, the pair turned on heel and hoof and marched away.

The grimalkyne didn't move, nor did he make a sound for several long seconds. Then he stomped a snow-white paw, balled up the flyer, and let out a sound somewhere between a scream and a roar. Another grimalkyne rushed up to him from some spot to the right, and the navy-blue cat who had initially greeted Deandra hurried past her now to join the others.

"What happened, Powder?" the navy-blue cat asked.

Without a word, he handed her the crumpled flyer.

She shared an uneasy glance with the third grimalkyne before unfolding the paper. She clearly didn't like what was on the sheet any more than Powder had, as she angrily thrust it toward the ginger grimalkyne.

"Goddess above," the ginger cat said before crumpling the flyer once more and tossing it over her shoulder in disgust.

The ball of paper flew out of Deandra's line of sight. She knew she should probably sneak away now; she felt bad about eavesdropping ... but she was also nosy.

Powder said, "I honestly thought *not* posting about the event on socials would keep them from finding us. You'd think completely ruining our most recent event would have tided them over for a while."

After a tense moment of silence, the navy cat said, "I was going to wait until after the festival to tell you this, but Scarlet called this morning. The shop in Robinson was vandalized last night. Thousands and thousands in damages."

"What are we doing?" a voice said in Deandra's ear.

Deandra flinched so badly that she crashed into the cage she'd been hiding behind. The cage's wheels were locked, which kept it from moving an inch, but it still rattled violently. A few bells hanging from cords attached to the cage's ceiling jangled so loudly, they might as well have been struck gongs.

All three grimalkyne whipped their heads toward the commotion, their ticked-off feline gazes landing on Deandra and the newly arrived Wendy.

"Oops," Wendy whispered.

Deandra swallowed hard, stood straight, and stepped out into the open. Wiping her hands down the front of her jeans, she offered the three cats a toothy smile. "Uhh … hi."

CHAPTER SIX

The navy-blue grimalkyne was in front of her so fast, Deandra bumped into the cage again, setting off the strings of bells. She assumed they were built-in toys for whatever animal would call the cage home.

"Are you actually a vendor assistant, or are you an ASA spy?" the cat asked.

Theodore stepped out from around the navy-blue cat. "You're a spy?"

"Are *you* a ninja?" Deandra countered, hand over her heart, before her brain could tell her to shut up. How did he disappear and reappear so dang fast?

Theodore crossed his arms. "You didn't answer the question."

Deandra swallowed hard, her gaze shifting from him and up toward the cat, unable to form a coherent thought for longer than a few seconds. She just gaped at the grimalkyne, mouth opening and closing as if she were a beached fish.

"She is!" Wendy said from Deandra's side. "An assistant I mean, not a spy."

The grimalkyne thankfully moved out of Deandra's space enough that she could comfortably take a breath. Wendy huddled closer to Deandra's side when the other grimalkyne joined the navy-blue one and Theodore, hemming the cousins in. With the cage to her back and three grumpy grimalkyne plus an equally grumpy sorcerer crowded in front of her, Deandra was finding it a bit hard to breathe again.

Deandra was quickly learning that not every fae or magic-touched being gave off something like magical pheromones, but many of them did, often when they were angry. She wasn't sure how many of them knew they did it. Perhaps it affected mundanes more than fae or the magic-touched. Either way, the more potent the invisible magical fog was, the more it felt like Deandra was on the verge of a panic attack.

After several long, tense seconds passed, a white paw wrapped around one of the navy-blue grimalkyne's arms. "Neela, ease up a little, huh? You're scaring the poor girl," Powder, the white cat, said.

That finally made the navy-blue cat stop glaring holes into Deandra's soul, and the moment the cat looked away, Deandra and Wendy expelled gusting breaths. An invisible weight lifted from Deandra's chest.

Neela said, "Sorry. It's just that the timing of your arrival and ASA's made me jump to conclusions. We've always felt welcome at this festival, but vendors don't usually wander through our booth. Not since the last event, anyway. And we see a lot of the same faces during the summer festival circuit—especially the Zombie Cactus ones."

Deandra chewed the inside of her cheek. "What happened at the last one? Powder, you said that ASA ruined it?"

The all-white cat crossed his furry arms over his black T-shirt that featured a band Deandra didn't recognize. She didn't even know if it was a mundane band or one only popular in the hub system. She wondered why Theodore was wearing a shirt for the cage business, but the cat wasn't. "How do you know my name? Now *I'm* wondering if you're a spy."

"Not a spy," she said, hands held up in placation. "I just heard, uhh …" She smiled awkwardly at the ginger grimalkyne. "I heard you call him Powder, is all. Not a spy. Just … nosy."

The ginger cat laughed. "At least she's honest, I guess. I'm Velma, by the way."

"Dee. And this is my cousin Wendy."

Wendy waved, remaining uncharacteristically quiet.

"Well, Dee," Neela said, "I'm guessing you overheard enough to figure out what happened. ASA has been targeting our company for years, but harassing us at events is relatively new. They think our cages are barbaric. But it isn't that they believe magic-enhanced cages are the problem and non-enhanced, mundane ones are fine. They believe in doing away with confinement of all kinds. I don't know if you noticed, but the faun wasn't wearing clothes. They believe clothes for any being with animal ancestry are also a cage."

Theodore scoffed. "He's insufferable. All of ASA is. They *should* have been disbanded ages ago. The Collective doesn't care enough to do anything about it."

Neela absently patted Theodore on the head with one of her big paws, and he smiled affectionately at her. Not in a romantic way, but in a quietly devoted way. Almost like how a dog gazes at its owner. The idea that some weird role-reversal thing was happening and this human was a pet to cats was creeping her out a little.

Velma picked up the thread, and Deandra was grateful to focus on something other than the image of Theodore curled up in a dog bed in front of a crackling fire while Neela sat on the couch watching TV.

"Depending on which end of the spectrum they fall in their belief system, some will say cars, telepads, and even buildings are a form of cage, as all animals should be free," Velma said. "Sapience, they say, shouldn't affect one's connection to their animal ancestry."

"There's quite a large subset who say societal rules are a cage and believe we should live in the wild," said Powder. "*Living in the wild* might have been more feasible in the fae realm, but it certainly isn't in this one. Fae and magic-touched are safer in the hub system, as far as I'm concerned. The less mundane some of us are"—he motioned vaguely to himself and his two grimalkyne companions—"the harder it is for us to live in the mundane world.

"Maybe we'd fit in just fine at an anime or comic convention, and we certainly would be—and some of us are—embraced by the furry community, but what about the rest of the time? Even the staunchest believers in the ASA organization still live in the hub system. The dome of magic enclosing each hub is just a larger version of our playpens, if one wanted to split hairs. We're all living in a cage in one way or another. ASA has developed very strong opinions about which cages they think are acceptable and which ones aren't, and now they make those opinions everyone else's problem."

Wendy awkwardly cleared her throat. "You said one of your store's locations was vandalized?" When she got several slit-eyed cat stares in response, she said, "I'm not a spy either! I'm also very nosy and well-versed in the art of eavesdropping. We're sleuths in our spare time."

Velma's plethora of whiskers seemed to be vibrating, and her pink nose twitched like a bunny's. "Are you two PIs?"

The cat sounded intrigued rather than irritated, like maybe she'd dreamed of being a PI since she was a kitten and wanted to be regaled with stories about cheating spouses and other assorted tomfoolery.

"Uhh ..." Deandra said, resisting the urge to elbow her cousin in the side. "Nothing professional. It's more of a hobby we keep stumbling into."

Velma's orange-and-white-striped shoulders slumped. "So you're just two mundane ladies who are obsessed with true-crime podcasts. Got it."

Somehow the cat sounded personally offended. Deandra wanted to tell her that it was only Wendy who was obsessed with true crime, but she didn't think that clarification would make Velma feel any better.

Neela spoke up. "We have four stores across the hub system. We started the business almost a decade ago. Powder and I grew up together, and he and Velma met at a sorcery convention. She met Teddy at a similar one a year before."

Theodore's hair was still being petted absently by Neela.

"Velma was at the convention as a panelist, talking about the various ways runework can be used to enhance life for hub system residents that go beyond basic talismans on one paw and maintaining the obelisks surrounding each hub on the other. Powder was so impressed with her discussion, he tracked her down during the convention to tell her about the enchanted cage business he and I had been trying to get off the ground for a year or so. We knew we needed to network with sorcerers to create what we wanted, but most were either too expensive or unwilling to work with grimalkyne."

Velma laughed, which sounded somewhere between a hiss and a purr. "There's an air of snobbery in every fae or magic-touched group, though some are worse than others. Sorcerers are often insufferable, but if you can find one who is fed up or disillusioned with sorcerer society as a whole?" She rubbed two digits together. "Those ones are like gold, and they're willing to help for a decent price, too."

"It also helps if the sorcerer," Theodore said, aiming a thumb back at himself, "is a graduate of a sorcery academy but hates everything the Collective stands for. I'd much rather be a freelance sorcerer than be caught up in Collective political BS."

Velma smiled down at him, nodding. "I had enough connections in the industry that I could call on several sorcerers to see if they'd be into doing more advanced runework for us. Most of them were, and Theodore pulled in some other disillusioned sorcerers, too. ASA only sees the negatives when it comes to our cages, but while they see confinement and imprisonment, we see safety."

Neela said, "There's a lot of freedom in the hub system for fae, even if we're restricted to only certain cities. But for some fae, we have freedoms that we'd *never* have had in the fae realm. Heck, even sorcerers got an upgrade in fae status here. They didn't run things in the fae realm. Elves and dragonkind did. There are fae like the avians who were hunted in some parts of the fae realm for their feathers. Others for their horns or scales or … fur." She frowned, her gaze distant for a moment. "We don't have those dangers here."

"ASA can claim they have the moral high ground," Powder said, "but if they did *any* research, they'd know that cages such as ours existed in the fae realm. And the conditions in the realm were often worse! It wasn't uncommon for there to be culling programs. Certain sapient and sentient animals who were considered too willful or opinionated or otherwise difficult to deal with often had their populations whittled down. Some animals were bred to be more compliant and docile, while others had those traits bred out to better suit a specific purpose.

"Our cages use magic to keep animals confined, but they're training tools, a safety measure to help both the animal as well as their owner or parent find the best ways to teach self-soothing and self-control and to prevent injury."

Deandra mentioned the cage she'd seen in Mythic Pet Kitchen and how Juniper believed the runework gave the kittens a safe place to exist while they learned to better control their phasing power.

Neela nodded. "Exactly that. Vibrissa cats are a perfect example. They're honestly their own worst enemy when they're kittens. There was an eighty percent mortality rate for vibrissa cats in the fae realm, most of them perishing before they reached six months old."

"Oh, that's awful," Deandra said, thinking once again of the shivering vibrissa cat who had phased to the top of its enclosure just to escape the stressful commotion happening on the ground floor.

Wendy leaned over and whispered, "No alien cats!"

Neela either didn't hear Wendy's comment or chose to ignore it. "The vibrissa were an endangered species. Here, they only have a *ten* percent mortality rate, thanks in part to our cages. We even have contracts with two mythical zoos. Fae and magic-touched animals are under a high threat of being endangered in this realm because we only have what species made it here before and during the Glitch. There were species of animals and insects that were gone within a few years after the Glitch, simply because there weren't enough of them to maintain a population and they weren't compatible with the native species."

Velma nodded. "The veils surrounding hubs allow mundane animals in and out; the magic doesn't repel them. Sapient animals like us often can't cross the veils without travel talismans, but some sentient animals can slip through. Vibrissa straddle the line, allowing them to freely traverse the veils. Life is dangerous enough for them as kittens, but at least in a hub system, they have a chance. An *alien cat* as you put it—"

Wendy winced.

"An alien cat like a vibrissa in a mundane setting could suffer any number of fates just for being too different. We truly believe our cages help provide protection for fae and magic-touched animals in a realm that wasn't meant for them." Velma sighed. "It's something we're all passionate about. But ASA only looks at the surface of what we do."

"And, to answer your previous question," Neela said, "they believe that by destroying our products—or keeping them from being purchased—we'll eventually take such a financial hit that we'll be unable to stay in business. Paying for custom runework is *not* cheap." Theodore grinned at this, and Deandra figured, even if he was treated as a human pet, he might not mind if he was making bank. "At an event last month, their flyer campaign was very successful. They often do that—hand out leaflets that rehash lies and false statistics. The flyers usually double as an invitation to one of their demonstrations, too. At the last event, they focused on highlighting the *one* case where one of our cages was blamed for the death of a pixie. And—"

"A *pixie*?" Deandra asked, incredulous, before she could stop herself.

Neela's eyes narrowed to slits like only a cat's can. "Pixies have their own laws and society, in large part because they're a species that straddles the line of what's considered sapient and what isn't. They're obviously *very* sapient in most respects, but their size often means they're treated terribly, assuming they're not ignored altogether. So they created their own society that they police themselves, even if it's not recognized by anyone else as legitimate. Anyway, we're occasionally commissioned to make what are essentially pixie jail cells that are used as part of their legal system.

"The pixie in question was on trial for murder. She was apparently *very* guilty, because instead of standing trial, on the day before she was supposed to be in court, she held on to the bars of her cage—which were magicked to issue zaps to discourage escape—until she short-circuited her own heart. Our cage itself didn't kill the pixie; the pixie used the cage to bring about her own death to avoid paying for her crimes. And yet, ASA finds ways to twist the facts to blame us and our cages.

"ASA members have occasionally been used during criminal cases as witnesses or experts—which is laughable—and they often trot out that pixie story. Last month was the first time they used it during a festival event, as the details are pretty gruesome, and festivals are family events. ASA always *pretends* to be sympathetic to the pixie cause. Which is extra sad, as the pixies would honestly make excellent allies for ASA, since there are a *lot* of them and a good chunk of their population is bitter about their treatment. And yet, ASA ignores them just as much as everyone else does."

"Is destroying property at your stores common?" Deandra asked, wondering if ASA was possibly escalating.

"It's only happened twice, but they were both within the last six months," Neela said, frowning. "We don't have definitive proof that this last attack was them. It's our newest store, and the security system was scheduled to be set up next week, so we don't have any digital proof. I went ahead and told Scarlet to call out the werecats *and* ACSI."

"Oh!" Wendy said. "I love *ACSI*!"

"She didn't mean the *show*," Powder said, sounding disappointed. "You were right, Velma. They're true-crime junkies."

In a stage whisper, Wendy explained to Deandra, "The A stands for alchemical. Alchemical Crime Scene Investigation." Louder, she said, "That's so cool. I mean, not the burglary part, but hearing about the real-life uses of ACSI."

"I'm still very new to the hub system," Deandra said, hoping to lessen the cats' general annoyance. "Does this all mean that the attack on the store was magical in nature and not a mundane smash and grab?"

Neela nodded. Deandra noted that Velma and Powder were eagerly awaiting Neela's explanation, too, as they hadn't known about the burglary until a few minutes ago. "The front windows were smashed, but all the glass is outside, as if a miniature explosion happened *after* they broke in. The lock on the front door was mundane, and that was melted to a puddle on the ground. There was also a locking array on the door that only the three of us and Scarlet had a talisman for. The vandals broke the array. That could only have been done by a sorcerer or someone with the right magical lock picks."

Neela glanced at Deandra and Wendy in turn. "Scarlet isn't a grimalkyne. She's not totally sure about her heritage, but she thinks she's got draken ancestry. Anyway, she's got a very keen nose. When she went to the shop this morning to assess the damage, she said there were faint scents of oranges, coffee, and horsehair—and that's *despite* the alchemical bomb that apparently went off in the place."

Velma, Powder, and Theodore all gasped.

"Is she sure?" Powder asked.

Velma scoffed. "Are you really doubting Scarlet's nose?"

Powder shook his head. "I just thought he went wild and *stayed* wild. Why would he be back? There have to be several alphabet groups looking for him."

"There are," Theodore said. "He's so legendary, there's a course at the academy practically devoted to him. Sorcery and alchemy aren't the same, of course, but they share a lot of the same building blocks. The Collective should be looking to find the guy rather than sensationalizing him in courses, but no one asked *my* opinion."

Neela patted his head again. "Maybe it's what we've all said a million times—living a wild life in the mundane world is not only difficult but very lonely. Especially for his kind. We're down to, what, ten in the entire hub system? It's possible that loneliness finally overrode the fear of getting caught. That, or he cracked mentally."

Deandra glanced at Wendy to see if she had any clue what was going on.

Wendy's expression was just as perplexed as Deandra felt. "Being *not* in the know isn't great."

"Tell me about it," Deandra muttered.

Velma chuckled. "Sorry. There's a species of ungulate shifter ... there isn't a proper earthen-realm translation. The closest thing you have in your lore is a unicorn. These hoofed animals aren't all rainbows and glitter, though. They breathe acid gas, have razor-sharp teeth, and are carnivores who prefer other hoofed animals to feed on. They were like the sharks of the forests in some parts of the fae realm. They left you alone as long as you left them alone, but attacks were ... they weren't pretty, let's put it that way. In the fae realm, they could shift between human and unicorn at will, but if they stayed human for longer than twenty-four hours, it would get more and more painful to switch back. If they went longer than seventy-two hours, they got *stuck* as humans. So most lived as unicorns.

"They had a unique magic skillset as humans, though, so they were often tempted to shift to use their magic. For whatever reason, maybe because the transition between their two forms is so intense, they're natural-born alchemists. Even still, alchemy takes a lot of practice, so many of them must choose the life of an alchemist *or* of a unicorn—not both."

Wendy asked, "You said there's only ten left in this realm? How many made it here before the Glitch?"

"A surprisingly decent number of them, actually. On the second day of the Glitch, a herd of them were running together when a giant portal opened up in front of them. They all ran in, and the portal snapped shut behind them before they knew what happened," said Neela. "They were compatible with some breeds of mundane horses here. But they were also hunted nearly to extinction by the native humans, so the last few of them went into hiding within a few years. They live a very long time, so it's possible there are a few pure-blooded unicorns still in this realm that are hundreds of years old. Because of their longevity and their ability to hide, no one knows the exact number, but ten is the one I see thrown around the most.

"Anyway, there was a unicorn colt named Lionax Orma who was part of that herd. He became very sick shortly after the Glitch, possibly because he was so young. Many earthen diseases new to the fae population either wiped out or severely changed the fae and magic-touched here in the years after the Glitch. Lionax became so ill, he had to be put into a medically induced coma. Three days came and went—assuring he was well and truly stuck as a human when he finally awoke a month later.

"Lionax was furious. Emotion helps fuel the transition in unicorn shifters, and his body's reaction to the mundane flu altered his fae blood and brain chemistry. He became volatile and violent, but he was also something of a prodigy in alchemy. He became as brilliant as he was nasty."

Powder jumped in. "History suggests Lionax is at least a hundred and twenty years old, with a life expectancy of around three hundred years. It's believed that he's one of the founding members, if not *the* founding member of ASA, which appeared on the scene out of nowhere about fifteen years ago.

"He's publicly said that he understands ASA's mission state-ment more than anyone, as he's trapped in the cage of his own body—a cage he wouldn't have been in had it not been for the Glitch. When ASA first started, it was a much more violent organization. They broke into zoos, pet stores, even veterinary clinics to free the animals there. Lionax was usually their spokesperson, chatting up reporters and doing interviews. ASA often used his alchemical concoctions in their raids and animal prison-breaks, and it was reported that the scents of oranges, coffee, and horsehair lingered in the air after ASA's reign of destruction.

"A couple of years after ASA's founding, one of those raids went bad when ASA released a mythical animal that's something like a hippo. Hippos might be depicted as tutu-wearing animals in your mundane cartoons, but they're deadly. The creature ASA released from the zoo was like that—but it could shoot lightning from its mouth. It was the only one in the entire earthen realm, and the zoo was doing what it could to make the animal comfort-able while it was here. It was too dangerous to set loose in the wild, as it could do untold damage to whatever flora and fauna was in its new environment.

"When ASA released it, it went on a rampage—destroyed large swaths of the zoo, badly injured many people, and even killed one of the ASA members. It took several Collective sorcerers, werecats, and powerful witches to finally capture the animal and get it back into the zoo."

Deandra was mildly horrified. "Did Lionax or the ASA members get arrested or anything? I'd think there would have been efforts to shut ASA down after that."

"Like I said," Theodore said bitterly, "the Collective should have shut ASA down ages ago."

The grimalkyne all nodded.

Neela said, "Several people went to jail, and one lady was even sent to the Antarctica prison hub. Only the worst of the worst go there. But Lionax wasn't put away. There were rumors that he was killed, or that he paid off Collective sorcerers to look the other way while he escaped into the wild. Lionax *did* have deep pockets. He's got to have half a dozen bounties on his head, though. He was the leader of ASA at the time of the incident—and apparently was also the one who got the cage open. By our laws, he's guiltier than the hippodynus who trampled that poor man to death.

"Regardless, ASA continued on. They were way less violent, though. The attacks on places like zoos and pet stores stopped entirely. Most of what they do to push their mission is behind the scenes.

"A handful of years ago, some wildly illegal alchemical concoctions started popping up on the arcane web. People think Lionax is the creator, because those concoctions smell like oranges, coffee, and horsehair. I don't think the magic itself even gives off those scents. So it's either him, reminding people he's still out there, or a very clever alchemist who admires Lionax adopted the calling card for themselves."

Deandra's mind spun. "So the scents being detected in your

store either means someone in ASA bought one of those concoctions, or Lionax did the damage himself."

Neela nodded. "The demon hippo fiasco happened around the time our business was just getting started, but he made enough comments online to suggest he thought we were terrible people. It's hard to know if ASA has been growing bolder and more violent again as an organization because they've found their footing, if they're becoming more frustrated with their perceived lack of success, or—most worrying—if Lionax is back, a decade after he disappeared from the public eye, and is possibly even more unbalanced."

They all fell into contemplative silence. Deandra certainly hadn't anticipated all this when she came wandering into the grimalkyne's tent solely out of curiosity about the cages' price tags.

"I feel like I should apologize again for eavesdropping," Deandra finally said.

Neela huffed a laugh. "And I'm sorry if I scared you. In hindsight, you showed up at the perfect time. You indirectly forced me to tell everyone about the break-in, which I'd been dreading. I probably would have held on to the details all day and given myself a stress-stomachache."

"Have you talked to the werecats here to warn them about ASA?" Deandra asked. "We kind of know Officer Sutter, if you want me to mention what I overheard earlier."

Powder cocked his furry head. "You're on friendly terms with the werecats?"

"I'm not saying we're police consultants," Wendy started.

"And you *shouldn't* say it, because it's a lie," muttered Deandra.

Wendy steamrolled over her comment. "But we *do* have a perfect three out of three sleuthing record."

"Officer Sutter doesn't even know about one of them," Deandra said. "We kept the magical coin mystery to ourselves."

Wendy shrugged. "We still have a perfect record, even if she doesn't know about it. If a tree falls in the woods, does it make a sound? Of course it does. And now these fine felines have first-hand … first paw … experience with our excellent on-the-job skills—"

"Job is a stretch …" Deandra said.

Wendy remained undeterred. "We're good at making people feel comfortable enough to get them to chat. Neela feels lighter now that she's told her business partners about the burglary, and now she'll be more relaxed at the festival."

Deandra's nose wrinkled. "I still think it's the nosy thing."

"Definitely the nosy thing," Velma agreed, but she was grinning.

"It *is* a good idea to mention ASA to the werecats—especially with the station so close to the park," Powder said. "Neela probably would have tried to sweep it all under the rug until the end of the weekend so as to not stress *us* out, but now that I know, I'll go talk to the cats myself."

Neela hiss-sighed.

With a knowing look cast Deandra and Wendy's way, Powder said, "That means I was right. You probably *did* save us a lot of headaches, sleuths. So thanks for sticking your noses into our business."

Deandra laughed. "You're very welcome. I'll be bouncing between a couple of booths this weekend, including the one for the Mythic Pet Kitchen. My dire wolf and I have been tasked with trying to convince festival-goers to adopt as many vibrissa kittens as possible. In exchange for selflessly helping you this afternoon, do you have any tips for me?"

"Oh. I have an idea," Powder said. "Be right back."

Deandra watched him go.

"They need exercise," Velma said. "So if they're cooped up and start to get bitey or mischievous, you'll need toys. Mundane laser pointers work great for them. They can also be trained to do basic tricks fairly easily; they're very smart. Either engage their brain or their body, and you'll avoid too much trouble. Assuming they don't get loose and start phasing, anyway."

"This is just a loan," came Powder's voice from behind the group. Velma, Neela, and Theodore turned around and stepped aside. Powder had a small harness and leash in hand. "Just a loan, okay? The runework on these things is *pricey* but they've been specifically crafted for animals who phase."

"You can thank yours truly for that," said Theodore. "It's some of my best work."

Powder continued, "Vibrissa can be trained to go on walks, so if you have a really unruly one, get it in a harness and give it some freedom, and it'll be a happy camper."

Deandra took the bright red leash and harness from Powder. "This is great. I really appreciate it."

Deandra suspected that letting her borrow the harness and leash set was self-serving on Powder's part. If someone at the festival decided to adopt a vibrissa cat, this was the kind of booth they should hit up for supplies for their new teleporting pet. He was probably hoping Deandra would be able to send a few new customers their way. Juniper had said full-grown vibrissa weren't that much bigger than the size the cats were now, so the kittens wouldn't quickly outgrow this pricey gear, either.

When Wendy's stomach loudly growled, the cousins bid the grimalkyne goodbye, wished them luck on the rest of their setup, and set off for Hogarth's Hoagies. Deandra admired the intricate runework etched into the supple red leather as they walked, hoping the items would help get some of the cats homes.

When she spotted an ASA flyer attached to a utility pole, she tore it down, crumpled it up, and tossed it into a trash can. Powder's words echoed in her head. *"They broke into zoos, pet stores, even veterinary clinics to free the animals there."*

What if ASA targeted the Mythic Pet Kitchen and attempted to release the phasing kittens from confinement, convinced they were better off loose in the world?

Deandra was starting to develop a stress-stomachache of her own.

CHAPTER SEVEN

Though they were *both* hungry now, Deandra and Wendy took their time walking through the aisles of booths. Deandra took in the sights as she listened to Wendy, who was deep in a monologue about Heather's micromanaging warpath.

"Deandra!"

The cousins both came up short in the middle of a wide aisle of grass.

The call had come from her left. A pair of draken were pulling a flat-bed cart topped with several pieces of oversize furniture, blocking her view of the booths. When the draken passed, she spotted Quinn and Rularo. Quinn waved, her smile bright.

Glancing at Wendy, Deandra said, "Those are Peril's owners. Parents? Whatever."

"Do you think Peril is in his beard right now?" Wendy asked, eyes squinted as if she could somehow see through Rularo's thick black hair. "Want to go say hi, or are you peopled out?"

"The social battery still has some juice in it, but it's getting low. You going to pass out from hunger?"

"I'll survive," Wendy said. "Maybe."

Remembering something, Deandra rummaged around in her purse—which now held the cat harness and leash among her other usual flotsam—until she found the half-consumed bag of strawberry fruit puffs. She handed them to her cousin and then immediately headed for the Greenwoods. "You're welcome, and I'm sorry!" she called over her shoulder.

The Greenwoods had a double booth, with their stationery— such as bespoke gift wrap, tissue paper, journals, and note cards— on the left side and the tattoo station on the right.

A freestanding wooden hutch stood in a corner of the tattoo half of the booth, and Deandra figured that was where the living inks would be stored. A black leather adjustable chair was already set up, as well as a flat table like one might see at a massage parlor. A cart and stool stood near the chair. Deandra assumed the cart would hold Rularo's supplies, like tattoo guns, paper towels, and inks, so he would have easy access while working on a client. A long table with several closed binders lying on top was the extent of the furniture on that side of the booth.

Rularo and Quinn were both in the stationery section of the tent, setting up shelves, baskets, and racks. The considerable stacks of boxes dotted around suggested they planned to set up the bulk of their wares today, but they'd probably bring the pricier items, such as living inks and tattoo guns, tomorrow.

"How's it going?" Deandra asked, stopping just outside the

tent. A dark purple tablecloth was draped over the box-laden table that stood between her and the Greenwoods.

"Hi, Dee," Rularo said a bit absentmindedly, scratching the side of his head. More to himself, he muttered, "I know I brought it. Maybe it's in that one?" He wandered off toward the tattoo side of the tent without another word, then crouched to presumably search a box.

Quinn blew a wayward curl off her sweaty forehead and propped a hand on her hip. "We're good. Still *so* much to do, but we've made some good headway. Festival setup day is always stressful, but honestly it's been nice leaving the store to our employees while we get to be outside all day."

Today, her shirt was beige and featured Earth with a smiley face etched over it. *"Good morning, Starshine,"* the text above the image said, with *"the Earth says hello"* below it.

Deandra wished she was as perpetually cheerful as Quinn and her T-shirts.

Wendy stopped beside her. "You and I need to have words," she said, then waved the empty fruit-puff bag in Deandra's face.

Wide-eyed, Deandra took the bag. "How ... how did you eat those so fast?" Glancing over at her cousin, she found her shirt dotted with little flecks of pink powder. There was a distant, haunted look in her cousin's eyes.

While focused on some spot in the middle distance, Wendy said, "It's like I blacked out. One minute, I was trying a single fruit puff, and when I came to again, the bag was empty." She turned her wide gaze to Deandra. "What the heck were those things? Were they drugs? Am I now addicted to ayahuasca?"

Deandra snorted.

"If it helps," Quinn said, "ayahuasca is usually consumed as a tea." She canted her head. "I have to say, though, that the speed at which you ate those is not something I'm going to be able to unsee for a long time. You were like a starved raccoon in a trash can ..."

"At least we're now bonded by trauma," Wendy said, and held

out a hand for Quinn to shake. "It's nice to finally meet you. I'm Wendy, Dee's cousin."

"Quinn," she said, laughing, and shook Wendy's offered palm.

The two ladies fell into easy conversation.

Deandra tried to join in, but her gaze kept drifting to the table topped with binders. While she was familiar with InkCraft's stationery, as they were the ones who'd designed Deandra's magic-animated business cards, she didn't know much about the tattoo half of their business. InkCraft's tattoo studio was in one of the building's back rooms.

She recalled Jackie's elaborate flower tattoo. Deandra had met the young woman last month. She'd ended up having an unexpected connection to the missing phoenix feather that had sent the whole town into a tizzy. Jackie's tattoo had shifted colors in a slow, hypnotizing way. Rularo had done the artwork for her. Deandra had never seen anything like it. She figured those binders were filled with designs festival patrons could pick for their flash tattoos.

Unable to contain her curiosity any longer, she stepped into the tent and headed for the table. One of the binders was actually a spiral-bound appointment book, while the other two were filled with plastic sleeves. One binder was labeled "B&G Flash" and the other "Color Flash."

She flipped open the appointment book and found the tab for this month. When she landed on the weekend in question, she noted that appointments were being scheduled every forty-five minutes, and most of the slots for Friday and Saturday were already full. It confirmed that Rularo, at the very least, would be at the festival until after eight p.m. each day. Hopefully Peril wouldn't go too stir crazy being on his own for most of the day.

Next to each name was written either "black and gray" or "color." She admittedly knew very little about tattoos, but she'd thought "flash" meant customers had a choice of pre-selected designs, and since those designs were typically less complicated and could be finished quickly, it was more of a drop-in situation rather than one you needed an appointment for. Perhaps the nature of an event like this changed that, though.

She closed the appointment book and moved to the color binder. The first page didn't feature designs, but rather a note to prospective customers written in bold text.

If you didn't fill out your design request and intake forms before your appointment, please know that your preferred live-ink colors might not be available.

Safety warning: Sage-versil ink (green) and myrobalan-iron ink (black) are known to cause allergic reactions in mundanes and draken. Jenipapo-versil (admiral #3 and azure #5, specifically) is not recommended for anyone with more than fifty percent elfin ancestry.

An allergy test is performed on everyone, regardless of species, if they select nacre inks, as there are often trace amounts of magic-touched mollusk shell dust.

Shatterberry ink can only be administered to trolls, draken, and ogres. It cannot be used on shifters or mundanes. No, we don't care how pretty it is. If you're unsure of your ancestry, it will not be used. Period. (Think of how wolfsbane affected werewolves. Shatterberry is worse.)

Not understanding most of that, Deandra flipped the page. There were roughly fifteen plastic sleeves featuring the tattoo designs on offer. They were arranged by category, given the tabs on the side. "Zombie cactus" was, fittingly, the first option, followed by "flowers," "celestial bodies," "mundane animals," "mythical animals," and "symbols."

As is, each design was relatively simple, favoring strong, bold lines. What made the designs truly shine was their color combinations showcasing InkCraft's legendary inks. Butterfly wings slowly flapped in a rainbow of colors. Hearts, anchors, skulls, and daggers could be filled in or surrounded with colors that shifted in a slow wave. She stared at a heart whose colors transitioned from yellow to orange to red. Dragons could breathe a gout of fire that left their mouth in a blast of red-orange that morphed to blue-white. Deandra had never really considered getting a tattoo before, but she was tempted now. Maybe she could talk Wendy into getting something with her.

Rularo, who had been rummaging through a box nearby, stood up now, issuing a triumphant, "I *did* bring it!" The sudden appearance of his bulk in the crowded space made the big man look like a giant who'd been stuffed into a dollhouse. He grinned at Deandra as if he'd forgotten she was there. "Hey, Dee!"

She chuckled. "Hi, Rularo."

"Call me Ru. We're practically family now."

Every time Deandra was around the Greenwoods, she was happy the two golden retriever-like people who were so different on the surface had found each other.

The big man's enthusiastic greeting had startled Wendy and Quinn out of their chat on the other side of the tent.

Rularo took a few steps toward Deandra, his grin growing wider. It was so wide, in fact, that it bordered on manic. He looked down at his own nose, his eyes crossing, before returning his focus to Deandra. His smile was giving cartoon villain. "Peril is super, *super* stoked to hang out with you tomorrow, Deandra," he said, drawing out all three syllables of her name. "So stoked, actually, that he squeals like a kit every time we mention it."

She stared at him blankly. Maybe the heat had cooked his noodle.

When Peril suddenly poked his little face out of the depths of Rularo's beard, Deandra understood what the man had been doing. "Don't exaggerate, Father! It's unbecoming." He turned a beady eye toward Deandra. "Greetings," he said after a beat. "I'm not excited about your visits, per se, but I don't hate the idea of them, either." He abruptly tucked himself away again.

Quinn beamed and clapped dramatically, though silently. Rularo was cheesing just as hard. Wendy's mouth was open in a little "o" of surprise, probably because she'd never heard a ferret speak in full sentences.

Before Deandra could think of anything to say, she was distracted by movement behind Rularo. She realized a moment later that there was a tent behind him, and the occupant was busy at work setting up their own space. They'd pinned up a tarp of some kind to serve as a backdrop. From what she could tell from this side, since the colors were more drab on the back, the back-drop had a blue background decorated with puffy white clouds. Occasionally, the edge of a piece of furniture or a body part would hit the tarp, making it flap and jerk.

There only appeared to be two or three feet of space between the backs of the two tents. It wasn't wide enough to form an alley for vendors to wheel carts through, but there was probably enough room to use it as a narrow walkway. Deandra assumed it was mostly used as a way for vendors to cover distances to the restrooms quicker than wading through the festival crowds. Even though the flapping artificial clouds were distracting, the tarp was far enough away that it wasn't hitting the Greenwoods' tent.

Rularo noted her line of sight and said, "That's what this is for."

Her gaze shifted from the lightly thrashing tarp to his hand, which held a folded chunk of white fabric.

"Keeping the area more enclosed will help anyone who's nervous about getting a tattoo feel a little less exposed." Rularo stooped to grab something out of the box near his feet and produced a bag of clips, then proceeded to get the white tarp pinned into place, starting on the tattoo side of the booth.

Deandra closed the binder of color tattoos and headed back toward the other ladies.

Quinn cocked a brow. "You considering a tat? I think Sunday

is the only day left with openings. Ru's better at keeping track of those than I am. We'd be happy to work you in at a later date, though, given all your help with Peril."

"It's not a no, but a *not right now*," Deandra said. "I was a little confused about something, though. I thought the whole point of flash was that they were drop-ins ..."

"Usually, yes," Quinn said. "But some of the living inks have a short shelf life, so we have to make sure we have what customers want on hand, and that means we need to know what they want before they get here. Ru's made a name for himself, and he rarely does flash, but we still didn't think appointments would fill up this fast. We posted on socials last night that we had an appointment form on our website, and almost every slot for the first two days of the festival was snapped up within three hours. I've got five inks curing in the kitchen right now, and I have to start another eight when we wrap up here."

"I'm glad you two are so busy, but I hope you don't burn out," Deandra said.

Quinn huffed a tired laugh. "Don't worry; we usually close the shop the Monday after the festival and sleep all day. It's a wild weekend for our employees, too. We make such good money at this event, though, being sleep deprived is totally worth it."

Rularo yelped. "Goddess above! What the heck was *that*?"

Whirling toward him, Quinn asked, "What was what?"

Squeal!

That didn't sound like a ferret squeal—it sounded far more ... porcine.

Rularo hadn't finished covering the back of the tent yet, so Deandra had a clear view of the backdrop of the tent behind the Greenwoods' flapping furiously. The tarp settled over something person-shaped for a few chaotic seconds before the shape lurched away again, followed by another squeal. Rularo yelped again, stumbled back, crashed into a stool, and pitched over it, landing in a heap. Peril had sensed the danger he was in and launched out of Rularo's beard before the man hit the ground. He skittered across the slippery binders, and a breath later he was perched on Quinn's shoulder. He heaved hard, his front paws over his mouth.

Despite Rularo taking a tumble in the tattoo half of the booth, Peril's focus soon shifted to the back of the tent, where InkCraft's back neighbors' tarp was still flapping around as if caught in a localized hurricane. He repositioned himself on Quinn's shoulder so his back faced Deandra. His black-tipped white tail swished in agitation.

Quinn, unconcerned with the commotion in the back tent, hurried toward Rularo, who was still on the ground, groaning in pain.

Before Deandra could get a question out, a squealing mass hit the tent's tarp, lifted it enough to gain clearance, and then shot directly at Deandra.

"Hit the deck!" Wendy shouted and dropped to her knees, but Deandra was too frozen in shock to move.

The creature squealed again, then winged upward at the last second, taking it toward the top of the Greenwoods' tent. It apparently didn't realize it could fly out the open sides. Deandra narrowly missed getting a wing to the nose.

She'd experienced being in a house with a terrified trapped bird, giant moths, and even a bat once. But this? This was something her brain could *not* process.

It was a copper-colored piglet covered in black spots and sporting all-black wings. Why did a pig have *feathered* wings? Why did it have wings at all?

She'd seen a few flying pigs before this at the flight park, but she hadn't interacted with them. And they certainly hadn't been zipping around near her head like an insect lured to a bright light.

It took a few more panicked seconds for her to realize the poor pig was scared out of its little mind. As she hastily climbed onto a table, she wondered if the tent behind InkCraft's belonged to the Mythic Pet Kitchen. She also hoped Quinn wouldn't be too upset if she got footprints all over her pretty purple tablecloth.

The piglet squealed in terror as it tried—for the tenth time—to get out the top of the tent, couldn't find an opening after it careened into the fabric a few times, and returned to flitting about wildly.

"Hey! Chill out!" Deandra said, simultaneously waving her arms to get the terrified pig's attention and also ducking out of the way periodically to avoid getting a hoof to the face. She was sure she looked like one of those waving inflatable arm-flailing tube men outside a car dealership. "Pig! Little piggy. Hey—ahh!" She squatted just in time for the squealing creature to zip overhead. It still hadn't figured out that, if it flew a few feet lower, it could shoot out the wide space between tent poles and into the open.

Would Parks Management have to be called if she couldn't catch it? How did one even catch a flying piglet? A net gun?

She could only imagine the pandemonium that would break out in the mundane world if the piglet were to cross the veil and mundanes learned pigs really *could* fly.

"You're going to hurt yourself!" Deandra called, a little frantic, when the piglet crashed into the top of the tent again. "Come here. I promise I won't hurt you!"

"Frankenswine! Where are you?"

Deandra froze, sure that couldn't have *actually* been the name she'd heard. Well, it was worth a try. Hands on hips, she looked up at the piglet. "Frankenswine! Get down here!"

The piglet abruptly stilled in the air, its beating wings keeping it aloft like a bird of prey. Lucidity returned to its eyes. It squealed once, as if to ask, "Who, me?"

"Yes, you! Get down here!" Deandra said.

Frankenswine squealed again, but this time the pig sounded excited. It tucked its wings and dove straight for Deandra like a porcine torpedo.

"Oh no," was the only thought Deandra could form before the winged pig slammed into her chest. Her breath went out in a whoosh, and she had no doubt she'd be bruised in the morning. She wrapped her arms around the pig as the force of the impact knocked her off the table, sending her backward. She slammed her eyes shut, hoping the grass was soft enough to prevent her tailbone from shattering.

She hit something solid a breath later, but it was much softer than the ground. When she cracked open an eye, she found herself staring up into *two* faces. One was the grinning face of Rularo, and the other was the terrified face of Peril, who was poking out of Rularo's beard again. The big man had caught her in his arms. She sagged in his hold.

Frankenswine issued a happy grunt.

"Holy crap," Wendy said from beside them, hands on her knees. "That was the most chaotic sixty seconds of my life."

Deandra huffed a laugh, which hurt a little on the way out. "Which is saying a lot, seeing as we almost got roasted to death in your car a few months ago."

"*Second* most chaotic sixty seconds of my life," Wendy amended.

By the time Rularo had deposited Deandra back on her feet, a wide-eyed Quinn was rushing toward them with an equally worried-looking Juniper hot on her heels.

"Frankenswine, you naughty pig!" Juniper said.

The piglet squirmed at the sound of his voice, kicking Deandra in the stomach and the bicep in his efforts to get to the goblin. Deandra handed Frankenswine over. Once he was in Juniper's arms, the piglet nuzzled the goblin's neck, snorting and grunting.

Juniper, now that he seemed confident his porcine charge was no worse for wear, finally paid more attention to the others gathered around him. Looking at Quinn and Rularo in turn, he said, "I do apologize for all the commotion." Addressing Deandra, he said, "Hello again. I promise, I take good care of my animals. Please don't let this dissuade you from assisting me tomorrow."

Wendy asked, "What happened, exactly? It sounded hectic over there even before the pig escaped."

Juniper's olive-green skin went a little darker at the cheeks, and he clenched his jaw for a moment in clear annoyance. "Someone snuck into the tent when my wife and I had our backs turned and opened the door to Frankenswine's pen! Kira—my wife—caught the little sneak attempting to get a birdcage open, too."

"Any idea who it was? A bored kid?" Deandra asked, though she feared she knew exactly who was behind this.

"At first I thought it was a child, but it turns out it was an adult—a gnome. He was about yay high," Juniper said, holding his hand at his chest level, which was around Deandra's mid-thigh. "He wasn't wearing his hat; it threw me off. Um. Do you, uh, know what was odd, though? After Kira whacked him good with a broom, he took off running and shouted, 'Let the lions roam free!' Super-duper weird, right?"

Deandra's brows smashed together. The only thing "super-duper weird" was how Juniper sounded so stilted all of a sudden.

"While Kira was chasing him away—oh, she was *hoppin'* mad! —the hooligan practically crashed directly into Officer Sutter. That's karma, for ya! Kira was reporting the whole thing to the werecats while I was trying to catch Frankenswine here."

The piglet had fallen asleep in the goblin's arms, worn out by his ordeal. He snored softly.

Deandra thought of how many vendors were keeping their high-value items with them until tomorrow, not wanting to leave them mostly unattended overnight, and couldn't help but wonder why Frankenswine had been penned up in the first place. "Do you, uh, leave the animals in their cages overnight?"

"Oh, Goddess, no! Frankenswine is our daughter's pet. We've been watching him for the weekend. Terrible timing, but what can you do? We have to keep him with us as much as possible; he's got terrible separation anxiety. We brought a few other animals with us, just to help them with socialization. The festival can be stressful for them, since there's so much activity, so bringing them on setup days helps desensitize them a bit."

She was about to ask something else when she realized that the Greenwoods had both gone very still.

Wendy had noticed it, too. "You two all right?"

The Greenwoods exchanged an uneasy look.

Rularo spoke first. "That phrase—*let the lions roam free*—is the motto for a fringe sapient-animal advocacy group."

"Ohh," Juniper said in that strange tone again. "How odd that such a group would be here."

Deandra narrowed her eyes. She knew a fellow terrible liar when she heard one. He sounded like she and Wendy did every time they attempted to discreetly interview a perp—which is to say they always sounded like they were in desperate need of acting lessons.

Wendy, however, didn't seem to notice. She asked what Deandra had been thinking the whole time: "ASA?"

Quinn's brows hiked. "You know about them?"

Deandra stared down the aisle of tents in the direction of the grimalkyne's tent, even though she couldn't see it from her current vantage point. "We were in a booth earlier that had a visit from ASA. They promised to cause trouble this weekend."

The usually always-cheerful Quinn scowled. "ASA posts up outside adoption clinics like the one where we got Peril."

The group at large cast a look at Rularo's beard, but the ferret didn't make an appearance.

Quinn said, "There are sapient animals that are as intelligent as you or me and can function normally, all things considered, in society. Beings like yetis. They wouldn't be able to live a normal life in the mundane world, but they can in the hub system." Quinn eyed Rularo's beard again, her expression a bit guarded. "But there are animals like salica and aeorci that—"

Deandra raised her hand like she was in school. "Sorry. What's an aeorci?"

Quinn smiled at her good-naturedly. "They're members of the avian species who have lost the ability to shift. It's not clear if it's a mutation or the result of interspecies mixing with native mundane populations, but some avians retain their sapient intelligence yet must live their lives as birds. Birds of prey have a better go of it than, say, a tiny sparrow.

"Animals like them, like Peril, are able to think like you and me, but they can't hold down what constitutes a normal job or anything like that. Living in the wild is what ASA thinks is best for them—*to let wild animals roam free*—but can you imagine how terrifying it already is to be an animal on the lower end of the food chain, and then to be saddled with the burden of contemplating your own mortality?"

"Zero out of ten. Do not recommend!" came a muffled shout from Rularo's beard, which made everyone crack up. It must have sounded like a roaring 747 in there for Peril, being that close to the source of Rularo's booming laugh.

Quinn said, "Animals like Peril are safer in this realm if they have a home to live in, which means they need to be paired with folks who can accommodate their needs. I understand that ASA sees our adoption of Peril as insulting to sapient animals, and that even if he's got an entire house and yard to live in, they still see it like a cage or as a prison, but he's happy with us."

Peril poked his head out. "They are my family," was all he said before he disappeared back into Rularo's beard.

The Greenwoods smiled warmly at each other, and Rularo grabbed hold of Quinn's small hand with his large one. Quinn's eyes had gone a little glassy.

Rularo said, "ASA was out in force the day we brought Peril home. They stand outside adoption clinics with signs, and they shout at you through megaphones—which didn't help Peril's nerves; you'd think they'd realize that. They even threw rotten food at us. A rotten cabbage clocked me in the back of my head. I spun around so fast, the faun who had lobbed it at me got startled and tripped over his own hooves. I think he sprained his knee or ankle when he fell. I must have looked *pretty* furious, because his buddies wordlessly scooped up the faun under his armpits, and they hobbled off, leaving their stuff behind on the sidewalk. I might have kicked one of their coolers down the street like a soccer ball."

Quinn wrapped her free arm around his elbow. "It takes a lot to make this guy mad, but when he *is* mad …" She gazed up at him. "He'd do anything for us."

Rularo nodded tightly. "I guess it's even better that we decided to keep Peril home for the festival. I don't want ASA anywhere near him."

Juniper, who had been quietly petting the top of Frankenswine's head as the Greenwoods spoke, cleared his throat now. "I do hope, Dee, that this nasty business with ASA hasn't changed your mind about tomorrow?"

He had even worse puppy-dog eyes than Havoc!

"We'll be there tomorrow," she said, fighting back a laugh. "I'm making it my mission to get every one of those vibrissa cats a home."

Juniper smiled, clearly relieved. "All except the one your dire wolf pup adopted, of course." He gave Wendy an elevator scan and his expression turned gravely serious. "This is the one we need to convince, right?"

"She's the one," Deandra said.

Juniper stared up at Wendy defiantly. "I'm going to break you, young lady."

Wendy swallowed. "We can't have a—"

"I. Will. Break. You," he said slowly, then turned on his heel and marched back toward his own tent. "Nice to see you again, Rularo and Quinn. And I'll see you tomorrow afternoon, Dee!" he cheerfully called over his shoulder before pulling up a corner of the tarp and slipping behind it.

Wendy's shoulders slumped. "It's only a matter of time before my apartment ends up as the headquarters for your menagerie, isn't it?"

As if issuing its own concerns, her stomach growled again.

Deandra hooked her arm around Wendy's, then eyed the Greenwoods. "Hopefully the rest of the setup goes smoother. We're heading out. Wendy needs food, stat, before she passes out from low blood sugar."

They laughed.

Leaning toward Rularo a bit, and with her focus homed in on his beard, she added, "See you tomorrow, Peril."

After a long beat of silence, he poked his head out. "You have a dire wolf? I should like to meet him." Then he was gone again.

Brows hiked, Deandra stood to full height. "Uhh … *is* it okay if I bring Havoc with me?"

Quinn's eyes were watery again. Rularo had a large arm around her slim shoulders now. He looked a little weepy himself. "Absolutely," she said. "Anything he wants."

Peril poked his head back out. "Even the—"

"Except that. *Never* that," Quinn told him.

Peril's little face scrunched up in irritation, and then he disappeared from view once more.

Deandra opted not to ask.

Waving at the Greenwoods, Deandra steered Wendy away, hoping they'd make it to Hogarth's Hoagies without incident—and before Wendy passed out from hunger.

CHAPTER EIGHT

The next day, Deandra sat in her car at the curb outside the Greenwoods' house. She'd already taken Havoc on a long morning walk, walked Barnaby at eleven, and gone to the flight park with Voidbringer for an hour. She'd then swung by the apartment to grab Havoc.

She'd spend the next hour with Peril, and then she and Havoc would have their first shift at the Mythic Pet Kitchen booth around three thirty. Cruz wouldn't be able to join her until tomorrow, as his vet clinic was always swamped on Fridays.

Glancing in her rearview mirror, she met Havoc's eye. "You ready for this?"

He chirp-barked.

Taking that as a yes, she got herself and Havoc out of the car and they made their way up the driveway. She stood on the porch with Havoc for ten full seconds, twirling her keyring around her finger over and over, before she got up the nerve to unlock the door and scoot inside.

There was something odd about letting herself into a house that belonged to someone she didn't know that well. Even with permission—and a key!—it still felt like trespassing. She wondered if it was a feeling she'd ever get used to.

Once inside, she heeled off her shoes and left them on the pile of various footwear by the door. "Hey, Peril. It's me," she called out from the middle of the foyer, feeling a little silly. "Havoc is with me, too. I'm going to let him off the leash. He's very friendly, but if you're scared, you can stay in your tunnels so he can't get to you, okay?"

The only sound in the house was the soft hum of the food dehydrators in the kitchen and the muted chatter of the narrator on the nature program playing on the living room's television. If Peril was currently scurrying around in his tunnel system, she couldn't hear it. She watched Havoc, who was still leashed and seated in the entryway with her. His head was cocked curiously, but his gaze was focused in the general direction of the TV, where a mouse was bounding across a field.

She unclipped his leash from his harness, and he set off in a slow trot into the living room, muzzle to the carpet.

Deandra wandered into the kitchen first, finding it just as chaotic as the last time she'd been here. What looked like a mad scientist's lab had taken over the counter on either side of the sink, though. There were small vials in a two-tiered wooden rack as well as mason jars of various sizes. Each was filled with ink, the colors varied and vibrant. Some of the inks were as still as pond water, some thrashed and foamed like contained tempests, and others bubbled, as if boiling. There were mason jars sitting in plastic tubs of ice, positioned under heat lamps, or lined up on the windowsill where they got ample sunlight. She kept her hands behind her back, worried she'd inadvertently bump into something and cause untold property damage or bodily harm.

She moved out of the kitchen and into the dining room, where the table was still covered in the pieces of Peril's latest puzzle. It had been about a third complete when she was last here, and it was close to half done now. As she stood behind one of the dining room chairs, she glanced up at the opening in the tunnel that ran along the top of the wall opposite. She half expected to see Peril peering at her from there, but the space remained empty.

As unnerved as Deandra still felt about a talking animal, she was a little disappointed that he hadn't shown his face yet. Perhaps all their previous interactions were a fluke, and she didn't, in fact, have the calming presence the Greenwoods were so sure she possessed.

She stepped into the den-like area next, eyeing the tunnel system that ran above the windows. Havoc rolled around on his back in a sunbeam.

Still no sign of Peril.

The Greenwoods had told her to make herself at home, so if he didn't materialize in the next ten minutes or so, she'd curl up on the couch to watch TV until her allotted time was up.

The den had an open doorway on either end—one leading to the dining room and the other to the living room. She walked up the single step that led her back into the living room, now having completed the circuit of the main part of the house. A toucan was on the TV now, its colorful beak taking up half the screen.

Glancing to the left, her gaze swept over the tunnel system that ran along the top and bottom of the wall, the trio of black-and-white close-up photographs of mushrooms, and the sectional couch.

She froze.

Peril was on the back of the couch watching her. He stood upright, reminding her of a meerkat. He was wringing his front paws. This was the first calm moment she'd had with him, and she wondered how she'd never noticed before that, while his whole body was white, his paws were black. The black fur stretched an inch up his limbs, as if he were wearing tiny crew socks.

"Hi," Deandra ventured, worried her voice would be too loud —like a gunshot fired in a silent room—and would scare Peril away.

He *did* flinch at the sound of her voice but otherwise stayed put.

Something about the way he watched her made her think this wasn't normal nerves. His anxiety only seemed to ratchet up when Havoc trotted into the room. It took him three tries, but Havoc finally jumped onto an ottoman. Despite being able to fly, Havoc seemed to instinctively know that he shouldn't show that ability to anyone not in the pod. Well, and to Wendy.

Perhaps Peril was regretting his declaration that he'd wanted to meet her dire wolf. The breed gave most people—mundane, fae, *and* magic-touched—pause. Even the size of Havoc's puppy persona made people uneasy. Havoc must have looked like a terrifying monster torn from myth to tiny Peril. She supposed she could leave Havoc in the car for the rest of the visit …

"Can I speak plainly, Deandra?" Peril asked, still wringing his paws as he looked from her to Havoc and back again.

Brows furrowed, Deandra nodded. "Sure. Uh … what's up?"

He didn't want Havoc in the house; she was sure of it. Even though it was summer, if she left all the windows down in her car, Havoc would be okay. He was a dragon, after all. Heat didn't affect him the way it would a dog.

Peril stood a little taller. "You must know that my … oh, I never know the right term. My parents, I suppose? Yes, my parents. You know my parents are the most important individuals in the world to me, yes?"

Not only was this line of questioning bizarre, but so was how badly the ferret's voice shook. And the fact that he was talking in full sentences!

"Yes, I know that, Peril."

"Good. So it's imperative that you answer my next question truthfully." He huffed a breath out of his nose, then balled his paws into little fists and held them at his sides. "Are you here not as my caregiver but because you're a charlatan in disguise? Have you come into our lives to swindle us? Are you perhaps the employee of a rival living-ink vendor sent here to learn the secret ingredients to my parents' inks so your bosses can undercut my parents' livelihood?"

Deandra just stared at him. Of all the things he could have asked her, none of that had been in the realm of her imagination. Peril looked equal parts terrified and incensed.

She knew she needed to say something, *anything*, to first calm him down—he was quivering with anxiety, or perhaps rage—and then she'd tackle the wild claims after that.

She thought long and hard about what to say. "*What?*"

Peril blinked. "Are you a witch? A sorcerer? A zoolinguist with a specialty in the mythical?"

"Uhhh …" Deandra said eloquently.

Peril's little nose bunched. "I shall try a different tack." He glanced over at Havoc, who still lay on the ottoman, but he was currently chewing loudly on his unmentionables, one foot in the air like a grooming cat. "Are you being deceived by Havoc, or is Havoc deceiving *you*?"

She noted then that, while most who looked at Havoc focused on some spot far above his actual head, Peril's gaze was fixed slightly downward. From Peril's spot on the back of the couch, Havoc's actual position was lower than the ferret's. As a dire wolf, Peril's line of sight would have been higher.

Oh.

Oh.

"Uhh, Havoc," Deandra said slowly. "Did you expand the pod without telling me?"

Havoc, with a back foot still in the air, looked up at her—then aggressively sneezed. Scrambling to his feet while remaining atop the ottoman, he cocked his head.

She knew Havoc well enough now to understand most of his body language. He comprehended what she said most of the time, but his non-verbal responses were rarely in line with human ones. He didn't shake his head for no or nod for yes. Currently, he was confused by her question. Which meant he *understood* the question but didn't understand why she'd asked it. Meaning that, no, he hadn't let Peril into the pod.

Could Peril somehow see *through* the glamour?

"Um. So," Deandra hedged as she refocused on Peril. "What do you see when you look at Havoc?"

Peril narrowed his eyes. His voice had stopped shaking, at least. "I don't see a dire wolf, I'll tell you that much. What do *you* see?"

Deandra chewed on her bottom lip. Havoc's secret wasn't hers to tell. As much as she wanted Peril to be comfortable around her, and to trust her, revealing Havoc's biggest secret—and frankly hers, too—wasn't a line she was willing to cross. Deandra truly liked the Greenwoods, but she didn't know either one well enough to know if they'd keep Havoc's true identity to themselves, no matter how appreciative they were about her willingness to help with Peril.

"Ah," the ferret said sagely and nodded to himself. He lowered to all fours and scampered along the back of the couch toward her until he was sitting only a few feet from her on the edge. He levered himself onto his back feet again. "The answer is neither, then. He shows you who he really is, and you're protecting that knowledge."

Deandra had no idea what to say. She still didn't want to utter the word "dragon," just in case Peril saw something else entirely.

Maybe there was a strange glitch in the glamour magic that specifically affected salica, and Peril saw a tiny moose in a tutu or something.

He sighed. "I may have lived a sheltered life, all things considered, but even *I* know dragons are supposed to be extinct."

Deandra's eyes dang near popped out of her head. She hurried forward and plopped onto the couch near his perch, sitting cross-legged. Peril scuttled back several inches, but he didn't bolt away. "*How* can you see him? Oh gosh, what if the glamour magic is starting to weaken? I have no idea if I can even get another collar made. And even if I could, I'm sure it's *way* more expensive than anything I—"

She was cut off when Peril jumped off the back of the couch and landed on her knee. He placed a digit to his mouth and shushed her.

Standing on his back feet again, he clasped his front paws in front of his chest. "My kind doesn't have many magical skills. We're faster and stealthier than a mundane weasel, but other than possessing sapient-level intelligence while trapped in a five-pound body, there's not much that's special about us." He paused —seemingly for dramatic effect. "Other than the ability to see through illusions and glamours, that is. I can see through veils, too. We were used in the fae realm by many royal families and paranoid rich elites specifically because of that skill. We make excellent spies."

She blinked at him. "Oh."

Peril, though he was wringing his hands and looking generally anxious, managed to sound a touch condescending when he said, "You're not very loquacious, are you?"

"Don't sass me, little guy. I'm trying to wrap my head around the fact that I'm chatting to a flippin' talking ferret—who uses SAT words, I might add—who also happens to know mine and Havoc's biggest secret. Sorry for not having enough words to express how much I'm currently freaking out."

"Ah," Peril said. "I suppose I can understand that."

They settled into thoughtful silence. The muted roar of a lion sounded from the television behind her.

"Do, uh, your parents know about this skill of yours?"

Peril nodded. "Oh, sure. We learned I could see through veils shortly after they adopted me and brought me to Axia. They helped me research my kind ... as much as one can on Forage, anyway. We've known for quite some time that I can see through illusions and glamours, because of that research, but it's never come into practice until today.

"Well, I suppose that's not entirely true. It's never come into practice in a manner this extreme before. The most common type of glamour magic is superficial at best—changing hair or eye color. It's a very rare magic. As is illusion magic. But this ..." He turned on Deandra's knee to study Havoc. Her dragon was still on the ottoman, but he was on his back, watching a moth as it gently banged against the dome light on the ceiling. His front paws were flopped over his chest, and his back legs were stretched out straight. "Your dragon isn't quite the fearsome creature one would expect, but he's magnificent all the same."

Havoc chirped, proving he was paying close attention to the conversation, even if it didn't look like it.

Deandra still didn't know what to make of this. "Listen, Peril. I don't want to ask you to lie to your parents or anything, but—"

He turned around on her knee to face her. "Say no more. This is not my secret to tell, any more than it was yours. Why you're keeping it a secret is also no business of mine. My parents trust you, so I do as well. Your secret is safe with me. I swear it."

While she felt relieved, she wasn't sure she believed he wouldn't blab this revelation to Quinn and Rularo eventually. A slip of the tongue during a casual chat could put Havoc in serious danger.

Peril began to wring his hands again. "I have a secret for you as well, though it's not as big as yours."

She couldn't fathom what secrets Peril might be keeping. "What's that?"

He fidgeted for so long, Deandra was sure he'd changed his mind. "You know that puzzle in the dining room?" When she nodded, he continued. "My parents got it for me for my gotcha day. I must confess that I hate it. I *loathe* bananas! If we could make some headway on it today—my parents have been too busy this week to help me—I can complete it sooner, and then they'll bring me a new one. Would … would you help me with it?"

Deandra was briefly baffled again. He seemed as concerned about his puzzle as he'd been when he'd feared she was a spy for a rival ink company.

"I'm not the best at puzzles, but I'd love to help you anyway," Deandra said.

She couldn't be sure, but it looked as if the ferret's eyes welled up a bit.

"That's cool." Peril sniffed. "Or whatever, I guess."

Quinn's words from a couple of days ago came back to her now. "*…he's not the best at freely expressing softer feelings. Poor guy's got some serious trust issues. If he's prickly, it's a defense mechanism. I guess he figures if the other person is prickly back, he at least got in the first jab, you know?*"

Without warning, he jumped off her knee and onto the back of the couch. He raced along it, hopped to the floor, and then onto the back of a dining room chair—all within a matter of seconds. He was frighteningly quick.

As she headed into the dining room to join him, she imagined ferret spies darting around fae castles and mansions, fast and silent, as they gathered intel for their owners about family members, friends, and enemies alike.

She just hoped that *this* ferret wasn't a spy gathering intel on her and Havoc.

CHAPTER NINE

Taking everyone's warning to heart that the parking situation in and around Oracle Park would be a nightmare, Deandra parked in her grandparents' driveway, then she and Havoc hoofed it the rest of the way. Her grandparents lived on the southwestern side of the park, so she'd either need to skirt the entirety of the park to get to the eastern side, where most of the vendors were set up, or take her chances with the walking paths that would take her through the middle.

Her grandparents and several other Mermaids Club members had been at the festival all day, either running their booth for the club or preparing for the evening's pie-eating contest. The club's booth was part information, part recruitment, and part bake sale. Every year, each club member pulled a zombie cactus–baked good assignment out of a hat. Some treats were apparently easier to tackle than others. It had become something of a game for them to see what new and unique recipes the members of the organization could come up with to pay homage to the almighty zombie cactus.

Deandra's grandparents had been saddled with making cheesecakes. Per her grandma during their phone call last night, the last iteration of her cheesecake wasn't even fit to be used as a frisbee. Pulling "cheesecake," according to her, was the equivalent of drawing the short straw. No one had come up with a decent zombie cactus cheesecake recipe in ages. Hopefully her grandma's most recent attempt had come out better, though her grandma was sure that her cheesecake offerings would end up on the freebie table—within the club it was known as the Abomination Table—where Mermaids Club members put their failed experiments. Zombie cactus cheesecakes, she said, often couldn't even be given away.

Between her grandmother's continual cheesecake woes and Eileen's declaration that zombie cactus refused to be freeze-dried, Deandra grew leerier about trying the various unique concoctions that would be for sale this weekend.

The raw kale flavor of the fruit puff still haunted her.

Instead of walking through the park that was no doubt swarmed with people, she planned to walk two blocks, then make a left onto Wheeler Avenue, which would take her in front of the police station before she finally made it to the vendor booths.

Both sides of the road were lined with cars, only allowing for a single car to travel in either direction comfortably. The sidewalks were equally stuffed, with people of all shapes, sizes, and species crowded in nearly shoulder-to-shoulder. Somehow, everyone who was headed away from the festival had piled onto the sidewalk on her left, while everyone who was festival bound was on the right. She didn't know if this was standard etiquette during busy events or if it was a hub system rule that people followed as naturally as green lights meaning go and red meaning stop.

The folks leaving the festival were loaded down with shopping bags, and many were sipping what appeared to be frozen lemonade, the color an odd shade of green. Cactus-shaped balloons bobbed along on pink or yellow ribbons held by sleepy kids who were being dragged along by equally sleepy parents. Deandra guessed those were the families who had gotten to the festival right when it started at nine a.m. and now were wrecked after six hours. The flood of people on her side of the sidewalk was probably the after-work crowd. The festival ran until eight p.m. tonight, with events, activities, and live music scheduled for most of it.

Several people ahead of her, a festivalgoer waddled along in an inflatable cactus costume. The couple directly in front of her were dressed like zombies, complete with blood-splattered rags. They each wore a plastic headband, to which a small flowerpot holding what appeared to be a real cactus was affixed. A man nearby wore a red T-shirt with a zombified cactus on it, along with the message: "Grab unlife by the thorns."

Deandra idly wondered if this festival had taken on a life of its own over the years. Had what originally started as a fundraising effort with a niche theme morphed into something else? It reminded her of the progression of mundane Black Friday. It used to mean steep discounts on select items that were available on a first-come, first-served basis during the wee hours the day after Thanksgiving. Now stores offered modest, if not negligible, Black Friday deals for a whole week. Some even nonsensically advertised Black Friday deals in the middle of summer.

She also wondered if working in the service industry for so long had prematurely turned her into a curmudgeon.

Havoc, conversely, happily trotted alongside her, head turning this way and that as he took in the spectacle. He had his zombie-hand toy in his mouth, as he'd refused to leave it behind. The squeaker had thankfully been punctured the night he got it. Now it just made an odd squelching noise, which seemed fitting for an undead severed extremity.

The sounds of chatter and laughter grew exponentially as she and the tide of tourists turned onto Wheeler. A sea of white tents took up a large swatch of the park, looking like a bank of low-lying clouds. Carnival rides and game booths had been erected in the park overnight. A colorful Ferris wheel slowly turned in the distance, the buckets swaying high above the treetops. Music blasted out of a stereo system.

Normally Deandra would have assumed a small town like Axia couldn't have this many people milling about inside it. There wasn't enough parking or hotels to accommodate them all. But with telepad travel, people could visit from the other side of the country in less than an hour and get home again just as quickly.

As she and Havoc made their way down the middle of Wheeler—which had been closed entirely to cars—she was overwhelmed by the sheer *number* of festivalgoers and the cacophony of so many people talking and laughing, of children shrieking, of canned music nearby and live music somewhere in the distance, of carnival barkers. It was like a wall of sound.

No wonder businesses loved this weekend—and tomorrow was sure to be even busier.

A giant balloon arch had been erected between two trees, marking the unofficial entrance to the festival. Several werecats—in both human and feline forms—loitered in front of the police station and near the arch, making sure folks were behaving themselves. As she passed under the arch, Deandra half expected the balloons to be cactus-shaped. They were standard ovals, though, the green, pink, and yellow balloons etched with the message "WELCOME TO THE 27TH ANNUAL ZOMBIE CACTUS FESTIVAL!" A few of the letters had been replaced with cactuses or cactus fruit.

It was slow going getting from the park entrance to the Mythic

Pet Kitchen booth, partly because of the crush of people and partly because Deandra was suffering from severe distraction. By the time she finally made it to Juniper, she'd purchased a bag of zombie-cactus-powder–dusted popcorn, a set of cactus-shaped potholders, and a box of cactus-flavored dog treats that were, of course, shaped like cactuses.

Deandra stopped at one of the long tables that ran along the front of the booth. There was an opening between the two tables, presumably to give Juniper and Kira an easy way to enter and exit the booth. A goblin woman who she assumed was Kira, Juniper's wife, was busy with a customer at the far end of the rightmost table. She was about the same height as Juniper. She was dressed casually in jeans, tennis shoes, and a dark-blue shirt with "Mythic Pet Kitchen" written across the front.

A cardboard box with airholes cut into either side and a handle at the top sat on the table near Kira and her customer. The box occasionally rocked and jumped. Sounds were issuing from the box, too, but there was so much noise around her, Deandra couldn't have said if it meowing, hissing, or growling. The surface of the leftmost table in front of her was dotted with binders, flyers, business cards, and adoption rules and suggestions. Two of the three binders were closed and had the words "Available For Adoption" written on the front.

"There's a line here, lady!" someone said, but before Deandra could reply or even turn toward the annoyed person, she heard Juniper's familiar voice.

"Oh! Thank the Goddess!"

Deandra heard him but somehow couldn't *see* him.

Granted, she'd been driven to distraction again.

The booth appeared to have similar magical properties to the grimalkyne's tent of magical cages. She knew this tent was a double, just like the one she'd helped Otis set up yesterday. And yet, her eyes were telling her that there were at least twenty people inside the tent who all appeared to have plenty of elbow room. There were also four large cages and a playpen that was closer in size to something she'd expect to see in a petting zoo. She blinked rapidly, as if that would make her brain reconcile with what she saw.

"Deandra?"

She took a startled step back as Juniper crossed the threshold of the tent and walked through the opening between the two tables. It was as if he'd been behind an invisibility curtain.

"Oh! Goodness me," Juniper said, staring up at her. He was dressed identically to his wife. Close up, she could see now that the words "Mythic Pet Kitchen" written across the front of their shirts were spelled out with sketches of various mythical animals making up the individual letters. "Did I not mention we have a magicked tent?"

"You did not," Deandra said. "Are the tent poles covered in runes the way the bars of the vibrissa cage are?"

He bobbed his head. "Very similar, yes. Makes your brain feel a bit scrambly if you stare into it too long, doesn't it? Your reputation precedes you so much, I forgot you're actually new to the hub system."

She couldn't imagine ever *not* feeling new here. If she thought about the way magic was bending physics—again—her mind would bend until it snapped, so instead she asked, "Where do you want us?"

His shoulders relaxed a bit. He seemed to spend most of his time around her worried she was going to change her mind about helping him and flee in the opposite direction. "We're currently keeping people's visits to half an hour before they're gently kicked out and need to get in line again. Some folks would spend all day in there with the animals if we let them! But the tent is set to fifty max capacity; otherwise, the magic gets fussy. Can't have the tent collapsing on us, can we?"

Deandra chose to treat that as rhetorical. She glanced to her left and right, and then her gaze snagged on the line of people standing behind a freestanding sign that said, "Wait here for your 30 minutes with the animals of the Mythic Pet Kitchen!"

She'd walked right past the line, so overstimulated that she'd missed it.

The man at the front must have been the one who was cross with her for cutting to the front of the substantial line. Currently, though, he was fussing over Havoc, who was on his back with that infernal toy in his mouth. It gave a few disgusting squelches as he chomped down on it. The man was giving Havoc belly scratches that had his back leg thumping the ground, making the man chuckle. His irritation had clearly been soothed.

"I didn't mean to ignore you earlier," Deandra said to the dark-blue-skinned man who looked completely human otherwise. His head of perfect brown curls filled her with envy. "My brain is barely functioning."

"No worries. I was probably grouchier than I should have been. I've been in line for over an hour," the beautiful-haired man said while staying squatting beside Havoc, dutifully scratching his stomach. "Please tell me this guy is up for adoption. If so, take my money right now."

She laughed. "Sorry, this one is mine."

The man frowned, then stood. "Bummer."

Havoc rolled to his feet and gave his beloved toy a few more squelching chews, his whole back end wiggling as he wagged his tail.

Juniper noisily cleared his throat to get Deandra's overtaxed attention back on him. "I'll have one of my assistants swap places with you, Dee, so she can help us manage the line. We've got an additional person arriving within the hour. The wristbands have been going off as they should, but we've gotten a bit behind on kicking folks out."

"I *knew* it," the beautiful-haired man muttered.

Kira ambled over and propped her fists on her hips, giving the man a hard stare. "You've been grumbling something awful for the past fifteen minutes. You know I could decide to kick your little behind to the back of the line just because I don't like your attitude, right?"

"I'm sorry, ma'am," the man said, properly chastised. "I came a long way just to visit this booth. Your stores have some of the rarest pets in the entire hub system, and all your charity work with mythical animal organizations and zoos is very commendable. I'm a big fan, truly."

Kira and Juniper shared a small smile.

"Thank you," Kira said. "That's very kind of you. We do our best. It's been a long road to get where we are, and we still face obstacles every day, but it's worth the blood, sweat, and tears." Turning to Deandra, she held out both hands. "You must be the infamous Deandra Hendricks."

Deandra took Kira's small hands in hers, even though one was currently holding a leash. Her shopping bag's handles slipped off her shoulder and landed on her forearm.

Havoc noisily sniffed one of Kira's tennis shoes poking out from the wide hem of her jeans. "It's nice to meet you. I heard you chased off Frankenswine's liberator with a broom."

Kira's olive-green cheeks flushed. "I don't know what came over me. Maybe I knew my daughter would never let me hear the end of it if we lost her beloved pig. Oh, those ASA people infuriate me to no end! Surely they have worse people than us to harass. I wish I'd had something stronger than a broom, I'll tell you that much. Frankenswine is just a piglet! How is liberating a piglet who's scared of his own shadow going to accomplish anything?"

"No trouble with them today?" Deandra asked.

"Nope! But honestly it's been so busy we've hardly had time to breathe, let alone check for anyone skulking about. I vowed not to let them ruin this weekend, though, no matter what crap they try to pull. We're going to persevere, whatever it takes. So far, so good!"

"Glad you've been having a good first day."

Kira beamed. "Me too. Best weekend of the year by a mile." She peered around Deandra for a moment. "My husband seems to be getting antsy behind you. He's got high hopes you can get those kittens homes. I don't doubt your skills, but you've got your work cut out for you. We appreciate the help." With a squeeze of Deandra's hands, she let her go. "Good luck."

Ugh.

Juniper laughed awkwardly. "Don't scare her, dear!" The goblin then grabbed Deandra by the elbow and all but yanked her, and by extension Havoc, all the way into the tent.

It wasn't until Deandra was past the two tables that the magic of the rune-etched poles kicked in, and the space before her expanded like a rolled-up rug being unfurled. The ceiling of the tent stretched an additional five feet. The four cages she'd seen from her vantage point outside turned into *rows* of cages, playpens, and shelving units stuffed with pet supplies. The tent was a miniature version of Mythic Pet Kitchen. How the heck had he and Kira managed all this since yesterday afternoon?

There were at least ten workers wearing Mythic Pet Kitchen shirts or aprons milling around the space, helping customers or tending to animals. Juniper had told her that mundane vehicles had been on their way to Axia for several days with their animal charges—maybe a wave of employees had arrived last night, too, and the pack of them had easily gotten the magicked tent set up.

Juniper only let her gape for a few more seconds before he ushered her forward. Beyond the freestanding shelves of food, treats, toys, harnesses, and leashes, and the giant playpen-slash-petting zoo, were large cages holding all manner of creatures. It wasn't until they were near the back of the tent that Deandra saw the cage full of vibrissa cats. This cage was twice the size of the one that had been in the store, had four platforms and ramps for the cats to play on, and had solid walls made of ultra-tough plastic.

Havoc yipped when he finally saw them, dropped his toy, and lunged forward until he hit the end of his leash. Deandra called him back to her, and though he dutifully turned on a dime to sit at her feet, he whimpered as if in pain. She unhooked his leash from his harness, but he knew better than to run off just yet, so he stared at her, quivering with barely contained anticipation. Laughing, she finally decided to put him out of his misery and said, "Release!"

He was off like a shot.

Reluctantly, she picked up his soggy, discarded toy that was now covered in bits of grass and dropped it into her shopping bag, though she'd have much rather dumped it in a trash can.

When Havoc reached the cage, he excitedly scream-chirped, then dropped into play stance. On the other side of the cage, four of the six kittens rushed up to him and either got into some version of play stance themselves or started hopping over their littermates in their eagerness to get a better look at the dragon. By the time Deandra and Juniper reached the cage, Havoc had started his sprint around the enclosure as the four social kittens matched his pace from inside.

The two less adventurous of the kittens were on higher tiers of the enclosure. One was watching the commotion below, but the most anxious of the litter was watching Deandra and Juniper's approach. The hubbub of the festival couldn't have been helping the kitten's already overloaded nerves. Deandra marveled, though, that despite looking like a mundane tent from the outside, this magicked one was so deep, Deandra could hardly hear the festival from here. She figured the Mythic Pet Kitchen staff might be having a hard time kicking people out not just because of the animals, but because it was so zen in here by comparison.

She *did* think she could hear the faint whine of a tattoo gun from the Greenwoods' tent behind this one, though. She wondered if tattoo guns were usually that loud or if there was something unique about tattoo guns that were filled with living ink. Maybe tattoo recipients had to wear earplugs.

Near the vibrissa cage was a playpen that appeared to be the same model as the one she'd seen in the grimalkyne tent. If so, it would mean the kittens could run around in an open-roof area without fear that they could phase away and get lost. A few chairs

—some fit for humans and some more suited to people who were goblin-sized—were in the playpen, as well as several toys. Deandra figured it was a meet-and-greet area for prospective adopters. The backdrop of the tent was a dark-blue fabric tarp that was decorated with puffy white clouds. This had been what she'd seen flapping around the day Frankenswine was released. She was unsure if the serene background was for the cats' benefit or potential adopters—probably both.

Deandra eyed the area around the cats, noting that there was a good twenty feet of empty space between the kittens and the rest of the animals. "They aren't, uh, dangerous or anything are they? Why are they so far removed from the rest?"

Juniper wrung his hands. "If I'm not mistaken, in the mundane world there's a stigma against black cats, no? People have superstitions about them, they're harder to adopt out, things of that nature?" When Deandra nodded, he said, "In fae society, that's sadly the case with green ones. It's a holdover from a world we can't even return to, so why should our superstitions persist? It's silly.

"To add insult to injury, the vibrissa are mischievous to a fault, can be even more aloof than the average cat, and while they're incredibly intelligent as adults, they're positively reckless as kittens. They're only suited for the right kind of owner, so it's best not to keep them up front. They're adorable, and adorable animals get snatched up based on aesthetics first and compatibility second. If we keep these *in the back*, so to speak, we can make sure we only send serious prospects their way."

Deandra deeply appreciated that Juniper, despite running a business whose success relied, at least in part, on getting his animal charges adopted, was making decisions based on their welfare rather than his wallet.

"What's the superstition about green cats?" Deandra asked, watching the kittens sprint around the inner edge of the cage while Havoc pranced along the outside.

"Oh, it was a combination of things, really, but it mostly

stemmed from folks being uninformed," he said. "The vibrissa originally hailed from a valley that was known for its lush landscape. Imagine the Amazon rainforest, and you're close to what their part of the fae realm is like. The vibrissa, despite their size, were one of the best hunters in that region. Legend has it that an exploration party came across the cats during one of their expeditions and managed to befriend a few of the tiny hunters.

"My guess is, they actually *captured* the cats and hauled them back as prizes in magic-dampening sacks, especially if they already knew of their phasing powers. Over time, they were domesticated and snapped up by wealthy people who wanted a designer cat. But, as I've told you, they're not fit for everyone. They filled shelters and zoos when folks realized they'd taken on an animal they couldn't handle. It's a story not unlike what certain breeds of dogs, especially, contend with in the earthen realm.

"In any case, stories about a misbehaving pooch who chews up your favorite shoes are one thing. Spooky stories told about a horned cat who can phase through walls and steal your children from their beds is quite another." Upon seeing Deandra's wide eyes, he laughed. "They're too small to snatch a child, even if that was something they'd do. And as I already told you, they can only phase to places in their direct line of sight. They can't phase through walls." He eyed her. "Want an example of what they *can* do? Let's say a vibrissa cat phases onto a high shelf, knocks a vase to the floor just to hear it smash, and then phases to the other side of the room and pretends they had nothing to do with the crash that woke their owner in the middle of the night.

"Then, while the owner is picking up the shards of a priceless family heirloom, the naughty vibrissa cat phases into the bedroom where the door was left open in the owner's haste to investigate the noise. The vibrissa cat curls up on the owner's bed. When the owner later tries to remove the cat, the cat merely phases out of their grasp and back onto the bed ... over and over and over, until the owner gives up and lets the cat stay. A little manipulation here, a little manipulation there, and the next thing you know, that cute little vibrissa cat is running the household like a furry green dictator."

Deandra blinked rapidly.

That decided it once and for all. Havoc was *not* taking home a vibrissa cat. Deandra didn't care how stinking cute they were.

"You're not doing the best job of convincing me these cats should be pets," she said.

Juniper laughed off the comment. "They just need owners who aren't pushovers, who have the patience of a saint, and who possess an iron will." He winced. "And who knows how to properly kitten-proof their houses and/or are willing to move all their valuables into storage for a year or two."

With that ringing endorsement, Deandra and Havoc got situated in the playpen and waited as Juniper skillfully got two of the kittens out of the cage without losing track of the other four. When the kittens were safely in the playpen with her and her dragon, Deandra noted that they were wearing collars that she assumed bore runes that kept them from phasing. She figured they were similar to the harness and leash that Powder had let her borrow, which were still stuffed into her purse.

"Is the collar made by the same people who make the cages?" she asked, watching as one kitten did her best to stalk a vicious, stationary flower poking out of the grass.

"We get the collars from the grimalkyne over at Feline Protected, yeah," Juniper said from outside the playpen. "There are other companies that make similar cages and gear, but theirs are the best in the industry. Pricey, but well worth it. They sell collars, harnesses, and leashes to us at wholesale prices—which are still exorbitant—that we can then turn around and sell here. It's been a good working relationship so far.

"On a personal level, it's been nice that they're just as passionate about fae species and helping to maintain their populations in this realm as we are. Not everyone in our industry cares about that as much these days, but the grimalkyne do. And they have incredibly talented sorcerers on hand as well, who take requests, giving us access to custom runework that the average business owner doesn't have, what with sorcerers usually being snatched up by the Collective or working in other high-level jobs."

"How did you meet them?" Deandra asked, smiling at Havoc who lay on his belly in a sploot position while the two kittens hopped on his back, bit the spade of his tail, and otherwise used him as a jungle gym. Havoc's eyes were wide with delight.

"Good ol' internet search. I told them what I needed, and one of the grimalkyne and one of their sorcerers actually came out personally to Axia to meet us! It was such a kind gesture. I almost hired them right on the spot, even though Teddy still makes me a little uneasy all these years later. Even so, Kira and I hit it off with them right away. I swear, within minutes of them leaving, Kira was already sending them a list of all the things we wanted to order."

"I'm glad it worked out," she said, watching as one of the kittens scaled the wall of the playpen like it was a ladder, only to be halted when it reached the top. A bright blue dome of magic flared to life over the top of the pen, and the runes on the kitten's collar flared the same color.

Deandra glanced up, marveling at the sensation of feeling like she was sitting inside a snow globe for a moment.

The vibrissa cat hissed, more so, it seemed, from being scared by the bright light than because it was zapped. She landed on her feet, then stumble-walked toward her sibling and Havoc.

"Juniper?" someone called.

Juniper and Deandra both glanced across the expanse of space between the vibrissa section of the tent and the rest to find a young goblin lady standing with the beautiful-haired man beside her.

"Warby here is interested in the vibrissa," the young lady said. "He had one as a kid."

"Ooh," Juniper said, waving enthusiastically. "Right this way, Warby."

Deandra, who had been sitting cross-legged on the grass, heard a slight rustle and glanced to her side to find the tail of one of the vibrissa kittens sticking out of her shopping bag, which she'd left beside her purse. She grabbed the cat and pulled it out, finding that it had the corner of the bag of cactus-flavored dog treats in its mouth. Before Deandra could do anything, the cat phased out of her hands and reappeared a breath later on the opposite side of the playpen with the bag still in its mouth. The collars didn't prevent phasing within the playpen, then.

"Kitty, can I have those back?" Deandra asked cautiously, then slowly got out of her cross-legged position to attempt to crawl as unmenacingly as possible toward the cat.

The cat kept its vibrant yellow eyes trained on her as it started to chew a hole in the treat bag. There was something very unnerving about someone—animal *or* human—defiantly doing the very thing you asked them not to do, all while maintaining eye contact.

"Aw, c'mon," Deandra said. "I'm sure Juniper has cat treats for you instead!" The hole in the bag widened. "Those things were twenty-five dollars!"

When Deandra was an arm's length from the cat, it phased out of sight with the treat bag again. Deandra whirled toward Havoc. The kitten had materialized on his other side.

"You're not going to help me?" she asked him. "Those are *your* treats."

Her dragon merely rolled his eyes up at her without otherwise moving, seeing as he had a vibrissa kitten curled up on top of his head while it groomed itself. Apparently even dragons were rendered immobile when a cat decided to use them as a place to sit.

Deandra played keep-away with the kitten for several more minutes—one of them enjoying the game far more than the other. Hint: It was not Deandra.

Juniper's warning from days earlier came back to her now. *"The worst version of keep-away one can play is with a mischievous vibrissa kitten, let me tell you."*

He wasn't lying.

In the end, she was left drained, the treat bag was left empty, and Warby, endlessly amused, had left with a new vibrissa kitten.

Success?

The one good thing about working in the Mythic Pet Kitchen booth was that after three hours, Deandra had been fully cured of any lingering desire to adopt a vibrissa kitten. They were *exhausting*.

Actually, there were *two* good things. The other was that the little menaces were completely wearing Havoc out, so currently there was only a slim chance he'd wake her up at four a.m. like usual with airborne zoomies.

Four of the vibrissa kittens had found homes. One had gone to Warby earlier. A couple, thankfully, had fallen in love with Havoc's kitten. Seeing the kitten and Havoc play had convinced them to seal the deal, as their Great Dane at home had a similar personality to Havoc. And a pair of bonded siblings had gone to a gigantic draken woman who had apparently traveled all the way from the Maine hub specifically for this breed of cat. She was excited to make the long trek back to Maine in a decked-out camper van she'd outfitted specifically for this occasion.

She'd used vehicle telepads to get the van to Axia in a matter of hours and would take the scenic—and mandatory—route back via mundane channels. The kittens seemed just as happy about this arrangement. Juniper was happy, too, as he'd talked the woman into a veritable boatload of "vitally necessary" kitten supplies, and he even gave her a coupon she could use to get a discount on a magicked cage from Feline Protected.

The remaining two kittens would be the most challenging to find homes for, as they were the shyest of the litter.

When Deandra's scheduled time was up, she was more than ready to go home and take a nap, but alas, she had to head back to the Greenwoods' house for her second visit with Peril. She'd tried not to think too hard about the fact that the salica knew Havoc's secret. The kittens had provided an excellent distraction, but now that her next visit with the ferret loomed, her buried apprehensions were beginning to resurface.

Standing outside the cage where the remaining pair of kittens dozed together in one of the beds, Juniper thanked Deandra profusely for her help. Apparently he was rarely able to adopt out even one vibrissa during the festival, when he was lucky enough to have them—this was the first time in three years—and he was thrilled that they might all find homes by the end of the weekend. If they *weren't* adopted, they'd have a stint at one of his sister-stores for a few months before being shuttled to the next one.

She was getting ready to head out the way she'd come with her tired dragon when a sudden upwell of voices sounded from behind them. Deandra and Juniper whirled toward the back of the tent. Even Havoc and the once-dozing kittens were on high alert now.

Deandra thought she heard … chanting? That was a little ominous. It didn't sound like the persistent noise of festivalgoers, that much was clear.

There was another spike in volume as several people shouted. She stilled when there was a sudden and dramatic drop in noise, as if someone had hit mute on a previously blaring television set.

And then the boos started.

"What the heck is going on?" Deandra muttered to herself.

"What do you say we sneak out the back here and ask the Greenwoods," Juniper said. "I'll warn you, though, that the Axian Town Council told us walking behind the tents is a safety hazard, and if we're caught using the back area as a walkway, we're in violation of rule such-and-such."

"I don't care about rule such-and-such," Deandra said.

That was apparently all the encouragement Juniper needed, and he scurried forward and lifted the blue fabric dotted with white clouds. Sound flooded in with such force, Deandra winced. She wasn't sure if Juniper's tent had been outfitted with noise-dampening runes or if the physics-defying magic really had moved her farther from the general hustle and bustle of the noisy festival. Between thinking about the magic involved and the sudden crash of sound, a headache was forming.

"The Axian Town Council is complicit!" someone shouted.

"Your rights are being violated!"

"Boooooo!"

"Don't let them treat you like mundane animals!"

"You hold the keys to your own prison!"

"Boooooo!"

"Let the lions roam free!"

That last one sent Deandra out of the tent and into the narrow walkway behind it. She was surprised to find a few other vendors had spilled out the back of their tents, too. People shot each other curious looks. Some scurried toward the tent behind theirs, while others hurried left or right, using the back walkway as a shortcut to get closer to the commotion. She hurried toward the white backdrop Rularo had pinned to their tent yesterday, then tentatively lifted the corner of the fabric on the stationery side of the tent, not wanting to possibly scare Rularo or a customer who was in the middle of getting jabbed by a tattoo gun.

"Quinn?" she whisper-shouted.

The spot Deandra picked put her face between two cardboard-box towers. If she turned sideways, she could squeeze through. Glancing down at Havoc, she said, "I'm going to unclip your harness, but you have to stay close to me, okay? I don't know if you getting spotted by ASA or Parks Management would be worse right now."

As usual, Havoc growled at the words "Parks Management," and curling plumes of white smoke wafted out of his nostrils. She unhooked his leash, wadded it up, and stuck it in her back pocket. Then she slipped into the Greenwoods' tent.

Quinn was on the other side of the table that marked the front of the tent, her arms crossed as she watched the commotion. She hadn't noticed that she had company.

Deandra held up the fabric backdrop so Havoc and then Juniper could make their way into the tent. By the time the three of them were inside, Rularo had spotted them.

He and a man stood at the table where the appointment book and flash-tattoo binders were laid out. The man was a handsome silver-fox kind of guy—probably in his fifties or so. He wore dark jeans and a white T-shirt. His arms were covered in full sleeves of tattoos, and given how some of them had shifting colors or moved periodically, he was either a regular of Rularo's and InkCraft's living inks, or he'd been to other tattoo artists with similar skill sets.

Deandra often tried to pick out details about people in Axia that might reveal what species they were. The guy was tan, six feet tall, and had salt-and-pepper hair. Nothing screamed fae.

Shrugging, she returned her attention to Rularo, having decided the customer was human, just like her.

"Do you know what's going on?" Deandra asked.

"ASA demonstration," Rularo said tightly.

The rage pouring off the usually chipper Rularo was making Deandra twitchy, so she turned away from them, letting the men get back to the tattoo appointment, though she wasn't sure how Rularo would be able to focus with all the noise.

A series of shrieking animal calls emanated from the assembled ASA members, though there were no animals present, from what Deandra could see from her vantage point. The noises also sounded canned somehow, as if they were a nature recording from a jungle or safari.

"We're behind you, Quinn," Deandra called out, hoping to be heard over the shouting beyond the tent. She deposited her shopping bag and purse on the table draped with the purple tablecloth.

Quinn whirled around, but her hardened expression softened when she saw who had spoken. "This is the kind of nonsense they did outside the adoption clinic when we picked up Peril."

Deandra, Juniper, and Havoc joined Quinn in front of the tent, standing in a horizontal line with Havoc seated between Deandra and Quinn.

There were at least a dozen ASA members, most of whom seemed to be fauns, though there were a few humans and elves mixed in. Most of the ASA members were in the throes of a strange interpretative dance. They were clustered so close together, flailing and thrashing, it was if they were one entity—a living knot of limbs and horns and faces. It was honestly impressive that they could "dance" so close together without elbowing and kneeing each other, which spoke to this presentation being highly choreographed, despite its chaotic nature. The "music" Deandra had heard earlier was blasting out of a portable stereo held above an elfin woman's head. It was more a series of discordant animal calls and screeches than anything with a rhythm.

"Why were people booing earlier?" Deandra whispered to Quinn.

"It was *ASA* who was booing. They were yelling at each other and booing to draw in a crowd," Quinn said. "It always works."

Deandra was mildly annoyed with herself for falling for it.

A lone faun wandered around the outer edge of the circle made by curious festivalgoers, many with their phones out as they recorded the flailing ASA members. He was the same faun who had handed the flyer to Powder yesterday, warning the grimalkyne that ASA was out in force and that they wouldn't be sparing the cats' booth this weekend. His bone-white horns seemed to gleam in the full sun, especially when paired with his shiny black fur.

Once he'd made a couple of loops, he shouted, "Tell me, my friends. Do you value freedom? Autonomy?"

No one in the crowd replied.

"Of course you do!" The faun had taken on a theatrical air that he hadn't shown when he'd been passing out flyers the day before. "Do you believe in a being's right to choose how they live their life? Do you believe every sapient being should have their own agency?" He paused for a long time, walking in a slow circle around his ASA members, who still flailed and thrashed. "Only a monster would say no. Only a *monster* would say living in a cage is a quality way of life."

Right on cue, as soon as the faun said, "living in a cage," the knot of roiling ASA bodies drifted away from each other as if a low impact grenade had exploded, revealing that they'd been shielding a caged creature all this time. Inside the cage was what initially looked so much like a human child that the crowd shouted in alarm. Deandra realized belatedly, just as Juniper had, that it was a baby-faced gnome sans his hat. He might be the same one who'd tried to liberate Frankenswine yesterday.

Rularo's massive bulk appeared in Deandra's periphery a moment later. The tattoo customer took up a spot between the big man and Juniper.

"Don't worry, friends," the faun said, furry arms held out. "Harold here is fine. The cage is big enough for him to crouch in comfortably. There's a water bottle attached to the side for him to ensure he doesn't get dehydrated. We'll put a bowl of food in there for him later." The faun, smiling smugly, continued his way around the circle, seemingly pleased that the overall mood of his audience had shifted. Clearly, no one was sure how they were supposed to feel. "Harold here is a little hyperactive, so we stick him in a cage to calm him down. If he talks too much, we'll lure him in there with treats. If he *still* talks too much, then we'll throw a blanket over him. He falls asleep eventually. There's nothing wrong with that, right? Just a bit of behavior control when *his* behavior doesn't suit *my* preferences."

Deandra's gaze bounced around the faces of the assembled crowd. People were shooting uneasy glances at their neighbors. She knew the faun was making the point that if it was cruel to put a sapient being who was recognizably not "just an animal" in a cage, then it was cruel to put *any* sapient being in a cage.

She thought back to what Neela had told her about vibrissa cats. "*There was an eighty percent mortality rate for vibrissa cats in the fae realm, most of them perishing before they reached six months old.*" Fae and magic-touched species that had ended up in the earthen realm because of the Glitch were all almost immediately put on endangered lists. Vibrissa might have been wiped out entirely without intervention.

One could argue that letting species like the vibrissa die out in this realm would be allowing nature to take its course and that no one should step in. But was that fair to the vibrissa when this wasn't their home realm, and they were here through no fault of their own?

Why did ASA get to decide what was acceptable and what wasn't, especially when not every situation was identical? Animals like Peril *should* have autonomy. But that autonomy also meant they could choose a way of life that suited *them*, not what ASA approved of.

"While you wander this festival enjoying your cactus-flavored treats, I want you to pay attention to those around you," the faun said. "Learn who your vendors are before you decide to part with your hard-earned money. Make sure you know whose interests and exploits you're funding."

Deandra sucked in a breath when the faun suddenly marched their way. Quinn's hand clamped around Deandra's forearm. Havoc was on his feet, a low growl vibrating in his throat and smoke pouring from his nostrils.

Rularo took a step forward. "That's close enough, goat," he said, his voice dangerously low.

The faun stopped several feet away, hands up in placation. His palms were light brown, and the backs of his hands and fingers were covered in dark fur. His nails were wide, thick, and filed into points. The faun stared at Rularo for a long beat, then a slow, knowing smile crossed his furry face.

Deandra didn't like that smile at all.

"Oh crap," Quinn said. "I think that's the same faun who Rularo scared the day we adopted Peril. The one who fell and hurt himself."

"*Hurt* myself?" the faun hissed, voice low, clearly having heard Quinn. "Your brute of a husband broke my ankle. I needed surgery. I was in a cast for months."

"Oh no," Rularo mocked. "Your hoof was in a *cage*? You allowed medical treatment where you were housed in a hospital? How awful that you needed confinement for your own safety."

The faun's nostrils flared, and spittle foamed at the corners of his mouth. Deandra resisted the urge to ask if he was rabid.

"You *know* that's not the same thing," the faun snapped.

"Do I?" Rularo asked. "Because it sounds like you pick and choose which rules to follow. If you want all sapient animals to be free, then go be free. Go live in the wilds and leave the rest of us alone."

"If I left, if ASA left, there'd be no one remaining to fight for those who can't do it themselves." The faun's creepy goat eyes focused on Deandra for the first time. "I don't have any idea who *you* are, but to turn a dire wolf, the most fearsome of fae canines, into a house pet is insulting."

Deandra merely glowered at him, wondering how fast he'd blow a gasket if he knew Havoc was actually a dragon. Havoc growled at the faun.

The goat man swallowed nervously as he eyed Havoc. He gave his furry head a shake and took several steps back. Rolling his shoulders, he turned toward his captive audience, arms out. His theatrical persona was back in place in an instant, and his voice rose in volume so that all assembled could hear. "We didn't stop in front of this particular booth by accident, my friends. It just so happens that we have *multiple* offenders all in one place. Someone is shining down on ASA today.

"First, we have the Greenwoods," he said, gesturing first to Quinn and then Rularo. "Did anyone who bought their wares or received one of their dangerous tattoos know they *own* a salica? Own. What a barbaric word! They *own* a rare breed of magic-touched ferret, who's locked up in their home day and night, unable to live to his full potential.

"Did you know that, in the fae realm, salica held positions of great power in high houses? They were intelligence gatherers, scouts, and even advisors to royalty. But what have the Greenwoods done with him? *Nothing.* He was funneled through system after system that didn't care about his potential, that didn't consult with him despite his sapience, that only cared about the hefty fee the Greenwoods were willing to pay to get a designer pet."

Quinn lunged forward.

Deandra clamped a hand on the other woman's arm to hold her back. "Don't," she whispered in Quinn's ear. "He *wants* you to react."

Deandra cast a look at Rularo, knowing he was more of a wild card than his wife. The man's face had gone a deep shade of red, and his massive fists were balled by his sides.

"Babe," Quinn said, her tone gentle but firm.

Rularo, jaw tight, glanced at his wife, then his customer. "Let's get back to your tattoo, yeah? No itching or burning at the test site, right?"

The man lifted his shirt to reveal his side, presumably to prove that his tanned skin *hadn't* broken out in a rash. "All good," he said. "Told you I'd had plenty of nacre tats before."

"Can never be too sure," Rularo said, then stalked back into the tent, his customer trailing after him.

"Aw, looks like the big man doesn't want to fess up," the faun said as Rularo retreated. Deandra held her breath, half expecting the man to come hurtling back out of the tent to dropkick the faun into next week. When that didn't happen, the faun spun on his hoof and gestured theatrically at Juniper. "I'm glad you joined us, goblin. I had a feeling you would, given your proximity to the Greenwoods' tent and your insatiable curiosity. My hunch was right."

Turning to his crowd, the faun said, "Second, we have the owner of the Mythic Pet Kitchen. Don't let the goblin's small stature and nervous act fool you. Did you know that his ancestors were among some of the fae who traveled between here and the fae realm in the years *before* the Glitch? Oh, yes. Juniper Thistlewick comes from a *long* line of unscrupulous goblins who made their fortune by plucking unsuspecting animals—many of them sapient—from the fae realm and smuggling them here for rich folks to domesticate, hunt, and even *eat*."

Deandra stiffened but refused to glance down at Juniper. Even if everything this nasty faun said about Juniper's family was true, it wasn't true of Juniper himself. She knew that down to her very marrow. And it wasn't just because the pathway to the fae realm had been closed for a century, meaning Juniper couldn't have been a sapient-animal smuggler, even if he'd wanted to. It was because she knew a fellow animal lover when she met one.

An odd humming sound was issuing from the goblin.

Deandra wasn't sure if he was horrified, furious, or scared. Maybe all three.

The faun continued his tirade. "Anyone familiar with the horrible mundane practice of puppy mills should think twice about purchasing an animal from the Mythic Pet Kitchen. Not only does he associate with seedy breeders, but he also continuously purchases torture devices from Feline Protected. He even offers discount coupons to his customers!"

On cue, the gnome still in the cage howled in pain. All attention swiveled to him.

He was either an excellent actor, or he really *was* injured. Holding up his hand that was marred with three nasty-looking burns across his palm, he turned in a crouched circle so the onlookers could see his wounds. The lines were puffy and red.

"Tell us, Harold," the faun called out. "How did you get those injuries?"

"I'll show you." Blowing out a calming breath, Harold touched his unblemished hand flat to the inside of his cage. Every mesh square of the cage lit up red, as if the metal had gone molten, and Harold yelped in agony before yanking his hand back. Tears slid down the gnome's face, though he clearly was trying to remain strong. It wasn't until that moment that Deandra realized that the hems of the gnome's shirt and pants were charred. Did he get zapped that badly every time he got anywhere near the walls of the cage?

"How is this humane?" the faun asked his horrified audience.

"You had that cage's runes manipulated, and you know it!"

Every head whipped in the direction of the voice. To the right, the circle of people surrounding the ASA demonstration began to part. The approaching newcomers stood a full head over the average festivalgoer, so it was clear with a single glance that the three grimalkyne had arrived. Powder, Neela, and Velma walked through the tunnel of people single file, and once they'd entered the makeshift circle formed around ASA, they fanned out into a horizontal united line. Velma looked even more ticked off than

Rularo. Definite orange cat energy. Teddy the sorcerer was not among them.

Neela took a step forward. "Our cages would *never* exert that level of magical charge—especially not one of that size. And our runes burn blue. *Yours* are red. You bought one of our cages, overrode the magic, and twisted it into something dangerous. Did you find an untrained sorcerer on the arcane web?" She thrust a fluffy digit in Harold's direction. "You're torturing a colleague—*in public*—to prove a point that you *made up*!"

The faun took an involuntary step back but otherwise held his ground against the three very angry felines who were a good foot taller than him. "*You've* just proven our point. Your cages aren't safe if it's this easy for us to buy one, have the runes altered for less money than it took to buy the horrible contraption in the first place, and then turn it into a torture device. Harold volunteered for this because it's a cause he believes in. What happens when someone who buys one of your cages has nefarious plans, hmm? What then? Shall I tell all these fine people about the pixie *killed* by one of your cages?"

Someone in the crowd gasped.

Oh, this was *not* going well.

Rularo appeared in Deandra's periphery again. Keeping his voice to a whisper, he said, "Just letting you all know the werecats are on their way. They've apparently been putting out little fires—figurative, not literal—that ASA set just before this so-called demonstration, so they've been spread thin. They've already gotten dozens of calls about this, though. They'll be here soon."

That was a relief.

Deandra wondered what ASA thought about werecats working as enforcers of laws set by both mundanes and the Collective—yet more cages, even if they weren't tangible.

"That's some of the shoddiest runework I've seen in *quite* some time!" came a shout, and the crowd parted once again to let Theodore into the open area around the faun and the caged gnome. The gnome didn't look like he was faring too well in there.

Theodore took up a spot beside Powder. The all-white cat leaned down and cupped a paw around the sorcerer's ear, whispering something. Theodore looked at the faun, and then his gaze slid toward the Greenwoods' tent. When Deandra offered him a small smile of recognition, the sorcerer's expression remained blank.

"I almost hired them right on the spot, even though Teddy still makes me a little uneasy all these years later," Juniper had said, and she was inclined to agree.

Theodore, still being whispered to by Powder, finally nodded. Seemingly satisfied, Powder stood to full height, arms behind his back. Theodore continued to stare in the direction of the Greenwoods' tent.

Deandra had been so unnerved by Theodore that she'd lost track of what the cats and the faun were yelling about.

A crash startled her, but this time the commotion came from behind her. As one, Deandra, Havoc, Juniper, Quinn, and Rularo turned around. The man who'd been getting a tattoo was stumbling around the tent, one hand to his side, and another to his throat.

"Whoa, whoa," Rularo said, hurrying to his side, but the man shoved him away, gasping. The man crashed into the table where the appointment book and binders lay, sending them to the grass. The table rocked onto two legs, then settled back, thudding onto the ground.

The man frantically tore off his shirt and threw it as if the fabric scalded him. Deandra and Juniper both gasped at the sight of the man's side. The outline of a horned beetle had been inked there, partially shaded with blue, purple, and green living ink to give the carapace an iridescent sheen. The beetle's shell was only half colored in; perhaps Rularo had taken a break to make a quick call to the werecats as things grew more heated outside.

The area around the beetle was so inflamed, it made Deandra's side itch in sympathy. Dark-red veins spiderwebbed away from the tattoo, like crimson forks of lightning.

"Goddess above!" Quinn said and practically vaulted over the table behind her. "That's shatterberry poisoning, Ru!"

"I know!" he said as Quinn jumped over the fallen binders, slid across the table, and landed in the tattoo half of the shop in a matter of moments. Deandra idly wondered if Quinn's fae ancestry had blessed her with the agility of a gazelle or if instincts had simply taken over.

The man screamed.

Deandra had no idea what to do. Havoc pressed against the side of her leg, apparently feeling ill-equipped, too. She placed a hand on Juniper's shoulder, and she felt him relax a little, though the goblin still wrung his hands.

"There are adrenaline shots in my bag under the cabinet!" Rularo said as he helped the thrashing, screaming man to the ground. His skin was coated in sweat.

Deandra felt the crowd surging forward, curious about the fallen man's plight more than whatever argument had broken out between the faun and the grimalkyne. Her neck prickled. Hushed questions swelled like a rising tide behind her.

She heard the distant thunder of cat paws racing along the ground.

The man's back suddenly and violently arched. The crowd seemed to suck in a collective breath. Angry red lines were crawling toward the man's chest under his skin. He screamed silently, the veins in his neck bulging, before he went limp in Rularo's arms.

Quinn slid to the man's side on her knees and plunged the needle of a syringe into his upper arm a breath later.

Deandra chewed on her bottom lip, willing the man to stir.

CHAPTER ELEVEN

The next several minutes passed in sheer pandemonium. Officer Sutter was the first werecat on scene, taking command of the situation with lightning-quick efficiency that was at least partly fueled by everyone being dang scared of the lady when she had her menacing werecat aura cranked up to eleven. Anyone with any sense got the heck out of her way. Other cats took on the task of crowd management so that only a select few remained in or around the Greenwoods' tent.

Which was how she, Havoc, and Juniper ended up standing well away from the action less than a minute after the cats showed up. Officer Sutter had told the rubberneckers, "I need everyone but Quinn and Rularo out of here. Now!" In a quieter tone only meant for Deandra, she'd added, "Haven't seen you in a while, Dee. Should have guessed you'd find your way into the middle of another weird incident." Her sardonic half smile suggested she was teasing. "Get on out of here. But don't go too far—we're questioning you next."

Deandra watched, her thumb's cuticle wedged between her teeth, as the cats interviewed Quinn on one side of the tent and Rularo on the other. Several other cats and a few human cops got Rularo's customer into some kind of stretcher-slash-hammock contraption, hooked that onto harness-like vests worn by two werecats in their feline form, and then the cats took off with the man, presumably racing him to the hospital.

The wounded gnome had been extricated from his cage by then, too. When he was freed, he all but collapsed on the grass. He, too, was loaded into one of the stretcher-like hammock contraptions and carted away.

Deandra had no idea if feline-powered ambulances were the norm or if it was a matter of necessity today, since the surrounding roads were packed with cars and/or people. The cats didn't imitate wailing sirens as they tore off with their wounded charges, but the occasional roar probably worked just as well to make people clear a path.

She hoped the man was going to survive. She didn't even know his name.

All she knew was that he'd been suffering from "shatterberry poisoning." The first and only time she'd heard of shatterberries was yesterday. She tried to recall what she'd seen on the disclaimer page of the color tattoo binder she'd perused. She couldn't be sure, but she thought it had said shatterberry ink was not to be administered to mundanes or shifters, that shatterberry was to shifters what wolfsbane was to werewolves—only much worse.

Was shatterberry a plant? A fruit? A pigment created from several other ingredients? Maybe it was an alchemical controlled substance, like Quowlaxliquin.

Was the guy a shifter and didn't disclose it? Did he have dormant shifter genes hiding in his family tree? Though she remembered the disclaimer saying that if anyone was unsure of their ancestry, shatterberry was off the table as a potential ink option, as it was too dangerous to risk.

An even worse possibility flitted through Deandra's mind.

Had Rularo been so distracted by ASA and the faun's harassment that he'd grabbed the wrong ink and accidentally poisoned the man?

Realizing then that she hadn't seen the white-horned faun since Rularo's customer collapsed, Deandra quickly scanned the vicinity, not finding him. He clearly hadn't stuck around to ensure his colleague was okay, leaving the wounded gnome in his magicked cage to fend for himself.

Another scan of the crowd revealed that none of the other ASA members were immediately visible, either. The fauns were hard to miss, but she supposed the humans and elves could more easily blend in with the growing mass of looky-loos, many of whom had missed the initial chaos and were creeping in now to check out what all the fuss was about. Had any ASA members been snatched up by werecats, or had they all scattered to the wind?

Two women entered the Greenwoods' tent. While they were in plain clothes, they moved with authority and a professional assuredness that was just as effective as an official uniform. Their demeanor wasn't quite the same as a werecat's, but there was no doubt that they felt comfortable at what was essentially a crime scene. They each carried a rectangular box, like a squat, bulky briefcase. Deandra figured they might be witches who were on some law enforcement team or other. The only specific kind of witch Deandra knew about who worked with the police were death witches. She genuinely hoped there would be no need for *that* type of witch and that the man would pull through.

"Oh, this is most distressing," Juniper said, wringing his hands. He'd said that *a lot* over the last few minutes. "I also … uhh … wanted to address the rather nasty things that—"

Deandra waved a hand covered in chewed-down cuticles to quiet him. "I don't care about rumors—"

"That's just it! They *aren't* rumors," Juniper squeaked out. "The Thistlewick family shame was aired publicly. People were recording it! It's probably on Forage already. My wife and I have been fighting off rumors like this for ages, knowing how much they could damage our business if animal activists caught wind of any of it.

"Many terrible things have been done to mundane, magic-touched, and fae animals under the Thistlewick name—both before *and* after the Glitch. I've done what I could to distance myself from it, especially since my life's calling is so closely tied to the shameful things my family has done. But no matter what I do, it seems to follow me like a poisonous fog."

That admission gave Deandra pause.

Given everything the faun knew about Juniper and his pet store franchise, and the fact that someone had tried to liberate some of Juniper's animals yesterday, Deandra suddenly had her doubts about this being the goblin's first altercation with ASA. "Yesterday, you made it sound like you'd never heard their motto before. *Let the lions roam free.*"

Juniper's eye twitched, and his jaw tightened. "Like I said, I've been trying to distance myself from that nasty business for a long time. I didn't want to outright say I suspected ASA let Frankenswine out of his cage and then get roped into discussing the whole sordid mess. I have a bad habit of blabbing the truth at the perfectly wrong time when under pressure."

"Same," Deandra said with a sigh.

His smile was brief. "I knew about the Greenwoods' salica, as they're frequent visitors to my shop. I figured it was just as likely that *they* were familiar with ASA, so I set them up for an easy laydown."

Deandra cocked her head. "A what?"

"Oh, you know," he said, and then proceeded to mime something Deandra eventually guessed might be tangentially basket-ball related.

"Oh! A lay*up*, not a lay*down*."

Juniper wrinkled his nose and flapped a hand. "Whatever. Sports. *Blech*." He stuck out his tongue as if he'd just eaten a zombie cactus fruit puff.

She chuckled. "So this *wasn't* your first run-in with them?"

"Sadly, no. They've staged protests outside my sister-shops for years. They've attempted to stop our vans as they escort our animals between sites. After the third time one of our vans was targeted, we started using unmarked vehicles. Targeting our transports is bad enough, especially if they ever succeeded in letting our animals out, but it could be catastrophic if they did so in the mundane world."

Deandra frowned. "Have they ever attacked your stores?"

"Once," he said, a distant look in his eye. "It was several years ago. They let out an *entire litter* of vibrissa kittens. We only have vibrissa available for adoption every three years or so. Despite what Jet might have said about Mythic Pet Kitchen obtaining animals through dodgy breeders, it's not true. No reputable vibrissa breeder would have kittens more than once every three or four years. Female vibrissa cats go fallow for upward of two years after they have a litter. There have been some upsetting practices —several by my own family—where magical means have been employed to shorten the fallow period, but it rarely ends well for the mother or her litter."

Deandra supposed that explained why the draken woman had traveled across the entire country just for the kittens—the breed wasn't an easy one to come by, especially if they were coming from reputable breeders.

"Anyway," Juniper said, his tone sad, "the incident happened during the early days of our flagship store in the Floridian hub. We'd only been open for a few weeks and had gone out of our way to get those vibrissa kittens. Then ASA showed up en masse. While my wife and I were distracted by the positively rowdy demonstration outside, someone snuck into the store and opened the vibrissa cage.

"We were only ever able to find one of the five kittens, and that was because the poor thing got clipped by a car, and we found it wounded on the side of the road. It thankfully made a mostly full recovery and was adopted by a lovely couple. Not knowing the fate of the others still haunts me to this day, though.

"We invested heavily in security that day and continue to do so for all our stores. We have dashcams in our vans as well, and I do believe that's what's prevented them from ever being full-on hijacked. ASA still wages protests outside our stores on occasion, and harasses our transport drivers, but we've thankfully managed to stave off any large-scale vandalism."

They fell quiet.

The grimalkyne had said that their newest store had been targeted, too, with ASA getting in before security was in place to record the perpetrators in the act. It spoke to the organization having a team of scouts and spies who gathered intel on their targets so that they knew the best times to strike.

Had that happened today, too?

What if ASA had been demonstrating in front of the Greenwoods' tent as a distraction, allowing someone from within the organization to sneak in through the back to poison the man's ink? If that were true, was it the tattoo customer who had been the target, or had it been Rularo, because ASA wanted to undermine his business for the supposedly egregious act of owning a salica?

Havoc, who had grown bored—and was possibly unwinding from the adrenaline high of not only this last incident but playing with the vibrissa cats for three hours—sank to his belly with a world-weary groan and wedged his muzzle between his front paws. He was out like a light and snoring softly a few seconds later.

Deandra pulled out her phone, noting the time. It was after seven p.m. There was still daylight, but it was growing darker and colder. String lights on tents and in some of the surrounding trees were beginning to wink on. She still needed to check on Peril, but she was unsure now if the Greenwoods would have to pack up early and go home, or if they were going to be stuck here for even longer than planned. Would Rularo be taken into custody until the Axian police force could prove one way or another whether he'd poisoned his customer on purpose? Perhaps if the man succumbed to his shatterberry poisoning, Rularo's intent wouldn't matter.

She had a flood of texts to read. She hadn't checked them since she'd left the Greenwoods' earlier. And all the recent excitement meant she hadn't heard her phone go off. The messages were all from Wendy and Cruz, both of them following the same general progression.

Wendy
The shop is bananas today! How did your visit with Peril go? I'm actually looking forward to running the booth later, just so I can get a break from this place. What time are you helping Juniper again? Maybe I can swing by before my shift starts at the booth

Wendy
Hey! How's it going? Please tell me you haven't adopted any alien cats

Wendy
Something hinky is going on in the vendor area. I keep hearing chanting or booing or something

Wendy
Are you near all that racket?

Wendy
ARE YOU OKAY?

She pulled up Cruz's thread next.

Cruz
Hey. The clinic has been a madhouse all day. Usual Friday chaos. How are things going for you? Did you get Peril out of hiding? Knowing you, you not only got him to come out, but you two probably finished that puzzle

Cruz
So. Tell me the truth...how many of the vibrissa cats have you adopted?

Cruz
I heard there was some kind of emergency at one of the vendor booths? You got any hot goss?

Cruz
Oh no. Are you the *cause* of the hot goss? Again?

Cruz
The lack of reply has me a little worried...

Deandra, for the sake of her thumbs, started a group text with herself, Wendy, and Cruz.

Deandra
Hi! Long story short, an animal rights activist group crashed the festival. In the middle of that, one of Rularo's tattoo customers was poisoned by shatterberry ink and was hauled away by a catbulance. I'm waiting outside the Greenwoods' tent (who are being interrogated by werecats) with Havoc and Juniper because Officer Sutter has to interrogate us next, since we were with the Greenwoods when the guy collapsed. I still need to visit Peril again!

Cruz
Was the group ASA, by any chance?

Deandra
Yep.

Cruz
Even we've had to deal with them at the clinic to some extent. They usually focus on the bigger hubs more than us, thankfully

Deandra
The lead guy (at least he seems like the lead guy) is a faun named Jet. He was probably two seconds from getting beaten to a furry pulp by the grimalkyne before the tattoo client collapsed. Jet took off, though. Didn't even stick around to make sure his gnome buddy got out of the magic cage

Cruz
We gotta work on your context skills

Wendy
Girl. How in the heck does the exciting stuff always happen to you?

Cruz
Exciting? Did you see the part about someone collapsing from a poisoned tattoo?

Wendy
Yeah! That's the exciting part! Is the customer okay?

Deandra
Don't know. I'm sure Officer Sutter won't tell me, either. It was really scary. He kept screaming, but by the end, he wasn't making a noise...

Wendy
That's awful. We don't sell shatterberry anything in the shop, but we have a few First-Aid Kits for Magical Mishaps (that's the brand name…isn't that cute?) that have shatterberry antidotes in them

Cruz
That stuff is no joke. We've had a few animal clients over the years who have come in needing to get their stomachs pumped because they ingested shatterberry that was in their witch-owner's stash

Cruz
Are you all right, Dee? You need anything?

Deandra
I'm okay. I think. I'm worried about the Greenwoods. Rularo is white as a sheet. Quinn is sobbing. I don't know if they need extra care for Peril

Wendy
I'm stuck in this booth for another hour at least, but if you're still there when I'm done, I can come keep you company

Cruz
I'm still at the office but should be out of here soon. I can be down there in half an hour, but it can be sooner if you need it. Send me an SOS and I'll be out the door

Deandra

Deandra
Oh gosh. Officer Sutter is heading this way. Update pending!

She pocketed her phone before either of them could reply.

Officer Sutter strode up to her and Juniper. Havoc snorted awake and blearily pushed himself into a seated position. He yawned widely, then gave his head a hard shake.

"Mr. Thistlewick, an officer will be joining me in a moment. I'll have you talk to him while I have a chat with Miss Hendricks, all right?"

Juniper wrung his hands some more. "Yes, ma'am. Of course, ma'am."

A few awkward seconds later, Juniper was led a bit away from Deandra by a male werecat. Deandra swallowed nervously when Officer Sutter fixed her with an unblinking stare. The officer was always professional, kind, and understanding, yet Deandra often felt like she was four seconds from being reprimanded when she was in her presence.

"No need to be so anxious, Deandra," Officer Sutter said. "This is just a chat, okay? It's not like we haven't done this before. Can you tell me what you saw and heard?"

Deandra started rambling. She told the officer about her three hours in the Mythic Pet Kitchen booth, sneaking through the back of the Greenwoods' tent with Juniper and Havoc, watching the ASA demonstration, and then finally the man collapsing with those awful, angry marks on his side. "I know you can't tell me much, because it's an ongoing investigation and everything, but can you tell me his name? I feel bad that I don't even know *that* about him."

Officer Sutter hesitated for only a moment before she said, "Conrad Osgood."

Deandra nodded to herself. "Thanks. Do … do you know if Conrad made it?"

The officer chuckled. "Can't help yourself, can you? We still don't know much. Shatterberry poisoning is treatable if it's caught in time, but the window is very narrow. Mrs. Greenwood administering the adrenaline shot as quickly as she did at least gave him a chance."

Deandra gusted out a shaky breath. "Thanks for letting me know."

"Did either of the Greenwoods mention a previous relationship with Conrad?"

The question threw her for a second, if only because Officer Sutter's ability to flip her intimidating werecat aura on and off in a blink was jarring. Deandra said, "Based on what little I saw, I wouldn't think they knew each other before this. They had a very professional kind of relationship, from what I could tell."

"Thank you. I'll be in touch if I have any other questions." Officer Sutter glanced over her shoulder. "Looks like the ACSI team is done in there, so you're free to speak to the Greenwoods. If you suspect either one of them is planning to skip town, please discourage that, hmm? I would rather *not* have to go on a multi-jump telepad chase—especially not during a festival weekend."

Deandra nodded tightly, unsure if Sutter was being facetious or not.

With that, Sutter strode toward Juniper and the officer still chatting with him. Deandra pulled Havoc's leash from her back pocket, hooked it to his harness, and the two hurried across the grass toward the Greenwoods.

A standing sign holder on a long pole had been positioned at the mouth of the tattoo side of the tent. The sign behind the plastic covering listed flash design categories, available living-ink colors, and pricing. A hastily scribbled note taped to the outside of the plastic read "CLOSED UNTIL FURTHER NOTICE."

Quinn saw Deandra coming and rushed to the front of the tent to meet her. "Did Sutter tell you anything? Did she accuse Ru of … I don't know … attempted homicide, or something awful like that? Gosh, I don't even know if that poor man is still alive." Her eyes were shiny with unshed tears.

"All she told me was that Conrad's condition is uncertain, and she asked if you'd had any dealings with him before today."

Rularo had been sitting on a stool on his side of the booth, his elbows on his knees as he stared at the ground. He pushed himself to his feet, walking over to join the ladies. He looked so ... defeated. They both did. Seeing the Greenwoods so dejected was like looking at a pair of kicked puppies.

"I'd never met Conrad before," Rularo said, his voice flat. Hands in the pockets of his jeans, he stared at the grass as if he couldn't bear to look at his wife *or* Deandra. "He was familiar with living tattoos, given all his other ink, but I'd never talked to him before today."

Deandra didn't know how to broach the subject of this horrible incident possibly being the result of negligence on Rularo's part, so she approached the topic from a side angle. "Do you know what his ancestry is?"

Rularo's gaze shifted to some point in the distance only he could see. "He said his mother is an earth witch who specializes in ink craft as well. That's part of how he got interested in living inks, as it was a hobby of hers. He said she comes from a long line of witches who were here pre-Glitch, so she's magic-touched instead of fae.

"As far as he knows, no one in his family had secret affairs with fae. That information alone means I wouldn't have had shatterberry anywhere near him." He turned his attention to Deandra, his brow furrowed. "I have a client who wants shatterberry ink for her piece tomorrow, but she's draken. I didn't even *bring* shatterberry with me today. At least ... at least I don't *think* I did."

Deandra wanted to hug the big guy.

Quinn's voice was soft when she said, "*I* packed the ink today, Ru. If shatterberry ended up in the crates this morning, it was *my* fault, not yours."

The two stared at each other. There was no malice, only regret and self-doubt. They were both clearly worried they'd screwed up and caused undue hardship for the other.

Deandra figured this would be a good time to slowly back away and leave the pair to sort things out themselves. But she was a nosy, curious person, and her next question was out of her mouth before her feet could move. "What exactly *is* shatterberry?"

The couple snapped out of their staring contest.

"Uhh … let's see. That's sort of an involved question," Quinn said, rubbing her forehead as if trying to rid herself of a headache.

"Oh, you've done it now," Rularo said playfully, though his smile was strained. "Fae flora is one of her favorite topics."

Quinn rolled her eyes good-naturedly, but her amusement seemed just as forced. "Before the Glitch, fae and mundanes—some combination of scientists and the wealthy—brought flora and fauna back and forth between the two realms. There was some interest in testing how fae flora in particular would do in controlled environments in this realm. Seed vaults were built in both places. I would guess there are seed vaults full of mundane seeds somewhere in the fae realm to this day.

"Anyway, there are a few wealthy fae families in this realm who hold a monopoly on fae seeds and plants. They're the reason zombie cactus exists here. It's possible to purchase certain seeds, plants, and fruit from them. They cater largely to restaurants who try to keep fae dishes as authentic as possible, given the situation."

Deandra recalled the strange-colored vegetables she'd eaten at the Drake Inn Café while on her first date with Cruz and the unique vegetables growing in the Greenwoods garden and piled on their kitchen counters.

Quinn continued, "They're based in a remote hub in Georgia. All they do there is cultivate fae plants. They sell the plants and produce at a premium because the supply is so limited. A law was inked in the very early days of the Glitch that basically makes the place untouchable. They have dedicated telepads, which very few people have access to, and a triple-reinforced veil. That's the rumor, anyway. Shatterberry is one of the rare fae plants you can only get from that hub."

Deandra wondered if Cruz's nerdy tendencies were rubbing off on her because she very much wanted to visit this secret greenhouse hub full of fae plants.

"Shatterberries come from a tree, and the fruit is about the size of a mundane orange, though they look a bit like raspberries. The rind hardens to something similar to a coconut shell," Quinn said. "Shatterberry got its name because if it's not picked before it's ripe—just before the rind hardens—it will eventually fall to the ground and shatter. The impact sends spores like dandelion fluff into the air. Once the rind hardens, the fruit becomes extremely bitter. Not even animals will eat it, and when the fruit first hits the ground, the spores give off a puff of noxious gas."

Talking about this seemed to be cheering Quinn up a bit, at least. "Anyway, the spores are very tasty to animals and insects, so that burst of gas is supposed to give as many of the spores as possible a chance to scatter into the wind. The shattered shell, the spores, and the fruit—before it turns bitter—can all be used in creating living inks. The extract has unique, unpredictable properties when it hits skin in particular, so you might get a splatter of any color in the rainbow. It also sparkles, a bit like glitter.

"It's absolutely gorgeous, especially since you never know what you're going to get. It makes for unique tattoos, and the inks are also used in paper products, textiles, and paints. Very specific curing processes make the ink safe to wear on your body in terms of fabrics, regardless of your species, but when using it in tattoos, it gets into the bloodstream *very* quickly.

"The FDMA classifies it as a Level 8 when it comes to consumables. That's the top of the scale. It can't be used as artificial coloring for food products or in glazes for pottery, because those could have contact with food. Some people have even gotten sick after licking an envelope if the paper had been colored using shatterberry ink, so it's even heavily regulated when used in stationery.

"At this point, when it comes to the general population, it's only used in textiles. Rules are a bit different for elephantine fae, though, since they're the only ones who don't seem to suffer from shatterberry poisoning. Ru has to take all kinds of extra precautions just to administer the ink to a client, to make sure he doesn't suffer from poisoning while doing the work. We're lucky he didn't get poisoned, too."

"Why use it at all?" Deandra asked, then mentally winced, as she hadn't planned to ask that out loud.

Quinn chuckled. "I know. It sounds nuts to even bother with it, huh? It is more trouble than it's worth sometimes—now being a perfect example—but the elephantine are *very* used to paying a high price for a piece using shatterberry ink."

"Maybe we were being too greedy," Rularo said, dejected. "I added shatterberry to the list of inks to choose from on the off chance someone might want it. I was surprised we had someone request it for Sunday." He stood a little straighter. "You know ... the more I think about it, the more I'm *positive* we couldn't have brought any of the shatterberry with us, hon. It's in the blackout case in the freezer, remember?"

Quinn snapped her fingers. "That's right! I put it in there last night so the galaxy variant would be properly chilled for your first client tomorrow morning."

"So ..." Deandra said slowly, "how would shatterberry have gotten into the tent at all, let alone into your tattoo gun?"

Rularo shook his head, expression distant. "I don't know." He looked at each woman in turn. "I'm not a conspiracy theorist, but I can't help thinking someone must have snuck in here and added it to the ink cup when we were distracted during the ASA demonstration."

Quinn flinched as if struck, but Deandra didn't react, seeing as she'd had that exact thought earlier.

"The question is," Deandra said, "was the target Conrad, or was it you?"

Quinn flinched again. "Wait. *Wait!* You think someone wanted to punish Ru, and they used Conrad as collateral damage or something?"

Deandra shrugged. "Maybe?"

Rularo, without a word, walked closer to the ladies. He looked left and right, left and right, as if he expected one of the werecats to drop from the tent's ceiling at any moment. The sign outside had kept any curious shoppers from venturing inside, so the area around the front of the tent was relatively empty.

Apparently having decided that no one was going to catch him in the act of whatever the heck he was doing, Rularo crouched behind the table covered in the purple tablecloth. He disappeared from view for a few seconds, bumped his head on the underside of the table so hard it jumped, then cursed before standing and rubbing the back of his head. In his free hand, he held the appointment book. Cheeks pink and eyes darting wildly, he whispered, "Over here." He speed-walked toward the back of the tent.

Deandra and Quinn shared a quick, bewildered look, then hurried after Rularo. Well, Deandra *tried* to hurry, but she was temporarily halted thanks to her dozing dragon. The sudden yank on his harness woke Havoc with a start. He scrambled to his feet, yawned, and then trotted along with her toward the Greenwoods, who huddled near the freestanding wooden hutch decked out with rows of ink and cleaning supplies and several tattoo guns.

Deandra assumed the compromised tattoo gun and ink cup must be in the custody of ACSI.

When she reached the Greenwoods, Rularo flipped open the appointment book, found the proper page, and balanced the book on an open palm. The ladies scooted closer. With his free hand, Rularo placed a pointer finger on the six-fifteen slot. The line was blank, though it was clear a name had once been written there. "I didn't show this to the werecats—please don't be upset, Quinny. I don't usually make it a habit to lie to the police, but I wanted to talk to you about it first, and I knew if I told them about it, ACSI would have taken the whole book with them."

Deandra remembered then that Conrad, in his throes of shatterberry poisoning, had hit the table and knocked the binders and appointment book to the ground. The tablecloth draping had shielded the appointment book from view. The binders, however, Deandra noted, had been confiscated.

Quinn gave her head a little shake. "I thought all the slots were filled as of this morning."

"They were," Rularo said. "The six fifteen was a no-show. Conrad showed up sometime after ten this morning. You'd run to the bathroom, Quinny, so you missed it. But Conrad dropped by between sessions to tell me how much he loves my work, and he signed up for a Sunday appointment."

Rularo flipped the page and pointed to the noon appointment.

Conrad Osgood

"He filled out his forms and selected his design and colors and all that. He said, though, that if we had any openings before Sunday, he'd be happy to go early, since he had an event Sunday evening in one of the Midwest hubs—can't remember which— and would like to get home as soon as possible." Glancing at Deandra, he said, "Clients are told to get here at least fifteen minutes early so we can get any allergy tests out of the way, and they can sign the liability waiver. When the client didn't show up by ten after six, I texted Conrad, and he rushed over to take the open slot."

Deandra's mind whirled. "Was the no-show anyone you had a previous relationship with?"

"Not that I know of," Rularo said, absently running a finger over the ridges and divots in the paper where a name had once been. "We only communicated through email. He was professional enough. He'd filled out the form, wanted a tree tattoo with fall colors and falling leaves—standard stuff. Do *you* recognize the name Axil Romano, Quinny?"

She shrugged and shook her head.

Deandra asked, "Are no-shows common?"

"Not really," Rularo said. "I'm not trying to toot my own horn here, but I'm a fairly well-known artist, and I rarely offer flash because of how complicated things can get with our inks. So when I *do* offer it, I fill up pretty fast. And I filled up even faster for this event than we expected. Cancellations happen, because life happens, but it's better etiquette to cancel with your artist than to not show up at all if you don't want to end up blacklisted." To Quinn, he said, "We were so slammed this morning, I forgot to even mention the schedule change. He didn't want anything too complicated, and because of Axil's planned appointment, we had enough ink to get Conrad's done.

"I really didn't think much of the no-show. It's annoying that this Axil person didn't have the common courtesy to email me, but Conrad filling in balanced that out. Plus, this is a festival, and festivals can be weird. I've never done flash at a market as big as this one. For all I know, Axil got lost, was frustrated, and then just went home."

"But ..." Deandra said. "Now you're wondering if *you* were the target, since Conrad being here during the six-fifteen slot was a fluke."

Rularo shrugged helplessly. "Unless they were hoping I'd get poisoned through accidental contact, since I'd be taking fewer precautions. I was still in gloves, though. I try to keep living inks off my skin as much as possible, anyway, but I use gloves that go past my elbows when I use shatterberry."

"Maybe it wasn't about hurting you physically," Deandra said. "Maybe they wanted you to be responsible for hurting someone else—if not worse. It would mean someone is targeting the business or your reputation more than you. I don't know if that's any better."

"It not being an assassin would make *me* feel better," Quinn said. "But someone trying to take down our business isn't exactly great, either."

He took hold of his wife's hand and turned fully toward her. "I need to know how safe you feel, Quinny. If we *really* think someone is trying to target me—target *us*—for some reason, we need to pack up shop and forfeit the weekend. I know this is our best weekend of the year, and we'd be out the money we paid for the booth space, but I'm not risking the business's reputation, my clients, *or* your safety. So I need to know: Do you think I'm just being paranoid? Or do we need to shut this all down? If you don't feel safe, we'll pack up right this second, drop the appointment book off at the police station on our way out, and call the weekend a wash."

Quinn chewed on her bottom lip as she regarded her husband. "That would be a lot of canceled appointments, Ru. We spent so much time and money making all the inks, and—"

"I don't care," he said gently. "I don't want to participate in any of this if you don't feel safe here."

She stared at him for a long time. "Shouldn't I be asking *you* that? Do *you* feel safe?"

He shrugged helplessly.

"If you want my advice," Deandra said, feeling beyond awkward again, listening in on what should probably be a private conversation. "I say you shut down for today. There are only a couple of hours left as it is. Take everything with you, tell the werecats about the no-show, and then let them decide how safe it is for you to participate this weekend. Heck, maybe they'll station werecats around your booth for protection. Or maybe they'll position stealthed agents around the tent in hopes the culprit will come back and try to sabotage you some other way."

It was possible that Wendy's love of not only true crime, but genre television, was making Deandra's imagination grow out of control, like a bramble bush.

Quinn nodded, seemingly unfazed by the idea of werecats holding stakeouts in or around the tent. "Let's do that, Ru."

"You take care of what you need to, and I'll go check on Peril," Deandra said. "I haven't gone over there for the second time yet."

Quinn slapped herself in the forehead. "I'm a terrible mother! I totally forgot about him."

Laughing, Deandra said, "If you need me to feed him or anything, just text me instructions, okay? Take as long as you need. He'll be fine."

"We appreciate you, Dee," Rularo said, suddenly looking exhausted.

"All good." She gave his arm a squeeze, exchanged a quick

hug with Quinn, plucked her purse and shopping bag off the table, and left the Greenwoods to their own devices, Havoc trotting alongside her.

After she was well clear of the festival grounds and headed for her car, she texted Wendy to say she was heading to Peril's. Then she called Cruz.

"Hey," he said before the phone had rung even once. "You all right?"

"I have *so* much hot goss for you." She remembered all over again that Peril knew Havoc's secret. "But first, we need to address the fact that you *once again* neglected to tell me important details about the magical breeds of animals I'll be sitting for. Namely that salica can see through illusions, veils, and glamours."

He was quiet for several long beats, clearly confused. "I don't know why that would—*oh crap.*"

"Oh crap, indeed!" Deandra said a little too loudly, startling a woman ahead of her. "Sorry," she said, wincing, when the woman shot her an annoyed look over her shoulder.

They agreed it would be best to discuss the "hot goss" in person—and away from prying ears—once she was done with Peril. Deandra resisted the urge to ask Cruz to meet her at Peril's house. It would be nice to have moral support when breaking the news to the nervous ferret that his parents were delayed because they were talking to the cops. Peril had already thought that Deandra was a rogue agent sent to ruin his parents' livelihood. What if this new development made him suspicious of her again?

She ultimately decided against inviting Cruz along, if only because Cruz had mentioned that he wasn't Peril's primary care veterinarian. And that was because all Cruz heard when he tried interacting with the ferret was screaming.

Nonstop screaming.

"I'll have a piping hot pizza waiting for you at my house when you're done," Cruz said, breaking through her scattered thoughts.

Deandra's stomach rumbled. "I demand an entire pizza for myself. Double pepperoni."

"Done."

"And cheesy breadsticks!"

"Obviously. With extra marinara dipping sauce," he said. "This ain't my first rodeo."

She laughed. "See you soon."

On the way to the Greenwoods', Deandra debated about what to tell Peril—assuming she told him anything at all. This was something he should discuss with his parents, wasn't it?

She'd just pulled up in front of the Greenwoods' house when a pair of texts popped up on her phone propped on the dash. They were from Quinn. The first included feeding instructions. The second was a little distressing.

> **Quinn**
> We might be here for a while. Officer Sutter said there have been some "developments" and that the appointment book throws some things into question. Looks like another set of interrogations are coming. Please tell Peril we miss him and that we shouldn't be home later than 10PM

The salica would no doubt ask why his parents were delayed. It wasn't like Peril was a mundane dog who'd be unable to tell Deandra was lying through her teeth when she said "Your people will be home soon!"

Dogs didn't have a true concept of time, anyway.

Peril was different.

As she walked up the driveway with Havoc, she decided that she'd tell Peril that the tattoo schedule had gotten thrown off because of overbooking. Or, uhh ... too many cancellations. So many cancellations, no-shows, and overbookings, in fact, that the schedule had become a tangled mess, and his parents would be stuck at Oracle Park for longer than planned to help make sure all of today's appointments were fulfilled. Yeah. That was believable. And it was kinda true. If you didn't think about it too hard. She'd distract him with a nice bowl of beef-and-gravy kitten chow, and they'd work on his puzzle, and all would be well.

Before she could open the door, another text message notif-ication sounded. She pulled out her phone, stalling like the coward she was, hoping it was Cruz asking if she wanted dessert as well.

Instead it was another text from Quinn. It was only six words long. Her stomach bottomed out.

> **Quinn**
> Goddess above! Conrad didn't make it...

Deandra swayed on her feet. Conrad was dead. Conrad, who

more than likely had been in the wrong place at the wrong time. Conrad, who had an unknown event in some unknown hub tomorrow, sure to be missed by friends and family. All because he'd taken an appointment slot that had been vacated by someone else at the last minute.

She had no idea how she was going to maintain any level of composure in front of Peril now, especially when her plan to skirt around the topic of his parents had already been terrible.

Telling herself that the ferret would probably hide for part of the visit anyway, she let herself into the Greenwoods' house. She'd use the first few minutes to center herself; then she could give Peril at least a half truth.

All her half-baked plans went right out the window the moment Deandra closed the door behind her and Havoc. Instead of hiding, Peril was standing in the foyer, his front paws held in front of his chest.

"Good evening," he said almost cheerfully as she slowly took off her shoes. "You arrived a bit later than I expected. Is everything all right? Did you see my parents at the festival?"

"Um. Hello there," Deandra said as she unhooked Havoc's leash from his collar. "Good, uh, evening."

Peril cocked his head. "Are you all right?"

"Hmm? Me? Oh, sure. Just a long day at the festival. Hey, you hungry?" Deandra beelined for the kitchen, and then for the cabinet that held Peril's expensive kitten food. "Where do you usually eat? Here in the kitchen?"

After placing the beef-flavored kitten food on the counter by the sink, she went rummaging for a can opener. She found one in a drawer on the opposite side of the kitchen. When she turned to head back for the waiting can of kitten food, she yelped and dropped the can opener, narrowly missing her socked foot. Peril was standing on his back legs on the counter now, paws on his hips. His black-tipped tail flicked in a way that was very reminiscent of a miffed housecat.

"Why are you acting dodgy?" Peril asked.

"Dodgy?" Deandra went to pick up the can opener that had slid halfway across the kitchen. "I'm not dodgy. Let's get your dinner ready, hmm?" Placing the can opener next to the kitten food, she opened the cabinet near the refrigerator where Quinn had told her she'd find Peril's dishes. They had unique designs—one covered in butterflies, one with palm trees, another with open books. She grabbed two and spun around, holding them up as if they were prizes on a game show. "You got a preference, big guy?"

She winced. *Big guy? Really?*

Juniper's admission from earlier repeated in her head. *"I have a bad habit of blabbing the truth at the perfectly wrong time when under pressure."*

Same, dude. Same.

The ferret's forepaws were crossed, and he tapped a foot. He was no more than five pounds, stood a smidge under two feet tall, and yet Deandra was panicking under his scrutiny. She didn't want to freak the ferret out. But she was also keenly aware that anything she did or *didn't* say could somehow backfire on her, putting Havoc's secret in jeopardy. She honestly wasn't even sure if that worry made sense, but no one said anxiety was logical.

"Deandra," Peril said slowly.

In hindsight, when she reflected on this moment later, she'd know it was the quaver in his little voice that broke her resolve.

"Did something happen to my parents? Are they okay?"

Deandra blurted, "Someone might have sabotaged Rularo's ink with shatterberry—"

Peril gasped.

"—and then the contaminated ink was unknowingly administered to someone with mostly mundane parentage—"

Peril gasped again.

"—and the ink sort of, um, killed him? Your parents are at the police station now going through a second round of interrogations because of recent *developments* and because we currently don't know if the sabatoger ... sabotogee ..."

"Saboteur," Peril offered helpfully, his tiny eyes huge.

"Right. Thanks. We don't know if the saboteur was targeting one of your dad's customers, your dad specifically, or their business in general."

This time, Peril didn't gasp.

He fainted.

Deandra lurched forward and caught the limp ferret just before he slipped off the countertop and onto the stone-tiled floor.

Sighing in relief that she'd grabbed him before he cracked his head open on the counter or floor, her heart racing a million miles an hour, she carted the unconscious ferret into the living room. Havoc was passed out on his back in the middle of the living room carpet, his limbs stuck out in four directions like a starfish.

Deandra managed to get a throw pillow laid flat on a couch cushion with some creative elbow work without dropping the ferret, then gently laid him on top of it. She knew the ferret was high-strung, and that he got stressed out when his parents were away, to the point that he forwent food and water. They often ended up needing to take him to the vet to get fluids by the time they returned home.

Fainting had to be somewhat normal for him, right? It was that worry that convinced her he needed the plushiness of the pillow rather than just a couch cushion, ensuring he'd be more comfortable when he woke up. Hands clasped behind her head, she stared down at his little unmoving body.

When two full minutes went by with no change, she was ready to abandon her plan to loop the couch for a fortieth time and call Cruz and beg him to rush over here to revive the salica.

Then Peril snorted awake.

She hurried over to the pillow where she'd left him and dropped into a squat beside the couch. Belatedly, she realized that having her face so close to his when he was coming to from being unexpectedly unconscious might not be the best choice. His eyes slowly blinked open. He registered Deandra's face looming over him, screamed, and then rolled off the pillow and into the space between it and the back of the couch.

His scream woke up Havoc, who scrambled to his feet and then launched straight into the air, chirp-shrieking in alarm. He'd zipped skyward so quickly, he bumped into the ceiling. He did a frantic perimeter check from up there, chirping up a storm at nothing in particular.

"Havoc!" Deandra said, getting to her feet and waving her arms like a member of ground crew guiding a plane into a gate. "It's okay! There's no threat. I scared Peril by accident."

By the time Havoc got his bearings and lowered himself back to the carpet, Peril had perched on the back of the couch, a paw over his chest.

Deandra held up her hands in placation toward the ferret. "My bad ..."

Peril huffed out a breath. "Goodness. Maybe next time you can give me the news in pieces instead of using a firehose."

Deandra grimaced.

The ferret said, "I'm more prepared this time. Start at the beginning and tell me everything. Spare no detail."

"Don't you want to wait until your parents get—"

"No." He stomped a foot. "I want to be fully informed so that when they return—and they *will* return; they will *not* be arrested for homicide—we can skip right to problem-solving instead of wasting time on minutiae." It still threw Deandra that Peril had a vocabulary that consisted of words with more than two syllables, given how little she'd heard him speak before this weekend. "And if you're about to make a comment about needing to cater to my delicate sensibilities, I would rather you didn't. My constitution is fine, thank you."

Deandra opted not to point out how fast he'd fainted when the news became too much for his constitution. Or the fact that he, much like Juniper earlier, had been wringing his paws a lot for someone who claimed their nerves were under control.

"Puzzles are my *thing*, Deandra," he said pleadingly when she had yet to speak. "My parents put this drivel on," he said, flapping a paw at the television where yet another nature program was playing, "because they think it soothes me. You know what I watch when they've gone to bed? One of the many, *many* twenty-four-hour crime channels. If you ever attend a trivia night about serial killers and need a partner, I'm your ferret! I'll sweep the floor with everyone."

All Deandra could do was stare at him. She turned to ask Havoc what he thought of the revelation that Peril the ferret was a true-crime junkie like Wendy, but he was passed out like a starfish again.

Defeated, Deandra laid out all the details she had for Peril. He was a good listener and only asked questions when he needed clarification. He paced along the back of the couch as she spoke, employing a sort of run-hop mode of movement that was so cute, she got distracted by it more than once. The only thing she left out was the fact that ASA had specifically called out the Greenwoods for owning a salica. She didn't want him to feel like any part of this could have been his fault, no matter how indirect.

By the time she finished talking, he had one forelimb crossed in front of his chest with the other propped on top. He tapped a tiny digit to his chin as he thought, contemplative gaze angled toward the ceiling.

"The name of the no-show was Axil Romano, you say?" Peril finally asked.

"Yeah. Why, does it sound familiar to you?"

"Come with me." In a blink, he was off the back of the couch and hop-running across the living room and into the foyer. A blink later, and he'd disappeared around a corner into the hallway.

She looked from Havoc to the hallway and back again. What on earth could the salica have to show her?

"Come now, Deandra, we don't have all night."

She yelped and whirled around, finding Peril's little face sticking out of the topmost tunnel that ran along the back wall of the living room. How the heck had he moved so fast? No wonder salica made formidable spies in the fae realm.

He scampered away.

Sighing, she left her dozing dragon in the living room and crept into the Greenwoods' hallway. She hadn't ventured down here other than the day of the initial walk-through of the house. Once she was in the hallway, there was a bathroom almost imme-diately to her left. She assumed Peril wasn't in there, so she kept moving. The only other doors were for a guest room coming up on her left and one she remembered led to the master bedroom at the end of the hall.

Deandra stopped outside the guest room that doubled as a craft room and home office. There was an artist table on each side of the room, the wide drawing surfaces propped up at a thirty-degree angle or so. She easily guessed which one was Quinn's and which was Rularo's, based more on the size and height of the table and stool than what was on or around them. The room was full of shelves, racks, and hutches crammed with art supplies like brushes, paints, paper, and pencils. There were jars of inks, baskets of dried herbs, rows of art books, and stacks of sketch-books. Somehow the space didn't feel cluttered, though.

Deandra slowly walked into the room, not seeing Peril, but assuming this was the room he'd wanted her to meet him in.

A simple desk sat below a window in the middle of the back wall. Other than a four-tier mesh desk organizer tray and a mesh cup filled with a bouquet of ink pens, nothing was on the glass surface of the desk other than a laptop. Folders and loose paper that at first glance looked like invoices filled the bottom three shelves of the desk organizer, while the top one was empty. She wondered if that was where they usually kept their appointment book.

Deandra started when Peril suddenly jumped onto the back of the black leather chair positioned in front of the desk. He'd appar-ently been sitting on the chair's cushion waiting for her. "Have a seat, Deandra. We have some research to do."

Her brows hiked. "We could just use my phone to research. I've got Forage set up on it. I feel a little weird about using your parents' computer."

Peril waved her concern away with a paw. "It will be much easier for me to read along on a bigger screen. They let me use the computer to play games sometimes. I have the password. I just don't have the reach needed to operate the mouse pad *and* the keys. The lack of thumbs is an issue, too."

What on earth kind of games could a ferret play on a computer? She laughed to herself at the image of him wielding a tiny controller while wearing a headset, yelling obscenities at internet opponents as he played war games.

He waved a paw again. "Come, come. We don't have all night."

Sighing, Deandra pulled the chair away from the desk, easily rolling it along the hardwood floor. She wasn't sure how she'd wound up getting bossed around by a talking ferret, but here she was.

As she sat down, Peril jumped soundlessly to the glass desktop. Deandra opened the laptop, squashed down the feeling that she was a hacker from a sci-fi movie hunting for state secrets, and scooted a little closer to the desk. "You never said whether the name Axil Romano was familiar to you," she said, unsure what the ferret had in mind.

"Means absolutely nothing to me. But that's what the internet is for. We'll use your hour of allotted time with me to scour the 'net for this Axil person. It's our only lead."

Deandra sat back and crossed her arms, eyeing Peril. "How do you figure it's the *only* lead? What if Conrad really *was* the target? He clearly knew a lot about living ink, since he was covered in it. He could have told someone in his life what he was doing today, or posted about it. Someone out there might have been keeping tabs on him, waiting for an opportunity to add shatterberry to the ink. The ASA demonstration proved to be a great distraction."

Peril bared his teeth. She didn't think it was a show of aggression; he was lightly disgusted by her ineptitude. "That's a *lot* of variables, and also a very complicated way to eliminate someone. If someone wanted Conrad out of the picture so badly that they were willing to follow him to Axia to hurt him, they could have added shatterberry to his drink or food just as easily. Heck, they could have pushed him in front of a moving car! I believe Conrad was just in the wrong place at the wrong time."

That sick feeling churned in Deandra's gut again. She also believed Conrad had gotten wildly unlucky, which made it even worse.

She pushed the feeling way down to process later. "Fine. I'll agree that Axil *may* have been the true target. But we also have to accept the possibility that the target might have been your dad."

Peril swayed a little on his back feet, but he stayed conscious. "I can't think about that right now. Investigating Axil as the intended victim is easier for me to swallow. Plus, if we can find something useful about this person, it could help take the heat off my father. I'm sure the werecats are investigating the possibility that Father poisoned Conrad on purpose—that there's some connection in their pasts and that my parents are lying about it. If we can come up with something credible, the werecats can stop wasting their time trying to pin any number of crimes on him. This is the only thing I can think of to do."

Deandra realized then that Peril didn't just feel uncertain about how to help his parents. Some part of him probably felt guilty, too. After all, he was usually *with* his parents, tucked away in Rularo's beard. If he'd been with Rularo at the time of the incident, he might have seen something that absolved Rularo of the crime.

"Okay," she said. "We'll start with Axil."

Peril stood a little straighter on his hind legs. "If you truly feel uncomfortable about putting in their password, just pick me up and hold me over the keys, and I'll type it in."

Deandra did so, feeling a bit foolish. This was the computer hacker equivalent of *Ratatouille*.

"Done," Peril said.

She deposited him next to the laptop just as the screen switched from the password box to a family picture of the Greenwoods. It showed Quinn holding Peril in her arms, but Peril was in the midst of trying to claw his way out of her grasp, his eyes and mouth open and his forepaws stretched wide, presumably reaching for the safety of Rularo's beard. Quinn's face was twisted in a rictus of fright, and Rularo was lurching away from Quinn and Peril, his eyes comically wide and his mouth in a little "o" of surprise. Deandra cracked up. It was such a chaotic picture, and it was even funnier that, of all the family photos the Greenwoods could have chosen, they'd chosen this one.

"Embarrassing," Peril muttered. "And none of that was even my fault! The photographer clearly thought I was a mere mundane animal who could be charmed by nonsense better suited to children. She waved some monstrosity in my face that squeaked like a creature in the midst of being eviscerated. My keen instincts for self-preservation kicked in, and I wisely sought safety."

"So the photographer squeaked a stuffed elephant, and you lost your marbles," Deandra guessed.

Peril crossed his forelimbs. "How *dare* you." He coughed. "It was a stuffed parrot."

She laughed again.

"They got perfectly acceptable pictures that day, and they even have framed ones in the living room and bedroom. I look positively regal in those, and yet my parents chose ..." He flapped a paw at the screen. "That."

"I think it's sweet," Deandra said. "The picture probably makes them happy every time they see it. They cherish the memory with you, even if it's silly."

Peril huffed. "I suppose. Anyway, pull up the Forage browser. Let's check their email first to see if this Axil Romano nincompoop emailed my parents after the fact, and they just didn't see it because of all the hullaballoo."

She cocked her head. "Where did you learn words like 'nincompoop' and 'hullaballoo'?"

Peril's nose twitched. "I *can* read, you know. I've taken many online courses. I technically have a GED. I read voraciously as well. My parents have a tablet for me. I can use my paws to turn digital pages easily enough; paper books are too hard for me to wield."

Giving her head a little shake, flabbergasted once again by how different Peril was from her expectations, she double-clicked on the Forage desktop icon. When the browser opened, the Greenwoods' email inbox was an already-open tab, so she didn't need to have Peril input another password. She didn't feel any better about snooping in their email than poking around on their laptop, but thankfully the email chain between Rularo and Axil Romano was near the top of the inbox.

Clicking the thread revealed that their interactions were just as Rularo had said: He and Axil had been maintaining a cordial back-and-forth about setting up the tattoo appointment, and Axil had returned his filled-out form detailing the flash design he wanted as well as the colors. There was also a reply that said, "I have filled out the intake form via your secure link. I have detailed all relevant medical details."

"Do you know anything about the intake forms?" Deandra asked.

"No. But I'm sure they're saved to the computer somewhere." Peril suggested they check the folders on the desktop, and after minimizing the browser, there was indeed a folder she hadn't paid attention to before. "Client Intake Forms" was written in bold. A little lock symbol in the corner of the file suggested that it was password protected, but she double-clicked it at Peril's behest anyway. A password box popped up.

"Drat," Peril said. "I don't know this one. My parents are pretty good about rotating passwords—for, uh, reasons. I know my parents; this password won't be any of the ones I know."

Deandra figured there was a land mine buried in that last

comment, and she didn't want to step on it. "We don't need to be snooping in people's personal files anyway."

"I'll bet there are juicy details in those files, though," Peril said, sounding grumpy. "What if the smoking gun is in there?"

"Then it's not ours to find." She happily pulled the inbox back up.

The last sent email in the thread was one from Rularo reminding Axil of the day and time of his appointment, including a map of Oracle Park. The Greenwoods' tent was circled in red.

Axil hadn't replied to that email, nor had he sent a follow-up stating that he'd miss the appointment.

Deandra hurriedly opened a new tab so she wouldn't be tempted to poke through any other emails, simply because they were available. Peril was a bad influence. She typed "Axil Romano Axia" into the search bar. The results weren't anything particularly interesting, nor did it seem like Axil was from this hub.

"What if he's a mundane who just happens to know about the hub system?" Deandra asked idly. "If he's from the mundane world, we'll probably never find him."

"Have faith," the salica said. His tone suggested he was telling himself that just as much as her.

They tried "Axil Romano tattoos" and "Axil Romano living-ink tattoos" to no avail. Deandra, concerned that perhaps the reason Axil hadn't shown up was due to no fault of his own, typed in "Axil Romano telepad accident obituary."

She wasn't sure if she was relieved or not that there were no immediate search results that pointed to Axil experiencing a mishap on his way to the festival.

Peril asked, "Is there any way that Axil had a personal connection to ASA? Maybe he found out ASA was going to be at the festival and opted not to attend because of it." He paused thoughtfully. "Doesn't it seem fishy that ASA planned their big demonstration outside my parents' tent, and then, around the same time, someone is killed by shatterberry poisoning?"

Under different circumstances, she might have written all this off as a series of unfortunate, and unrelated, events. But she feared the Greenwoods were being set up somehow—she just couldn't figure out the why of it yet. "So you mean, instead of the killer using the ASA demonstration as a lucky distraction, you think it's possible ASA held *that* demonstration in *that* location specifically to supply *the killer* with a distraction?"

"It's just as likely as anything else, isn't it?" Peril asked. "Do we know if ASA announced the demonstration was going to occur? I don't know much about the organization myself. My parents said there was an altercation with them on the day they adopted me, but so much of my time before then ... and even several months after that ... is fuzzy, if not gone entirely." He wrung his paws. "Anyway, from what I've heard, they schedule these demonstrations in advance, hoping to have an audience already in the area when it kicks off. They're as spontaneous as a flash mob."

Deandra searched for ASA's social media next, figuring it would be the best place to advertise such a thing if they wanted to lure in as many people as possible. There were at least four social media sites that ASA used, all of them with posts as recent as this afternoon. Deandra was only familiar with Picayune, which was similar to mundane Twitter, so she clicked on that one.

Sure enough, the pinned post at the top of the feed announced there would be a demonstration today around six o'clock. The post included a map similar to the one Rularo had sent Axil, with a circle drawn in red in the aisle made between the Greenwoods' tent and the one across from it. The post had been made on Thursday—a full day before the festival began.

Where had ASA gotten a vendor map? She supposed any number of vendors advertising their participation in the festival could have posted the map on their own feeds, and someone in ASA had saved a copy for their own purposes.

The fact that ASA had picked out their location for the demonstration days in advance made Deandra wonder again if it had been Rularo who had ultimately been the target of the incident. Could someone want to discredit the man and his business? If so, someone either wanted to demonstrate that Rularo's living inks were unsafe, or the killer was willing to treat InkCraft *and* Conrad as collateral damage in their mission to punish the Greenwoods for owning a salica.

Unless, of course, there was something else in Rularo's past that was catching up to him now. That was the same line of thinking Peril assumed the werecats were erroneously investigating now—and the reason they were being interrogated for a second time.

"So …" Deandra said slowly as she sat back in the chair, arms crossed. "There's a little piece of the puzzle I haven't mentioned yet."

Peril turned so quickly, he almost lost his footing. He stumbled wildly, but managed to stop himself at the edge of the desk, his forelimbs pinwheeling as he teetered on the precipice. Once he was on steady footing again, he marched in front of the laptop and stood between it and Deandra. "I told you not to spare a single detail!"

"I know, but I didn't want you to pass out again!"

He gasped *very* dramatically. "How *dare* you."

She merely cocked a brow at him.

"I'm not fragile," he said, stomping a foot.

"You *fainted*, my guy. You were out cold for two minutes. I almost called a vet to come revive you."

Peril had one tiny digit upraised, clearly about to make another argument, but then paused, squinting. "Wait. Which vet?"

"Dr. Caddel."

Peril vigorously shook his head. "No! Not him! Don't you *ever* call him!"

Startled, Deandra involuntarily rolled the chair back a couple of inches. "Whoa, whoa. What's your beef with Dr. Caddel?"

Peril tightly crossed his forelimbs. "His … *zoolingual* powers are too strong." He said the word "zoolingual" as if it were a fatal communicable disease. "I don't want someone in my head listening to my thoughts! Do you know how invasive that is? My mind is a sacred temple, and the only one who's been granted access is *me*. Dr. Jasper is acceptable because her mind-reading skills are weak. She can read emotions, which I find acceptable. I mostly wear those on my figurative sleeves anyway. But Dr. Caddel?" Peril shuddered, then gave Deandra a scrutinizing scan. "I suppose it makes sense a pet sitter would be aware of local veterinarians. But to have him on speed dial? What exactly is the nature of your … *association* with the miscreant?"

Deandra stifled a laugh. His guarded tone suggested he already had an idea about the "nature of her association" with Dr. Cruz Caddel, but he clearly wanted her to prove his assumptions were incorrect. Her brief amusement faded quickly, though, as she braced herself for the very real possibility that her next admission could give the ferret the vapors again. "He's kind of my … boyfriend."

Peril sucked in a great lungful of air, his mouth hanging open in horror, and he stumbled backward as if she were a fearsome monster who had just crawled out of a lagoon. He tripped over the edge of the laptop, his butt hitting the keyboard. A long string of nonsense letters rapidly filled the search bar. He scrambled off the laptop and slowly backed away across the desk's surface, eventually scaling the desk organizer to stand on the empty top shelf. The expression on his little face was some combination of disgust, shock, and disappointment.

In a tight voice, he asked, "Is he going to … pick you up later?"

"What, because you think he'd be able to read your mind through the walls?" she asked, laughing.

Stone-cold serious, Peril bobbed his head.

Oh boy …

Deandra decided not to tell Peril that she'd almost asked Cruz to join her here. Some part of her had wanted to pawn off the job of explaining the Greenwoods' situation on her zoolinguist other half. Now she was especially glad she hadn't. Peril would have pitched a fit to end all fits.

"No, he's not coming here. I'm going to go see him later," Deandra said, and stifled another laugh when the ferret bared his teeth in disgust. "Tell me something ... he said that, in your limited interactions, all he heard from you was screaming. Is that something he's picking up on with his too-powerful skills, or is that you preemptively mentally screaming to drown out any thoughts he could possibly hear? Like, I don't know, when people in a movie turn on the faucet to help distort their voices if they fear their house is bugged."

The way Peril hiked his nose in the air while simultaneously looking deeply embarrassed told her she'd hit the nail on the head.

"You know he's not *actually* a mind reader, right?" Deandra asked gently. "It's more like telepathy, where you have a mental conversation instead of an audible one. But he can't hear or read anything you don't want him to. He can't pry into your mind and steal your secrets."

Deandra didn't actually know how deep into an animal's mind Cruz could go, especially when creatures like shifters and salica possessed a human-level consciousness. Maybe when it came to the more sapient of animals, Cruz's ability *did* creep toward mind-reading territory, but she also knew him well enough to know that he'd never violate a patient's privacy that way. She voiced that last part out loud.

"Well of course *you'd* say that," Peril said. "You're snogging the mind-invading miscreant!"

Deandra's cheeks burned. She refused to be shamed and chastised by a talking ferret!

They'd also gone very far afield of their task at hand. "*Anyway!* As I was saying ... I left something out earlier. There might be more evidence that ASA was targeting your father."

In a blink, Peril was in front of her again. "What do you mean?"

"I didn't think it was that important until I saw that they planned the demonstration days in advance. But ... during the demonstration, the faun leader specifically called out your parents. They wanted the audience to know your parents own a salica, and that they think you're essentially a prisoner here because your kind is destined for bigger and better things than being someone's, and I quote, *designer pet.*"

Peril's mouth dropped open. "How offensive!"

She supposed outrage was better than the reaction she'd feared he'd have.

The ferret was quiet for a long moment. "Do you think *I* could be the reason Conrad was killed? Some thug in ASA decided they understand my life better than me and punished my parents and a total stranger because of it?"

That was the reaction she'd hoped to avoid.

"I don't know, Peril," she said truthfully, her tone as gentle as she could manage. "I truly don't understand what ASA could have wanted out of the demonstration if it was related to you. I think they're just trying to get attention in as flashy a way as possible.

"I'm honestly surprised the videos of the demonstration aren't pinned to their Picayune profile by now, but maybe they're holding off because of what happened to Conrad. I'm willing to bet they're either avoiding posting anything to save their own butts—that gnome was in a really bad way—or ACSI considers the footage evidence, and ASA can't post it if it's part of an active investigation."

"Depending on how injured the gnome really is, he could sue ASA for negligence. Maybe the footage can be used as evidence against them," Peril said, smiling. "One can hope, yes?"

Yes, one could hope.

They returned to their internet search. Deandra only had a few minutes left before her time was up, and as much as she didn't want to abandon the ferret to fritter away the hours alone until his parents came home, she was starving. She had a whole pepperoni pizza to devour—*and* cheesy breadsticks. She wanted to see Cruz, too, of course. She missed him. Yadda yadda. But also … *pizza.*

She tried "Axil Romano Alliance of Sapient Animals" next.

"Oh! Look at that," Peril said, hurrying to the side of the laptop to practically press his snout to one of the search results. "Click this one," he said, tapping the third result with a claw.

She did as the pushy ferret bade.

It was another Picayune profile. The bio read "Born: Luma. Work: Robinson. Resident: The world."

"Ugh," Peril said. "Everyone is a resident of the world, you absolute turnip."

Deandra opted not to comment on the fact that Peril sometimes used British slang. It must have seeped into him via osmosis as he watched shows and movies in the dead of night while his parents slept. Maybe he was a connoisseur of British cozies in addition to serial killer documentaries.

The bio continued with "Let the lions roam free. Release ASA from its shackles."

"Huh," Deandra said. "What do you think *that* means?"

Peril shrugged his furry shoulders. Most of his focus was on reading the posts below the bio. "Scroll down, please."

She complied. The posts were infrequent. Three a week here, once a month there. Some were about ASA, but others were about disappointment with sports-team losses, thanking friends for birthday wishes, and memes about hub-related things, such as telepad travel and getting the wrong spell enhancement in your morning coffee. Overall, pretty boring.

She kept scrolling when Peril requested it, but she'd mostly zoned out. She decided she'd give the salica five more minutes of reading time before she fed him his kitten-food dinner and then skedaddled to Cruz's house. She idly wondered if Havoc was still knocked out on his back in the living room or if he was awake and getting into quiet mischief.

Oh gosh. What if he's in the kitchen eating his way through the Greenwoods' entire supply of vegetables? Peril might not be able to digest that smorgasbord of plant material, but Havoc certainly could.

The sheer terror of finding the dragon glutted on the kitchen floor, having eaten all the vegetables the Greenwoods had painstakingly grown and procured for this weekend's ink supply, was moments from sending her out of the chair.

Peril's voice stopped her in her tracks. "A motive!"

"What?"

The ferret was standing on the laptop in the square of space to the right of the mouse pad. He tapped a paw on the screen. "This post here from two years ago."

In a flash, Peril was perched on her shoulder. She only *slightly* flinched.

The post read: "ASA is an incredible organization. They do work that matters. But the leadership is populated by a bunch of buffoons. I stepped down today as a board member. This breaks my heart. But elevating Jet Kettle to board chair? Really? Mark my words, friends! He's going to run this organization into the ground."

Deandra was a little bummed now that the more recent posts had nothing to do with ASA, as this very likely was the guy they'd been searching for. Axil could have simply cut ties with the organization once Jet became board chair yet still kept tabs on them. Axil might have had every intention of getting his tattoo done today, but perhaps when he caught wind of the ASA demonstration happening just outside the tent where his nemesis would be posted up, Axil decided it wasn't worth potentially running into the faun.

Deandra eyed the time at the bottom of the screen. "As interesting as this all is, I've gotta get going, okay? And you need to eat dinner."

Peril sighed dramatically. "Fine."

He remained on her shoulder while she closed the laptop and headed back out into the living room.

Havoc, thankfully, was still out cold on the floor.

After filling the butterfly-covered dish with kitten food and leaving it on the counter for Peril—who actually settled in to eat—Deandra went searching for her phone, only just now having realized she'd misplaced it. The search turned a little frantic when its location remained elusive for what felt like half a century. She eventually found it wedged between two couch cushions. It likely had ended up there during Peril's fainting spell, seeing as Deandra had been panicked that the ferret's heart had given up for good due to her overloading his "delicate sensibilities" with too much information too fast.

There was a check-in text each from Wendy and Cruz, as well as a goodnight text from her grandma. Her mom had sent a picture of the sunset from her back porch.

Nothing from Quinn or Rularo. It was getting close to nine. She crept into the open doorway of the kitchen to snap a picture of Peril eating. After typing a quick update telling the Greenwoods that Peril was fine, she sent the message and the picture to them in a group text. She chewed on her bottom lip, staring at the text thread for three full minutes. No reply.

After scooping her dead-weight dragon off the floor, getting her shoes back on, and calling a goodbye to Peril, she headed for her car.

Havoc didn't stir as she placed him in the back seat.

Once in the driver's seat, she attached her phone to her dash and tapped the screen. Still no answer from the Greenwoods.

Deandra
Is it too late for pizza?

Cruz
Nope. I actually ordered it ten minutes ago, so it should be here soon

Deandra
On my way. Havoc has been out like a light for over an hour. He'll probably get the zoomies as soon as I get there

Cruz
Max is also charging her zoomie batteries

After pulling up in front of Cruz's house, she checked her phone again.

No response.

None had come in an hour later, either …

Deandra woke with a start, disoriented. There was a crick in her neck. Pushing off the hard surface under her cheek, she sat up and rubbed her neck. Slowly the dark masses in the room solidified into recognizable shapes.

She was in Cruz's living room. Cruz was passed out next to her, his mouth agape in sleep. A mostly empty pizza box sat on the coffee table, the only thing visible below the propped-open lid was a few discarded crusts. Maxine and Havoc were both on their backs in one of Max's beds across the room. Havoc was using her belly as a pillow. The bed wasn't big enough for the two of them to share, but that rarely deterred them.

Rubbing the heel of her palm against her eye, she crept off the couch to use the restroom. Her eyes still hurt a bit from crying. She'd been recounting everything to Cruz as she'd stuffed her face with pizza when it had suddenly hit her all at once: She'd witnessed a man caught in the throes of being consumed by rapid-acting poison. Though he hadn't died in front of her, he had fallen unconscious—a state he apparently had never woken from. She couldn't get over how tragic it was that he'd unknowingly ended up in the middle of an ASA vendetta.

And poor Rularo! He was probably being treated as a murderer until the werecats and ACSI could prove otherwise. Quinn would probably be considered an accessory. That, or she'd be cleared of any suspicion and then be left to worry about the fate of her husband.

When Deandra emerged into the dark living room, she gave her eyes a moment to readjust. She'd splashed cold water on her face, but her eyes still felt raw. Cruz was awake now, too, looking just as exhausted as she still felt.

She eyed the world beyond his windows. It was still the middle of the night. She wasn't sure what had woken her up, other than the pain in her neck. But it wasn't like this was the first time she and Cruz, party animals that they were, had passed out on the couch while watching a movie.

She tiptoed to the side table where she'd left her phone charging. A series of long texts from Quinn had finally come in just after midnight. She quickly scanned the messages, heart pounding.

Cruz must have seen her expression in the blue glow of her cell phone, because he whispered, "Porch?"

That was code for "let's talk outside so we hopefully don't wake the 'dogs.'" Cruz had only experienced two of Havoc's four a.m. airborne zoomies so far, and now, like her, he tried to avoid them at all costs.

They made it outside and got the front door closed without waking up either animal.

They sat on the bottom step of his porch, and he pressed his shoulder against hers. "Good news or bad news?"

She unlocked her screen, internally grumbled at the 3:15 a.m. time display, and handed the phone to him with the text thread already pulled up.

Out loud, he whisper-read, "Hi, Dee. I finally made it home. Thank you so much for taking care of Peril. Ru is still at the station. They're holding him overnight until more info comes in, just in case he's a flight risk. The potency of shatterberry found in both the ink cup and the cartridge of Ru's tattoo gun was so high, they're treating it as an illicit street drug. They've got to trace its origins to prove Ru didn't buy it himself, since our license from the FDMA doesn't cover the potency they found. I guess some living-ink tattoo artists will buy raw shatterberry extract off the arcane web, since that's easier than going through the trouble of getting an official license for the weaker stuff. He could be booked for intent to distribute a Level 8 consumable! Raw shatterberry is apparently also a common additive in counterfeit prescription pills. Did you know that? I sure didn't. Neither did Ru! Now they're treating him like he's a drug kingpin *and* a murderer. I'm so scared for him."

Deandra grimaced, just as she had the first time she read the message.

Cruz said, "I didn't even think of all the ways the werecats might interpret the negligence angle. I guess it makes sense that they need to rule out that the shatterberry ink wasn't some illegally concocted substance the Greenwoods made, trying to cut corners."

"Me either," Deandra said. "Keep reading."

He returned his attention to her phone. "You and the werecats were on the same page about something, though. They told me to run my half of the booth like usual tomorrow, and they'd keep a few guards hidden in or around our tent to see if anyone else tries something sketchy. They haven't ruled out the possibility that someone is trying to discredit the business as a whole, so whoever this is might target the booth again. If Ru gets cleared of whatever nonsense they're accusing him of, they'll have him go back to work at the tent, too, in case the person strikes again. I have a feeling they'll assign him to work in the booth regardless, both to keep an eye on him and to use him as potential bait.

"Two of our employees were running the shop yesterday while we were at the festival. They've been called in for questioning, too. As of late last night, the werecats got a warrant to search InkCraft, so the brick-and-mortar is closed until they're done with their investigation. They're looking for more raw shatterberry, I guess. Or a receipt from superillegalsubstances.com 🙄 Anyway, all this to say, if you could still help out with Peril tomorrow, that would be great. We appreciate you so much!"

Cruz suddenly flinched. "Another message just came in." He handed her the phone, but she waved him off.

"You can read it," Deandra said, a little concerned that Quinn was still awake—or maybe she'd never gotten to sleep.

Cruz scanned the message, then read it out loud. "I hope this doesn't wake you up, but I couldn't sleep. Peril didn't talk much when I got home. He was very affectionate, though. It's like he could tell I had a rough day and knew better than to make me talk about it. It's helping me miss Ru a little less. Anyway, he's curled up on Ru's pillow right now. Sometimes Peril talks in his sleep. He just said, 'Axil Romano.' Should I assume you and Peril discussed what happened?"

Deandra's stomach flipped, and she let loose a world-weary sigh.

Cruz was quiet for several long seconds. Hesitantly, he asked, "Are you worried Quinn is going to be upset you told Peril too many scary details?" His tone implied that he could tell that she was filled with a minor sense of dread but couldn't fathom why. "Quinn seems like a fairly levelheaded person. It's not as if you told a child inappropriate things. Peril, despite what ASA might think, is an adult with his own agency. *He's* the one who decides what's too much information for him to handle."

"It's not that. I honestly think Quinn will be happy Peril knows—not necessarily because she'll be grateful that she doesn't have to tell him all this herself, but because Peril is comfortable enough with me that we had full-on conversations." Deandra paused, staring out at the dark, quiet town beyond Cruz's fenced-in yard. "I'm worried that, even if Peril doesn't intend to tell his parents about Havoc while he's conscious, he can't really control what he does when he's asleep."

Cruz leaned against her shoulder. "I didn't think of that. For what it's worth, the Greenwoods don't seem like the type to go blabbing other people's business all over town. Even if Havoc's secret *is* pretty big—especially for people like them. Fae fauna is to me what fae flora is to them."

They fell quiet for a while.

"So this might sound awful …" Deandra said, trailing off.

"Say it anyway."

"What if there really *is* something sketchy in Rularo's past, and that's why he's currently holed up in the station right now? What if there's a connection between him and Conrad they're trying to hide?"

Cruz wrapped an arm around her shoulders and kissed her temple. "Okay. Be honest. Do you *really* think Rularo is a bad guy who would throw Havoc to the wolves to save his own hide. Split second decision. First answer."

"No," she said without hesitation, her shoulders slumping as she leaned against him.

"So what are you actually worried about then?"

She thought about that for a while. "It feels like I lose more and more ground on who knows Havoc's secret every day, and it's getting harder to control. Peril literally seeing *through* the glamour really threw me for a loop. I didn't even know that was possible. What if there are people who have the same ability that I don't know about? The wrong person could see what Havoc really is while we're out for a walk or something and use that information against him." She shrugged, still pressed to his side. "I guess I'm just anxious in general."

"And anxiety is always worse at three in the morning, too," Cruz said.

Truth.

Deandra asked, "Speaking of anxiety, do you think it would help or hurt Quinn's if I called her right now?"

"I vote help."

Nodding, she said, "Okay. I think I'll need to pace for this one."

"No worries. I'll be here when you're done."

She got up, then turned around and bent down to quickly kiss him. "Thank you."

He smiled up at her. "Not sure what I did, but I'll take it. And you're welcome. I'm great."

Laughing and rolling her eyes, she walked away, dialing Quinn as she slowly walked down the pathway that bisected Cruz's dog toy–covered lawn.

"Dee?" Quinn asked breathlessly after two rings. "Hi. Are you okay? What happened? Did you somehow get news before I did?" The sound of a door gently closing sounded in the background.

"Oh gosh. Sorry. I didn't mean to scare you. I probably should have sent a warning text first. I just couldn't sleep, either."

Quinn fell quiet, and the silence felt heavy somehow.

"So … about your last text," Deandra said, needing to break the tension. "Peril, uh, kind of knows, you know, everything? He's very intimidating when he wants to be. I think it's because he has a more extensive vocabulary than most *people*."

Quinn burst into tears.

"Oh no. Quinn. Wait. What did I say?"

"He … talked to you … in … full sentences?" Quinn blubbered.

Deandra, stifling a laugh, told Quinn all about her investigation session with Peril. Quinn, as she'd guessed, was delighted that she and Peril had bonded so quickly, even if the reasons for it were less than ideal. She also didn't sound noticeably cross that Deandra had used her laptop or had briefly snooped through her email inbox, either.

"Gosh," Quinn said, sniffling, "I really wish I knew more about the hierarchy within ASA. It's wild to think that this Axil Romano person once held a high office in the organization. I wonder if Axil knew about Peril. That post was from two years ago, you said? He was calling ASA a great organization back then, so I would assume he shared the belief that someone owning a salica is an insult to their kind.

"I feel like Axil wouldn't have booked the tattoo if he knew about the adoption. Because of the rarity of salica in general, news of the adoption really seemed to set ASA off. When we picked up Peril, there were at least fifteen ASA members out front. It was the most I'd ever seen outside that clinic, and we'd been there several times during the adoption process."

Deandra chewed on the inside of her cheek. "I guess it's possible that Axil did some last-minute research on Rularo and jumped ship when he didn't like what he found. Do you have anything on your website about Peril?"

"Nope. We do what we can to keep our personal life private. Neither one of us likes social media much. We only have accounts for the store, since showing my stationery products and Ru's artwork are the best tools in our advertising arsenal."

"Were there articles written about the adoption?" Deandra asked.

"Hmm. One or two, I think. The clinic obviously wants people to know it exists, since that's the only way they can stay open, but they don't let reporters into the building. There were pictures of Peril on the website when he was up for adoption, as well as what little history is known about him, but they specifically asked us if we were okay with leaving that information up, or if we'd prefer it to be taken down. Peril is still so sensitive about his past, we asked them to remove him from the site. As far as I know, they did."

Deandra mulled that over. "One thing that keeps bugging me …" she said, then chuckled sardonically to herself. "Okay, there's more than one thing. But … when Jet turned toward us—after he said it was no coincidence that their demonstration was happening outside your tent—he called out Juniper, too."

"Oh yeah," Quinn said. "He accused Juniper's family of being animal smugglers and friends of unscrupulous breeders or something, right? What an awful thing to say! The Thistlewicks are such kind goblins."

Briefly debating whether she should broach the subject, given how protective she was about Havoc's secrets, Deandra said, "Juniper claims those *aren't* rumors. I don't think for a second that Juniper or Kira have done any of those things, but it's apparently true that Juniper's family once did. What I'm wondering is … where are Jet and the rest of ASA getting their information? The Thistlewicks' history, your adoption of Peril, and even the case of the pixie dying in one of the grimalkyne's cages, is all information they'd have to do a lot of digging to find.

"I get that they're doing research on people they're harassing, but it seems so … involved. They've also vandalized buildings owned by Juniper and the grimalkyne, attacking when the business is just being established so security is light or nonexistent. Their MO seems to be creating big distractions so that someone from within their ranks can sneak in the back and cause trouble when no one is looking."

Quinn choked back a sob. "If that's really the case, it's *so* cruel that they were willing to kill Conrad just to make a point, or seek revenge, or whatever they're doing."

Deandra's already tired, itchy eyes welled up again. She couldn't break down and set Quinn off even more. She sniffed once, willing the tears pricking the backs of her eyes not to fall. "Agreed."

Yawning, Quinn said, "I think talking this out helped. I still don't know what the heck is going on. I can't even entertain the possibility that they're going to lock Ru away for murder *and* drug manufacturing. If they took the time to get to know him, they'd know how completely ridiculous this all is. I'll just keep my head down, work the festival as planned, and believe that Ru will be let out in the morning because he *didn't do anything wrong.* Whoever is doing this to us won't win. They can't. I won't survive it."

"They won't," Deandra said with an air of confidence she didn't quite believe but hoped Quinn did. "The werecats will figure it out. ACSI is working on it, too. Officer Sutter is a very fair person. If I was caught up in something like this, she's someone I'd want on the case. So you go do your thing at the festival tomorrow, and I'll do some more sleuthing with Peril. He seemed to enjoy it. I think having something to do keeps him from spiraling. And he *does* like his puzzles—even figurative ones."

Quinn sounded like she might be crying again. "Thanks again, Dee."

When Deandra hung up and headed back toward Cruz, she found him slumped over on the porch steps at a very awkward angle, snoring. And here she'd thought Havoc slept in weird positions. She gently shook him awake, and they crept back inside.

Standing on the coffee table with a piece of pizza crust in her mouth was Maxine. The grease-splattered pizza box lid was flipped all the way open now. Her eyes bugged.

"Maxine Lilith Caddel!" Cruz whisper-hissed. "Drop it!"

Max, her eyes as wide as saucers, gobbled the crust down as if it were a spaghetti noodle.

"Lilith, huh?" Deandra asked him.

"I'm giving the whole full-name thing a try when she's in trouble. It lets her know I mean business."

Maxine quickly snatched up the last discarded pizza crust.

Cruz groaned. "And Lilith seemed fitting, what with Maxine being a *demon.*"

Max barked once, tail wagging so hard it was going in a circle.

She sniffed the inside of the now-empty box, apparently got breadcrumbs up her nose, and sneezed so violently she fell off the coffee table.

Something thudded to the floor somewhere behind Max. Reluctantly, Deandra looked around her to find Havoc with an entire slice of pizza in his mouth. What had hit the floor was a chunk of cold cheese. He'd apparently helped himself to the pizza box that Cruz had left on *top* of the refrigerator, as placing things on counters to keep them out of the reach of your counter-surfing dog wasn't terribly effective when your dog was actually a flying dragon.

Havoc shriek-barked upon Deandra spotting him near the ceiling, which sent the rest of the pizza slice careening to the floor, where it landed with a splat.

Deandra's shoulders sagged. At least Cruz had hardwood floors and not white carpets. "I'll get the duffel bag of tennis balls."

Maxine, who was snuffling around *under* the coffee table now, unleashed a howl of joy at her favorite phrase. She hadn't found the slice Havoc dropped on the other side of the room yet.

Cruz sighed. "And I'll start the coffee."

Since the following day was Saturday, Deandra didn't have to look after any of her usual charges. Cruz had to work until two, and then he would meet her to help out in the Mythic Pet Kitchen booth around three. Up until last night, she'd thought her Saturday morning would be blissfully lazy.

Unfortunately, somewhere between bites of pizza and cheesy breadsticks and random crying jags, Deandra had gotten a text from Wendy last night asking—nay, *pleading*—for morning-shift help at Heather's booth because Otis was out sick. Deandra wondered if the guy was *actually* sick, or if he was just sick of

Heather. Wendy had her bets on the latter. Madison, by some miracle, was still employed, consistently showing up on time, and hadn't broken down in tears yet. But it was all hands on deck in the store, and Heather couldn't spare anyone else for the festival.

Deandra agreed, of course. Because Deandra was a sucker.

And because Wendy offered her another free dinner. Deandra realized that she was as easy to bribe with food as all her animal companions …

Cruz and Deandra took Max and Havoc on a long walk around his neighborhood first thing in the morning. Afterward, he headed off to work, and she went home to drop off Havoc. Wendy had already been at the booth for an hour by then. Though Deandra was exhausted thanks to the "dogs" being amped up until five this morning, Havoc was currently sufficiently worn out. He'd no doubt sleep the day away on the couch while Deandra tried to survive day two of the festival on caffeine and sheer force of will.

It was nine a.m. when she reached the Heather's Elixirs booth, and she'd yet to receive another update from Quinn about whether or not Rularo had been released from werecat custody.

Since Wendy had only gotten part of the Greenwood story so far, Deandra regaled Wendy with all the sordid details of yesterday's fiasco, in between the trickle of early morning festival shoppers. The only part she left out was Peril knowing Havoc was a dragon. The main reason for the exclusion was because Deandra didn't want to be overheard. Plus, a small part of her feared Wendy might be offended that yet another person could see Havoc's true form when she couldn't, even if in this case it wasn't because Peril had been let into the pod.

"Excuse me," a woman said, startling the cousins out of their conversation.

Tables ran along the inside edge of the tent on three sides, allowing shoppers to walk in and peruse the many items on offer as if the booth were a miniature version of the brick-and-mortar store.

The new customer stood by a table on the right side of the tent holding a bar of soap in each hand. "Which one of these would work best to ward off evil spirits?"

Deandra cocked her head. She'd learned on day one in Axia not to make any assumptions, even when completely baffled. For all she knew, the woman's question was perfectly reasonable.

"Uhh …" Wendy said. "Those are just mundane soaps, ma'am. One is lavender, and the other is shea butter. They don't have any magical properties. They just smell good."

The woman had long silver hair that fell to her midback in soft waves. She wore a long, flowy gray dress and cloth sandals of the same color. A massive black purse hung from her forearm. She was both ethereal and regal. "Yes, but what smells the *worst* to an evil spirit? I need something that gives them a coughing fit so I can triangulate their location."

Wendy glanced pleadingly at Deandra for help.

Deandra hesitated, then asked, "Can, uh, spirits actually smell anything?"

The woman glowered at Deandra, slammed the soaps back into their basket, and hiked her purse onto her shoulder. "My review of your store will *not* be kind." She stalked off.

Wendy huffed a laugh when the lady was out of sight.

"What did I say?" Deandra asked, bewildered.

"Nothing," Wendy said, still chuckling. "Vending is weird, my friend. Buckle up."

Over the course of the next hour, Deandra was flirted with by a teenage boy who couldn't have been older than fourteen *and* by a guy old enough to be her grandfather, was shown pictures of children and pets for seemingly no reason, and was asked where to find the bathroom by at least five people. A man asked if Heather's Elixirs sold "those sparkly feather boas I saw yesterday." A draken woman asked if Robert's Libations was a vendor this year, as she really liked the zombie cactus water she'd bought two years ago. And she was told a sob story by a man who'd come into the booth looking for a locking talisman, who then ended up telling her about a break-in last month where the robber only stole the condiments out of his fridge and his favorite houseplant.

When the man left with his talisman, Deandra grabbed Wendy by the elbow and pulled her into a back corner of the booth. They were alone for the moment.

"Is the festival always this weird?" Deandra asked.

Wendy cracked up. "*People* are always this weird. You're just getting a concentrated dose right now. At least you didn't have to talk to the dwarf who not only told me about the, and I quote, *rotting pustules* on her feet, but she *showed* them to me so I could better recommend an herbal remedy for her. I wanted to be like, honey, you need a doctor, stat."

Deandra's nose wrinkled. Now she knew what the odd smell had been earlier when she'd been trying to help a woman decide which ten travel-sized lotions to pick, as there were over twenty scents. She'd told herself it was probably the zombie cactus lotion she'd sampled and kept getting a whiff of every time she moved her hands while she spoke—which didn't say much for the lingering aroma of the lotion.

"You didn't deal with weird people at the coffee shop?" Wendy asked.

"Sure. But they were usually more on the rude side than straight-up strange. Though, there *was* the guy who told me that, since I was wearing green on a Thursday, I was more likely to lose my teeth."

Wendy blinked. "Like ... lose all of them at once? Lose them that day?"

"You really think I asked for clarification?"

"Right, right," Wendy said, shaking her head as if mentally chastising herself. "The last time I asked for clarification on a really weird question from a customer, I ended up signing up for a hot yoga class at a place called Swamp Alley. It was run by a bog witch, and the place smelled like old tofu.

"I was convinced during most of that class that I was going to be reduced to a puddle of goo. I assumed the smell of the place was from all the liquefied bodies of the patrons before me who had seeped into the stained, threadbare carpet. I saw sounds. I heard colors. The next day, I felt like I'd been hit by fifteen buses," Wendy said, her expression distant and a little haunted. Then she shrugged, lucidity returning. "Best sleep of my life, though."

Deandra was at a loss again.

"Good morning, ladies."

Thankful for the excuse to not think about stinky Swamp Alley, Deandra turned, a greeting on her lips. Her mouth dried up when her gaze landed on the newly arrived customer.

Holding out a flyer, he said, "I'd like to invite you to our event this afternoon. Tell your friends and colleagues. The more the merrier. It won't be in Oracle Park, as the Axian werecats are cowards who yield to the whims of the weak-spined mayor. Shameful. But the parking lot of the Axian Nights Hotel will suffice for our purposes."

All Deandra could do was stare at him. At his sleek black fur and slightly curved white horns.

Recognition dawned in his strange goat eyes a moment later, and he tucked the flyer under his arm. "You're the one with the dire wolf, aren't you? Friend to the Greenwoods. Friend to Juniper Thistlewick." He gave her an elevator scan before extending his hand. "I don't think we formally met yesterday. I'm Jet Kettle. And you are …"

"Not shaking your hand," Deandra said, crossing her arms instead of reaching for his offered palm. "I'm surprised you're at the festival today after the stunt your group pulled. How's Harold, by the way? You know, your *friend* who you abandoned in a *cage* as soon as the werecats showed up?"

Jet dropped his hand to his side. He smiled smugly, revealing two rows of perfect square teeth. "I'll figure out who you are soon enough. I like a challenge. Dire wolves aren't common in the hub system. Rarely does Parks Management allow people to own dire puppies, given how unpredictable they are. How wild. As they should be, as far as I'm concerned. But they should be *in* the wild, not crated in someone's tiny apartment while their captor hocks baubles and foul-scented soaps to fools who think a couple of mundanes know the first thing about magical, well, anything."

He gave her another scan. "In which hub system did you register your dire wolf? Because there isn't one registered in Axia as of this morning, I'll tell you that much."

Deandra *had* sent in that registration form Cruz had started for her a couple of months ago. He'd given it to her on their first date. She'd been trying not to worry too much that she hadn't received Havoc's official registration paperwork. She figured it just took a while to process such things, as was usually the case when jumping through bureaucratic hoops. And yet, things in Axia moved at lightning speed compared to the mundane world. She recalled how quickly Parks Management had acquired a warrant to seize Havoc. Less than a day. They'd even had her name.

Now she wondered if there was a specific reason for the hold-up on Havoc's paperwork—such as an investigation. What if someone from the higher levels of Parks Management showed up in Axia to check out Havoc for themselves?

"Are you just passing through for the festival? Or are you illegally harboring an animal that shouldn't be in your possession?" Jet held up a hand to stop a reply that hadn't been coming. "Don't fret. I'll find out. And if I can't, I'm sure Parks Management will be happy to assist me. Records suggest there was an incident a couple of months ago here in town where a dire wolf was on the suspect list during an arson case. Even if the wolf wasn't ulti-mately blamed for the crime, clearly at least one ranger thought the pup was dangerous. Can't imagine there's more than one fire-aligned dire wolf in this little hub. Your name was redacted, but that's easy enough to find. Sounds like maybe you're not *suited* for being its captor—I can't imagine any *mundane* who would be."

Wendy lunged forward, and Deandra barely got an arm out in time to stop her from attacking him. "You done, goat? If you're not going to buy anything, you can go. Actually, no. We have the right to refuse service to anyone, and this is me refusing."

"There's nothing in here I'd waste my money on." The faun only had eyes for Deandra. "I'll see *you* later—one way or another." He turned on his hoof and left.

Deandra glared in the direction of the retreating faun long after he'd been swallowed up by the crowd.

CHAPTER FOURTEEN

A head poked around the side of the tent. "You ladies all right?"

Deandra tore her furious gaze away from the crowd and toward the woman peeking into the booth. It was Eileen from Enchanted Bite.

"Mostly," Deandra muttered.

Eileen looked left and right, then said something to someone behind her. She hurried into the booth with Deandra and Wendy, long ponytail of box braids swinging. "I would have come to check on you sooner, but I had a potential big fish on the hook. When I saw how that faun marched out of here, I figured he'd said something terrible to you ladies, and I felt bad I let capitalism win earlier. You don't need me to slap anyone on your behalf, do you?"

Deandra laughed despite herself. Eileen reminded her a little of her mom, and she missed her a lot in that moment. If she called her mom and started sobbing, she'd probably take the news of Deandra's sleuthing hobby and her new pet a little better. It might even sway her mom to come visit.

Wendy said, "We're okay. Kicked his little goat butt out of here."

"I reported that brute to the werecats on Thursday," Eileen said. "And then I heard he was part of that group that was doing some kind of interpretive dance or something where someone got hurt? I don't know. The details from the rumor mill are fuzzy. But if that faun was in the middle of it, I'm not surprised that whatever it was went bad."

"What happened on Thursday that made you report him?" Deandra asked, wondering what on earth ASA was doing here on Thursday when the vendors weren't even set up yet. Then again, someone from ASA more than likely had let out Frankenswine, so ASA's little minions were definitely in the area that day.

"This is gonna require some back story. Bear with me. We told my daughter that when she turned sixteen, she could have a pet. The agreement was that she had to pay for it herself with her allowance money and all the responsibility was hers." She paused. "I promise this is related to the malevolent goat. So a few days after her sweet sixteen, my daughter tells us that she wants a hamster. There's a pet store she walks past on the way home from school every day, and there was a hamster in there she'd fallen in love with. Great, I thought. Hamsters are small and low maintenance. It meant that if she fell down on her duties, my husband and I wouldn't suddenly have a dog we needed to walk every morning at five a.m. before work like the suckers we are. About a week later, she tells us she officially decided she'll buy the hamster on the way home from school, as well as all the supplies, and she'll even get it home on her own. My baby is taking care of business, I thought."

She shot Deandra and Wendy a *look* that made them both laugh.

"My precious baby girl, who I love with my whole heart, forgot to mention until she got the adorable ball of fluff home that this was a *magic-touched* hamster. A sticky-foot hamster, to be precise. As in, a hamster that was descended from *Spider-Man* and can climb vertically up walls like a dang gecko with the speed of a cheetah. This hamster cannot be contained by mundane cages. It can barely be contained by *magical* ones.

"Chews through plastic. Gnaws through those thin metal bars as if they're made of butter. Mister Flash is a night owl and likes to make his great escapes in the wee hours. When I tell you ladies that nothing in life prepares you for waking up thanks to a hamster falling on your face from where it was previously stuck to the ceiling by its feet? Believe me.

"My husband was not prepared—as no one would be. *I* was not prepared for the way that man screamed bloody murder when the hamster landed on his face. So I screamed bloody murder. My older brother, who was staying with us at the time, came charging into the room with a baseball bat, sure someone had broken in and was doing us great harm."

Wendy was snort-laughing under her breath. Deandra had tucked her lips over her teeth to keep her reaction in check. Her eyes watered from the effort.

With a knowing smile, Eileen continued. "Just last week, we found a company that makes cages specifically for magic-touched and fae animals. Mister Flash is given free rein of the house during the day. But at night, when he can no longer control his invasive thoughts, he needs to be caged up. He's never been able to bust out of that cage. Absolute miracle.

"Fast forward to Thursday, and my daughter, Ricki, well before you started setting up this booth on Thursday, was walking around taking it all in. She stumbled on a booth run by three grimalkyne who sell those *same* incredible magic cages. In fact, it's the same company. The cages are *very* expensive but worth their weight in gold, let me tell you. I happily gave her extra cash to buy a bigger cage for Mister Flash. That very cage was sitting in the corner of the tent when that nasty faun stopped by on Thursday while we were setting up."

Deandra asked, "Did he want to buy fruit puffs or something?"

Eileen shook her head. "At first, I figured he was a vendor, so I was planning to offer him one of our vendor discounts. But then he started asking a bunch of questions. He had someone with him —an elf, I think. She had a clipboard and was scribbling stuff on it. He asked how long we'd been in business, if we were based out of Axia, if this was our first festival—all normal enough stuff to ask.

"Then he asked if we were full-blooded mundane, which isn't necessarily a rude question, you know, but it's borderline. And I didn't appreciate his tone. I told him I was, but that my husband is a kitchen witch—you know, unnaturally good with plants? There's never been a paper cut, scraped knee, headache, or stomach bug that man can't cure with one of his herbal remedies and poultices."

Deandra was learning that, when it came to witches, a "kitchen witch" was the most common. Sounded like it was folks who had a green thumb, but on steroids—possibly even more so in the case of Eileen's husband.

"The faun turned to the elf then and said something to her, and she lifted the pages of her notes to pull out a flyer. It sounded like he was planning to invite me to some event or other, but before he fully had the flyer handed to me, he saw that cage. That faun went still as a statue when he saw it. He asked what the cage was for. My daughter was more than happy to talk to him about her beloved hamster.

"She picked up the cage and brought it over to him, showing him the built-in tunnel system, the ladders, the platforms, and told him how the runes etched into the bars kept the hamster from being able to escape at night. She said something along the lines of 'Can't let him roam free at night or he gets into trouble,' and you would have thought she told the faun that we planned to cook that little fluffball up for dinner.

"He went ballistic. Zero to sixty. Screamed at her. Screamed at *me*. Called us names. No one talks to my kid that way. I laid into that goat so bad, he finally tucked his tail and stormed off." Eileen shook her head, face screwed up in disgust. "Ricki didn't break down crying, but it was a near thing. She's a sensitive girl, and she *loves* that hamster. That little menace is living the life, no matter what that awful goat says. Who yells at a child?"

Deandra frowned. "What did the werecats say when you talked to them?"

Eileen rolled her eyes. "Whole bunch of nothing. Said they'd look into it. I guess you can't exactly lock someone up for being a jerk, seeing as a good chunk of the population would end up behind bars."

Wendy said, "Sounds like the werecats are cracking down now, at least."

"How so?" Eileen asked.

"The faun is the leader of ASA—Alliance of Sapient Animals," Deandra said. "They're the ones who held that demonstration yesterday where a gnome was hurt. They're planning another demonstration today, but the werecats banned them from congregating in the park."

Eileen nodded absently. "I guess that's something. The ASA minions were all over the vendor area on Thursday. I talked to at least three other vendors who had run-ins with them, too. Asking a lot of probing, borderline-inappropriate questions, and if they didn't find whatever you said offensive, they invited you to that demonstration.

"One vendor said she'd been setting up alone, so she had to leave her booth unattended while she made runs to and from her car. During one trip, she got back to find a faun in her booth—said he seemed young, just little nubs for horns. Anyway, the vendor sells homemade pet treats that have mild magic-enhancing additives. Anxiety control, calm dreams, joint pain relief—stuff like that. The faun was looking through one of her pamphlets that detailed the nature of the magic additives, so at first she thought he was a fellow vendor. But when she said hi, the faun screamed, tossed the pamphlet on the ground, and sprinted out of the back of the tent like his fur was on fire."

"Weird," Deandra said.

Eileen nodded. "Anyway. Sorry for the verbal vomit. I really *did* feel guilty that I left you two to fend for yourselves with the faun when I'd already had a bad experience with him ..."

Deandra asked, "I gotta know ... did you reel in the deal on the big order?"

Eileen grinned, though she clearly tried not to. "I did! It's with a mom-and-pop shop who has a section of their store dedicated to goods made by small businesses like mine. Could turn into a monthly gig."

"Nice," Deandra said. "No hard feelings. Promise. And I appreciate you checking up on us."

"Can I pay down my guilt by giving you a bag of fruit puffs?" Eileen asked.

With a level of enthusiasm that was frankly embarrassing, Deandra asked, "Do you have more strawberry?"

Wendy whimpered, "Please say no. I ate half a bag in record time. It was scary. Delicious, but scary."

Amused, Eileen said, "Good news, bad news. I sold out of the strawberry yesterday. Happened even faster than last year. My husband is actually trying to get a few more batches done today so we can have them tomorrow. Poor man is working overtime back at home and doesn't even get to experience the festival today. Anyway, our second and third best sellers are black cherry and peach. I'll give you ladies one of each."

"Can we at least pay you half?" Deandra asked Eileen's retreating back.

The woman flapped a hand, waving off the question. She was back a few seconds later with the promised bags.

"By the way," Eileen said to Deandra, "we changed out the label on the zombie cactus fruit puffs to kale klusters, and ... they sold out!"

"No way!" Deandra said, laughing, then realized a moment later that it might have been a rude response.

Eileen lightly elbowed her arm, chuckling. "Right? Those things were *nasty*! I would have called them a loss and tossed them all out if it wasn't for your suggestion. So these bags are on me. I appreciate you."

"*Mooooom! The card reader is acting up again!*" came a frantic call from next door.

Eileen's eyes went wide. "Gotta go! Nice chatting with you ladies. You need me to kick any goat butt, you know where to find me!" Then she hustled off.

A new wave of strange customers swept in a few minutes later.

The worst thing that came out of the next few hours at the booth was that, even though she and Wendy were very busy, Deandra still managed to eat almost half a bag of the black cherry fruit puffs. She considered the very real, very sad possibility that, much like the mom-and-pop shop, Deandra might need to start a monthly order.

DEANDRA HAD JUST MADE IT TO HER CAR IN HER GRANDPARENTS' driveway when her phone rang. She expected it to be Cruz, as he should be getting off work soon. She was pleasantly surprised to be wrong.

Practically flinging herself into the driver's seat and closing the door, she hit Accept.

"Rularo! Hi! Are you okay?"

The big man chuckled. "Quinny answered the phone the same way. I'm fine. The werecats released me about half an hour ago. I was mostly calling to let you know you don't have to check on Peril midday. I went straight home after the cats let me out because I was starving." He paused, then laughed. "Yes, yes, I wanted to see my boy, too."

"*Hello, Deandra!*" came a distant, tinny greeting from the ferret.

She laughed. "Hi, Peril. Do you still need an early evening visit, Ru? Quinn said if you got released today, the cats would likely tell you to go back to business as usual."

"Guess I shouldn't be surprised you ladies already talked logistics. Granted, I'm not exactly firing on all cylinders at the moment."

Deandra frowned. "Have you been cleared of the accusations, then?"

"Yes and no. They haven't found any evidence from the booth or the shop that we're in possession of raw shatterberry, or any ink with a shatterberry potency above the limit we're permitted to have. I have no idea if they think I'm Conrad's ... if they think I purposely ..." He sighed. "I don't know if I'm their number one suspect for murder. Goddess above, I still can't believe that happened. I've never actually seen shatterberry poisoning in person. It was ... awful."

"Agreed," Deandra said, the image of Conrad thrashing on the ground easy to conjure.

"Anyway, I haven't told Quinny this part yet, since I just got off the phone with Officer Sutter, but they're working on getting a warrant for the house next. I suspect they're going to seize our computers too, to try to find any searches or purchases of shatterberry on the arcane web."

Deandra's heart rate doubled, trying to remember if she and Peril's sleuthing session had included anything about shatterberry.

Rularo chuckled. "If you're worried about your search history on the laptop while you and Peril were playing detective, don't be. Peril already told me about it. Glad you two found something to bond over."

There was a bit of rustling on Rularo's side of the call, and then Peril's voice rang out so loud in her ear, she pulled the phone away. She put her phone on speaker too and laid it on her thigh.

Rularo said, "Not so close to the speaker, Peril! We need to work on your phone etiquette."

"Hello, Deandra. Hello. Hi. Can you hear me?"

"Hi, Peril."

"Oh good. Yes, hello. I have a bit of news! Not even Father knows this yet. Mother set me up with the tablet late last night, because neither of us could sleep much, and I resumed my internet investigation!"

"I am intrigued," Deandra said.

"I am apprehensive," said Rularo. "I know you think we limit your true crime viewing because you're … uh, excitable, but it's because of the Zodiac killer incident."

"Water under the bridge. Why bring up old news, Father?"

"It was last year."

Peril coughed awkwardly.

"You were so convinced you knew the killer's identity after bingeing documentaries and researching for a month that you emailed *thirty-five* reporters, Peril. Someone was calling my cell phone—the number of which you gave without permission, I'll remind you—day and night begging for an in-person interview. I had to change my number! For as smart as you are, I'm still amazed you overlooked the slight issue of a mundane reporter living in the mundane world being able to interview *a talking ferret in a hub.*"

Peril coughed again.

"Oh no," Deandra said, laughing. "Did I make you fall off the true-crime wagon, Peril? You framed this all a little differently to me …"

"Do you want to hear my news or not?" Peril asked, clearly miffed.

"Proceed," Rularo said. "But if this gets out of hand, I'm changing the passwords. Again."

"Yeah, yeah," said Peril. "So! I ended up deep in the weeds on Quarrel."

"On what now?" Deandra asked.

"It's similar to the mundane Reddit," Rularo explained. "Kind of like a message board. Lots of niche discussions happen on there. It's, incidentally, where Peril spent a lot of his time when he was searching for the Zodiac killer."

Peril apparently chose to ignore that comment. "There's a Major Quarrel about ASA, and then a veritable mountain of Minor Quarrels within it. I found a Skirmish that was active as recently as this week about the relationship between Jet and Axil over the years. Turns out, Axil had been Jet's mentor. Apparently one of the 'secret' ways ASA recruits members is by volunteering at troubled youth facilities. They search for magic-touched and fae youth— specifically ones who feel stifled by the hub system and are mad there's a whole world out there they'll never get to see because they're too different."

Deandra said, "The ones who feel like the hub system is a cage."

"Right. ASA recruits them, fosters their hatred of the system that's locked them behind veils, and then gives that hatred a direction. All this comes from Quarrelers who were sharing stories of friends and loved ones who got pulled in by ASA. Quite a few of these already-troubled kids got thrown into centers for wayward fae youth because they were caught committing minor, and sometimes major, property damage in ASA's name."

Rularo said, "I know not all ASA members are terrible people, but hearing stuff like this makes it harder not to think that."

Peril made a noncommittal *hmm* noise. "Jet, as you might have guessed, was one of those troubled fae youths Axil plucked from a detention center. From what I've been able to find, it sounds like Axil started working with ASA ten years ago and rose through the ranks quickly. Jet joined about two years later, which makes the goat about twenty-five years old. The two were very close. Though it sounds like once Jet was older and making a name for himself within the organization, the relationship became strained."

"Is Axil a faun, too?" Deandra asked, wanting a mental picture in her head of this phantom person she only knew by name.

"I'm getting there," Peril said. "Don't ruin the reveal!"

Rularo groaned. "Do you have all the info laid out in your head like a *Dateline* episode again? Get the audience to think one thing in the first half, then pull a switcheroo in the second that makes all their assumptions fly out the window?"

Peril's prolonged pause spoke to a twinge of embarrassment. "I'm a riveting storyteller, Father!"

Deandra bit back a laugh.

"As I was saying! The relationship between Axil and Jet became fraught over the years. There are conflicting accounts from many Quarrelers, leaving me puzzled as to which account is true. Some say Axil became too extreme in his ideas about ASA's future, and that's what ultimately led to the board voting him out —not that he left voluntarily. Others say it was *Jet* who was too extreme, and that the board bullied Axil out because he kept trying to stifle Jet's out-of-the-box thinking."

"I obviously don't know either one of them," Deandra said, "but I've at least interacted with Jet one-on-one. That guy is terrible. I'm Team Axil, just because I'm absolutely *not* Team Jet."

"Seeing as I'm pretty sure Jet is the one who clocked me in the head with a rotting cabbage," Rularo said, "I'm not that guy's biggest fan, either."

"You two interested in a conspiracy theory?" Peril asked in a fittingly conspiratorial tone.

"Ah, here's the ol' switcheroo," Rularo said.

"Hush, Father," Peril said, though he sounded a touch amused. "*Way* down in the Minor Quarrel about Jet and Axil is a Skirmish about how strange it is that Axil has very little online presence. One theory is that he used to have one but scrubbed it after the falling out with ASA. All accounts suggest Axil has a pretty big ego and likes being the center of attention, at least in person. But from what anyone can tell, there are no photos of him. What social media he *does* have doesn't even have a profile picture, and posts are sporadic. Across the whole Major Quarrel, people have mentioned numerous times that they don't remember the last time he was seen in public. My question is: How would anyone outside of ASA even know what he looks like if he doesn't post much online and hasn't for years?"

Deandra grew antsy, realizing now that the sneaky little ferret was absolutely building to a big reveal and was drawing this out to keep his audience—all two of them—on their toes.

"Now that you mention it," Deandra said, "his Picayune profile picture was just the default gray circle with a newspaper icon in the middle, right?"

"Yep," Peril said. "More than one Quarreler in this buried discussion said they have it on good authority that who everyone refers to as Axil Romano is actually someone else entirely."

"*Who?*" Deandra asked, immediately annoyed with herself that Peril had so thoroughly sucked her into his story.

"A shifter who has been trying to stay out of the limelight for a while because of his many previous run-ins with the law. There are rumors there are actually warrants out for his arrest in several hubs, and that's why he's been MIA for years," Peril said. "One *very* active poster across the Master Quarrel thinks 'Axil Romano' is actually an anagram."

Rularo blurted, "*Of what?*"

At least she wasn't the only one who had been sucked in.

Deandra imagined the ferret standing a little straighter as he said, "Lionax Orma."

Wait.

She knew that name. Where did she know that name? Lionax. Shifter. In trouble with the law. "Oh. Wait. Um ...the ... gosh, what was he again?" she asked herself, thunking herself lightly in the forehead a few times as she willed her memory to kick out the right word. "Oh! Unicorn shifter, right? One of the original founders of ASA?"

"Ding, ding!" Peril said.

Neela's words replayed in her head. *"It's hard to know if ASA has been growing bolder and more violent again as an organization because they've found their footing, if they're becoming more frustrated with their perceived lack of success, or—most worrying—that Lionax is back, a decade after he disappeared from the public eye, and is possibly even more unbalanced."*

Rularo came to a conclusion before Deandra's whirling thoughts could get there. "Oh. *Oh.* Okay, let's say that this conspiracy theory is right, and Axil Romano and Lionax Orma are the same guy. Shatterberry ink would have been *devastating* to a unicorn shifter. I'm talking possibly-fatal-in-a-matter-of-thirty-seconds devastating. Shatterberry is incredibly poisonous to shifters in general and ungulate shifters in particular.

"That's something any hoofed shifter or hoofed sapient would know. I know 'shatterberry' is probably not something you'd ever heard of before this weekend, Dee, but for shifters, it's the equivalent of a mundane with a severe peanut allergy needing to check the menu at every restaurant they go to. Hoofed shifters have to check clothing labels and the labels on any magical consumables. Shatterberry is highly regulated, but it's fatal to them, so that's not the kind of thing you want to be lax on double-checking. When you two were snooping on my laptop, did you try to read Axil's intake form?"

Deandra's cheeks burned. The fact that Peril had coerced her into trying to open a locked folder made her feel awful. The love of the hunt couldn't be allowed to turn into her prying into people's private lives. Sure, she and Peril had been poking around online for anything they could find about Axil, but they'd only been looking at publicly available information as well as information Axil had posted himself. That was all fair game. Locks, however, were there for a reason.

"I tried a couple of passwords last night to no avail," Peril said.

The ferret clearly didn't feel the same way about privacy. Which didn't make her feel any better about him knowing Havoc's secret.

"*This* is why we rotate passwords, you nosy ferret," Rularo said, laughing.

Deandra realized that those vague "reasons" the Greenwoods had for maintaining security had less to do with worrying about hackers and more to do with a sapient ferret with an unquenchable thirst for knowledge.

Rularo said, "Axil stated on his form that he's an ungulate shifter."

"Aha!" Deandra and Peril said in unison.

"He even asked me if shatterberry was going to be used the day of his tattoo, and if so, what safety precautions we employ to make sure there's no cross contamination."

"Oh dang," Deandra said. "So are we thinking the person who snuck in to add shatterberry to the ink thought they were poisoning Axil-slash-Lionax and somehow didn't know he was a no-show?"

"If that's the case, it couldn't have been anyone in ASA, right?" Peril asked. "Anyone familiar with ASA would know who Axil-slash-Lionax is, so when they snuck in, they'd know Conrad wasn't him."

Dang it. Deandra had been ready to fling open her car door, march over to the police station, and tell Officer Sutter she was sure the poisoner was Jet. After all, as a fellow ungulate, Jet would know shatterberry would prove fatal.

And even if Jet and Axil were no longer communicating, there were ways Jet could have found out about Axil planning to attend the festival. ASA members had been poking around tents as early as Thursday. Deandra had easily flipped through the Greenwoods' appointment book, so someone else could have, too. Could someone have seen Axil's name in the Greenwoods' appointment book and recognized his alias?

ASA had first announced the demonstration on Thursday. Would someone like Jet throw together an elaborate demonstration in front of the Greenwoods' tent just to provide cover for one of his minions to sneak in and take out one of ASA's former leaders?

Deandra thought it unlikely. Not to mention that Jet, of all people, would have seen Conrad and known Axil wasn't in the booth at his scheduled time.

As Peril had told her the other day, this theory had too many variables.

"Still there, Dee?" Rularo asked.

"Still here," she said, feeling a little dejected that she couldn't pin the whole thing on Jet, get justice for Conrad Osgood, save the Greenwoods from further stress, and call it a day.

Peril's last comment looped in her mind. *"Anyone familiar with ASA would know who Axil-slash-Lionax is ..."*

"Did you happen to find any old photos of Lionax, Peril? If Lionax and Conrad look nothing alike, it would even further suggest that the killer wasn't someone from ASA." Deandra was fairly certain Peril would have searched high and low for everything he could find about Lionax online once he learned the unicorn shifter's name—assuming there was anything left to find. If Lionax had gone out of his way to create a new identity to distance himself from the one with a murder charge tied to it, he might have found ways to thoroughly bury much of the old him. "I figure once that conspiracy theory took root in your head, there was no stopping it from growing out of control."

Rularo boomed a laugh. "She knows you so well already!"

"Yes, yes," Peril said, half annoyed and half distracted. "I only managed to find a few, and they're not the best quality—as if they're pictures of a picture. One is an old staff photo from the ASA website, and the other two appear to be group photos taken at what very well could be ASA holiday parties. Father, can you send these to her somehow?"

There was some rustling on the other end of the line, muffled conversation, and the sound of Rularo's thumbs tapping on his phone screen. Deandra scanned the rearview mirror. Both sides of her grandparents' street were lined with cars, and the sidewalks were crammed with people either coming from or going to the festival. Even from this distance, she could make out the faint sound of music. It was relatively early, but it was already clear today would be a magnitude busier than it had been yesterday. Hopefully that meant she, Cruz, and Havoc could work their magic to get those last two vibrissa cats homes.

"Okay, Dee, I just sent the pictures to your phone," Rularo said.

Her phone buzzed on her thigh a few seconds later. The three pictures were, as Peril said, not the best quality, but the staff photo was clear enough. Lionax was a handsome guy in his thirties or so, at least according to her human eyes. If Neela was right, Lionax was actually one hundred and twenty years old, meaning he'd ended up here *during* the Glitch. As in, he'd only been a few years old when he'd found himself in an unfamiliar realm just before the door had shut behind him for good. He'd been part of a herd, but now there were only ten of them left. Did the remaining unicorn shifters in this realm include his parents? Siblings?

Maybe someone like Lionax didn't just consider the hub system, but the entire realm, a cage he couldn't break out of. Then, to add insult to injury, sometime after getting marooned here, he'd wound up trapped in his own body, never able to shift into his ungulate form again. If he'd lost a bit of his sanity—or even most of it—in light of all that, Deandra wasn't sure she could blame him.

She studied his photos a bit more. Despite being fae, on the surface, Lionax looked mundane. His hair was a coppery russet brown, and while it was short, appeared to possess effortless waves. She wondered if his mane would have been the same color. He had a short beard, a nice smile, and brown eyes.

The group photos suggested he was taller than most of the others who were grouped around him, but not by a wide margin. One arm slung around the shoulder of the man next to him bore several tattoos. They were colorful, but he was too far from the camera for Deandra to make out any of the designs.

When comparing her memory of Conrad to the man in the photos, it was clear they were different people, if only because Lionax's features were obviously younger. But if someone unfamiliar with Lionax had been sent into the InkCraft tent with the task of adding shatterberry ink to an ink cup at around six fifteen and then getting back out as fast as possible, seeing a brown-haired man with a sleeve of tattoos might have been all the confirmation the killer had needed that they were in the right place—especially since Conrad's back had been facing the tent's interior, as everyone had been distracted by the ASA demonstration.

"Do you see a resemblance?" came Peril's voice. "I didn't get the opportunity to meet Conrad, so I don't know how the two compare."

Deandra didn't miss the hint of bitterness in his tone, but she did ignore it. She repeated her thoughts out loud.

"I agree," said Rularo. "Side by side, I'd say it would be hard to confuse the two. But they have the same basic body type and coloring, and both have living ink. I can tell from the color composition in Lionax's pieces that they're living-ink art, even if you obviously can't see movement in a still. Without close scrutiny, I'd say one could pass for the other."

Deandra chewed the inside of her cheek. "So the two main possibilities are, one, someone was targeting Axil-slash-Lionax but wasn't familiar enough with him to know it wasn't him at first glance, or two, someone is trying to discredit Ru, and the ASA part is mere coincidence. In either case, the person—whether they did it themself or coerced or bribed someone to do it for them—

had to not only know what shatterberry is, but where to find raw extract, *and* have a means to add it to an ink cup."

"I'd be willing to bet," said Rularo, "that they also knew Axil is a shifter. If they wanted to severely injure or kill whoever was on the table during the six-fifteen appointment slot, there are easier substances to get a hold of. Even mundane arsenic can make an elephantine fae sick if you use enough of it. Shatterberry, though? Shatterberry is personal."

Deandra mulled all that over, intrigued by the mystery but still unsure what to make of it. She eyed the time on her dashboard. It was just after one. Now that she didn't have to check on Peril, all she had to do was go home to grab Havoc—who was clear on the other side of town—and then circle back here. Even though she didn't love yo-yoing across town, she at least had a guaranteed parking spot in her grandparents' driveway.

"Well, as fun as this all was," Deandra said, "I should probably get going. I'll see you a little later this evening, okay, Peril?"

"Uh … I had a request," the ferret said hesitantly. "I will likely keep, you know, researching this, and I was wondering if it would be okay to text you if I happen across anything interesting before I see you this evening. My parents will be busy with the festival and keeping an eye out for poison-wielding assassins. I figure you'll have more downtime and can possibly chat about any new discoveries."

An alarm bell went off in Deandra's head, but she couldn't have said why. Peril usually sounded a bit hesitant, regardless of the subject matter, but there was something even cagier than usual about his tone.

Rularo either didn't pick up on it or didn't find it particularly noteworthy. "If that's something she agrees to, you have to promise not to blow up her phone all day. You already have restricted permission with us because you abused the privilege one time too many."

Grumbling, Peril said, "Most fathers applaud their children's passions."

"There's passion, and then there's obsession," Rularo said. "Plus, as adorable as your paws are, they produce epic typos that are only made worse by autocorrect."

His last comment, she knew, was more of an indirect warning to Deandra. Now she felt apprehensive for a whole new reason. Even still, she said, "Sure, you can text me, Peril. But if you get out of control, I'm blocking you."

Peril gasped.

Laughing, she told them she'd talk to them later. Rularo said he'd get her phone number loaded into the texting app on Peril's tablet before he headed out to the festival.

After hanging up, Deandra checked the messages she'd missed while on the phone, finding a few from Wendy detailing more weird customer interactions. There was a picture from her grandpa of the Mermaids Club's baked-goods table where a good chunk of the goodies on offer were gone—though her grandma's three cheesecakes were untouched save for a very narrow wedge cut out of one. A small chalkboard sign was propped up near the pies. The visible build-up of chalk residue suggested that messages had been written and erased with great frequency. The message now read "ONLY $0.25 A PIE!"

Not a slice. A whole *pie*.

Deandra wondered how long it would be before the price was dropped to free.

Cruz
It's a Zombie Cactus Festival miracle! I'll be out of the office a little early. I just need to swing home to let Max out for a few minutes and then I can head over. It's such a madhouse, it might actually be better to walk. I'll never find parking in this

Deandra
Better idea! I'm done early, too, so I can come pick you up. 1. It'll save you a walk. 2. I've got princess parking at my grandparents' house. *And* 3. I can get you caught up on the latest. I also agreed to let Peril text me, so consider this your warning that I may decide to chuck my phone out the window, and this could be the last text you ever receive from me

Cruz
Okay, sounds good. But also…WHAT?

Deandra
I don't know how this happened either!

She was seconds from turning on her car when a text came in from an unknown number.

Unknown
Hello, Deirdre. This is Peter.

Deandra blinked at her screen.

Unknown
I meant hi, Dana. This is Percival.

Shoulders sagging with the weight of instant regret, she programmed the number in as Peril.

Deandra
Hi, Peril

Peril
Oh, Goodyear it went thorough! Please forgive any maleficence. My farmer was not wrong when he said my typecast gets Confucius

Resisting the urge to block the ferret immediately, she started up her car and slowly backed out of the driveway. After a drive that took twice as long as usual, Deandra pulled into her parking spot and sighed dramatically—not because of the traffic, but because yet another text notification had popped up on her phone attached to the dash.

There was a little "33" in the corner of the notification bar.

This would no doubt be a very long afternoon …

Deandra, Cruz, and Havoc sat in the car outside her grandparents' house. Deandra had her head pressed to the headrest, her eyes closed. Cruz, presumably, was still holding her phone, as dismayed as she was that the little ferret could text with the frequency of a teenager under the influence of too much caffeine. From the last update Cruz had given her, though, most of the messages remained unintelligible.

"I didn't tell you this last night," Deandra said, eyes still closed, "but Peril told me why he's always mentally screaming when you're in his presence."

She'd originally opted to keep Peril's admission to herself, but the constant barrage of texts had whittled down her loyalty. Cruz at least had the wherewithal to turn off the ringer after the tenth chime in a row when he first got into the car.

Her eyes opened when she heard him adjust his position in the passenger seat. She rolled her head along the headrest until her face was angled toward him. He was watching her expectantly, brows raised. "You can't tell him I told you, okay? He'd surely consider this a betrayal most foul."

"Well *that's* dramatic." Cruz's forehead scrunched. "This almost sounds like he's screaming at me on purpose."

"He is," she said, then told him that Peril thought Cruz was a miscreant mind reader.

Cruz opened his mouth, closed it, opened it again. "Wow. I … wow. I don't even know what to do with this information. So he considers his screams to be protection against a mind probe? Like wearing a tinfoil hat to keep out aliens?"

"Oh, that's a good example. I used the one where people in TV shows run water to make it harder for anyone listening through planted bugs," Deandra said. "But yes."

"Huh," Cruz said. "I've met some paranoid sapient animals, but this is new, even for me."

"Glad I can keep things interesting," she said, gaze shifting to her phone in his hand, where the lock screen had just lit up with another notification. "Is he saying anything of note, or is it just stream of consciousness? No *wonder* his parents took the privilege away …"

"He's got to be lonely," Cruz said, unlocking her phone so he could check the latest wave of messages. "He has the mind of a person, and yet while he's able-bodied, it's safer for him to remain almost exclusively indoors unless he can be tucked into a bag."

"Or a beard," she added.

"Or a beard," he agreed. "He *does* seem happy; Dr. Jasper

thinks so, anyway. But he doesn't have in-person friends. Sounds like he's got several online contacts, but I doubt many of them know he's a talking ferret."

Deandra frowned, now seeing the flood of texts as someone reaching out with all four paws for companionship. "Aw, *man*. Now I feel bad! He … just wants to be my friend, doesn't he?"

"Yep. And I don't see this as desperation, by the way. It's a combination of not having much experience—or desire, honestly—with interacting with anyone other than his parents, and him just … liking you. Ultimately, he's an introvert, but when introverts find their tribe, it can awaken dormant extrovert tendencies." Cruz cut her a look. "I promise I'm not saying you have the social skills of a talking ferret, but I think you two are alike in a lot of ways. You're most comfortable around your people. He is too. So now you're getting love bombed. Nerd bombed?"

As if on cue, three new messages popped up in the open thread, punctuated by a trio of rapid-fire *whooshes*.

"This *is* excessive, though," Cruz said, returning his focus to the phone. "Okay, let's see if we can figure out what he's talking about. By the way, the previous thirty or so were, I think, about an Ed Gein documentary? He texts like my friend's ten-year-old—only a few words per message. We can just *not* talk about the part where a ferret is obsessed with serial killer lore, right?"

"I would prefer that, yeah."

"Good," he said, laughing. "Uhh, okay, he says that he beehives—no, believes—that Axel Rose is in town. Wait, what? Oh. No, he meant Axil Romaine. Romano! Good grief. *Oh!*" The significance of that last part hit them at the same time and they shared a surprised look. "He thinks Axil is in town."

"Safe to assume, then, that Axil is unaware there might have been an assassination attempt?" Deandra asked.

Cruz shrugged. "For all we know, Axil has no idea the shatterberry incident even happened. Maybe he was a no-show because he got sick and can't leave his hotel room."

"Why does Peril think he's in town?"

Cruz refocused on the phone. "So … there's an *Axil R.* who left a comment on the Zombie Cactus Festival Picayune page as recently as an hour ago. Obviously the way Peril recounts this is decidedly incoherent and he used five texts when he only needed one, but I get the gist. I think. The post was about a live band that was starting …" Cruz glanced at the time on the dashboard, "a little over an hour ago. Axil R. commented that if the band's warm-up routine is indicative of what their live set will be like, he recommends going to the food truck circle in the middle of the Oracle Park instead, because the gaggle of screaming children there will drown them out. He also said that he resorted to drinking hard liquor to numb the pain."

"Ouch," Deandra said. "But that's also a good clue. Peril really *is* good at this sleuthing stuff. He and Wendy would be an unstoppable force."

A *whoosh* sounded from the phone.

Cruz read, "The profile pectoral on the Axil R is a unicorn. Europa! We've found him!" He snorted a laugh. "I'm going to start using *Europa!* instead of *Eureka!* upon my many great discoveries."

"Such as?"

Cruz thought long and hard about that. "Europa! Pineapple on pizza is actually delicious!"

She stared at him. "First, that's not a new discovery for you, and second, get out of my car."

He grinned. "You gotta try it! *Really* try it. You'll be yelling Europa in no time."

"You're exceedingly clear on my views that hot fruit on a pizza is an abomination," she said.

"So you *are* still mad about me sneaking a piece of pineapple under a pepperoni?"

"*Yes*, Cruz. I'm still mad. It was ten times worse than the time I bit into a chocolate chip cookie and the chocolate was actually *raisins*. It was a package of cookies! How did a rogue raisin cookie get in the bag? I'm still scarred, and then you callously reopened a hidden wound before grinding salt into it."

His nostrils were flaring from how hard he was trying not to laugh at her theatrics, which had been her intention.

Whoosh!

Whoosh!

Whoosh!

Cruz glanced at her phone, eyes scanning the new messages. His forehead scrunched, and he cocked his head to the side as he worked to decipher the nonsense. Then he sat up straight, winced, and glanced at her. "Uh-oh."

"Uh-oh? What do you mean *uh-oh*?"

"Uhh … if Axil didn't know he'd been part of a potential assassination attempt, he does now. Peril, uh, DM'ed him. And he told Axil he's got information he needs. Then he, uh, gave Axil your phone number so you can set up a meeting."

Deandra's eyes bugged. "You're kidding."

Cruz handed her the phone so she could read the messages herself.

> **Peril**
> The lack of massages must meant your
> Byzantine, so I'm being procreation

Deandra's head hurt already.

> **Peril**
> Axil R has been informative that someone
> attempted to shatter bury his tattoo

> **Peril**
> He's very intravenous in details, so I let him
> beehive I am a member of the press working on
> an article about SOS

Peril
He is now in position of your phone number and will call to set up a Renaissance

Peril
When you come to visit me this evening, you can put me in your purse and cartography me to the meeting so I can listen in

Good grief.

Deandra
Peril! You have to ask before you give out people's phone numbers. Your dad wasn't thrilled when you gave out *his* number, remember?

Peril
I'd give out mime, but farther blocked applications for phone calls

Deandra
So not the point I was making

Peril
I'm sore

Peril

Peril

Deandra clapped herself on the forehead. "Oh no. He found the emojis."

Cruz said, "We still have half an hour before we need to be at the Mythic Pet Kitchen booth. Is it time to get a new phone? We can drop yours in a porta-potty. Also, the offer to flee the hub system entirely to take a stab at making a living off scrap metal art is still on the table. We can back out of here, pick up Max, then go creepy-van shopping."

She laughed despite the headache that was forming. The bubble that meant someone was typing had been flashing for longer than usual, and Deandra feared the incoming message would be a mile long.

> **Peril**
> I meant to say that I'm sorry if I crossed a line

Huh. So he *could* type coherently when he took his time, then. She'd been starting to wonder if he wasn't correcting his typos due to being a terrible speller. Turned out he was just impatient.

The next message took even longer.

> **Peril**
> Father told me, even if he's cleared of any suspicious, the werecats and ACSI found a couple of minor violations at the shop that will mean lots of paperwork to update licenses, as well as fines. Axil may have insight into the ASA situation that wraps up this case faster, and then their business can resume as usual, so they'll no longer be bourbon with this. On a shellfish note, it's still unknown if my adoption was somehow the catalyst. It will test me apart until I know

Frowning, Deandra read the message out loud to Cruz.

"Kind of hard to be too mad at him, eh?" Cruz asked. "Though I'm assuming you'll be legitimately mad if Axil actually calls you. What are you going to say?"

"Can't I just block him and pretend this didn't happen?"

"Sure," Cruz said slowly. "Or, and hear me out, maybe you can convince him to tell the werecats what he knows? Though, if it's true that he's been on the lam all these years because of his connection to the hippodynus attack—"

"The *what*?"

"The hippo on steroids that ASA let out of the zoo."

Oh, right. The grimalkyne had told her about that.

Cruz continued. "That attack was so horrific, it was actually a big part of my zoolingual schooling. Major teachable moment for all kinds of reasons—it illustrated the role of mythical zoos, the reality that many animals and insects were doomed to be introduced to this realm only to become extinct again thanks to the Glitch, and how important it is to find out which fae and magic-touched animals are compatible with earthen-realm species.

"Scientists and veterinarians have to determine how realistic it is to devote time and resources to try to save certain populations. The hippodynus was the only one of its kind here and wasn't compatible with any earthen-realm animals. Hippopotamus was the closest we had, and yet they're somehow not remotely genetically similar, even down to, uh, the reproductive bits."

She felt bad for the marooned demon hippo, even if it *was* unpredictably violent. "Did someone really die during that attack?"

"Yep. It ... wasn't pretty. We had to study the images of his wounds as part of our course. The hippodynus passed away in captivity, so we can't study it directly anymore. Not that the hippodynus let anyone near it—not while it was conscious, anyway. Quowlaxliquin was originally created specifically to keep the hippodynus sedated; it was the only way to examine it. They had to launch food over the walls of its massive habitat using a catapult."

Deandra recalled what the grimalkyne had said about unicorn shifters and that they were described as sharks of the forest. Were there also packs of hippodynuses roaming the fae realm? It sounded like a wildly dangerous place.

"If I recall correctly, at least ten people were injured, too. Many critically," Cruz said. "A few people in ASA have been prosecuted for the attack. Not only were people injured and one killed, it resulted in hundreds of thousands in property damage. There were trespassing and breaking-and-entering charges, too.

"Lionax was never caught or directly tied to the attack, despite him supposedly being the founder of ASA. It's believed multiple members of the organization were either bullied into taking or happily took the fall for him. That, or Lionax's deep pockets got him out of hot water because he paid off the right people. Then he vanished from the public eye. Well, maybe. He might have just quietly come back as Axil years later."

Deandra mulled all that over. "That opens up the suspect pool of who would want Lionax dead. Even if he was keeping his Axil identity separate from Lionax, it's obviously not a totally contained secret anymore. The killer could be someone who was a loved one of the guy who was killed in the hippodynus attack. Or a newer member of ASA who didn't know Lionax back then could have figured out who Axil really is and is upset about being deceived. Heck, maybe someone who took the fall for the guy is ticked off that Lionax has been running around free all this time while they or a loved one was locked up."

Cruz nodded. "The most obvious person to me is Jet—especially if he's worried that Axil decided that, after all these years, he wants his job back. Maybe there's been enough of a shift in leadership since Axil left that he thinks he can resume his old role."

Deandra wrinkled her nose. "It sounds like Axil got ousted, though. He either really didn't like the direction ASA was going with someone like Jet at the helm and he bounced, or he got kicked out. And trust me, I *really* want it to be Jet, because he's a jerk, but I don't think it was him. Conrad was standing next to Rularo during that demonstration.

"If Jet was as tight with Axil as it sounds, there's no way Jet could look Conrad in the eye and mistake him for Axil. And unless he's truly a psychopath, he would have found a way to call off the minion armed with shatterberry. Plus, ASA seems to have spies scattered all over the festival. When Axil didn't show up for his appointment, Jet would have known."

The phone rang then, and Deandra flailed, almost losing hold of it. That happened to her entirely too often. In her defense, phones were meant for texting, searching the internet for new restaurants, and playing Lollipop Jumble—*not* phone calls.

It was an unfamiliar number.

"Oh no!" she said, as realization dawned, and she tossed her phone into Cruz's lap as if it had scalded her. "I can't talk to a unicorn shifter! What would I even say to him! I'm going to wring Peril's little neck!"

Cruz yelped, grabbed the still-ringing phone, and tossed it back into her lap.

Havoc chirped-barked from the back, clearly hopeful it was time to play catch instead of just sitting in the boring car.

"You're the sleuth here, sleuth!" Cruz said, hands held up, palms facing her. "Answer it. For Peril. You can pretend it's the wrong number."

"I could just *not* answer it at all," she tried.

Grinning, he said, "True. But your curiosity will eat you alive."

With a groan, knowing he was right, she snatched up the phone, blew out a fortifying breath, and accepted the call. She would have put it on speaker, but Havoc was currently rolling around in the back seat making *very* weird noises. "Hell-hello."

"Uh. Hello," the male voice on the other end said. He sounded normal enough, though Deandra had no reference for what a hundred-and-twenty-year-old unicorn shifter was supposed to sound like. "I'm calling for a Deandra Hendricks?"

Peril gave him her full name?!

"That is I," she said, then mentally winced. Why did she always have to be so *weird*? She was not good under pressure. "How can I help you?" She shot a pained look at Cruz, who offered her two enthusiastic thumbs up.

"Right. I'm half expecting this to be a scam, but someone on Picayune said you had information about something that went down at the InkCraft booth yesterday. You work for the Greenwoods or something?"

"I'm their assistant." She was their assistant caregiver, so it wasn't totally a lie. "This is Axil Romano, correct? You were scheduled for a tattoo with us yesterday but didn't call in with a reason for your failure to attend."

The pause on the other end was so long, Deandra wondered if the call had dropped.

"I paid the deposit. I know it's not refundable. There's nothing on the website that says I'm obligated to pay the rest of the fee if I don't make the appointment." He sounded ticked off. Maybe he thought this whole thing was a roundabout way to get money out of him. "So this *isn't* about the incident in the tent?"

"I was only asking about the no-show because we suspect that the shatterberry ink that killed Conrad Osgood—the man who took your slot—was actually meant for you." There she went, blurting the truth again instead of being a savvy wordsmith who kept everything close to the vest.

Axil gusted a quick breath. "It *was* shatterberry, then? I tried calling the werecats as an anonymous concerned citizen, but they wouldn't tell me anything."

"It was, yeah," Deandra said. "Is there any reason someone might have been targeting you specifically? Your paperwork said you're a shifter. Shatterberry is fatal to your kind."

"Well aware," Axil said, laughing bitterly. "And yeah, you can say I've got a few enemies. Planning to make a few more before this festival is over."

Deandra's eyes widened. "What does *that* mean?"

Axil's tone suddenly morphed from cautious and suspicious to confident and a little intense. "Do you have any idea what kind of *people* your bosses are? Rularo is worse than his little elfin wife, but she's just as complicit." He paused. "Granted, I don't even know who I'm talking to. You could be just another subjugator of sapient animals."

Havoc chirp-barked as he flailed around in the back seat, the car rocking slightly. She suspected he was so bored that he was now chasing his own tail.

"*Yeah*," Axil said, drawing the word out. "You're probably just as bad as the rest of them. The attempt on my life has only solidified my resolve, though. I suspected as much when I got the news that someone had died in that tent. I'm glad I trusted my instincts not to show up when I found out the Greenwoods are harboring a salica. Disgusting. They need to disclose that kind of thing on their website. It's unprofessional not to let customers know such things. Tell them that for me, yeah?"

Deandra didn't reply.

"You can also tell them that they and everyone else who subjugates the sapient are what's wrong with hub society. You tell them that, when things get … *interesting* later, they can blame themselves."

As if the alarm bells hadn't already been blaring—now they were screaming. Deandra shot a wide-eyed look at Cruz, then jabbed a finger in Havoc's direction before she scrambled out of the car. Thankfully Cruz understood that she meant they needed to move, and they needed to move *now*.

Neela's words replayed in her head. *"We're down to, what, ten in the entire hub system? It's possible that loneliness finally overrode the fear of getting caught. That, or he cracked mentally."*

Deandra was leaning toward "cracked mentally."

"How are the Greenwoods to blame when you're the one with all these ominous-sounding plans?" she asked, hoping he'd keep talking.

Cruz had a leashed-up Havoc by her side in record time, and they headed in the direction of the festival.

Deandra pulled the phone away from her ear long enough to hit the mute button. To Cruz, she said, "Axil sounds like he's planning something. That's why he's still here. He's not working with ASA, though. We have to get to the werecats. I'll see if I can get anything out of him about where he is."

Before he could reply, she unmuted the phone again. With Cruz's hand in her free one, they speed-walked toward Oracle Park.

Axil had been ranting up a storm while the phone was muted and apparently wasn't thrown off by the sudden upswell in background noise. "—cowards, all of them. You know what I just real-ized? Someone trying to take me out means I'm on the right path —that I've *always* been on the right path. They only try to stifle the voices of those who speak a truth they're too scared to hear. Well, I'm done hiding. I'm done being quiet."

Going out on a limb, she asked, "Are you hiding because of your connection to the hippodynus attack?"

"Huh," Axil said, almost sounding impressed. "Your online lackey wasn't lying when he said you know who I am—who I *really* am."

Peril needed his online privileges revoked. Who knew what else the little ferret had said to Axil—to Lionax—that he conve-niently forgot to mention.

"His spelling is atrocious, by the way. Might want to work on that if he's the one operating the Greenwoods' online presence. I almost discounted everything he said because I thought it was a bored kid using his mommy's computer."

Oh, how Lionax would blow a gasket if he knew the "person" he'd been chatting with was a "subjugated salica."

"You're not worried that coming out of hiding is going to land you in a jail cell?" Deandra asked.

He barked a laugh. "Those incompetent fools won't find me. And even if they do, this might be just what the cause needs. It'll shake ASA out of its complacency. They'll be at a crossroads. They'll have to decide once and for all if they actually mean everything they say. If it was one of *them* who tried to kill me, though, then they aren't safe, either. I'll wipe the whole slate clean and start fresh."

"What if sapient animals get hurt while you're wiping the slate clean?" she asked. "Is sacrificing innocent animals worth the risk?"

That actually gave Lionax pause. "Death while free is better than death in captivity. I'm sure the hippodynus would have agreed, if anyone had let it choose for itself. Instead, it died behind walls. Caged. *Alone.*"

His tone had been so grave, she'd almost stopped walking. Chills raced down her spine. She redoubled her pace, Cruz and Havoc matching her speed.

"Do you think it was someone in ASA who tried to kill you?"

A teenage boy shot her an incredulous look as she hustled past him. All Deandra could offer was a toothy grimace before she hurried by and then quickly sidestepped a man in yet another inflatable zombie cactus costume. She caught the faint sound of him heaving in there, and she wondered how much he regretted stuffing himself into that contraption during summer.

"I'm not sure," Lionax said casually. "It makes the most sense. That organization took the best of me, so it seems fitting they'd try to take what's left. But honestly? It feels like too bold of a move for them. Too carefully planned. Discreetly killing a shifter with shatterberry is diabolical. It's one of the worst ways for a shifter to go. The extract does something catastrophic to our bodies. It's like it turns the magic in our blood that fuels our transformation into gasoline and immediately sets it on fire. An awful, *awful* way to go."

Deandra's eyes pricked with tears as the image of Conrad thrashing on the ground slammed back into her head. "An awful way to go" was an understatement.

"You're not worried someone is going to try again?" she asked.

"I dare them to try," he said. "I'm wiser now. I'll see them coming before they ever see me. And the alarm on the door will give me all the warning I need, anyway. Clever device, this. Guess this town isn't *entirely* useless."

Her temporary distraction as she avoided a gaggle of kids running in the opposite direction of everyone else had apparently given Lionax enough time to realize he'd been freely chatting with a stranger. "Well, Deborah. Lovely talking to you. Thanks for the intel. If I can repay the favor a bit, might I suggest you distance yourself from your bosses as soon as possible? Never a bad time to start a new career."

Lionax abruptly ended the call.

She pulled the phone away from her ear to stare at the screen, bewildered, for a few long seconds. Glancing up at Cruz, who was valiantly keeping up with her frantic pace, she said, "That guy is *bananas*."

"Just hearing your half of it illustrated that pretty well," he said. "How worried do we need to be?"

"I honestly don't know. Maybe he's just loopy, but he's the kind of loopy where you don't want him to be proactive, you know?" Deandra broke her hold of Cruz's hand so they could stream around a couple who'd decided that the middle of the sidewalk was a suitable place to have a heated argument. "I gotta make one more call."

First, she texted the three images of Axil-slash-Lionax to Wendy, then called her once they went through.

Wendy answered almost immediately. The background was quiet, so she clearly wasn't in the Heather's Elixirs booth. "Hi! Who's the smoke show?"

Deandra almost tripped over her own feet. "Really? A smoke show?"

"So this *isn't* you setting me up on a date?" Wendy asked.

"Absolutely not," she said. "Given your reaction, I'm assuming he didn't come into the booth during the rest of your shift today?"

"Don't think so. It's kind of a blur, to be honest, but I like to think I'd remember that hair."

"Is there any way you can text the images to everyone else who's worked the booth this weekend? If you can send it to everyone who worked in the store this weekend, too, that would be great. Sounds like he bought an alarm talisman that can be used on a door sometime this weekend. We're trying to track him down. Anything we can find will help the werecats. And just, I don't know, keep an eye out for him. If you see him, don't approach him. Just call the sighting in to the werecats."

"I have so many questions, but I'm on it," Wendy said. "I'm at home eating lunch, but I'm heading to the store after that. I'll send a group text to the staff."

"Cool. Thanks. I'll tell you everything later," Deandra said.

"Exciting stuff always happens to you, I swear," muttered Wendy.

Deandra disconnected the call and shoved her phone into her back pocket. Once they rounded the corner onto Wheeler Avenue and the police station was visible in the distance, the knot in her stomach loosened a little. The cats would find Lionax before he executed his plan, right?

"Go," Cruz said, squeezing her hand. "We'll catch up."

Deandra only hesitated for a second, then she dropped his hand and took off at a jog. There were only two werecats outside the station, as far as she could tell. One was at the end of the block directing traffic away from Wheeler Avenue. There was a lot of honking and yelling coming from that end of the street. The other cat was standing at the balloon arch entrance of the festival, having a heated conversation with a woman while her young daughter sobbed openly, head thrown back. The little girl looked human at first glance, but a thin tail whipped around behind her. Was she part succubus? Deandra mentally chastised herself for getting overstimulated again and ducked into the police station.

The same receptionist she'd interacted with the last time she was here was behind the reinforced glass. That time, Deandra had been with Mavis, Lydia's grieving best friend. Deandra eyed the two sets of four plush chairs—one set upholstered in red and the other in navy blue. The chairs faced each other, with an oval wooden coffee table positioned between them. Just like last time, all the chairs were unoccupied.

The reception window was positioned in the center of the lobby. To the right, a sign reading HUMAN DEPARTMENT sat above a pair of doors. Above the left set read WERECAT DIVISION.

Deandra hurried up to the receptionist's window, taking in her mint-green skin and her tiny, curved, dark-blue horns. The lines around her bright light-brown eyes deepened as she smiled at Deandra.

"What can I help you with, dear?" she asked, her calm energy at war with how hard Deandra's heart was thumping.

"Is Officer Sutter in?" she asked, breathlessly. "I have some information about the shatterberry poisoning incident."

The woman sat up straighter. "I'm not sure if she is, but I'll track her down, all right, hon? Just have a seat."

Deandra sat in one of the red chairs, perched on the edge of the seat. Her leg jiggled. She had no idea what to do with herself. Cruz and Havoc joined her a minute later. Cruz took a seat on one side of her, while Havoc scrambled ungracefully into a chair on her other side. She recounted her conversation with Lionax in a whisper that she was sure the receptionist heard every word of. Despite the chaos just outside the front doors, it was quiet in the lobby. Plus, Deandra just assumed at this point that anyone magic-touched or fae probably had a heightened sense or two.

"Jeez," Cruz said when she was done. He was quiet for only a moment and then sat up, as if physically struck with an idea. "Oh. What did Peril say was in the Picayune post again? That Lionax was easily able to hear the warm-up of a live band, right? If we look up who was playing around that time, that might help narrow down where Lionax is, where he was staying, or at least where he was hanging out."

"Ooh. *See*," she said, nudging him with her arm. "You're pretty good at the sleuthing thing, too. We're basically a sleuthing *team* now. Things currently seem to be run by a sapient ferret, though, which is a problem."

He laughed, then pulled out his phone, tapping and swiping at the screen. "Okay, it looks like the band that was scheduled for two thirty is Reanimated Werewolf. There are two stages—one in the south of the park and one in the west. Reanimated Werewolf is on the western stage."

Deandra, with her own phone in hand, had started looking up Reanimated Werewolf as soon as Cruz said the name. She was hoping that they'd have social profiles with pictures from the gig. It didn't take long to find what she was looking for. In the background of one shot in particular was a small hotel. An overlarge freestanding sign propped on a thick pole displaying Axian 8 loomed behind the lead singer. The caption said *"Cassie rocks hard, even during warm-up. Come check out Reanimated Werewolf at 2:30 across from the Axian 8. Come party with us after our set at Axian 8's awesome rooftop bar!"*

When he was recounting the details of Lionax's posts told via an excitable ferret, Cruz had said, *"He also said that he resorted to drinking hard liquor to numb the pain."*

From what Deandra could tell, there were no other hotels in the immediate vicinity of where Reanimated Werewolf was playing. Since Lionax was from out of town and apparently planned to be here for at least a few days, it made sense that he'd be staying in a temporary location like a hotel. If he'd been staying with a friend or relative, it seemed less likely that he'd feel compelled to purchase an alarm talisman. Axian 8 had a bar, and Lionax had at least joked that he'd been drinking to make Reanimated Werewolf's music more palatable.

She nudged Cruz to get his attention and then laid out her theory.

He nodded. "Nice. That's a solid lead for Officer Sutter to check out."

A text came in a few minutes later, interrupting her perusal of Reanimated Werewolf's photos. She sighed to herself at seeing Peril's name on her screen.

Peril
Did he call you? Are we going to have a clementine meeting? Is the unicorn a miscellaneous or an ally?

Deandra assumed "clementine" was supposed to be "clandestine" and "miscellaneous" should have been "miscreant," one of Peril's favorite words. She'd always wanted to learn another language, but Peril Textspeak hadn't been what she had in mind.

Peril
I fear he's not an alley! He's been posting odd things on Picayune over the last ten minutiae. He said ASA will regret their choices. Then he said that he'll do what their too sacred to do. The last post said "Not all lions can roam free the same way. Some need help to spread their wings." What in the whirlpool does that mean?

Deandra was developing another headache. She definitely wasn't anywhere close to fluent in this language yet.

She'd planned to ask Cruz to make his best attempt at a Peril translation when the woman behind them spoke.

"Hon?"

Deandra quickly got to her feet and walked to the reception desk. "Hi. Did you hear from Officer Sutter?"

"All she told me was there was an incident at the Axian Nights Hotel, and she'll be tied up until she can take care of the issue. Most everyone else is working right now who could possibly talk to you. We're stretched pretty thin here today. It's always a bit nutty during festival week. Officer Lyle can come talk to you in twenty minutes or so if you can hang tight?"

Deandra honestly didn't know what the best course of action was. She, Cruz, and Havoc were due to help at the Mythic Pet Kitchen booth in a few minutes. Could she just ignore the fact that Lionax was unraveling? If the answer was no, what could she do about it, anyway? She didn't know where he was. And even *if* she found him, how did she expect her mundane self to fare when squaring off against a unicorn shifter with a chip the size of a small country on his shoulder?

She didn't like *at all* the fact that Lionax was apparently crashing out on social media at the same time that the werecats were being pulled to another part of town to deal with ASA.

Because she was sure that was what was happening right now. Jet had told her himself that ASA wasn't allowed to hold another demonstration in Oracle Park and that they'd been moved to the parking lot of the Axian Nights Hotel.

"Hon? If you need to report a crime, I can help you with that," the receptionist said gently. "Did … something happen that you need to report?" She cast a couple of wary glances in Cruz's direction. He was too busy trying to keep Havoc occupied to notice. Keeping the dragon occupied consisted almost exclusively of gratuitous belly rubs.

Deandra shook her head. "Nothing's happened. Not yet, anyway."

"Did someone make threats against you?" Now she sounded alarmed.

Shaking her head again, Deandra said, "Just vague posts on social media. I have a bad feeling, is all. I know having a bad feeling isn't exactly the most useful of evidence."

The receptionist shrugged. "It is if you're an empath."

Oh. Right. Deandra nearly forgot where she was. Empaths— *legit* empaths who could be certified as such—lived in places like Axia. Deandra was *not* an empath. She was a pet sitter whose phone had been blowing up all afternoon thanks to an excitable sapient ferret.

Deandra asked, "Can I report a series of odd circumstances? I guess it would be like calling in a tip to a tipline …"

The woman sat up a little straighter and smiled. "Absolutely. I can document it all and then pass it on to the next available officer. How's that sound?"

Deandra had no idea. "Sounds great."

"Perfect. Go have a seat and I'll meet you over there in two shakes of a faun's tail, okay? More comfortable out in the lobby."

Over the next few minutes, Deandra detailed everything she could think of. Cruz interjected when needed. She told the receptionist—who was named Emma—that, based on research performed by a salica, they had reason to believe Axil Romano was actually the infamous Lionax Orma. Lionax, she told Emma, was disillusioned with ASA, and he was now emboldened by the attempted assassination. Even though it wasn't relevant, Deandra added that she felt guilty for confirming the shatterberry poisoning detail for Lionax, fearing it was that knowledge that had pushed him over the edge.

Granted, she wouldn't have been in this situation at all had Peril not given out her phone number, but blaming the ferret now wouldn't do anyone any good. What was done, was done.

Emma, to her credit, took this all in stride. Either Deandra's strange tale wasn't that strange to a receptionist at a police station with both mundane and magical departments, or the woman had an exceptionally unbreakable poker face.

Deandra felt better after purging it all, though, so there was that.

"Is that everything?" she asked when Deandra finally ran out of steam. When Deandra nodded, she said, "If this Axil Romano character really *is* Lionax Orma, there will be quite a bit of interest in this information. We may even get Collective bounty hunters flooding into Axia!" Leaning toward Deandra, she added in a conspiratorial tone, "All the departments across the hub system are linked. There will be an alert in the database that there's been a possible sighting of Lionax. The bounty on him is *pretty hefty*, given how long he's been evading capture. I'll get this inputted right away, okay, hon?"

Deandra bobbed her head. "Thanks, Emma."

"No sweat. I've got your contact info, too, so we're all good. You may get a call from someone about the report if they need to ask any clarifying questions. Don't be alarmed if you get a call from an unlisted number. Bounty hunters are big on secrecy," Emma said, grinning.

Emma was as excited about the possibility of bounty hunters pouring into Axia as Peril was about a new serial killer documentary appearing on his favorite streaming channel.

With that, Deandra, Cruz, and Havoc headed out of the police station and toward the Mythic Pet Kitchen booth. They'd be a little late, but late was better than pulling a no-show like Axil-slash-Lionax had done with the Greenwoods.

The feel of Cruz's warm hand slipping into hers grounded her a bit. She smiled up at him as they walked. He smiled back, giving her palm a reassuring squeeze.

Comforted or not, Lionax's voice still lingered in the back of her mind. *"And yeah,"* he'd said, *"you can say I've got a few enemies. Planning to make a few more before this festival is over."*

She had to hope she'd done enough. Someone would stop Lionax before he did something rash.

Right?

CHAPTER SIXTEEN

Deandra, Cruz, and Havoc stepped up to the row of tables at the front of the Mythic Pet Kitchen booth—which was even busier than yesterday. The line to get in for visiting with the animals was ridiculously long. There were at least ten people waiting in line in front of Kira or one of their employees as they rang up customers. Several cardboard, plastic, and metal boxes were lined up in a neat row along the tables. Each had an information sheet taped to it that had the word "Adopted!" stamped across it in red. Maybe the vibrissa had already found homes, and Deandra could go home to take a stress nap.

Kira looked over just as her latest customer walked away with a colorful bird on her shoulder, and she waved. "Go on in!" she shouted. "Juniper is waiting for you. The kittens have been *very* naughty today. Only bit two people so far, though!"

Great.

With a wave to acknowledge that she'd heard her, Deandra stepped through the space between two tables and into the tent. Just as it had yesterday, her mind spun when the interior expanded before her eyes.

"Oh wow," Cruz said from beside her, his head tipped back as they walked toward the back.

The number of employees in the tent seemed to have doubled overnight as well. Mythic Pet Kitchen sold bedding—pellets made from recycled newspaper, straw, hay, and fire-resistant cotton—dishes, harnesses, collars, food and treats, and of course magic-enhanced cages, terrariums, and crates. There were customers shopping for pet supplies, customers visiting with the animals up for adoption, and there was even a lecture stage today.

The small stage had four rows of chairs positioned in front of it. The woman on stage wore a Mythic Pet Kitchen T-shirt and had a headset microphone. She slowly paced the small stage as she gave her rapt audience an intense lecture on the best practices for nail, claw, and hoof trimming. Not only were all the seats full, but several people stood around the filled chairs.

Deandra still couldn't understand the physics-defying magic that let this tent exist. The space was a cacophony of talking, laughing, the happy shrieks of kids, and animal noises, but it was still nowhere near as raucous as the festival itself.

It wasn't until they'd moved past the lecture stage and an aquarium filled with what honestly looked like a dozen tiny mermaids that Cruz spoke.

"I've lived here most of my life, and I honestly usually avoid the festival. I can't remember the last time I attended. I don't know if that's a lifelong-resident thing where you take your hometown for granted," he said.

Deandra shot him a "Please don't be mad at me" look before saying, "You also have a bit of a workaholic problem, remember?"

His head tilted side to side. "Okay, that's fair. I absolutely worked through the festival most years. But, still, it's cool to see this. Even *I* sometimes forget that magic can do stuff like this."

A thought suddenly occurred to her. "Is your zoolingual ability going wacky in here with so many animals in one place? I don't know why I think of them like wandering ghosts who are suddenly desperate to talk to the one person who can finally see them."

He laughed. "Without training? Absolutely. But I'm good at putting up walls. A lot of magic-touched and fae animals can sense I can speak to them, and sometimes they'll reach out mentally. I usually don't hear them, though, unless they're being really pushy. The overall vibe I'm getting is excitement, that they're having fun, with a few of them being extremely nervous. Normal nervous, though. An introvert forced to mingle at a party where they don't know anyone kind of nervous."

When she glanced at him sharply, he was grinning at her. He knew that scenario was quite possibly the scariest thing in the world to her and he was delighting in it.

"You monster," she muttered.

He laughed again, though it cut off abruptly a moment later. He stopped walking, too. They'd reached the secluded area where the vibrissa were being kept, the background the dark-blue tarp covered in renderings of fluffy clouds. Cruz's gaze was locked on the vibrissa cage that was still a good ten feet away. From what Deandra could see from here, one kitten was grooming itself in one of the beds on the ground floor of the cage, while the other sat on the topmost platform, staring right back at Cruz.

The shyest of the kittens was emerald green. She had pink tufts of fur that stuck out of her ears, and her eyes were so yellow, they were almost orange.

After several beats of silence passed, Deandra asked, "Is she talking to you?"

"Not quite," Cruz said slowly, still staring at the kitten. "She thinks mostly in emotions. She's … anxious, which I'm sure even you can sense. But it's not that she's anxious to be alone or away from the noise of the festival. She's anxious because she feels cooped up. The time in the playpen isn't enough. She wants … out. To stretch her legs. She actually wants to *see* the festival. To go on an adventure. She … she keeps smelling what I think is a hamburger?" He laughed. "She just showed me an image of a pile of burger patties and her diving into them as if they were a pile of leaves."

Deandra stared at the side of his head. It was wild that he could see and sense all that. "That's so cool," she said after a long beat.

He finally tore his gaze away from the kitten. His cheeks went a little red. It wasn't as if he was shy about his ability, especially when he'd made a successful career out of honing it, but he still got a little embarrassed with her when he zoned out while reading an animal.

"You know I like it when you talk nerdy to me," she said a little huskily, knowing he would get even more flustered now.

The tips of his ears went pink, too. He took a step closer and cupped her face. "Oh yeah? How *much* do you like it?"

Someone very noisily cleared their throat behind them, making them jerk apart. Havoc shriek-barked in alarm. Juniper stood there, looking *deeply* uncomfortable.

Now Deandra was flushing furiously. "Oh. I … uh, hello."

Juniper couldn't seem to look at either one of them. "Hello, Dr. Caddel. How lovely it is for you to join us on this fine day," he said to his shoes, in a haltingly awkward tone.

"Hello, Juniper," Cruz said, hand held out. "Nice to see you outside of the veterinary office. How are Tiramisu and Parfait?"

"Oh, fine. Fine," he said, shaking Cruz's hand while keeping his eyes diverted. "The tuna pâté is a hit, just like you said. Wonderous, that ability of yours. Ha-ha. Just wonderful."

Deandra didn't know either of the Thistlewicks well, but she found it endlessly amusing that Kira was assertive and sassy, while Juniper was shy and awkward. She wondered who had pursued whom when they first started dating.

"Speaking of, our shyest vibrissa just talked to Cruz—er, Dr. Caddel," Deandra said.

Juniper's head snapped up. "Truly?" he asked Cruz. "What did she say?"

Deandra unhooked Havoc's leash and gave him his release word, allowing him to trot around the vibrissa cage. He seemed to sense that the remaining two kittens were apprehensive, so his temperament around them was far more subdued than when the rowdier of the kittens had been here yesterday. She, Cruz, and Juniper made their way to the cage while Cruz recounted what the kitten had told him.

"Oh, the poor dear," Juniper said as he stopped just outside the cage, where he was eye-level with the kitten on the topmost platform.

She stared at him for a long moment, eyes wide, before she phased to the next lowest platform.

Juniper turned his back to the cage to address Deandra and Cruz. "I would love to give her some freedom, but I don't have a safe way to do it. I don't have any anti-phasing harnesses in the booth—none her size anyway."

With a flourish, Deandra pulled the red harness and leash set Powder had lent her out of her purse. "Ta-da! It's on loan from the grimalkyne."

Juniper's mouth dropped open and he held out his hands for the gear, presumably to inspect it. Deandra handed them over. He ran his fingers over the runework, muttering to himself about the excellent craftmanship. "I didn't know they had any of these in vibrissa size!"

A worrying thought hit her. "So there are *other* types of phasing animals?"

"Oh yeah," Cruz and Juniper said in unison.

Her mind conjured up a very disturbing image of an animal the size of an elephant phasing its way down a street, crushing cars as it went.

"I trust both of you implicitly," Juniper said, handing the harness and leash back to Deandra. "If letting this little one get some freedom and fresh air takes the edge off, it'll make her all the more likely to find a home today. She really needs to stop biting if she wants someone to adopt her. If you'd like to take her on a little outing, that's fine by me."

The rate at which he was wringing his hands suggested that was only partially true.

Cruz angled his head so he could see around Juniper's bulk, which was blocking a good chunk of the cage. His eyes glazed over a bit, as they often did when he was communicating telepathically with an animal.

To Deandra's amazement, a few moments later, the kitten phased back to the top platform, got on her hind legs, and pawed lightly at the glass. It was the liveliest Deandra had seen her yet. Juniper slowly turned around and sucked in a little gasp of delight when he spotted the kitten with her front paws still on the side of the cage. The pads of her paws were dark pink, while the small horns that sprouted from the middle of her head, one by each pointy ear, were teal. She also had antennae that stretched above the tips of her ears, and they swayed about independently of each other. She didn't have any scales, from what Deandra could see, unlike her brother on the bottom floor.

Deandra handed Cruz the harness and leash, then called Havoc to her. She and her dragon gave the cage a wide berth while the two men set about getting the nervous vibrissa kitten out of the cage and into the magicked harness. Based on what Juniper had told her about the manipulation skills of a vibrissa, she was half convinced this was all an elaborate ploy by the kitten to trick the silly non-felines into letting her out of the cage so she could phase herself to freedom.

Deandra shouldn't have doubted Cruz's skills, though. The kitten was so calm with him that she simply lifted this paw or that to better aid Cruz in getting the contraption on her. Her brother was so freaked out by the new arrival, however, that he phased to the cage's top platform and cowered in a corner.

Once Cruz had the harnessed kitten out of the cage and Juniper had secured the door again, assuring the last kitten was safe, Cruz turned toward Deandra, the tiny green kitten held to his chest. Her heart melted a little at the sight, if she was honest. The kitten had her paws balanced on his forearm and she had her side pressed to his chest. She visibly trembled in his hold, antennae flailing about.

"Don't let the trembling fool you. She's actually just purring," Cruz said. "Loudly."

The kitten tipped her head back and gazed up at him, eyes slightly squinted. Uh-oh. Deandra knew a look of adoration when she saw one. To make matters worse, now that she could examine the kitten up close, there was a patch of white on her chest that formed a perfect heart.

Cruz and Juniper were talking, but Cruz was startled out of the conversation by one that was apparently happening in his head. He glanced down at the kitten. He listened, cocked his head, then shrugged.

"Sure, if you want to," he said.

The kitten chirruped, and then she was scaling his shirt like a gecko. She perched herself on his shoulder and gently nuzzled his neck.

"Oh boy, oh boy," Deandra said. "You are in *trouble*."

He shot a fierce side-eye at the kitten who had her head pressed against his neck, her eyes closed. He mouthed, "I can't have a cat!"

"That's what they all say. The cat distribution system works in mysterious ways," she said, enjoying teasing him as much as she enjoyed tormenting Wendy.

Cruz couldn't take on a phasing kitten with his work schedule. Plus, if he thought Havoc and Maxine were a bad influence on each other, how much worse would it get with a vibrissa cat in the mix? Given the stricken look on Cruz's face as the kitten continued to nuzzle his neck affectionately, if he took this cat home, he would be wrapped around her little green paw in no time.

They needed to get her adopted ASAP.

"We'll just take a little stroll around the festival, okay, Juniper?" Deandra asked. "I'm sure seeing how affectionate she can be with the right person will lure in prospective owners left and right."

Juniper's eyes were a little glassy. "Oh, I'm just so happy to see her come out of her shell. I have high hopes this shy girl will find the perfect owner. Take your time out there." He leaned toward Deandra conspiratorially. "If you still don't care about rule such-and-such, I suggest you take the back way out of here, just in case she gets spooked after all. You'll have a quicker way back."

He reached into the back pocket of his jeans and produced a small stack of business cards that also had the booth number and location on the back.

Deandra took the cards, leashed up Havoc, and led the way to the cloud-covered tarp. She stopped when she reached it and glanced over her shoulder. The kitten was now on her back, being cradled in Cruz's arm like a baby. With his free hand, he rubbed her belly. She purred loudly, her orange eyes closed. Her antennae had curled up on top of her head, so now they sat in spirals next to each horn. They reminded Deandra of the curled fiddleheads on the ferns hanging from the eaves of the Greenwoods' house.

When Cruz reached Deandra, he looked up, dismayed. "Don't even say it. I *know*. I can't. I mean I *could*, but I absolutely cannot."

She cracked up, lifted a corner of the tarp, and slipped underneath it, hoping that once they were out in the hustle and bustle, they wouldn't manage to lose the kitten in the crowd. But when Cruz joined her in the back walkway, and the kitten was not only still on her back, but the tip of her tongue stuck out between her teeth, Deandra knew the kitten wasn't going *anywhere*.

THE KITTEN WOKE UP AFTER A FEW MINUTES, LIKELY ROUSED BY THE noisy festival. To her credit, she was more alert than outright terrified. She scrambled back onto Cruz's shoulder, her antennae unfurled from the top of her head and resumed their independent flailing about, and her big orange eyes took everything in.

While Cruz kept the leash's loop around his wrist, just in case the kitten got spooked and made a run for it, the leash hung loose across his chest. The kitten got a ton of attention, and Cruz ended up stopping to chat with person after person, telling them about the breed. Quite a few tentatively stopped to ask to pet Havoc, too. When the big menacing dire wolf flopped onto his back to get his belly rubbed, apprehension went out the window.

The kitten didn't want to be handled, and she mostly remained aloof when strangers fawned over how cute she was, choosing instead to keep close to Cruz's neck and watch the sights rather than pay her audience any mind. Deandra passed out several Mythic Pet Kitchen business cards to folks whose toxic trait was that they believed they, too, could woo the strange green cat, just as Cruz clearly had, if they were given the chance.

When their latest wave of admirers moved on, Deandra asked, "Has she been chatting with you at all?"

"Not much, really," he said. "I just get the sense that she's very content up there. If she was a person, her favorite pastime would be people watching."

Deandra was about to ask something else when her phone vibrated in her back pocket. Startled, she quickly pulled it out, both hoping and dreading that one of the Greenwoods was calling with an update.

Her stomach dropped when No Caller ID scrolled across the top of the screen. She turned her phone to face Cruz. "This is even worse than getting called by a unicorn shifter!" she hissed at him.

He took a step back, hands up, the red leash loop around his wrist like a bracelet. "I'm not catching that if you throw it!"

She whimpered.

Head tilted to the side, he did his best to look at the kitten. "What?" After a beat of silence, he looked ahead of them. "Oh. Good call. Dee, there's a 'Be back in 10 minutes' sign on that popcorn kiosk across the way. I'll bet you can hide behind that to block out some of the noise while you take your call."

She glared at him. "Are you trying to push me into being braver? Facing my fears?"

He closed the distance and kissed her quickly. "Yes," he said, mouth still close to hers. "But I also want the hot goss, so answer it before they hang up. What if you end up on a bounty hunter's hit list for resisting a phone call?"

Despite how ridiculous that sounded, her stomach still flipped. "That's not a thing!" A split second later, she hit Accept on the call and clapped the phone to her ear. "Hello!" she said too loudly.

Cruz stifled a laugh.

When she squinted menacingly at him, she noticed the kitten had a bemused smile on her adorable green face, too. At least it seemed like a smile.

"Miss Hendricks?" came the female voice on the other end of the line, redirecting her focus.

"Yes, that's me," she said, then thrust Havoc's leash at Cruz before she hustled across the grassy expanse toward the popcorn kiosk as if it were a verdant oasis in a desert. She got around the side of the kiosk in record time and pressed her back against it. The sign promising that the popcorn vendor would return shortly was at least temporarily repelling people, giving her a modicum of quiet. "How can I, uh, help you?

"This is Ruth Howard. I'm a Luma-based bounty hunter. I just read your report about a man you believe to be Lionax Orma?"

The woman was friendly enough, but she was also professional and all business. Deandra's inherent fear of authority of any kind had her in a choke hold. Plus, Ruth's question wasn't really a question. What did she even want Deandra to say?

"Yes. I filed that report. Uh, statement? It doesn't really seem like I can call it a police report, since I wasn't reporting anything other than weird behavior. Creepy behavior, honestly. Did the report mention what he said in his last Picayune post? I don't actually know if it was his *last* post, since I haven't gotten an update from Peril in a while. I don't know if that's something I should be concerned about or not. He's a ferret. A talking ferret. A salica. That's the proper term. I'm his pet sitter." She took in a gasp of air, her mouth dry.

Ruth smothered a chuckle. "You're the kind of person who would crumple in an interrogation after the first question, aren't you?"

"Yes, ma'am." She swallowed again. "And the question probably wouldn't have to be anything too prying, either. Like, *what's your name?* It's a good thing I don't have a taste for crime because I would be caught before I even got started."

"And that's probably because you'd turn yourself in."

Deandra laughed. "That's fair."

"What was this about a Picayune post?"

"Oh! Um. What did he say again?" She rubbed the spot between her eyes. When she was stressed out, she either vomited words like a faucet or her brain locked up altogether. "Oh! *Not all lions can roam free the same way. Some need help to spread their wings.*"

"What proof do you have that this is *the* Lionax Orma and not someone pretending to be him?" Ruth asked. "There have been countless false leads over the years."

"Did those leads ever link Axil Romano with Lionax Orma?

Because I think Lionax has been living under a different identity for years, right under people's noses. He's just gotten sloppy recently. He talked about the hippodynus attack and everything. I mean, I guess anyone who knows about Lionax would know that detail, too. But Axil, even if he's someone *pretending* to be Lionax, is a shifter who has ties to ASA. Someone tried to kill him with shatterberry extract. Even if Axil *isn't* Lionax, he's done such a good job of pretending he is that it convinced at least one person that Axil and Lionax are one and the same. He's gotta be a pretty good actor if he was so convincing that this person went through the trouble of finding a poison that was specific to his kind."

"I'm definitely intrigued by this," Ruth said. "My colleagues think it's another bogus lead, but I have a good feeling. Do you have any idea where Lionax is now?"

Deandra vigorously shook her head even though Ruth couldn't see it. "Everything I know is in the report. We have a few ideas of where he might have been this weekend, but that's it. I have a friend keeping an eye out for him, too."

"It's a good start," Ruth said. "I'll be in Axia in the next twenty minutes, hopefully with back up. I'll send you a text here in a moment. Anything comes up, you call or text, all right?" There was a long pause. "I need you to know, though, that if you share the number with anyone, I'll be forced to kill you."

"Ha-ha!" Deandra said.

The answering silence on the other end was somehow hollow. She pulled the phone away from her face, revealing that the bounty hunter had disconnected the call.

She didn't have "getting threatened by a bounty hunter" on her Zombie Cactus Festival Bingo card, but this weekend remained full of surprises.

CHAPTER SEVENTEEN

C all over, she peeked around the side of the popcorn kiosk, caught Cruz's eye, and waved him over. He dropped Havoc's leash and apparently told him to run to her, because the dragon sprinted toward her like a greyhound on a racetrack.

When Cruz and the alien kitten reached them, she filled him in on the brief, though mildly terrifying, call with the bounty hunter.

"Do you think I should send Peril a check-in text?" Deandra asked. "He could be taking a nap. Or he could have a pile of intel, and he's just waiting for me to restart the conversation. Then I'll get flooded with autocorrected madness."

She recalled how odd Peril had acted when he first asked for permission to text her. It wasn't his usual odd behavior. He'd acted as if he'd been hiding something. Sure, it could have been the secret that his own parents had severely restricted his ability to contact them throughout the day because he abused the privilege.

She thought it was more than that, though. She was figuring now that he'd wanted to text her not to keep her informed on his findings, but to have her phone number—a number he planned to give out to potential suspects and allies so she could be his proxy while investigating.

She hadn't heard a peep from the ferret in over an hour! Goodness knew what trouble he'd gotten himself—and by extension her—into in that time.

"Ooh, train of thought took the scary track," she said, and hastily pulled out her phone.

> **Deandra**
> You've been quiet. Should I be worried? It's like when a toddler stops making noise and then you find out they've tried to flush several bath towels down the toilet

> **Peril**
> Rudimentary

> **Peril**
> Rude8

> **Peril**
> Rude8

> **Peril**
> I don't know how to make an asteroid!

She assumed he meant "asterisk" to denote that "rudimentary" had been a typo for "rude." If he was still using the tablet, there was most likely an easy way to toggle to the symbol keyboard, but would he be able to get out again? Then she'd end up getting texts that looked like they were written in Wingdings.

Clearly, he was fine.

> **Peril**
> I felt gilded about my overstretch with you earlier, so I took a break from being a detection and started watching a Ted Bundy documentary to unravel

> **Peril**
> Unwind8

She sent him a catch-up text to let him know there were potentially bounty hunters on the case but that currently no one knew where Lionax was.

> **Peril**
> 😨

Aha! A successful use of the correct emoji!

> **Peril**
> Give me a few munitions and I'll see if I can find anything on his Pickleball

She looked up from her phone to find Cruz standing by a tree, his head tipped back as he watched the kitten traverse a branch like a tightrope. He still held the leash, but the hold wasn't tight, and there was still slack in the leash. The shy girl really *had* just wanted some fresh air.

Havoc sat on his haunches by her feet, intently watching a swallowtail butterfly flit about.

She basked in the relatively peaceful few minutes that

followed until she was snapped out of it by her phone buzzing in her hand.

Peril
Oh, great Scotsman!

Deandra
What?

She meant that question in every possible way.

Deandra
Take your time so I can understand you!

Peril

Deandra honestly wasn't sure if he'd used that last one on purpose or not.

Peril
First, he only posted once more on Picayune. It says With me, you'll spread your wings and be free. That was half an hour ago. Sectional, there seems to be some chatter about strange activity at a place called Weatherstone? Why do so many of the posts there have no contextualize?

Deandra
What kind of strange activity?

Peril
It doesn't make much sensory, honestly. There are many posts wondering why it smells like oranges and coffee.

Deandra's brain glitched, then kickstarted back into gear. *With me, you'll spread your wings and be free.* *Weatherstone.*

Oranges and coffee.

"Oh crap!"

Cruz was by her side in an instant. "What is it?"

"I think I know where Lionax is and what he plans to do. I gotta text the scary bounty hunter."

Deandra
Hi, Ruth. This is Deandra Hendricks. I think Lionax is at the Weatherstone Flight Park and he plans to compromise the dome over it to release the animals inside

Ruth
I'm still fifteen minutes out. Rounding up help. Alert your werecats.

Deandra scrambled to pull up her text thread with Officer Sutter next.

Deandra
Officer Sutter, it's Dee. Axil Romano/Lionax Orma is at the Weatherstone Flight Park

A new text from Peril popped up.

Peril
Now there are reports of the place smelling lichen horsehair as well. Why would that be considered strange? Aren't there often flying peonies there?

She reopened her text thread with Officer Sutter. No answer. Deandra chewed on her bottom lip. She called her.

Six rings. Voicemail.

Deandra disconnected the call. Whirling toward a worried-looking Cruz, she explained her new theory.

"Call Sutter again," he said. "I'll call the flight park. I'll give them a description of Lionax and find out if he's in there."

They made their respective calls. Officer Sutter didn't answer. Deandra texted her again. Waited thirty seconds. Called back.

Frustrated with the lack of reply, she looked to Cruz, hoping he had better news.

"No answer there, either," he said.

Peril
There was just another post on Pickleball. Someone is reporting that they can't get out of Weatherstone. The pass cards needed to operation the doors aren't working. No one can get out

Deandra
As carefully as you can, reply to that person and ask how many animals and people are inside

She stared up at Cruz. "I have a really bad idea."

"I'm listening."

"We try to get to the flight park so you can calm the animals enough so they don't make a break for it if Lionax is successful. And maybe we can even distract *him* until the bounty hunters get there."

Her phone buzzed.

Peril
8 owners. 6 flying ponies. 4 fae birds. 2 pygmy phoenixes. 2 flying pigs.

Crap. That was too many. She showed the text to Cruz.

"What's the range of your zoolingual power?" she asked. "Could you potentially talk to them from the outside?"

"Possibly," he said. "Quite a few of those animals would be able to effortlessly pass through the veil and into the mundane world if they got loose. It would be hard enough to catch them if they were loose in town, even if they were kept in by the veil. The flight park is fairly close to the veil, too."

Deandra waited him out.

"Let's go. You drive. I'll keep making calls."

They took off in the direction of Deandra's grandparents' house. The festival wasn't over for several more hours, and this was the busiest day. She had to hope that the roads wouldn't be too clogged with people. Most of the festival wasn't happening beyond the thoroughfare of McClaren Way, so if they could just get past that, getting to the flight park shouldn't take too long.

When they reached the car, and after they got Havoc in the back, they both realized at the same time that they'd accidentally stolen the vibrissa cat. She'd ridden on Cruz's shoulder like a furry parrot the whole way, apparently not issuing a peep of protest.

They'd bring her back. Plus, this was what the kitten had wanted: to go on an adventure. They were just being thoughtful caretakers. Or something.

They got across McClaren Way in eight minutes.

Cruz had called Weatherstone from his phone on a loop for half of those minutes, never getting an answer. What if something had happened to the staff of the flight park?

He switched to calling the police station when they still hadn't received a reply from Sutter.

"Oh! Hi. Is this Emma? This is Cruz Caddel. I was there with Deandra Hendricks earlier, who gave the report about Lionax? Yeah. Yeah. Hi. Good, thanks. Listen. We have an idea of where Lionax is. The Weatherstone Flight Park. Bounty hunters are on the way, but they're not in town yet. Officer Sutter isn't answering her phone. The bounty hunter said to alert the werecats. Yeah. I know. I think that was part of his plan. Got it. Thanks. We're headed there now. No one is answering at the Weatherstone office, and I'm worried someone might need medical attention. No, we won't, ma'am. Yeah. Okay, thank you."

He disconnected the call and heaved out a long breath. "She's contacting as many werecats as she can find. She's going to send EMS, too."

Deandra's stomach was in knots, unsure what on earth they would possibly find when they arrived. It wasn't until she'd practically Tokyo drifted into the half-full parking lot that she remembered she knew the owner of the flight park.

Heck, she even had a pass card that granted her access to the park hanging from her rearview mirror. Paula Fallow had let her hang onto their extra card because of how often Deandra brought Voidbringer to the park. The card wouldn't do Deandra any good, though, if all the doors were compromised.

Throwing the car into park, she plucked her phone off the dash. Her hands were shaking so badly, she hit the wrong person in her address book twice before she successfully dialed the right one. She put the call on speaker.

"Well, this is a surprise, Miss Henricks," drawled Grant Hornsby in greeting. "Typically it's the client who initiates contact first, no?"

"Are you in town?" she blurted, not wanting to waste time, especially since the incubus's voice was making her brain go fuzzy. Dang incubus powers.

"Yes. Why?"

"Have you or your wife talked to your staff lately? Are there security cameras on the property? Do you have a way to remotely access the feed?"

Mr. Hornsby clearly sensed how urgent this was, so he didn't ask any questions. She could tell he was on the move from the sharp click of his hard-soled shoes. "Give me a moment."

Deandra eyed the exterior of the flight park. The parking lot was set back from the building by a wide expanse of grass dotted with poop-bag stations. A walking path led from the lot to the front doors of the main office and then curved around the circumference of the building to give flight-park patrons a paved path to reach their loading pod of choice.

The office didn't have all its windows blown out or anything, but the windows were dark. Maybe there were black sunshades that were pulled down all the way to the floor? But why would the staff do that in the middle of the day?

"*What* is going on?" Mr. Hornsby asked. "All of the cameras went dark about an hour ago. Why wouldn't the security company contact me about a power failure?" He muttered to himself a bit. "Wait. The timestamps are still running. The feed hasn't stopped. The lenses themselves are all black—as if they were sprayed with paint. I'm going back in the feed two hours to see if I can see the culprit … Goddess. They simultaneously went black an hour ago. How is this even possible?"

As a mundane who asked herself that in Axia on a daily basis, she kept her snarky "magic, probably" comment to herself.

"I don't know, but it sounds like all the doors into the park were compromised, too. No one can get out." Deandra didn't know how the incubus would react to this next part. "I believe someone inside is trying to blow a hole in—if not totally destroy —the dome to let the animals out. There are over a dozen inside right now. We can't get a hold of anyone in the front office."

The silence was long. "How dangerous is the person inside?"

"I honestly don't know. The windows to the office are blacked out. The doors are jammed. We can't get in to see what's happening."

"Okay. Give me a second," he said, then muttered to himself a bit as he presumably checked his security system from his computer. "From what I can tell, one of the entrance pods isn't offline the same way as the others. All of them have a key hidden in the wall that will allow the doors to be opened if the power or magic fails. All but one are compromised that way and currently can only be opened with a key. This other one, though …I'm guessing the vandal treated it differently to give themself a way out. Whoever this is either is a sorcerer who knows their way around complicated rune arrays, or they employed a very complex rune-breaking talisman. I can get this particular door open remotely if you're willing to get me some information."

Deandra glanced at Cruz. He nodded vigorously. They scrambled out of the car.

"Which door?"

"Loading pod 9 on the far side of the park. The opposite side as the parking lot. The outer door will be stuck open if it's opened remotely, so I'll keep the inner one closed, as that causes just as much of a flight risk. Let me know when you're there, and I'll unlock it. Then I'll head to you. If I fly, I can be there in two minutes."

Deandra and Cruz took off at a jog toward the flight park. Havoc raced ahead of her, leash taut. The kitten jumped off Cruz's shoulder, hit the ground running, and easily kept pace with Havoc.

All at once, Cruz, the kitten, and the leash connecting them disappeared and reappeared five feet ahead. Cruz immediately doubled over and noisily vomited into the grass.

"Kitten!" he gasped, hands on his knees. "Holy crap. No phasing the human!"

Deandra and Havoc caught up. "Oh my gosh! You okay? I didn't know they could phase themselves *and* other beings."

"Honestly, I didn't, either. I don't think that's common." He levered himself to standing. "Oh, Goddess, that was horrible."

"What's happening over there? Did you make it to pod 9?" came Mr. Hornsby's voice through her phone's speaker. "Please don't dillydally when my very expensive park is in jeopardy."

Cruz made a rude gesture at the phone. Deandra bit back a laugh.

"You good?" she asked Cruz.

"Yeah. Good. The kitten is suitably apologetic."

They took off running again. They went left, passing the blacked-out front office, and then skirted the circular building until they made it to the right pod. At first glance, Deandra wouldn't have been able to tell just from looking at the doors that they weren't functioning normally.

"We're at pod 9," Deandra said.

A few seconds later, three nested circles of runes flashed blue on the door. An unseen mechanism whirled to life, something clicked, and the familiar keypad-like rectangle to the right of the door lit up.

MANUAL OVERRIDE:
Successful!

The door slid open.

ERROR:
Critical rune array malfunction!
Please call Runeworx to schedule maintenance.

"Leaving now," Mr. Hornsby said, then abruptly disconnected the call.

Deandra, Havoc, Cruz, and the vibrissa kitten rushed into the rectangular space that always reminded her of a cross between a glass elevator car and an oversize telephone booth. Though the thick reinforced plastic door that sat opposite the loading pod's outer entrance was scuffed from claws, nails, horns, and hooves, it was easy to see through it and into the flight park beyond.

The park had two terrain types. On one side of the wide pathway that bisected the park was the forest area, and the lagoon sat to the other side. Loading pod 9 opened nearest the lagoon area, but it provided a decent view of the thoroughfare where pet owners usually hung out, as it was dotted with benches and held racks for leash and harness storage.

Deandra had never entered the park from this side of the building, as it was easier to access the pods closer to the parking lot. Owners with shyer pets often used the farther entrances to allow their animals a chance to ease into the whole flight-park experience instead of entering through one of the doors that saw more frequent traffic.

If she craned her neck just right and peered to the left, she could see the backside of the mountain-like structure from which the waterfall fell into the lagoon. The back looked like a sheer rock face covered in pulsing runes, further confirming that what powered the waterfall was magic more than anything else.

Deandra's gaze swept back to the right. No animals were in the air, from what she could tell. Several owners sat on the benches, but they weren't doing much. It was a little unnerving, honestly.

One of the animals—a flying pony Deandra didn't recognize— trotted up to one of the seated owners and nuzzled their knee with its muzzle. At first the person didn't react, and then, ever so slowly, the person tipped to the side and collapsed onto their shoulder on the bench. Deandra gasped.

The pony's head suddenly whipped in their direction, and after a moment's hesitation, it zipped over. Cruz dropped to one knee. The pony on the other side pawed at the ground and shook its mane in irritation. Havoc sat close to the door, head cocked as he gazed at the pony. As far as she knew, he'd never seen one before. He'd probably love to have a flying animal to play with.

She willed herself to focus on the task at hand; she could worry about Havoc's social life later.

"He says all the owners fell asleep about five minutes ago," Cruz said. "One apparently pitched headfirst into the lagoon, and he and another pony had to pull her out so she wouldn't drown."

"Where's Lionax?" Deandra asked.

Cruz refocused on the silver-and-white flying pony. Several agonizing seconds later, he said, "He's on the other side of this mountain. He poured some kind of concoction into the lagoon, and it's bubbling now. It's giving off a cloud of green fog that's so thick, the pony can't see anything behind it. It's slowly rising upward." Cruz glanced up at Deandra from his spot in front of the pony. "If Lionax really *is* as talented at alchemy as rumors suggest, I'm guessing that cloud is either going to eat away at the dome like acid, or it's going to detonate and literally blow the top off this place." His focus returned to the pony. "Uhh, he says the vapor occasionally crackles like lightning? So I'm leaning more toward the exploding angle. We need to get *everyone* out of there."

"Do we think the sparkly green cloud of doom is what made all the people pass out?" Deandra asked, eyeing the edges of the door, wondering how airtight the seal was. She was somewhat comforted that she couldn't smell oranges, coffee, or horsehair. "As in, if we get through this door, are we gonna get knocked out, too?"

She watched as Cruz spoke to the pony telepathically. The pony pawed at the ground and shook its head some more.

Cruz said, "He doesn't know. Clearly whatever it is isn't affecting the sentient and sapient animals."

She didn't know what Mr. Hornsby planned to do when he got here. What if he went in there and passed out? Maybe just rushing in wasn't the solution. The werecats would be there soon. Perhaps if they went in as cats, they'd be immune to whatever was in the air.

A muted thud sounded behind Deandra, and her whole group whirled around. Havoc woof-barked in alarm. Her eyes bugged the moment her gaze landed on Mr. Hornsby. His black leathery wings were so wide, they stretched far beyond the opening of loading pod 9. It wasn't the width of his wings that was surprising so much as the fact that he *had* wings. How did she not know he had wings!

She watched, fascinated, as the wings folded against his back. The tips still poked up above his shoulder blades. "You have wings," she said.

Mr. Hornsby's lips thinned. "Are we going to do that thing where you state the obvious for no discernible reason? I'm well aware that I possess wings, Miss Hendricks. I told you I was going to fly here. How did you expect that to happen?"

"You own a fleet of flying thoroughbreds!" she said, cheeks hot.

"And I've told you more than once that I don't use those thoroughbreds as a means to get around as if they're mundane pack mules."

She was grateful that, if nothing else, both of the gorgeous man's power-suppressing thumb rings were in place. It was nice that she could be as annoyed with him as she wished without also making a fool of herself in front of Cruz as her mundane senses were hijacked by incubus magic.

Mr. Hornsby huffed an irritated breath and then turned around. The back of his shirt was open down the back, as if someone had taken a pair of scissors and sliced it from collar to midback. His thin tail whipped about.

She watched, mesmerized, as his wings shrunk until they were no bigger than her palm. It took less than five seconds. Mr. Hornsby reached up to grab the split collar of his shirt and pulled the two halves together. There must have been hidden magnets lining the edges of the shirt's cut—or something decidedly more magical—because as soon as he fastened the button that connected the two halves of his collar back together, the vertical slit in his shirt seemed to knit together, hiding his shrunken wings from sight.

Mr. Hornsby turned back around. "One shouldn't keep their wings out for all to see. It's uncouth."

She resisted the petulant urge to mutter *"You're* uncouth" just because he was such a condescending brat. She'd called him to let him know his precious flight park was in danger, and snark was how he repaid her.

Mr. Hornsby's gaze flicked to a spot behind her. "Ah. Hello, Dr. Caddel. I don't think we've ever met in person. My wife handles all the veterinary visits for Starshadow."

Cruz awkwardly cleared his throat. "Yes. Hello."

At least she wasn't the only one thrown off by the fact that Mr. Hornsby was ... *a lot.*

It sounded as if Cruz was going to say something else when he yelped.

Deandra whirled around, and Mr. Hornsby hustled into

loading pod 9 after her and Havoc. At first, she couldn't process what she was seeing. She looked at Cruz, into the flight park, and back again. Cruz was staring at the loop around his wrist and the fact that it was currently attached to only *part* of a leash.

The rest of the leash was still attached to a harness, which was wrapped around a vibrissa kitten, who was now sprinting toward the main thoroughfare of the flight park. The silver-and-white pony was galloping along next to her. Havoc chirped in distress, his nose pressed to the plastic and leaving twin circles of condensation where his nostrils blew out warm air.

"Wait. What the heck just happened?" Deandra asked. "Vibrissa can't go through walls! Juniper told me that half a dozen times."

Cruz was shaking his head, bewildered. "That harness isn't supposed to let her phase at all, and she already phased me *with* her. They aren't supposed to be able to do that, either."

Mr. Hornsby said, "She just reached a spot where she can see the lagoon. Can she tell where this Lionax fellow is?"

Giving his head another shake, Cruz closed his eyes. Deandra wasn't sure if he *needed* to do that, or if he was doing what he could to stay focused. "Oh, wow. Okay. She's sending picture-thoughts. I can see what she's seeing. Uhh … oh. There. Lionax is at the top of the mountain, near the waterfall. He just dumped in another bucket of powder."

Deandra craned her neck, pressing her temple to the reinforced plastic. A figure moved along the top of the mountain. "I see him."

Mr. Hornsby gently nudged her out of the way so he could see for himself.

"What is the kitten doing now?" Deandra asked.

Cruz's eyes remained closed. One hand was pressed flat to the see-through door. The leash loop still hung from his wrist, the severed red leash swaying gently a couple of inches from the cement floor. "She seems to be checking on the passed-out people inside. Four people on benches. One lying near the lagoon. Two slumped near one of the doors closer to the parking lot side. And one slumped near a door a few feet down. The ones by the doors all have their pass cards next to them. They were clearly trying to get out when they succumbed to the sleep potion. They all look human. No sapient animal owners or elephantine fae."

Deandra assumed the staff in the front office were similarly knocked out, probably succumbing to whatever sleeping agent Lionax deployed before they knew what had hit them—and well before they could get a warning phone call out to the werecats or even to the Hornsbys.

Speaking of phones … she glanced down at hers. What they needed more than anything was to keep Lionax distracted until the cavalry arrived. The unicorn shifter was clearly losing his hold on sanity, was probably exceedingly lonely, and liked to talk. So she'd let him talk. Before she could talk herself out of it, she dialed the second-to-last person she'd spoken to.

"Hello, Deborah," he said. "Calling for career advice?"

"Yes," she said, because why not, and ignored the odd looks Mr. Hornsby and Cruz shot her way at the sound of her voice. "What do you think I should pursue next? Are *you* looking for an assistant? I've always been curious about alchemy."

He scoffed. "One doesn't pick up alchemy as a casual hobby. It's a delicate art that requires deep study, dedication, and patience."

"Where should I start?" she asked.

He started listing off books she should buy as well as a video series a retired alchemist had posted on the arcane web. She made the requisite noises to imply she was paying close attention and taking dutiful notes.

Mr. Hornsby grunted. "The louse is moving in this direction, but he's still atop the mountain."

"Oh," Lionax said, sounding truly deflated. He must have heard Mr. Hornsby, even if his voice had been soft. Freakin' fae and their freakin' enhanced senses. "I see what's happening here. You've tracked me down and you're attempting to distract me. Is that it? You don't actually want advice. Who sent you? The Green-woods? No. Couldn't be. Do you even work for them, Deborah? Are you the world's worst undercover cop? Perhaps you're the kind of agent the Collective hires when they're facing steep budget cuts."

"*Hey!*" she said, not knowing why that offended her.

"Why don't you come on in and say hi in person, hm?" Lionax asked. "It's a little humid, but I needed to test this on a large quantity of water to make sure I've got my calculations right. Even if I'm a little off, this will give us a *lot* of data. And we need a lot of data, given the area of effect for the next one. Nothing will teach you more about alchemy than on-the-job training."

"This seems like a lot of work just to release a dozen animals," Deandra said.

He laughed. "On second thought, maybe you're just where you need to be career-wise, Debbie. I'm sure your lack of creativity makes you a perfect assistant for the Greenwoods. The current job market requires far more out-of-the-box thinking."

"Have you reached out to your buddy Jet? He's been causing all kinds of trouble this weekend. Seems like whatever shenani-gans you're planning would be right up his alley," Deandra said. "You two were like brothers once, weren't you?"

Lionax paused. "Jet is the worst thing that ever happened to ASA. You think what he's been doing this weekend constitutes trouble? In my day…"

Deandra quickly put the phone on speaker, and then muted the call, letting Lionax rant. "He says he needs water for whatever he's planning to do, but this is just a test run. He just wants to make sure he did the math right. There's only one place I know of in Axia that has both a lot of water and a lot of people nearby—especially this weekend."

Cruz and Mr. Hornsby both looked at her sharply. "The pond at Oracle Park," they said in unison.

The word pond was a bit of a misnomer, as it was closer to a small lake.

"I don't know what the range is on this sleeping potion," Deandra said, "but what if using something as big as the pond can create a fog that covers a large swath of the town? Maybe he wants to craft something stronger, so it knocks out elephantine fae, too. If the whole town is asleep, he could open every cage, every front door, and set loose as many animals as he can find. Which is admittedly bad and dangerous for everyone's pets.

"But he said I was thinking too small. What if *Axia* is a test run, too? This is the smallest hub in the system, right? What happens when he scales this and takes it to bigger cities with rivers, lakes, water towers, and reservoirs? To cities with rescues, and farms, and zoos ..." She glanced up at Mr. Hornsby, "And stables." His jaw ticked. "I don't know how big ASA is, but maybe some of the members would join him if he's successful here. Maybe he already *has* followers. The scale *and* scope could increase if he's got help across the hub system.

"I also don't know if there are any animals left in this realm as dangerous as the hippodynus, but I'm guessing there are still several that shouldn't be set loose on unsuspecting populations."

She took the phone off speaker and then unmuted it, placing it back to her ear as Cruz and Mr. Hornsby hustled outside to whisper about what they thought they needed to do next.

The werecats still weren't here. It had been over twenty minutes since Cruz last spoke to Emma. Where in the heck were they?

"—no one appreciates what we used to do back then," Lionax said, still ranting away. "That was back when ASA actually could make a difference. They're too soft now. Everything is performative. If Jet truly believed in ASA, he'd be here. I gave him a choice. Join me or face the consequences. Now he's trapped in a cage of his own making. And that's sad. I taught him everything he knows."

Putting the phone back on speaker, she pulled up her text thread with Wendy, and detailed what little she knew about whatever alchemical madness Lionax was cooking up, then asked her to check with Heather about what they might be able to do to counteract it. She sent a similar text to Paula Fallow, a kitchen witch, hoping the woman wouldn't ask too many questions, despite the message coming out of nowhere and there being very little context.

Deandra probably needed to make more witchy friends, just in case she ever got caught unaware by a loopy unicorn shifter trying to liberate animal-kind via alchemical warfare again. Or, you know, in case she was ever on *Who Wants to Be a Magical Millionaire?* and she needed to phone a friend about the basics of potion making.

Lionax was still rambling on, but he seemed to be running out of steam.

She asked, "Don't you think it might be time for some self-reflection if you can't get anyone to help you? Maybe Jet and the rest of ASA aren't here for more personal reasons."

Lionax fell quiet. "I *made* ASA," he said, voice low. "I built that organization from the ground up. They took my hard work, my blood, my sweat, my tears, and once I was used up, they cast me aside like trash. Jet is a two-faced liar and a sneak. He smiles in your face while sinking a dagger into your gut. He lied to ASA— lied about what he saw as ASA's future, lied to the board about me. The organization is a pale shadow of what it used to be, what it *could* be. And if none of them can see that, then I'll show them myself. Well, mostly by myself. I've found that the only way to guarantee loyalty is to buy it. Mercenaries come in all shapes and sizes—and I have the cash to pay for them."

"What happens when you run out of money and your loyal followers go looking for someone else with deeper pockets?" she asked, which set him off again.

A text came in from Wendy, and as she pulled up the thread, she craned her neck to check on Lionax. He was pacing the top of the mountain. The more distressing sight, though, was the cloud of green that was rising from the lagoon. It was somehow as solid as Jell-O yet as fluid as water. It had risen a good ten feet off the water's surface by now and was slowly inching its way toward the dome of the flight park. It had to be twenty feet across. At the rate it was going, it would probably reach the top in five minutes. Lightning forked through it occasionally, illuminating the gelatinous mass from within in bursts of lime green.

Wendy
Heather says she can't give advice on how to dispel something like that without knowing what went into the concoction in the first place. She does have talismans for better breathing, though. They're used to increase lung capacity—they can be used to help you swim or run longer if you're training for a race, though they're considered cheating in an actual race. They're mostly used to help promote better health, but she thinks if the air is compromised, it could help someone stay conscious in it for longer. We have some in the shop, but it would take someone at least ten minutes to get here and back from the flight park. Is that enough time?

Hitting mute on the phone again, she poked her head out of the door where Mr. Hornsby and Cruz were still brainstorming.

She looked at the incubus. "Go to Heather's Elixirs to pick up talismans for better breathing. With your incubus constitution, it might allow you the time needed to get to Lionax and stop him. We have maybe five minutes before that mass hits the dome, though."

He stared at her for a beat, and then what seemed like seconds later, his bat-like wings were unfurled, and the man was airborne and flying away at incredible speed.

Deandra
Incubus comin' in hot!

Wendy
Oh! Something exciting is happening to me, finally!

"You and Mr. Hornsby come up with anything?" Deandra asked.

"Not really. The kitten says the pygmy phoenixes and fae birds are down for the count now. Only the flying pigs and the ponies are still standing, though the ponies are drowsy," Cruz said.

"How is *she* doing?"

"Strangely? She seems totally fine," Cruz said. "Vibrissa were one of the few semi-domesticated animals from the fae realm that were bred to be more aloof, better hunters, stealthier, etcetera. The docile ones were usually culled. They bred out what they thought were weaker traits. I think this kitten, who is shyer, more cautious, and more observant, is more in line with how vibrissa are without intervention. Now I wonder if they're actually more magically inclined than we thought, and while they were breeding out certain personality traits, they were also breeding out some of their magic."

"You fall asleep on me, Debbie?" came Lionax's voice through the phone.

Wincing, she hurried back to the see-through door while simultaneously taking the phone off mute. Havoc still sat near the door, staring forlornly after the kitten—or possibly the pretty silver-and-white pony. "Still here," she said, angling her head to get a view of Lionax. He was still atop the mountain, but he was turned toward the back of the giant boulder, not the waterfall. His head was tipped back, as if he were gazing out the dome.

"It's cute you think you could distract me while reinforcements show up. I'm impressed you're sending them by air. But the potency of the alchemical potion wafting around in here is so strong, it would even fell a troll," Lionax said. "So do your worst, Debbie. It's too late."

"How is it not affecting you?" she asked.

"Would be stupid of me to not craft an antidote, wouldn't it?" he asked. "I need to stay conscious while the town sleeps. Lots of ground to cover for us, but we'll manage."

"You keep saying *we*," she said. "Do you have a friend in there after all, or are you talking in the second person like a true psychopath?"

In a calm, controlled voice that made the hair on her neck stand up, he said, "I'm *not* a psychopath. You're just narrowminded."

The call disconnected.

Deandra tried to call back, temple pressed to the door. Lionax walked toward the edge of the mountain, then hit Decline. He cocked his arm back and then swung it forward. Light glinted off an object as it tumbled off the mountain and out of sight, presumably into the lagoon below. The giant green mass was halfway to the ceiling now.

She whirled toward Cruz. "Not only did I trigger him into hanging up on me, he threw his phone into the water."

Cruz didn't get a chance to reply because Mr. Hornsby was back. He didn't bother retracting his wings.

Holding out two necklaces, one in each hand, the incubus said, "Put these on. I'll unlock that second door. You go in through here, and I'll go through the top. Do what you can to distract him until I can get to the dome. Heather gave me a few suggestions of what I can try once I'm up there." He pulled a few earthy-smelling satchels from the pocket of his slacks. "You need to buy me at least a few minutes."

Deandra and Cruz each took a necklace. They looked similar to travel talismans, but the hollow in the middle was filled with a slightly undulating, sparkly purple substance. Mr. Hornsby was already wearing his.

Before Deandra could ask anything, like "What about the flight risk of this door standing open?" the incubus had already taken off again. A mechanism in the inner door to the flight park groaned. Deandra and Cruz hastily put on their necklaces. The wide metal disc rested just below her collarbone. The necklace was too heavy, and for a moment she felt like she was hyperventilating, unable to get in *any* air, let alone having increased lung capacity.

Just when her wide gaze met Cruz's equally panicked one, the tension in her chest loosened, and she sucked in a huge, *huge* lungful of air.

The door opened and Deandra was hit full in the face by the overpowering smells of Lionax's magic. It was like walking into a humid coffee shop housed in a stable that had just been disinfected by an overzealous janitor who loved the scent of oranges.

Havoc sneezed.

"One sec," Deandra told Cruz, then she sent a quick text to Ruth the bounty hunter detailing where they were. It wasn't that she was worried that the moment they walked in there, they'd pass out, Lionax would steal her dragon, and then he'd nuke a sleep bomb in Oracle Park's pond or anything.

Okay, that was exactly what she was worried about.

> **Ruth**
> Five minutes out. Telepad traffic was awful, even with our clearance. We're in Axia now.

Deandra didn't know how well her dragon would fare, given how the gas was even taking out the flying ponies now. But if the fae kitten was still doing all right, maybe Havoc would be okay, too.

After giving each other a wary look, she and Cruz jogged into the park.

CHAPTER EIGHTEEN

They made it all the way to the first passed-out person before Lionax realized she, Cruz, and Havoc had joined him. Deandra did everything in her power not to look straight up and give away Mr. Hornsby's location.

"Oho! You decided to join me after all, have you, Debbie?" he called out, his voice easily carrying across the distance.

There were passed-out people and animals scattered all over the place. The ponies were all flopped on their sides. Even the flying pigs were starting to succumb to the sleep-potion-laced air. They slowly flew in circles only a few feet from the ground, like newly hatched, drowsy flies.

Deandra didn't understand how increased lung capacity

would keep her from also succumbing—wouldn't being able to take in *more* air make her pass out even faster? But she didn't feel any different. Not yet, anyway. There was also now a vent in the domed building thanks to loading pod 9's door being stuck open, so maybe the tainted air was rushing out and would dilute once it was out in the open.

She and Cruz stood back to back to keep an eye out for any of Lionax's minions who might be lurking. Havoc stood in front of her, his attention focused squarely on Lionax.

Lowering her voice, she asked Cruz, "Can you tell how many of the animals are still conscious?"

"Two pigs and the kitten," he said. "I just don't know where she is. She told me she was hunting about five minutes ago, and I haven't gotten anything from her since. Apparently she can block the mental link at will, but I can still sense her."

Her phone buzzed in her hand.

> **Ruth**
> At the door. My team is going in as cats. We're
> going to circle around the back of this mountain.
> Lionax will have defensive alchemical tools with
> him, so keep your distance

Voice raised so Lionax could hear her, she called out, "Maybe you'll succeed in destroying the flight park, but you'll be snatched up by werecats and thrown in a Collective prison soon enough. You know that, right? Maybe even the Antarctic one."

"I've eluded those idiots for decades, girl," Lionax called back. "You don't think I have—"

At first Deandra thought the unicorn shifter had already been caught somehow, but she realized he was staring at her with his head canted.

"Oh, I'm *so* disappointed, Debbie! I should have assumed you were just as despicable as the Greenwoods because you worked for them, but *this*?"

Deandra craned her neck to peer at Cruz, but he had his eyes closed again, apparently in communication with the kitten. As cool as his ability was, this going into a trancelike state when danger was afoot seemed like a real downside to the skill.

Her focus returned to Lionax just as he threw something again. But this time, his other arm was in motion, too. A small shiny object was hurtling toward her. She grabbed Cruz by the arm, trying to push him back, to snap him out of his link with the vibrissa kitten. She'd only succeeded in getting him to stumble forward a step when the glass object, no bigger than her thumb, hit the packed dirt path in front of her. The vial shattered, and with it came a plume of white smoke that smelled of oranges. A similar plume, like the vent of a geyser, shot up from the mountain where Lionax stood.

Nope. Where he *used* to be standing.

Because now the unicorn shifter was a mere few feet from her, the white smoke billowing around his shoes.

"Did you just use smoke to teleport?" she asked, incredulous.

Lionax grinned. "Cool, right?" Then his gaze slid down to Havoc.

Her dragon stood in front of her, stance wide, growl low, and smoke very similar to the kind that had poured from Lionax's thrown vial billowing from his nose. *That* smoke smelled like a campfire.

"You're keeping a fire-aligned dire wolf as a pet, Debbie?" he asked, sounding like a disappointed parent. "You know, these are exceedingly rare. Where did you get it? A little mundane like you being able to find a dire wolf puppy, let alone tame one, is—well, frankly I don't believe it. So either you're not who you appear to be ..." He stared intently at Havoc. "Or *he's* not."

Lionax dropped to a squat. Deandra stumbled back a step, bumping into Cruz, who was still zoned out. She still felt fine, so she figured his zombie-like state was because of the kitten and not because he was being put to sleep by the fog in the air. Havoc growl-barked—and for the first time ever, it sounded dangerously close to a roar.

The unicorn shifter just grinned at him. "Interesting. So you *do* have claws, little pup. Your kind is fearsome. You don't belong in a harness tied to a human, of all things. I can show you what you were meant for."

Deandra hazarded a glance past Lionax, noting that three werecats were slowly prowling toward them. It was unnerving that she only just now sensed they were there, given their size.

Then Lionax sensed them, too, and he whirled, glass vials already being thrown. He must have grabbed them from his pockets as he turned around. Two of the cats leaped out of the way in time, but a third caught a vial to the side. It shattered on impact, an explosion of green gas erupting from it. The cat was unconscious before it hit the ground, skidding along the packed earth and crashing into one of the posts holding up a leash-and-harness station. The wood cracked from the impact, but the board otherwise stayed upright.

The two remaining cats quickly got to their paws, shook their heads, and hunkered lower to the ground. Oh, they were mad. Deandra needed to get the heck out of there.

She turned, took Cruz by the arm with both hands, and gave him a very hard shake. "I need you to snap out of it!" Lightly slapping his face didn't work, either. She didn't know what to do. It wasn't like she could toss him over her shoulder and cart him away like a sack of potatoes. And where the heck was the dang kitten that had such a hold on him?

Then several things happened at once.

A massive shattering of glass sounded from above, followed by the falling form of a man with bat-like wings. Lionax tossed two more vials, and Deandra recognized them as his teleporting ones. The moment a great burst of white smoke exploded between him and the snarling werecats, he spun on his heel, scooped up Havoc as if he weighed nothing more than a loaf of bread, and jumped into the smoke. The leash went taut, yanking Deandra with it, but seconds later, the leash loop, much like Cruz's, dangled from her wrist, the leash cut off in the middle.

No harness. No Havoc.

Another series of crashes sounded from above, but she was too worried about Havoc to look up.

She spun in a frantic circle, unsure of where the second vial had landed—where Lionax's second teleportation vial had shattered, marking his next location.

A yelp sounded behind her, and she darted around the still-unresponsive Cruz to find Lionax closer to the loading pods on the parking-lot side of the building. Havoc was on all fours, his scales a muddy brown, black smoke pouring from his nostrils. She'd never seen him so enraged.

Lionax looked mildly terrified, and he was clutching his elbow with one hand. Blood seeped between his fingers.

She inched toward her dragon, knowing full well that she had no resources at her disposal to help him, but feeling compelled to move toward him all the same.

The unicorn shifter cackled. "Oh! You're no mere dire wolf are you? Look at you!" His gaze flicked to Deandra. "What secrets are you keeping, mundane? I only got a brief look at his collar, but I know glamour runework when I see it. It's the only way to stay hidden. I would have figured out just what you two are hiding if he hadn't bitten me. Good on him, though! He's a beast underneath the domestication you're forcing on him. Let loose, friend! Be wild! Take no prisoners!"

Havoc, as if he'd been waiting for permission, unleashed a gout of fire so bright, Deandra had to shield her eyes.

Lionax had gotten out of the way in time, if his deranged laughter was any indication. "Yes! Come with me, beast! We'll burn it all down together!"

At the same time Cruz let out a frantic, "Deandra? Dee! Where are you?" from behind her, Lionax shrieked in pain.

He looked down. Flailed. Screamed. Looked behind him. A blur of green. A screech from Lionax. Another blur. Lionax kicked out, lost his footing, and hit the ground. The vibrissa kitten phased next to his head, chomped down on his ear, then phased to his other ear.

His frantic flailing around let the two conscious werecats make their move, sprinting past Deandra and Cruz before pouncing on Lionax. They got him flipped over, and in one fluid motion, the puma that had been pinning him to the ground shifted into a woman who snapped sparking blue handcuffs on Lionax's wrists. Deandra assumed they were magic-nullifying cuffs. The werecat hauled a furious Lionax to his feet.

Another werecat trotted past Deandra, shifted into a human, and grabbed Lionax's arm. The werecat who had aided the puma in apprehending Lionax exchanged a few words with the woman before taking hold of Lionax's other arm. They hauled him back the way they'd come.

Lionax ranted and raved. "I never should have contacted you, Debbie!" he shouted as the cats dragged him toward her. "Actually, I never should have replied to that pimply child doing your online dirty work. He can't even spell! Why did I respond? He ruined everything!"

"This mean you don't want to hear that he's not a pimply teen, but the Greenwoods' salica?" she asked.

The unicorn shifter howled in rage. His elbow was still bleeding from where Havoc had bitten him. It was all quite satisfying.

A warm hand settled on Deandra's waist a moment after Lionax was escorted past her, and she twisted around, fearful. She met Cruz's worried expression. She was so relieved to finally see lucidity in his eyes, she almost burst into tears.

Havoc bounded over, chirp-barking as he circled them, as if to ask *"Did you see that, Mom? I nearly barbecued him!"*

Deandra laughed, though it was shaky. "You were very brave."

He abruptly sat on his haunches to attend to an itch.

Deandra returned her focus to Cruz. "Are you okay?" She pulled him into a tight hug.

He squeezed her back. "Yeah. It's like I *became* her for a while. I didn't have any control over it. Maybe *that's* the kind of thing Peril is scared of. Getting your mind hijacked isn't great."

Deandra pulled away, studying his face. "You sure you're okay? What was she showing you? You said she was hunting, right?"

His eyes bugged. "Oh crap." He peered over her head. "Bounty hunter … Miss. Um. Ma'am? Ma'am."

Deandra started to turn toward the sound of a throaty laugh, but she did a double take at the scene playing out behind Cruz. At least six other werecats were in attendance now. Cruz turned, too, then cursed.

There were magic-wielders here now, too. Four of them stood around the curving shore of the lagoon. Their hands whipped about in the air as if conducting an orchestra. Gold discs of magic, like massive translucent coins, hovered in front of each, filled with nested circles of runes. High above, Mr. Hornsby was flanked by four enormous flying horses. Their arrival must have been the additional crashes she'd heard earlier. While the gust of wind from the collective power of their beating wings wasn't pushing the gelatinous mass of green magic back toward the lagoon, it was at least keeping it stationary.

"Loose!" one of the magic-wielders called, and all four of them thrust their arms forward, sending the magic discs hurtling upward and then through the green mass.

The lightning within sparked so brightly, Deandra briefly worried the magic that had just been launched into the concentrated mass was going to detonate it instead of defuse it.

All at once, the ball of magic broke apart like storm clouds that had rained themselves dry, further aided by the wind gusts provided by Mr. Hornsby and his horses. Seconds later, the flight park's patrons—owners and pets alike—began to rouse.

Lionax had continued ranting all the way across the park. His distant shout now suggested he knew his plan had failed. "Where is that useless sorcerer! Rochester! Don't think I can't ruin you from prison!"

The werecats yanked him out of the building.

The EMTs who had apparently been waiting outside until the magic-wielders, who Deandra now assumed were sorcerers, were finished, rushed in to check on the wounded. Werecats morphed from feline to human. The incubus and his personal herd of horses lowered themselves to the ground near the lagoon.

The flight park had become very busy, very quickly.

The puma-turned-human bounty hunter made her way in front of them. "I'm guessing you're Miss Hendricks."

"Hi, Ruth," she said.

Then Ruth's gaze slid to Cruz. "Did you have a question?"

"Oh!" he said. "Yes. My ... our ... the vibrissa cat located—"

Deandra sucked in a gasp when something hit her shoulder. Or, more accurately, *landed* on her shoulder. A deep rumbly purr filtered into her right ear, and then the kitten was nuzzling her neck. She reached up to give it a scritch under the chin. Her purr deepened.

Ruth gaped, some of her rough exterior melting under the presence of a very cute kitten. Deandra had no clue what her ethnicity was—her skin was a dusky brown, her hair was sandy blond and hit just below her chin, and her eyes were almost gold. They were all feline. "That *was* a vibrissa cat! Franklin owes me twenty bucks. How do you two have a trained vibrissa *and* a tame dire wolf?"

The dire wolf in question was currently rolling around in the dirt.

Cruz said, "The vibrissa isn't ours. She's kind of on loan at the moment. She *is* up for adoption, though."

Ruth stared at the vibrissa. "Really? I've always been enamored with the breed. They're the most successful of feline hunters, despite their size. Tenacity in a small package." She took a step forward, hand reaching for the kitten still purring in Deandra's ear as she scratched the kitten's cheeks and chin.

The vibrissa sensed the bounty hunter coming, though, and suddenly swiped at the woman's approaching hand. Then she hissed for good measure.

Cruz coughed down a laugh. "I am absolutely *not* telling her that," he told the kitten.

The kitten hissed in reply, though with less force, then resumed nuzzling Deandra's neck, purr back up to a ten.

"Uh," Cruz said, glancing at the kitten, and then Ruth. "The kitten says she, uh, doesn't … like you."

Deandra winced, wondering what the kitten had actually said if "she doesn't like you" was the watered-down version of the message.

The bounty hunter, thankfully, didn't appear to be offended. Instead, she turned all her intensity on Cruz. "You're a … zoolinguist, then?"

She said it as if the label were lewd somehow.

"Uh, yes?"

She took a step closer. "Zoolinguists and shifters make quite the dynamic pair. Has that been your experience? Being *in* the mind of your partner?"

Deandra knew that she, as a mundane, couldn't clock a shifter —and a bounty hunter from the big city of Luma to boot—but she was seriously considering it.

Cruz caught on three seconds later that he was being aggressively hit on and wrapped an arm around Deandra so tightly, she might as well have been stuffed into his shirt. "Oh, I'm sure that's quite true, but I'm very taken. Really, *really* taken."

Ruth sighed. "Of course you are. There are so few of you—it's like discovering a new species. Girl has to shoot her shot, no?" She eyed Deandra. "Are you a zoolinguist too? You must be, with this menagerie."

"Boring ol' mundane." When Ruth just stared at her like she was starting to wonder if Deandra wasn't actually exceedingly honest, but rather an evil genius playing 3D chess and keeping everyone fooled, Deandra added, "There's one vibrissa left at the festival. He's at the Mythic Pet Kitchen booth. If he's still there, you could tell Juniper Thistlewick that Deandra and Cruz sent you."

"And how does he compare to the adorable assassin on your shoulder?" Ruth asked, back to her professional demeanor from earlier as if the last few very awkward seconds hadn't happened.

"I have a very unsubstantiated theory," Cruz said, still keeping his arm around Deandra's side, "that the ones who are more docile in nature might actually be more magically inclined. He and this one here were the last ones left, in part because of how shy they are."

Ruth's brows hiked again. "Her? Shy?"

"Once we knew what she wanted, she opened up," Cruz said.

"I'll bet she did," Ruth said, eyeing Cruz like he was a steak and she was starving.

"Oh my! How far we've gotten off track …" Deandra said, her tone stilted and her face hot. "Didn't you say, Cruz, that the kitten located something?"

"Oh!" he said, sounding just as uncomfortable as she did. "Yes. A second perp!"

Ruth stared blankly at him. "Why didn't you *lead* with that? We've just been here casually shooting the crap when there's another asset nearby? What if they got away?"

The kitten hissed so loudly and abruptly that even Ruth flinched.

"She says that she made sure he's not going anywhere," Cruz said. "Well, that's ominous. He's in the forest area." He leaned forward to address the kitten. "Can you show us where he is?"

A blink later, and the kitten was gone.

Startled, all three of them looked around, finding the kitten several feet away, on the path leading toward the loading pods closest to the parking lot. The kitten chirruped when she saw they'd located her, and then she phased away again.

They took off after her, Havoc racing ahead of them. He and the kitten both still wore harnesses with only a fraction of their leashes attached to the clasps. Deandra and Cruz had both lost track of their severed leash pieces a while ago.

Running across grass, skirting boulders, and doing their best to not trample the flowers as they raced after the kitten, they eventually came upon a man sprawled on his back, half his face covered by a bandana. Since everyone else who had been under the effects of the sleep concoction had started to awaken as soon as the ball of magic was dispelled, Deandra was a little worried this guy was in a more permanent state of sleep.

Ruth squatted next to him and checked his wrist for a pulse. "He's alive." The bounty hunter glanced over her shoulder. "Might want to give him some room. I can already smell what the banana lying over his face is soaked in—an alchemical version of chloroform. Once I take it off his face, he might wake up swinging."

Deandra and Cruz took several steps back. Havoc was noisily sniffing the unconscious man's shoes, so she called him to her side. He bounded over and sat by her feet. The vibrissa kitten, however, took a seat in the middle of the man's chest, staring down at him.

When Ruth tried to speak to the kitten, all she got in response was a spitting hiss.

Without further ado, Ruth pulled the fabric from the man's mouth. Almost instantly, he woke with a gasping inhale—and then he nearly choked on it when he spotted the vibrissa cat looming over him.

"Ahhh! Get it off me!" the man exclaimed.

Recognition smacked Deandra in the face. *"Theodore?"*

Rochester. That's who Lionax had been shouting about— Theodore Rochester.

His head whipped to the side, trying to find the source of the voice. Deandra, Cruz, and Havoc walked over so the guy wouldn't get a crick in his neck. A neck, she noted, that was dotted with several bites and scratches. "Oh. It's you. You want to get this little monster off me?"

Deandra crossed her arms. "I think you should probably answer a few questions first. That nice lady next to you …" Ruth shot him a finger wave. "Is a bounty hunter, and her colleagues just cuffed Lionax Orma and took him out of here. So I'm guessing she's going to want to know what the heck you were doing here, because I don't think it was because you were taking your pet out for a nice outing."

Theodore's brain was clearly working overtime. "Hey. Uh. Listen. It's not what you think. I—*ow!*"

The vibrissa kitten had phased to Theodore's side. His hand shot up, a snarling green kitten latched onto the pad of his thumb. The faint glow of golden light dissipated from his fingertips.

Ruth laughed. "Ah, so you're a sorcerer. And you were trying to craft a quick rune array to get your butt out of here …"

Deandra glanced at the kitten. "Good girl!"

She phased back onto Theodore's chest, but facing Deandra and Cruz this time. She squinted her eyes closed and chirruped. Then she whirled around to presumably glare daggers at Theodore again.

"I *am* very interested in what you were doing here, sorcerer," Ruth said. "As talented as Lionax is, he's an alchemist. I doubt his runework is on par with what an academy-trained sorcerer can do."

"How did you know—"

"I didn't," Ruth said. "Lucky guess. And you just confirmed it."

Theodore sagged, as if he hoped to melt into the ground. "I go where the money is, all right? Lionax pays well. So when he asked for rune arrays that could take out over twenty-five cameras simultaneously, I didn't ask why. I just told him how much. You can't blame a guy for going where the jobs are, can you? Is being an entrepreneur a crime now?"

Ruth scoffed. "That's your argument? Really?"

Theodore's lips thinned.

"How'd you end up passed out with that bandana on your

face?" Ruth asked. "Trying to give yourself sympathy points? Oh no, the poor entrepreneurial sorcerer was just doing his job, and then his big evil boss attacked him? Or did you knock yourself out, like a tame version of a cyanide pill?"

Cruz, inexplicably, burst out laughing. "Theodore was aware the kitten was stalking him. He took the bandana out of a satchel and was keeping up a running commentary, letting her know that he was going to catch her, knock her out, and sell her on the arcane web. He assumed she couldn't understand him. She attacked him, much like she attacked Lionax, until he hit the ground. She let herself be caught, and just before he used the bandana on her, she stole it and phased with it onto his face."

Theodore groaned. "So embarrassing."

Ruth, still squatted beside Theodore's supine body, gazed at the kitten. "Are you *sure* I can't adopt you?"

She got another spitting hiss in response.

In an effort to get the crestfallen look off Ruth's face, Deandra asked, "Did Lionax have any idea you're also the sorcerer for hire at Feline Protected? Seems like knowing that would make the former leader of ASA lose his cookies."

"Which is exactly why I didn't tell him," Theodore said. "He's as good at not asking questions as I am."

"What exactly were you doing in here when you were ambushed by a five-pound kitten?" Ruth asked.

"It's a *kitten*?" Theodore asked.

The kitten hissed in his face. He flinched.

Ruth said, "Better start talking, or I'm going to let her bite you again."

"I was his contingency plan," Theodore said quickly. "If his *alchemical masterpiece*s didn't work as intended, I was to dispel the magical clouds. One was the sleep potion, which he'd never tried as an aerosol before. I was on standby with rune arrays for sleep if it didn't keep the pet owners down. It didn't need to be that strong, all things considered, since there were only a handful of people in here."

"And the other magical cloud?" Cruz asked. "Would the lightning-filled Jell-O have exploded if it reached the top of the dome?"

Theodore clenched his jaw. "You're a bounty hunter, too? You look like an accountant …"

The kitten phased onto his face, bit him squarely on the nose, and then took up her place on his chest once more. Theodore howled in pain.

"Listen, Teddy," Ruth said. "This place is full of bounty hunters, the local werecat police, and even a few Collective sorcerers."

Theodore visibly swallowed.

"Truth serum is in your future, either way," Ruth said. "I have it on good authority that when you willingly confess, rather than having it magically pulled from your lips, the courts look on you more favorably. Your goose is still cooked, but it won't be *as* roasted if you fess up."

Theodore mulled that over. Deandra wasn't sure if it was Ruth's words or the kitten's soft growls that got the rogue sorcerer talking again. "The lightning-filled Jell-O, as you called it, was a corrosive gelatin that wouldn't have exploded so much as oozed across the entire dome and turned all the metal and glass into goo. You're lucky you're all still alive. If the wrong kind of magic had hit the gelatin?" Theodore whistled. "That's where the lightning inside came in. It was an amplification spell. If anyone used an offensive spell against it, *that* would have made it explode."

Deandra's stomach flipped. If the quartet of sorcerers hadn't chosen the right spells to throw at the mass to defuse it, they could have blown the flight park—and everyone in it—to bits.

Honestly, she was glad to know that little tidbit *after* the fact.

Ruth asked, "How did you and Lionax end up working together?"

"The arcane web. It's where I get all my clients. There aren't too many sorcerers working in the private sector, in the grand scheme of things, who are as trained as I am. I'm very busy."

Theodore studied her. "You're a bounty hunter. You know what it's like to take on gigs based on the payout. You help me stay out of the Antarctic prison, and I'll lead you to *every* sketchy person on my client list. I wouldn't doubt that at least half of them are in the system. You could claim a dozen bounties, easy. You'll clean up."

Ruth glanced over her shoulder at Deandra and Cruz, then shot a thumb at Theodore. "Can you believe this guy?"

Deandra recalled something Lionax had said. *"I've found that the only way to guarantee loyalty is to buy it. Mercenaries come in all shapes and sizes—and I have the cash to pay for them."*

To that, she'd asked, *"What happens when you run out of money and your loyal followers go looking for someone else with deeper pockets?"*

Now she had her answer: Any perceived loyalty went out the window in hopes of saving their own hide.

Ruth pulled a cell phone out of her back pocket and stood. "Kitten, if he tries anything fishy, you bite him again, okay? And hard."

The kitten chirruped.

"Hey," Ruth said into her phone. "Orma secure? Good. We've got his accomplice. Rogue sorcerer." She laughed. "I know. The Collective is going to have a field day with this one. Slimier than an anuran shifter on two-for-one elfin wine night."

"Well, that's just rude," Theodore said. "I'm a businessman!"

Ruth glanced down at him. "Same thing."

Theodore gasped. The kitten phased onto his forehead and bapped him on his already punctured nose five times in quick succession, as if she were trying to kill a small rodent.

Ruth sighed at the kitten as if she were a long-lost love. "She's so perfect."

The kitten phased back to Theodore's chest and pointedly ignored Ruth.

The bounty hunter cocked a brow in Cruz's direction, her expression hopeful.

"Sorry. She still finds you … uh … detestable," Cruz said.

A thought struck Deandra. "Theodore … when I saw you with the grimalkyne, you acted as if you hated everything about ASA. How could you turn around and work for its former leader?"

"I *do* hate everything about them. And I hated Lionax even more—in a bone-deep kind of way. He literally got away with murder because the Collective is populated by spineless elites," Theodore said. "But he also had a *lot* of cash he was willing to part with, and his requests were mentally stimulating. I liked the idea of taking his money and then turning around and doing runework for folks like the Thistlewicks and the grimalkyne, knowing it would enrage Lionax if he ever found out."

He said it all so casually, as if taking jobs from anyone willing to pay, regardless of his own morals, wasn't anything to lose sleep over. He did work that ran counter to his clients' interests and lied to their faces about his interests aligning with theirs, simply because they were keeping his bank account full. He was opportunistic to a fault. He might have hated the Collective for having no scruples, but he clearly didn't have any, either. She resisted the urge to tell the kitten to bite him a few more times.

A faint rustle was the only thing that gave away the approach of two loping werecats. They seamlessly shifted into their human counterparts. Deandra, Cruz, and Havoc backed up as the newly arrived women got the squirrely sorcerer cuffed. He'd tried once more to cast a rune array to get his opportunistic butt out of trouble, but the vibrissa cat bit him in numerous places until he was secure. Once it was clear the guy wasn't getting away, the vibrissa kitten phased onto Cruz's shoulder.

Ruth was the last of the werecats to leave, and she turned to try one more time to win the affections of the kitten—who began to nonchalantly lick her own paw as soon as Ruth started speaking to her. "You know, the ruder you are to me, the more I love you."

The kitten phased to Deandra's shoulder then and nuzzled her neck, purring away.

"Manipulative, passive-aggressive little monster," Ruth muttered. "I will grieve this loss for the rest of my days."

Deandra was only half sure the woman was being overly dramatic on purpose.

Ruth nodded a goodbye to Cruz, and then Deandra. "If I have any follow-up questions, I'll give you a ring. Try to stay out of any more criminal activity, okay? At least for the weekend."

"No promises," Deandra said. "And don't forget there's still one vibrissa kitten up for adoption at the Mythic Pet Kitchen booth."

Ruth walked off, waving over her shoulder to acknowledge that she'd heard.

Once they were alone, Deandra sagged against Cruz's side. "Well, that was … a lot."

Cruz laughed. "Speaking of the Mythic Pet Kitchen, we should probably get you-know-who back before Juniper reports us for cat-napping."

Deandra opted not to bring up the slight problem of the kitten being able to phase while in a harness that supposedly prevented it. If the kitten decided she didn't want to go back to the Mythic Pet Kitchen booth, Deandra wasn't sure they could make her. But they'd cross that bridge when they got to it.

Hand in hand, Deandra and Cruz headed for the main part of the park, which was still full of activity. Havoc trotted ahead. The kitten phased back onto Cruz's shoulder.

Mr. Hornsby was speaking with a pair of werecats. His four horses were grazing nearby. They were so massive and so colorful, Deandra could hardly comprehend they were real. It was hard to imagine that little Starshadow and Voidbringer might one day get to that size. They certainly wouldn't fit in her back seat anymore.

Most of the owners and their animals were gone, from what Deandra could tell. Several of the people milling about, Deandra realized, were witches, sorcerers, or some other type of magic-wielders turned maintenance workers who were attempting to get the runework on the doors back to full power.

The Hornsbys worked quickly.

She figured that while Mr. Hornsby had been flying to Heather's Elixirs, he'd contacted his wife to let her know what was happening at their flight park. Since the park was Mrs. Hornsby's family legacy, she likely would have wanted to do everything she could to not only save the park, but get repairs started as soon as possible. How they'd gotten four of their prize horses here so quickly was beyond Deandra. She'd ask Mr. Hornsby, if she didn't think he'd just meet her questions with more snark.

As they began their trek across the center thoroughfare, one of the werecats broke off from talking to Mr. Hornsby to head their way. Officer Sutter.

The blond woman stopped before them, hands on her hips. Havoc noisily sniffed her boots, which the werecat pointedly ignored. "I honestly don't even understand how you got mixed up in this one, Dee."

Deandra laughed despite herself. Mostly because the woman didn't sound upset so much as flabbergasted.

"Don't think this is going to become a habit ..." Officer Sutter hedged. "But I do apologize for our late arrival. It was good thinking to call for help from all angles you could think of." Deandra could tell the woman was warring against her instincts to not divulge anything to civilians, so she waited her out. "ASA held a demonstration in the parking lot of the Axian Nights Hotel, but this time, instead of just one of them being in the cage like the gnome yesterday, almost all of them were. Except the runes on the cages were compromised, and at some point during the demonstration, they were all trapped in the cages and getting zapped and burned. We were caught up in getting them out before they all got themselves killed. Ten of them are in the hospital now! Fools."

Deandra stood a little straighter, remembering something.

"What?" Officer Sutter asked.

"I think Lionax and Theodore were behind that, too. At some point during his ranting, Lionax said something like, 'If Jet truly believed in ASA, he'd be here … now he's trapped in a cage of his own making.' I think he meant that literally," Deandra said. "I'm sure there are several companies that make the kind of cages that ASA used, but the grimalkyne at Feline Protected are said to make the best ones. Theodore is their main sorcerer. It's not like ASA was keeping their demonstration location a secret—they passed out flyers and posted about it online. If Theodore is skilled enough that he could compromise that many cameras and doors in this place—which sounds like he was using heavy-duty magical lock picks—breaking into whatever storage room ASA was keeping their cages in probably wouldn't be that difficult for him. I'm guessing he did it on Lionax's orders when Jet and the rest of ASA refused his invitation to join him here today."

Officer Sutter said, "I heard a couple of the bounty hunters talking when they were hauling Theodore out of here. He's been a suspect in several vandalism cases—he's apparently very skilled in breaking runes and wards. He's got multiple outstanding bounties, but he's also good at minor glamour magic. He's been eluding capture almost as long as Lionax has. The hunters scored big today, thanks to you. They might throw you a parade."

Cruz said, "I don't know about that. One of them really wanted this little one." He reached up to scratch the kitten under her chin. "The kitten refused her, and now she's heartbroken. We might end up with bounties on our heads because of it."

Officer Sutter chuckled.

Deandra didn't. "He's only half joking."

He winced. "It might only be a third."

"I'll be in touch if we need anything else from you," Officer Sutter said. "It's just too bad Conrad got caught up in this ASA feud. Wrong place, wrong time. We're hoping ACSI finds evidence to pin that on Theodore as well—or even Lionax—but my gut tells me it wasn't either of them."

Deandra nodded. "Mine doesn't think so, either. I'll let you know if I come up with any brilliant theories, though!"

Officer Sutter grinned. "I have no doubt about that. Have a good night, you two."

As they headed for loading pod 9—the only door that wasn't magically stuck shut—Cruz said to the kitten, "You've got to be hungry, girl. Let's get you something to eat and go see your brother."

The kitten phased a few feet in front of them, back arched, tail poofed out.

"Whoa," Deandra said, hands up. "Is it *not* her brother?"

"Hey, girl," Cruz said gently, taking a step forward.

The kitten phased backward a few more feet.

In a low whisper, Deandra said, "I thought they could only phase to a location in their line of sight. How is she phasing *backward*?"

"I have no idea," Cruz whispered back. In a louder voice, he said, "Don't you want to—"

He staggered back a step, hand on his forehead.

Deandra hurried in front of him, hands on his hips. "Hey. Hey. What is it? Look at me."

It took a moment for Cruz to snap out of whatever the kitten had shown him. His wide gaze met Deandra's. Without looking away from her, he shouted, "Hey, Officer Sutter?"

"What is it, Caddel?"

"Can you meet us at the Mythic Pet Kitchen booth?" he called, hand still pressed to his temple. "There's someone you need to talk to."

CHAPTER NINETEEN

Half an hour later, Deandra and Cruz, their two animal charges in tow, strolled up to the Mythic Pet Kitchen booth's entrance. She and Cruz had taken off their too-heavy enhanced breathing talismans in the car. They were stuffed into one of her cup holders. Her lungs felt heavier or thicker now in the talisman's absence. She hoped that sensation faded quickly.

Patrons oohed and aahed at the sight of the dire wolf puppy and vibrissa kitten. Instead of waiting for one of the Thistlewicks to usher them in, Deandra walked straight through the opening between two tables. She hardly broke stride when the tent's interior opened and stretched out before her.

They'd made it halfway into the tent when shouts of alarm

sounded behind them. Deandra figured Officer Sutter and a few of her fellow werecats had shown up in cat form. That was confirmed when the officer called out, "We're looking for Juniper and Kira Thistlewick!"

It wasn't long before the startled-looking goblins came rushing over from different parts of the tent.

"Oh, goodness me," Juniper said, ringing his hands. "What's happened? Did the vibrissa—oh. I see she's still with you."

Officer Sutter asked, "Is there a slightly quieter place we can talk?"

The pack of them followed the Thistlewicks to the back of the tent, where the lone vibrissa cat was currently snoozing in a bed in the see-through enclosure. He woke out of a dead sleep, though, upon the arrival of three werecats, two humans, two goblins, a dire wolf, and the kitten's sibling. He phased to the top of his enclosure.

Could their kitten have phased through her clear enclosure all this time and had chosen not to? Or was their cage magically reinforced to prevent such a thing—and succeeded in doing so— while the door into the flight park wasn't?

Officer Sutter remained standing beside Deandra and Cruz, while the other two circled behind the Thistlewicks, hemming them in.

"What in all the realms is going on?" Kira asked, glancing over one shoulder at one looming werecat, then the other. "What's happened?"

Officer Sutter asked, "Do either of you know anyone by the name of Axil Romano?"

Juniper cocked his head. "No. Should we?"

Kira, however, flinched. It was slight, but Deandra saw it. "I don't know him, either."

"What about Lionax Orma?" Officer Sutter asked.

Kira scratched the side of her neck.

"Isn't that the unicorn shifter who founded ASA?" Juniper asked. He coughed nervously when no one else spoke. He was sweating, but Deandra thought that was more of a social-anxiety thing than a guilt thing. She recognized the panic in his eyes. And then he started to ramble. "He's the one who orchestrated the release of the hippodynus. Did I tell you that Kira was at the zoo that day, Dee? Isn't that wild! She told me about it on our first date. I fell in love with her that day. I'd never met anyone who cared about preserving the fauna of the fae realm as much as I did. I worried that when she found out the horrible things done in the Thistlewick name, she wouldn't believe me when I said I wanted to do the *opposite* of what my family did. I believe in education and preservation, not exploitation. But she *did* believe me.

"We've worked so hard to give fae and magic-touched a chance to thrive in this realm." He sucked in a gulp of air. Sweat trickled down his temple, and he hadn't stopped wringing his hands. "I say all this to illustrate that we are very committed to our animals, fair breeding practices, and our belief that all our animals are suitable for adoption. If somehow the vibrissa cat did something unspeakable and that's why you were gone so long, please know that we take full responsibility for it."

Deandra wanted to hug the goblin.

Officer Sutter asked, "How long have you been acquaintances with Theodore Rochester?"

The goblins were both temporarily flummoxed by the change in topic.

"Oh, I wouldn't say acquaintances," Juniper said. "We have a working relationship, certainly. He does most of the runework for the grimalkyne at Feline Protected, as well as some magic-enhanced gear, such as harnesses and leashes. He's an exceptionally competent sorcerer. Little on the … odd side, otherwise. Not that I'm one to talk! Ha-ha! I don't wish to speak ill of anyone, but he does make me uneasy. Most things do, though! Ha-ha!"

Deandra was slowly dying from secondhand embarrassment, but Officer Sutter was unfazed.

Turning to Kira, she asked, "And you, Mrs. Thistlewick? What is the nature of *your* relationship with Theodore Rochester?"

"Oh. I, uh, the same?" Kira said.

"Are you unsure, Mrs. Thistlewick?"

Kira cleared her throat. "No. I'm—I'm sure. Strictly professional."

"That's interesting," Officer Sutter said, pulling a cell phone–like device out of her utility belt. A few taps and swipes later, she swung the device around. "Theodore has become a person of interest lately. We've been scouring CCTV footage from across the town. This looks to be you and Theodore sitting together drinking coffee. I don't see any paperwork, laptops, or tablets on the table. It looks like you're laughing at something Theodore just said. Can you explain this? Because this isn't the only image we have. And they date back months—always at the same coffee shop. Always on Mondays at three p.m."

Juniper looked as if someone had just slapped him. He was probably thinking this was going to turn into an ambush where his wife was forced to admit she was having an affair. But Deandra knew it was much worse than that. "Kira?" he asked, his voice wobbly when she didn't answer right away.

"We, um, sometimes had coffee to discuss custom runework orders," Kira finally said. "He's in town for other clients on Mondays, so he adds me to his rotation."

"You need custom runework so often that you have a standing weekly coffee date with him?" Officer Sutter asked.

Now Kira was wringing her hands, too.

"Not only is he a consistent coffee date for you, but he's also a frequent purchaser of shatterberry extract off the arcane web. Did you know that, Mrs. Thistlewick?"

Kira's eyes welled up. After her gaze bounced around the assembled group for several agonizing seconds, she turned to Juniper and took his trembling hands in hers.

"We were working together to take down Lionax Orma," Kira told him. "Teddy learned that the man he'd been working for for months was *the* Lionax, so we were trying to figure out the best way to do it. I know Teddy makes you uncomfortable, so that's why I didn't invite you, love. I wasn't trying to keep it a secret, not really. Teddy agreed that keeping this between us was best. You can get so anxious, love. We needed level heads. We both knew, when all was said and done, you'd agree with us. Teddy feels just as passionate about protecting fae and magic-touched animals as we do. That's why he *jumped* at the chance to work with the grimalkyne. And why he felt betrayed when he found out Lionax hadn't divulged who he really was when he first hired Teddy.

"So when he told me he found out that not only was Lionax going to be at the festival this weekend, but he'd been living under the false identity of Axil Romano, we hatched a plan to get rid of him for good. ASA is a scourge on our industry. They've been harassing us for years. They drudge up old wounds tied to your family. They won't leave us alone. And I was just so *sick* of it. You have to cut off the head of the snake, right?"

Juniper snatched his hands out of his wife's and took a stutter-step back. She reached for him, but he recoiled.

Kira's arms dropped to her sides. "Teddy knew that, even if Lionax couldn't shift anymore, shatterberry would be effective against him."

"You're talking about … *homicide*, Kira," Juniper said, voice low. "How is that a solution? You nearly ruined the livelihood of the Greenwoods. For what? Why wouldn't you talk to me instead of cavorting with that … with that sleazeball? An innocent man is *dead* now, Kira. *Dead.*"

Kira's bottom lip wobbled. "I never meant for that to happen. I didn't know Lionax canceled his appointment. I took the shatter-berry Teddy gave me, snuck into the tent during the ASA demonstration, just like Teddy suggested, dropped the shatterberry extract into the ink cup, and then got back out again. How was I supposed to know the man in the tent wasn't the right one?"

Juniper clutched at his head. "You could have just *not resorted to homicide*, Kira! I can't believe this is even something I have to tell you!"

Deandra recalled something Kira had told her. *"Oh, those ASA people infuriate me to no end! Surely they have worse people than us to harass. I wish I'd had something stronger than a broom, I'll tell you that much."*

Shatterberry was certainly stronger than a broom.

Kira, clearly desperate now, asked her husband, "Did you know Lionax was slated to become the next leader of ASA? They were going to kick Jet to the curb and give the role back to Lionax. There would be a reign of terror again with Lionax at the helm. We have to deal with them enough as it is—the protests, the harassment of our delivery trucks, the vandalism of our stores. I know the loss of those vibrissa kittens from years ago still eats away at you. It was all going to get worse with Lionax in a position of power again. I couldn't let another incident like the hippodynus attack happen—not if Teddy and I could do something to stop it."

Deandra sagged against Cruz, who had an arm around her waist. She could hardly fathom how thoroughly Theodore had manipulated Kira—how he'd taken her hatred of ASA and weaponized it.

"And I hated Lionax even more—in a bone-deep kind of way," Theodore had said. *"He literally got away with murder because the Collective is populated by spineless elites."*

Theodore had worked with Lionax, the Thistlewicks, the grimalkyne, and heck, he probably even supplied ASA with his services, breaking runes on buildings that weren't yet fully outfitted with security cameras. Since he was one of the few academy-trained sorcerers working in the private sector, his client base spanned both sides of the ASA fight, making him acutely aware of details he otherwise wouldn't have known. She thought of the way Neela had petted Theodore's hair as if he were a pet, and the way he'd gazed up at her as if he adored her. He was an opportunistic con man who learned the needs and wants and sordid desires of his clients and then pitted them against each other for his own gain.

At least he was in bounty hunter custody now, but that didn't help poor Conrad.

"He lied to you," Deandra said before she realized she'd opened her mouth. The statement didn't come close to encompassing the enormity of Theodore's actions, but it still efficiently summed them up.

Kira's tear-rimmed eyes turned to her. "Who?"

"Teddy. He lied to you about all of it. Lionax was cast out by ASA. He tried to get Jet to join him on some new fool's errand, and Jet ignored him. Teddy was working *with* Lionax. He was helping him tonight to destroy the flight park—and that was just a test run for a large-scale plan. Teddy was loyal to only one thing: money. If you were paying him, he told you whatever you wanted to hear. But he clearly wanted Lionax out of the picture, and he tried to get you to do the dirty work for him."

Kira was vigorously shaking her head. "No. No, that's not true. He's on our side."

"He isn't," Officer Sutter said gently. "He and Lionax were both apprehended by bounty hunters tonight. They both have rap sheets a mile long. You were merely another one of their victims—and now Conrad Osgood is one of yours."

Tears streamed down Kira's face now. "I was doing this for us, Juni. For the future of our business. For the industry as a whole. I never meant for this to happen. Oh, Goddess above, what have I done?"

The goblin sank to her knees, but the two werecats behind her caught her under the arms before she could collapse. They gently hauled her to her feet, then escorted her toward the front of the tent. She didn't fight them. She didn't look back, either. She probably couldn't stand the sight of her crestfallen husband, whose world had just been upended. Deandra could hardly look at him herself.

Officer Sutter placed a hand on the goblin's shoulder. "I'm

going to need you to come into the station too, Juniper. We need to have a more thorough discussion, okay?"

He bobbed his head but didn't say anything.

Officer Sutter turned toward Deandra and Cruz then, though her focus was on the vibrissa cat on Cruz's shoulder. "Thank you for sharing what you saw, little one. We deeply appreciate your help. The Osgoods will, too. Unraveling the details of Conrad's death would have taken much longer without your insights."

The kitten chirruped.

With a nod in parting to Deandra and Cruz, Officer Sutter guided the dejected goblin in the direction of his arrested wife.

"*Woof,*" Deandra said. "Well, that was awful."

Moments later, they were swarmed by Mythic Pet Kitchen employees who were asking—*begging*—for the tea on their bosses. They did their best to give a condensed, slightly sugarcoated version to appeal to their curiosity, leaving Juniper with the terrible task of filling them all in later. Assuming he ever felt able to.

Deandra tried to use words like "allegedly" and "supposedly." She agreed with Juniper that his wife resorting to murder was the worst solution she could have come up with—but Deandra possessed half an ounce of sympathy for the woman because she'd been so thoroughly conned.

When the last of the employees finally drifted away, Deandra rubbed at her eyes. "I'd give anything for a nap, but I need to go check on Peril. He's going to want a very detailed update, and I'd much rather do that in person than through texts."

Cruz gently took the kitten off his shoulder and held her in front of him, his hands under her armpits so her little feet dangled in the air. "Are you going to be okay staying here now that Kira is gone?"

The kitten chirruped, but it sounded sad somehow.

He walked her over to the cage and got her deposited inside. She and her brother greeted each other with immediate rough-housing. "She'll be okay," he told Deandra as he walked back to her, but she wasn't sure if he was trying to convince her or himself.

Deandra said, "I'll drop you off at home, and you can spend the rest of the day trying to explain to Maxine why you smell like another lady."

They headed out with Havoc trotting ahead.

Deandra and Cruz looked back at the kitten at the same time, finding her with one pink-padded paw on the enclosure's wall, as if waving goodbye.

Deandra and Cruz spent a very lazy Sunday morning with the "dogs." Her appointments with Peril had been canceled, as the Greenwoods had apparently been bullied by Peril into allowing him to attend the final day of the festival. Deandra figured the salica was being overly paranoid, worried that the threat to the Greenwoods wasn't really over and wanting to be with them should anything go sideways.

She and Cruz made breakfast, took Havoc and Maxine for a long walk, and watched an epically terrible sci-fi movie that made Cruz laugh so hard, at one point he cried. It was a good morning.

Then they decided to explore the Zombie Cactus Festival as tourists. Deandra had been scheduled to help the Thistlewicks at their booth today, but given the events of yesterday, that was no longer in the cards. Deandra had no idea if Juniper would be back in the tent today or not. She couldn't imagine he'd want to be there if his wife wasn't, but perhaps he was the type who distracted himself with work.

Leaving their cars at Cruz's house, they walked Havoc and Max to the festival. Havoc had one of Maxine's leashes attached to his harness, since his had been severed when Lionax had tried to steal him via potion-powered teleportation.

They shopped, sampled countless zombie cactus treats, and played carnival games. During one game, Cruz tried to win a gigantic stuffed zombie cactus and instead won a goldfish—a goldfish who mentally screamed bloody murder at him until he released it into Oracle Pond.

After standing up with an empty plastic bag in his hand, he said, "In hindsight I probably should have found out if the water was safe for a goldfish, but he called out 'Thank youuuuu' as he swam away, so I'm guessing he's fine?"

"You live a strange existence," she said, a leash in each hand.

He kissed her before taking Maxine's leash. "Like you have room to talk. Did you already forget that yesterday we were almost blown up in a flight park while surrounded by flying horses, an incubus, a dozen werecats, a con man of a sorcerer, and an off-his-rocker unicorn shifter? Not to mention the mildly terrifying vibrissa cat."

"I was also dealing with the fact that you went full zombie on me while your brain was overtaken by a five-pound furry assassin," she said.

"It sounds crazy, but I'd actually love to set something up with whoever adopts her so I can train with her. She challenges my ability in ways that I didn't even know were possible. I haven't been that out of my depth since college."

"Nerd," she said affectionately.

They stopped by the Greenwoods' booth next. Both Rularo and Quinn were in the tent, and Rularo had resumed doing tattoos. Deandra and Cruz hung back until Quinn was no longer busy.

What surprised Deandra more than anything was that Peril was perched on Quinn's shoulder and remained visible, even while she interacted with customers. Granted, he looked four seconds from passing out, flinching and jumping at any loud sound, but he stayed out of Rularo's beard. He even occasionally run-hopped along the table, helping Quinn with bagging up items.

Quinn waved them over when the last of her current customers bustled off with their purchases. "Hi, Dee. Hi, Dr. Caddel."

Peril was distracted by a sticker affixed to his foot. He'd been so preoccupied with trying to remove it that he didn't realize Cruz was nearby until he was at the table.

"Hi, Quinn," Cruz said. "How's the festival going for you, now that things have settled down a little?"

Quinn wasn't able to get a word in, because Peril had spotted Cruz. He stood stock still, like a statue, then unleashed a high-pitched scream with such force, it sent him off the table and onto the grass below.

"*Oh, heavens! No! Deandra! No! We talked about this! La la la! No! Stay out of my head, you miscreant!*" came Peril's freaked-out voice from out of sight. Then his ears and half his face were suddenly visible behind Quinn's 'fro. "Be gone! My thoughts are my own! Hiss!"

He actually said the word "hiss" instead of just hissing, which made his theatrics ten times more ridiculous.

"Oh, Peril!" Quinn said, trying to reach for the ferret, but unable to grab him because he kept dodging her hands. "Don't be so silly! Dr. Caddel is nice!"

"Miscreant!"

Deandra tried next. "Peril, you like figuring things out, right? Test Cruz. Think of something, and see if he can guess what it is."

Peril stopped flailing around and took up a standing position on top of Quinn's head. There would be ferret-feet-size holes in her beautiful curls. "He could hear me and just guess incorrectly on purpose to throw me off."

"Why would I do that, Peril?" Cruz asked.

"Don't speak to me, miscreant!"

Deandra buried a laugh by coughing into her fist.

"Okay, fine," Peril said, forepaws fisted in front of his chest. "What am I thinking?"

After a few seconds, Cruz shrugged. "No clue. This time, think it *at* me. Imagine you have a card with whatever word or image you want me to see, and hand it to me mentally. Or chuck it at my face. Whatever feels right."

"Don't try to appeal to my sense of humor, miscreant. It shan't work."

Deandra and Cruz looked at each other and mouthed "shan't?" at the same time.

"Don't canoodle in front of me, either. I'll lose my lunch," Peril said. "What about—"

"A purple cantaloupe," Cruz said.

Peril gasped. "Incredible. No! Deceitful and invasive!"

This went on for several more minutes until Peril seemed relatively satisfied that Cruz wasn't actually reading his mind.

"I wanted to thank you, Dee," Quinn said, once the testing session seemed to be concluded. "We're officially cleared of any suspicion of foul play. We have a few obscure licenses we need to renew, and we have to pay a couple of fines, but that's nothing compared to what we were facing. Officer Sutter didn't exactly say it was all thanks to you, but she said we're lucky to have you in our corner."

"Aw," Deandra said. "Good to know she doesn't think I'm a menace. And I can't take too much credit—it was a group effort. Including Peril, here. He was a great help with research."

"When she told me about everything last night," Peril said, still atop Quinn's head, "she said I was essential to the investigation. Isn't that nice, Mother? Actually, I believe she said *integral*."

"I certainly didn't," Deandra said. "You were *helpful*. Don't get it twisted. And helpful is still kind of a stretch, since you were actively at war with autocorrect the whole time and I was fighting for my life trying to make sense of it all."

"So dramatic," he said, then hopped off Quinn's head and onto the table. With his back to Deandra and Cruz, he glanced up at Quinn. "Mother, may I attend the festival with Deandra? You know I love you and Father dearly, but it's a bit dull here. I'd like to *see* the festival a bit. Perhaps sample a meat delicacy or two."

"I don't know if delicacy is the right word for festival food," Cruz muttered.

Quinn looked like she was about to cry. "Are you sure? You're not scared?"

"I'm quivering in my proverbial boots, but I mustn't hide forever. I want to try. I trust Deandra will bring me right back should I get … overwhelmed. Or if Dr. Caddel proves to be as unscrupulous as I fear."

"Hey!" Cruz said, but Peril completely ignored him.

Deandra said, "If Peril gets spooked by another stuffed parrot and faints, I'll bring back his limp body."

Peril whirled around. "How dare you! I faint very infrequently."

"That's not a thing folks usually need to qualify. The fact that you need to speaks to an excess of fainting."

He gasped. "Slanderous."

"We doing this or not?" Deandra asked.

"Yes, please," he said. "Can I ride atop your wolf, as if he is my powerful steed and I'm a knight?"

Deandra blinked at him. He was a very strange ferret. After checking that Havoc didn't mind having a passenger, she gave Peril the go-ahead. He launched off the table, hit the grass on all fours, and then jumped onto Havoc's back in two blinks.

When Deandra glanced at Quinn, she saw she was near tears again. She mouthed a thank you. Rularo probably would have thanked her, too, but he was deeply focused on his tattoo work.

With a wave, Deandra, Cruz, and their growing menagerie set off to explore more of the festival.

AFTER A ROUND OF TRYING THREE NEW ZOMBIE CACTUS–FLAVORED treats, they headed for the Heather's Elixirs booth. Deandra thought the word "treat" lightly, as the cactus-flavored taffy she'd tried was possibly worse than Eileen's zombie cactus fruit puffs. She'd been surprisingly neutral on the chocolates filled with zombie cactus crème. Cruz had loved them.

The zombie cactus frozen lemonade, though? Top tier.

Last night, Wendy had mentioned that the team at Heather's Elixirs had decided that it was high time they got Heather into her booth at the festival and out of the store before half the staff quit in protest. Wendy had a feeling that Heather hadn't slept more than ten hours total in three days, and the woman was unraveling from sheer exhaustion more than anything else.

They'd drawn straws on who would be paired with Heather for the latter half of the festival today, and Wendy had drawn the short one. Deandra had planned from the start of this little festival-going mission to swing by around the start of Wendy's shift to give her some moral support.

The two ladies were already inside the booth by the time Deandra, Cruz, Max, Havoc, and Peril arrived. Peril had been doing relatively well so far, but he snapped at anyone who tried to pet him—both physically *and* verbally.

One tended to skedaddle as soon as one was told, "*Excuse* me. Does no one ask permission to invade someone's private space anymore? I don't know where your hand's been, madam!" by an indignant talking ferret. He seemed to be getting great pleasure from the perceived power his attitude afforded him.

To be fair to the handsy strangers, seeing Peril sitting astride Havoc—in dire wolf or dragon form—*was* pretty cute. Though, Havoc's collar *was* doing some heavy-duty physics-defying magic to make it look like Peril was riding on the back of a wolf. Deandra tried not to look at them too often, otherwise her brain would short-circuit.

Thankfully, Havoc had yet to flop over on his back to have those handsy strangers rub his belly. Deandra could only imagine how scandalized Peril would be if he was flung from his mount.

Wendy was standing forlornly in the middle of the booth while Heather flitted about, rearranging everything and muttering about the "atrocious aesthetics." Wendy's face lit up when she saw their little entourage arrive. It lit up even further when Deandra showed her the extra frozen lemonade she'd purchased for her. She rushed out to meet them, making grabby hands at the drink.

"How's it going?" Deandra asked, biting down on her bottom lip to keep from laughing when Wendy practically sucked down half of the drink in one pull, then pressed a palm to her temple, one eye squinted, as she was assaulted by brain freeze.

"It's been five minutes," Wendy said once she recovered. "And this is already the longest day of my life."

Cruz chuckled. "That good, huh?"

Wendy cast a look over her shoulder to where Heather was busily rearranging soap. Lowering her voice, she said, "Her husband isn't doing great. He's a fire witch, and his magic isn't aging well—I heard that's common with fire witches. Anyway, medical treatment for the magical doesn't exactly have a long history in this realm, you know? So there's a lot of guessing and experimenting going on. None of it seems to be working. And mundane medicine doesn't work for someone who feels like their bones are literally on fire. Mundane doctors think that's a flowery way of describing inflammation or bad arthritis.

"There are experts in other parts of the country who could probably help him, but that either requires telepad travel—which can be debilitating if he's having a literal flare-up—or very long travel days by mundane means, which is expensive and time-consuming. She's just falling apart. I'm guessing she keeps it all bottled up when she's with her husband, but all that anxiety has to go somewhere eventually. And it's going to us. The festival is already stressful, and then there were the delayed shipments ..." Wendy shrugged. "I feel for her. I really do. But I also want to strangle her and watch the light go out of her eyes."

"Strangulation takes much longer to do successfully than television and movies would have you believe."

Deandra, Wendy, and Cruz all slowly turned to look down at the ferret.

He stood on his hind legs on Havoc's back. "You can achieve unconsciousness in a few seconds with the right pressure points, but death might not occur for several minutes."

Wendy dropped to a squat in front of Havoc, who happily licked her chin. She scratched him behind the ears so she could distract him while staying eye-level with the salica. He looked exceedingly nervous, shifting his weight from foot to foot as he clearly warred with his natural instinct to flee the moment he felt uncomfortable. She held up one hand. "You either need very strong hand and upper body strength or a lot of patience. I don't have either, sadly."

Peril relaxed a bit, then held up his own paws. "I, too, will never know what it's like to attempt such a thing—not with these tiny things. What could I feasibly strangle? A mouse? That just seems cruel."

Deandra glanced up at Cruz. "I fear introducing those two was a grave mistake."

"Don't look now, but for some reason they're both miming stabbing the air."

"And I thought the *vibrissa cat* was scary," she said, and instantly regretted it.

Cruz frowned slightly. They'd been trying not to talk about the assassin kitten. They were both animal lovers at heart, so even though they'd left the kitten in the hands of the very capable staff of the Mythic Pet Kitchen, they were still bummed out. The kitten would be fine. Someone like Ruth, who the kitten *didn't* hate, would come along soon enough.

Hopefully.

She needed to think about something else.

"Can you hold down the fort for a second?" she asked him, handing over Havoc's leash. "I have an idea. But if it doesn't go well, I'm calling in the stabby twins over there for backup."

"I am once again alarmed and concerned."

She grabbed the front of his shirt to pull him down for a quick kiss. "It'll be fine. You know … probably."

Deandra walked next door to Enchanted Bite, waiting off to the side while Eileen chatted up a customer. Two teenagers—one boy and one girl—were bustling around the tent. The girl was helping a customer choose a candy flavor, while the boy was ringing up a stack of purchases. A man, who Deandra assumed was Eileen's husband, was restocking one of the shelving units with more bagged treats he pulled from a plastic tub. Their supply was running low. Deandra wouldn't be surprised if they sold out by the end of the day.

After a minute or two, Eileen noticed Deandra. She wrapped up her conversation a few seconds later, then came over.

"Hey, sweets," Eileen said. "What's up? I'm out of black cherry and peach now, but the lemon ones aren't bad. Little too tart for my personal tastes, but the kids love them."

"I was wondering if you could spare a few minutes?" Deandra asked.

Eileen eyed her curiously—but in that Mom way, where she was trying to assess how concerned she should be. With a nod, she glanced over her shoulder. "Martin, kids, I'm going to step out for a few. I've got my cell if you need anything."

Martin looked up and smiled. "We got it, hon." Addressing Deandra, he said, "You the one that suggested the raw kale label? Brilliant."

Deandra laughed. "Glad it worked out. I'll have her back in a few." To Eileen, she tipped her head to the side. "This way."

Deandra led Eileen into Heather's booth next door, where the woman was still muttering and fussing with the displays. She had her back to them. Deandra guessed that Heather's flustered energy was scaring away customers, as everyone seemed to be giving the tent a wide berth.

"Heather?" Deandra ventured.

Heather whirled around, a bar of soap in one hand and a satchel of herbs in the other. "It's a wonder we sold *anything* this weekend with the way—" She broke off when she realized that the person she was snapping at wasn't Wendy *and* that Deandra had company. She awkwardly cleared her throat. "Uh, sorry. Um. Hello. Is there something in particular you're looking for today?"

"Heather, this is Eileen from Enchanted Bite," Deandra said. "She has the booth next door. She told me that your temperature-control talismans changed her entire business model. She was hoping you'd be here this weekend so she could at least shake your hand."

"Oh! Oh, that's so lovely to hear," Heather said, her eyes welling up.

Deandra glanced over at Eileen when the usually chatty woman remained quiet. At first, she worried Eileen had been so put off by Heather's initial grouchy attitude that she'd either stalked off or was staring at Heather in disgust. Instead, Eileen stared at her like a starstruck teenager.

One beat, two ... Eileen closed the distance and grasped Heather's hands in hers. "I cannot thank you enough for your incredible talismans, Ms. Wittly. Truly. Mundane freeze-dryers just don't work the way I need them to for our magic-enhanced candies, and being able to modify the machines with your talismans changed everything. I mean that. You're so talented."

Heather burst into tears.

"Oh, goodness," Eileen said, pulling the woman into a hug.

Deandra stood nearby, feeling like a bodyguard who was on standby in case things got too emotionally charged. But after a few minutes, as often happens with women, the two got to talking about their lives, their families, their businesses. It wasn't long before Heather was telling Eileen about her husband's condition and the struggles they'd been having with finding medical treatment for him.

Soon Eileen and Martin had switched places, and he was giving Heather a list of potential herbal treatments to try, including one of his own making that had worked wonders for a friend's fire witch grandparent who had suffered from the same affliction. They exchanged personal information with a promise to be in contact at the end of the festival.

After giving a tearful Heather a hug goodbye, Martin headed out of the tent, giving Deandra's shoulder a reassuring squeeze on the way.

Heather turned to Deandra. "Thank you. You're not even one of mine, and you're still looking out for me."

"I'm just in it for the exorbitant monetary bonus," Deandra said.

Heather pulled her into a hug. Into her ear, she said, "The offer still stands to fire my niece and hire you instead. Just say the word, and I'll kick her to the curb. I'm willing to overlook the extortion."

Laughing, Deandra hugged her back.

Pulling away, they glanced over at the assembled group watching them. Peril had even jumped onto Wendy's shoulder to better spy on the goings-on in the tent. "Thanks, but I've got my hands full already."

A few minutes later, Deandra and Cruz left Wendy and Heather to their day at the booth and set off again with their animal companions.

Cruz, hand in hers, lightly bumped her shoulder as they walked. "You're such a softie."

She laughed. "Yet another self-serving act. Do you know how much easier I just made my life by calming Heather down? If Wendy was yelled and snapped at by Heather all afternoon, then *I'd* get yelled and snapped at all evening when she got home. Just preserving my sanity, is all."

"Yeah, okay. Tell yourself whatever you need to," he said, chuckling. "But I saw you wiping at your eyes. Softie through and through."

"Yeah, yeah," she said, though she was secretly pleased that introducing Eileen and Heather had gone even better than she'd hoped.

"I don't want to ruin the moment," Cruz said, "but you know there's one more stop you need to make, right?"

Deandra groaned. "But I don't wanna! What if they're mad? Or worse! What if it's a 'you break it, you buy it' situation? I don't have enough organs to sell to pay for that."

"You don't need *both* lungs, do you?" Cruz asked.

"Don't try to appeal to my sense of humor, miscreant. It shan't work!"

"How dare you mock me," muttered Peril.

Cruz cackled. She knew he'd start using "It shan't work!" at every available opportunity.

"*Fine*," she said with a sigh.

"I think they'll be understanding, given everything," he assured her.

She had her doubts.

A few minutes later, they stood outside one of the entrances to

Feline Protected's tent. She blew out a long, controlled breath, then stepped inside.

She was initially so dazzled by the interior of the tent that she forgot for a moment why she was there. The area expanded, just as it did when she entered the Mythic Pet Kitchen booth. There was a maze of crates, cages, and terrariums. Cages stood on the floor, on tables, and on elegant stands. Some hung from the tent's ceiling.

"I wonder if they have tunnel enhancements," mused Peril from Havoc's back. "One that expands into a den could be quite nice."

"We absolutely could, but we're going to be backed up on custom orders for a while until we can find an additional sorcer-er," came a voice from behind them.

"CAT!" Peril bellowed with all the force of a foghorn.

Deandra looked over just as Peril launched off Havoc and onto Cruz. Peril realized a moment after pawing at Cruz's face that he didn't have a beard and then frantically tried to get into Cruz's shirt via the collar.

There was much screaming from all involved. Peril eventually passed out in sheer terror, and Cruz ended up cradling his limp body in his arms, his eyes wild and his neck red with scratches.

It had been Neela who had spoken, but the screeching of ferret and man had brought over the other two grimalkyne, as well as a few curious patrons.

Neela, paws up, said, "Whoops."

"I'd, uh, hoped for a less dramatic entrance," Deandra said, hand clapped to her chest. "I was also hoping to ease into this, but ..." She reached into her purse and handed Powder the harness he'd given her. Only the clasp and two inches of the leash remained, and the harness was marred by grass stains. "You said it was just a loan, and then it got sort of ... ruined. The harness should still be fine! Though the vibrissa cat who was wearing it was still able to phase."

"Really?" Powder asked, touching a furry digit to the shorn-off end of the leash.

Cruz explained how the kitten had phased with him *and* had phased through a see-through wall. "Granted, she's a unique case, as far as I know, but it also suggests the runework could use some adjustment." He grimaced. "And I realize that's probably a touchy subject, since your go-to sorcerer was a con man …"

Velma hiss-laughed. "I appreciate that he's just as honest as you are, Dee."

Powder flapped the paw that still held the harness. "And don't worry about this. We're still reeling. We honestly don't even know what happened, just that it's all over the news that Lionax Orma is alive and was picked up by bounty hunters, *along* with Teddy. It doesn't make any sense …"

"How much honesty do you want?" Deandra asked cautiously.

Velma crossed her furry orange arms. "All of it."

So Deandra launched into the whole sordid tale, including the fact that Theodore had manipulated Kira Thistlewick into killing Lionax, only for her to poison the wrong man. Velma left at that point, paw to her stomach. It seemed she didn't like the firehose approach to receiving upsetting information any more than Peril did.

Velma also probably felt some measure of guilt, even though it was completely unwarranted, since she was the one who'd brought Theodore into the Feline Protected fold.

"Warn anyone who had a business relationship with Theodore that he's bad news," Deandra said. "And I know it's impossible, but try not to beat yourself up too much that you trusted him. A lot of people did. Taking advantage of people was his MO."

Neela and Powder stood there shell-shocked for a long moment.

Powder said, "I guess I should thank you again for sticking your nose in other people's business. I didn't love hearing all that, but I appreciate you letting us know what happened. We have some serious reevaluating to do."

Neela nodded. "Velma appreciates it, too. This will just take some time to adjust to. He really *did* feel like family."

Deandra frowned. "I'm sorry."

"Not your fault," she said. "If you're ever in the market for a cage or playpen, you let us know, okay? We'll hook you up."

Deandra hugged each of the cats goodbye, asked them to pass on a farewell to Velma on her behalf, and then they left the tent, hoping to escape before Peril woke back up and had another meltdown.

The ferret finally gasped awake ten minutes later, while they were standing in line for zombie cactus ice cream. Cruz and Peril were in the middle of a heated discussion about the ferret's "delicate constitution" when Deandra's phone buzzed in her back pocket.

She was surprised to find a text from Ruth.

> **Ruth**
> Your kitten's been adopted. Just wanted to let you know, in case you wanted to say a final goodbye. Her brother is going home with me. He's bitten me hard enough to draw blood twice in as many minutes. I love him!

Included was a picture of the two kittens sitting side by side on the topmost platform with a sign taped to the glass below them. "Sorry! We've been adopted!" was written in big red letters across the paper.

She showed the messages to Cruz.

"I wouldn't mind saying goodbye," he said. "Maybe give her a pep talk about not giving into her intrusive thoughts as often?"

"We should probably warn the new owner about her unique skills, too," Deandra added. "You know, for everyone's safety."

They abandoned their pursuit of ice cream and headed for the Mythic Pet Kitchen booth. As curious as Deandra was about the ice cream and its unsettlingly green hue, her stomach probably needed a break.

An employee who recognized them told them to head to the back. Juniper was nowhere in sight. The poor guy would probably need a long time to reconcile with the fact that his wife had gone to unforgivable extremes, even if, in her mind, she'd done it to protect her family and their business's future.

Some of Deandra's sadness over the fate of the Thistlewicks faded in light of the childlike delight Peril experienced upon seeing the tent expand. He liked this one far more than the grimalkyne booth, but to be fair, there weren't monster-size cat people roaming this one. He stood directly on top of Havoc's head, his forepaws pressed together as he took in the sights, his eyes wide with wonder.

When they reached the back of the tent, Deandra was a little surprised that the only people there were Ruth and a Mythic Pet Kitchen employee. The two kittens sat on the top platform of their cage. Deandra eyed the sheet of paper tacked to the side of the enclosure with "Adopted!" written in big red letters.

Ruth grinned. "I knew you'd come running."

Deandra glanced around. "Where's the other kitten's new owner?"

Ruth nodded at the employee.

The young goblin walked up to Cruz and held out the clipboard she'd been holding. She beamed. "You are."

"Wait, what?" Deandra asked.

Ruth laughed. "Adoption fees are paid for, as well as a magicked cage like this one if you want it. I put my name down as a backup, so on the off-chance things with you and the assassin kitten don't work out, I'll happily take her in. But I think she should choose who she wants, and that person is clearly not me."

Cruz laughed, his head cocked to the side. "She said she still doesn't like you, but she no longer finds you detestable. I'm honestly not sure how that's the word that's constantly in my head when she doesn't actually think in words, but she's fond of it."

"It's an excellent word," Peril said, then glanced over his shoulder at Cruz. "Miscreant." The label almost sounded affectionate that time.

Cruz didn't even react. Granted, he'd returned to staring at the clipboard the goblin girl was still holding out to him.

Deandra poked him in the arm. "What's going on in that head of yours? If you really don't want to take on another pet, Ruth will do everything in her power to wear the kitten's reservations down. I have no doubt about that."

"She's not wrong," Ruth said.

"I'd have to see how she'll interact with Max," Cruz said, but she could already tell he was losing ground with himself.

The employee helped everyone, minus Ruth, her new kitten, and Peril, into the playpen area. Peril watched from on top of the vibrissa kittens' cage, refusing to be handled by Ruth because he "didn't like her aura."

Hopefully Ruth wouldn't develop a complex.

Deandra knew that the collar around the kitten's neck probably wasn't strong enough to keep her from phasing out of here and to the next county if she really wanted to. The fact that she didn't attempt to leave the pen spoke to the kitten's willingness to cooperate for Cruz's sake.

The employee placed the kitten on the ground in front of a wiggling Maxine, but the kitten phased onto Cruz's shoulder the moment her paws hit the grass. Cruz pried her off and held her under her armpits in front of Maxine. Deandra had hold of Maxine's harness, while Havoc lay on his belly nearby, his face between his paws. Maxine was so excited to meet her potential new sister, her tail was practically whacking herself in the side of her head with every enthusiastic wiggle of her butt.

The kitten hung there, looking a tad offended, while Deandra eased the excitable dog forward. Max gave the kitten's belly an exuberant sniff, shriek-barked, and dropped into play stance.

The kitten vanished from Cruz's grip, then reappeared in front of Max and Havoc. The kitten just stood there, trembling for a moment, before she dropped onto an approximation of a play bow, too. Max scream-yelped in happiness and hopped toward the kitten, who immediately popped away again. Havoc lurched to his feet and bounced around in a circle, then charged for the kitten when she reappeared.

The next few minutes were so chaotic that the employee, Deandra, and Cruz hastily vacated the playpen while the trio was distracted. The humans, goblin, and bounty hunter ringed the playpen while the animals played the most hectic game of keep-away Deandra had ever seen. Given the chirrups from the kitten, Deandra figured she was having just as much fun as Max and Havoc. The small smile on Cruz's face as he watched them was reassuring, too.

When Ruth managed to get her own kitten into the playpen without any of them escaping, the game really got under way. Peril climbed off the cage and eventually made his way onto Deandra's shoulder.

"Heathens," he muttered in disgust as he watched the other animals roughhouse, though she wondered if some part of him wanted to join in.

Twenty minutes later, all four animals were sprawled out and panting—even the kittens.

"I'll throw in a playpen, too," Ruth said. "I'm not saying the bounty from bringing in *the* Lionax Orma was life-changing money, but it wasn't insignificant, either. I figure you can cover the vet bills yourself, though, given that you *are* the vet."

Cruz laughed.

He only hesitated for a moment longer before he held out a hand to the goblin teen. She passed the clipboard to him. The ladies watched the exhausted animals while Cruz filled out the necessary paperwork. Once done, he handed the board to Deandra.

"One thing left to fill out," he said.

She took the clipboard and stared at the only blank space.

Name: ___________

"I know you already have one locked and loaded," he said.

She scoffed. "I do not." Pausing, she chewed on the inside of her cheek. "Okay, fine. I was thinking Fern."

"Why?" he asked, amused.

"When she's relaxed, her antennae curl up. They remind me of fiddleheads on a fern."

Peril sniffed. Begrudgingly, he said, "I quite like that."

Cruz jutted his chin at the board. "Write it in."

"You sure? She's *your* cat."

"As if you're not going to be spending a ton of time with her," he said. "You're her default pet sitter, and I travel *a lot*." He glanced at Ruth and angled his thumbs toward his own chest. "Recovering workaholic."

Ruth gazed at him. "Do you happen to have a single brother? Asking for me."

"Sorry. Only child."

"Drat," Ruth said.

Deandra wrote "Fern" in the name box, then handed the clipboard back to the goblin teen.

"I'm only a text away if you need to rehome her," Ruth said. "But I have a feeling she'll fit in just fine."

Fern was on her back, her antennae curled on top of her head, and she was using Maxine's heaving stomach as a pillow. Max was flopped on her side, her lolling tongue lying on the grass. Havoc was on his side, too. The other kitten attempted to pounce on his wagging tail.

Deandra gusted a long, weary sigh.

What a weekend!

A couple of hours later, after they'd placed an order for delivery with the goblin teen for a cage, playpen, and a harness with more robust anti-phasing runework; returned Peril to his parents; and purchased zombie cactus ice cream—which was delicious—Deandra and Cruz were seated on his couch with yet another terrible sci-fi movie on the TV. Havoc was on his back on the ottoman, passed out and snoring. Maxine was in one of her beds chewing on a yak stick, and Fern was curled up in a tight ball in Cruz's lap.

Cruz kissed Deandra's temple. "I have no idea how all of this happened so fast, but I'm not mad about it."

She wasn't sure if she meant them as a couple or the fact that he'd adopted an alien cat—or both.

All she *did* know was that, while Zombie Cactus Festival season was far more perilous than Pumpkin Spice Latte season had ever been, she'd never been happier.

Want to see what chaos Fern brings to Deandra and Cruz's life? A Mythical Case of Kidnapping is up next! You can also join Melissa's mailing list to be notified about upcoming releases.

A Mythical Case of Kidnapping

To find out what happens when Dee pet sits for Fern the vibrissa cat, you can find the book here: https://melissajacksonbooks.com/a-mythical-case-of-arson/a-mythical-case-of-kidnapping

While waiting for the next book in the Mythical Pet Sitting Mystery series, you can check out the Witch of Edgehill series. There are five books—and the series is complete! (They're all in audio, too!)

Book 1 is *Pawsitively Poisonous*.

Every town has its secrets, but no one has a secret like hers.

Amber Blackwood, lifelong resident of Edgehill, Oregon, has earned a reputation for being a semi-reclusive odd duck. Her store, The Quirky Whisker, is full of curiosities, from extremely potent sleepy teas and ever-burning candles to kids' toys that seem to run endlessly without the aid of batteries. The people of Edgehill think of the Quirky Whisker as an integral part of their feline-obsessed town, but most give Amber herself a wide berth. Amber prefers it that way; it keeps her secret safe. But that secret is thrown into jeopardy when Amber's friend Melanie is found dead, a vial of headache tonic from Amber's store clutched in her hand.

Edgehill's newest police chief has had it out for Amber since he arrived three years before. He can't possibly know she's a witch, but his suspicions about her odd store and even odder behavior have shot her to the top of his suspect list. When the Edgehill rumor mill finds out Melanie was poisoned, it's not only the police chief who looks at Amber differently. Determined to both find justice for her friend and to clear her own name, Amber must use her unique gifts to help track down Melanie's real killer. A quest that threatens much more than her secret …

Get it right meow at https://melissajacksonbooks.com/witch-of-edgehill-mysteries/pawsitively-poisonous

ACKNOWLEDGMENTS

I'm starting to sound like a broken record in these, but! I have a new thank you to add. Shut Up and Write! I'm so glad you exist. I honestly wouldn't have gotten this book done without SUAW. So thank to you the hosts who show up every week and keep everyone accountable.

Now, to the usual suspects … thank you to Mom, Margarita, Kayla, and John for sticking to another too-tight deadline. I keep promising to give ya'll more time. One of these days, I'll actually mean it!

Thank you to my editor, Cyndi Sandusky, for *also* putting up with my too-tight deadlines. I'm a monster. I appreciate you putting up with my nonsense.

Thank you (a billion times!) to Molly Burton for the covers! I keep thinking you can't outdo yourself and then I saw Fern! *swoon*

Thank you to Sarah Waites for all your hard work keeping the Axian map updated. We're running out of buildings!

Thank you to Etheric Tales for the new drawings of Peril and the zombie cactus (it turned out even cooler than what I had in my head!).

Thank you to all the readers who continue to follow Deandra and all her zany animal-related adventures. I hope you're having as much fun as I am!

And, finally, thank you to Sam. I worry every day that by writing all these kooky animals, I manifested Bunny into our lives. I'm sorry / you're welcome.

ABOUT THE AUTHOR

Melissa has had a love of stories for as long as she can remember, but only started penning her own during her freshman year of college. She majored in Wildlife, Fish, and Conservation Biology at UC Davis. Yet, while she was neck-deep in organic chemistry and physics, she kept finding herself writing stories in the back of the classroom about fairies and trolls and magic. She finished her degree, but it never captured her heart the way writing did.

Now she owns her own dog walking business (that's sort of wildlife related, right?) by day … and afternoon and night … and writes whenever she gets a spare moment. She alternates mostly between fantasy and mystery (often with a paranormal twist). All her books have some element of "other" to them … witches, ghosts, UFOs. There's no better way to escape the real world than getting lost in a fictional one.

She lives in Northern California with her very patient boyfriend and way too many pets.

You can find out more about her upcoming books and join her newsletter at: https://melissajacksonbooks.com